HE CALLS BY NIGHT

Copyright © 2025 Shannon Hamilton

All rights reserved.

This book or any portion thereof may not be reproduced or used in any manner whatsoever without the express written permission of the author, except for the use of brief quotations in a book review.

This novel is entirely a work of fiction. The names, characters, locations, and incidents portrayed in it are the work of the author's imagination. Any resemblance to events or actual persons, living or dead, is entirely coincidental.

ISBN: 978-1-7384022-4-3

I want to take a moment to extend my appreciation to my beta readers; Marguerite Labbe, Robbie McLister, Alan McKnight and Ray Sullivan who offered encouragement, sharp eyes and picked the necessary holes. A special mention goes to this book's editor, Bea Syer, whose steady hand left me with a workable final product.

My thanks too, to my wife, Sophie, whose patience for my little hobby is endless.

And lastly, I want to save the final, most important acknowledgement for you, the reader, for taking a chance on an indie author. Your time and attention mean more than you know.

Glossary

If you are not native to Irish shores, you may stumble over a few words and sayings during your journey through *He Calls By Night*. I've put together a brief glossary to assist in your navigation of the wild and wonderful world of Northern Irish slang:

Auld	Old
Dander	Take a walk
Gander	Take a look
Headcase	Crazy
Hoak	To search
Peeler	Police Officer
Prod	Protestant
Root	Sex Offender
Sheugh	Water-filled ditch
Sleekit	Sly
Scunnered	Fed-up
Skedaddle	Leave
Stolie	Stolen
Tout	Informer
Thran	Stubborn
Wee	Small

1

Three days into the new year and Belfast was firmly in the clutches of a holiday hangover. The cue for a white Christmas had been missed. The snow arrived a week late and lasted a day until the previous night's storm washed it into dirty slush streaking the roads and footpaths.

The surviving Christmas lights in shop fronts and apartment windows were garishly offensive against the grey, miserable morning as people hunched against the weather and hurried to wherever they needed to be.

A woman concentrating on a losing battle with her umbrella forced Jacob off the pavement and ankle-deep into a freezing puddle. He used the last reserve of his Christmas cheer to swallow the appropriate swear word, pulled his sodden foot out of the water, and pushed on.

Mercifully, the queue at the coffee shop was light. Jacob squelched his way towards the counter, ordered two cappuccinos and took them up the stairs connecting the cafe to the first-floor office of Kincaid Investigations.

The security grille was locked back and Helen was already at her desk, flanked on either side by two electric heaters. The radiators in the office were slow to get going, having been installed around the same time the Titanic had set sail from the city.

"Colder than inside my mother's knickers," Jacob said, handing one of the coffees to Helen who closed her eyes and gave a patient shake of her head. It was only then Jacob realised they were not alone.

The woman rose slowly from one of the two seats on the far side of the room. She was old, touching eighty by Jacob's guess, and her thin coat would have done little against the bitter January morning. Her posture was stooped, fatigued by time and weather, yet her eyes, when they met Jacob's, were vibrant and bright.

"Mr. Kincaid." She offered a small, liver-spotted hand. Jacob shook off his glove and took it. Her touch was like ice. "My name is Deirdre Skelly." The woman spoke softly, as if raising her voice to be heard was an effort she couldn't muster the energy for. "I'm looking to engage your services."

Jacob gave a polite smile and guided her back down to her seat. "Mrs. Skelly," Jacob said quietly. "Would you excuse me and my associate for a minute?" He indicated for Helen to follow him into his office and waited until she closed the door behind them.

"A little heads up would have been nice."

Helen leant against the cast iron radiator, savouring its warm touch. She was his only employee, and her actual role in the business had never actually been given a name. Her coat buttoned over a range of duties, from admin to research, to just about anything else Jacob required.

"I thought we agreed," Jacob continued, pulling off his hat and running a hand over his thinning hair in an attempt to flatten it down. "No more walk-ins."

"You wanted me to turn her away? Look at her."

"Did she even say what she's after?"

"Missing person."

Jacob relaxed slightly. Missing people were bread and butter for private investigators. Helen watched as Jacob raised his cup of coffee, waiting until she was sure he had a mouthful. "From forty years ago."

"Jesus, Helen!" Jacob spluttered out the words, along with most of the coffee.

"Oh!" She slapped his shoulder. "Just hear her out. She

seems genuine."

"Well, that's nice, wonderful actually, that she seems genuine, but does she seem like she can pay?" He knew Helen would have noticed the old woman's worn clothing just as he had, and decided one of them needed to be the pragmatist.

Helen answered by folding her arms and fixing him with a measured stare. For someone who never had children, she had the look of a disapproving mother down pat and Jacob, knowing perfectly well what she was doing, wilted every time.

He set his cup on his desk and walked to the door. "Mrs. Skelly!" he said brightly as he opened it, "So sorry to keep you waiting."

"Deirdre, please."

She shuffled past Jacob and slowly lowered herself onto the chair across from his desk. By the time she had made herself comfortable, Helen had reappeared with a mug of strong tea which she placed within easy reach for the old woman.

"Helen says you're looking to hire someone to investigate a missing person case?"

"My son. Finbar."

"And he went missing forty years ago?"

"Forty-four, but I suppose there comes a point where four years doesn't make much of a difference."

Jacob nodded but didn't speak, wanting Deirdre to direct the conversation.

"My niece, Cathy, was talking a few weeks ago about this, whatyacallit? Podcast? I didn't hear it, but she mentioned the private detective on it, and how hard you chased that investigation, and I decided that's the man I need to look for my Finbar."

Jacob pursed his lips. He had been hired the previous summer by Natalie Amato, the creator and presenter of Miss Gumshoe, a popular mystery and true crime podcast. Natalie had hired Jacob to look into the death of a colleague inside a locked apartment, adamant what had been written off by police as a tragic accident was in fact, murder.

Their investigation had almost cost them their lives but it had resulted in a hell of a story when all was said and done. Natalie had suggested Jacob join her on the podcast to tell it.

He had agreed, and over three recording sessions they detailed a story of murder, extortion, coercion and kidnapping, all controlled by The Followers of Eden, a shadowy cult of Ireland's social elite.

The show was deep in the editing stage when they were approached by Cora Adebayo, the woman who had saved their lives in a dingy factory on the outskirts of Carrickfergus. Jacob had never been able to pin down exactly who Cora worked for, other than a government agency she never named. He could guess of course, but Cora would never confirm it. She operated in a world where deniability was currency, and Jacob was just another civilian.

Cora had made her pitch. The legal case against the Followers, built in large part on what Jacob and Natalie had uncovered, had not reached court and if the podcast was released before the trial date, it could be prejudicial, and potentially fatal, to the prosecution case.

Natalie had agreed, reluctantly, to delay the release and Jacob, who had been anticipating a dramatic upturn in business after appearing on the podcast, saw those hopes rapidly fade. Natalie had thrown him a bone and brought him back as a guest for a single episode, rehashing an old case of his, involving a painting stolen from a local art gallery and a looped security tape that almost allowed the thief to get away with her crime.

Miss Gumshoe attracted an audience of close to one hundred thousand listeners per episode, and Jacob's lone appearance, or rather, Natalie's description of some mildly thrilling heroics, was a boon to business. His client list shot through the roof, as did the number of loonies and headcases darkening his door with imagined cases and slights.

His initial assessment was that Deirdre Skelly did not fall into either loony or headcase category, but there were other concerns. For one, a forty-four-year gap between her son going missing and the opening of the investigation didn't inspire much hope of success.

"What you're asking is a tall order, Deirdre," Jacob said, choosing his words carefully. "Memories fade and records then weren't to the standard as they are now." He drummed his fingers on the table, uneasy about the next part but knowing it needed to be said. "Not to mention the money required to fund an investigation. Any investigation."

"I have savings."

Jacob shifted in his seat, uncomfortable with the thought of parting the old woman from her money. "I'm sure you do, but this is not a cheap proposition. Even for a basic investigation, costs add up fast."

Deidre slapped his desk with surprising force. "I have enough. I can't take it with me, Mr. Kincaid, and I need answers. I've waited too long already."

"Alright," Jacob said gently. "Help me out then. Where should I start?"

"Hartley House."

The name had a vaguely familiar ring, but Jacob wasn't sure why.

"It's in Millisle," Deirdre said, sensing his struggle. "The prison service has their training college there, but it was a borstal before then." She stopped. "I suppose they don't call them that anymore but do you understand what I'm talking about?"

"I think they'd be called young offender centres these days," Jacob replied.

"That's right. My Finbar was there back in eighty, and eighty-one." Her eyes were lost at an unseen spot on the wall behind Jacob. "He hated the place, ran every chance he could, but he always ran to me. I was his mammy. I kept him safe until the peelers came. He was predictable, so they knew where to find him. None of the rest of the family wanted him under their roof. He had a good heart."

Jacob hid a knowing smile. A mother describing a son as having a good heart was usually a solid indicator that the person being referred to was a toe rag of the highest order. House breaker, drug dealer, joy rider, or probably all three. Still, to the doting mothers it was always someone else's fault. It was the teachers bullying them, or the police having the temerity to arrest them. Or possibly in Finbar Skelly's case, the borstal staff likely trying to control an up-and-coming criminal.

Still, he reminded himself, he wasn't being hired to cast judgement on the long lost Finbar Skelly. "So the police knew where to find him?"

"They'd show up with the army. Couldn't come into the area by themselves. They dragged him out. Always kicking and screaming. Always crying." Her lip began to quiver. "Always afraid."

Jacob opened the drawer of his desk and rummaged around until he found a notebook. He flipped it open on a blank page and lifted a pen. "Did you tell the police about Finbar's disappearance?"

"Just an initial report. I didn't have any contact past that."

"Why?"

Deirdre didn't answer but Jacob could already guess. If the police needed an army escort into an area then it wasn't police friendly. Indeed, any engagement with the police would likely have been met with hostility, if not violence, towards the reporting party.

Jacob, who had just written POLICE on the top line of the page, put a line through it. "What about friends at the borstal?"

"Just the one. Matthew Connelly was his name. Met him once or twice when I got down to visit. He was a Prod but sure, nobody's perfect. Finbar and him were as thick as thieves, according to Father Pettigrew."

"Father Pettigrew?"

"Jeremiah Pettigrew. He was from our area, but he served as the Catholic chaplain down at the borstal. He looked out for Finbar. Knew him from back home and knew the place was getting on top of him."

"He still around?"

"No," Deirdre replied with a shake of her head. "No, he moved away, God, must have been back in the nineties. Suddenly."

Jacob kept his eye on the page. He didn't want to cast aspersions that would cause offence. Still, if it was one thing churches were good at, Catholic or Protestant, it was hiding dirty secrets. The sudden re-assigning of a man of God to a different parish pointed to a wide number of uncomfortable possibilities. He wondered if Deirdre was hoping he would make the connection and spare her saying it outright.

"Would Father Pettigrew..."

"He would have been close with some of the local boys, yes" Deirdre said quickly, taking a keen interest in Jacob's floor. "Last I heard he was still alive, up the coast towards Larne."

Jacob noted the priests name in his notebook. "When exactly did Finbar disappear?"

"December of eighty-one. Christmas Eve." Deirdre paused before continuing, "Christmas is always hard. This year though..." she shook her head. "Not sure why, but I don't think I'll see another one. Doesn't bother me much, but I want my answers before I go."

She reached into her bag and produced a tissue which she dabbed at her eye. "I had no car. His father was a drunk and nowhere to be seen, so I didn't get down as much as I wanted, as much as I should have. It was the twenty-third I last saw him. Finbar was pale, withdrawn. He was never a big boy, and I know some of the other lads would pick on him. When time on the visit was called, he wouldn't let go of my hand. He said he wanted to come home. He was begging me to take him with me, as if I could. The screws had to drag him out."

"You never saw him again?"

"I got a phone call the next morning. It was the Assistant Governor. Turner, I think his name was. Told me Finbar had done a runner during the night. That I should call the peelers if he turned up." Deirdre managed a smile. "He always did. Laid low for the first few hours then hitchhiked back to Belfast. It was usually the day after he escaped before he appeared. When the Governor called, I knew Finbar would be standing in my kitchen for Christmas Day."

"But he didn't show?"

"No. My brother, Adrian, saw him walking towards our house early in the morning. He called around that evening expecting to see Finbar but he never appeared."

"Whereabouts did Adrian see him?"

"The Falls," Deirdre said, naming perhaps the most well-known road in the city, the main arterial route through predominantly republican West Belfast. "We lived off the Whiterock. Do you know the area?"

Jacob pointed with his thumb to the wall behind him, where a couple of pictures of him in his old PSNI uniform hung. "Spent five years up in the West."

Deirdre glanced at the pictures and then away. Whatever her thoughts on the police might be, she kept them to herself. "He was walking home," she said, her voice dropping slightly. "Not even five minutes away but he never made it. I sat up all night and then waited all next day too. Christmas turkey drying out on the table. Not a morsel on it touched."

"And no one has seen Finbar since?"

"Not a soul."

Jacob tapped his pen on the notebook page. The Falls Road in the early eighties, the Troubles in their full violent swing. People were suspicious, wary of outsiders in their territory. It hardly seemed possible a teenage boy could be snatched off the street with so many eyes watching for anything remotely out of place.

"There's one more thing." The old woman moved her hand to her mouth and then pulled it away slowly. "The last time I saw Finbar, he screamed a name."

Jacob glanced up from his notebook. "A name?"

"A name." Tired, shining eyes met his. "Ned by Night."

2

"You see the old dear off?" Jacob asked as Helen entered his office and reclaimed her spot by the radiator.

"Walked her down to the taxi rank. She's going to get her niece to sort payment. Should be with us by the end of the day."

"Good." Jacob picked up a stack of yellow post-it notes and considered the old woman who had just been sitting across from him. Deirdre Skelly's physical frailty belied a steely determination. She had come to Jacob knowing she would not be taking no for an answer.

"So, anything interesting?"

"Paper trail job," Jacob replied, running his thumb over the edge of the post-its. "Run down a few dead ends until I have enough to give Deirdre. Simple."

Helen laughed. "Simple? Oh come on! This is Jacob Kincaid we're talking about. You make hitting the ground after tripping complicated."

"Thanks for that, Helen."

Her smile remained. "What do you have for me?"

"For now, two names." He ripped off the top post-it from the deck and handed it to her. "Matthew Connelly, sixty or thereabouts, and Father Jeremiah Pettigrew. Well into his seventies and a long time dead, knowing my luck. Look up the NCA's missing people database, anything from the early eighties onwards that matches Finbar's age. Check the Gardai's too."

She winked at him. "I'll jump right on it, boss."

"Helen," Jacob said as she reached the door. "You're a person of a certain age."

"Careful now."

"You ever hear of Ned by Night?"

She thought for a second before shaking her head. "Who or what?"

"Some old local ghost story apparently."

"Ah, I see. You think my parents might have told it to me around the firepit of our dirt hovel?"

"Something like that."

"Sorry, can't help. Must be doting in my advanced age, which is forty-nine by the way, you cheeky shit."

She closed the door, and Jacob turned to his computer. A misper investigation was never particularly cheerful work. Most people who went missing did so by choice, and had no inclination to be found. Even so, almost all left some kind of trace, even those who took measures to hide their tracks. But after forty-four years, Finbar Skelly's tracks were well and truly covered by the passage of time.

Jacob's feeling was that he had three threads to tug on: Finbar, the borstal, and this Ned By Night.

He started with Finbar. Deirdre had provided a picture of her son on the solemn promise that it would be returned to her undamaged. It was hard for Jacob to match the mental image he had already built of Finbar Skelly against the boy who looked back from the blurry, under-saturated photograph. Deirdre had told him that it was taken the summer before he had disappeared. Finbar was standing in what looked like a tidy back garden, wearing a pair of denim bell-bottoms and a patterned shirt. He was squinting against the sun, arms crossed over his skinny chest, a row of uneven teeth offering a cheeky smile for the camera.

Jacob took the picture over to the office printer, carefully set it face down on the scanner screen, and sent a copy over to his computer. Returning to his desk, he opened the scanned image, increased its size to fit onto an A4 page, and then printed it. He lifted the black and white image of Finbar from the printer tray and attached it with two thumbtacks to the empty pinboard on the wall.

The pinboard was archaic, bordering on cliche, Jacob knew. Anytime he used the board he felt as though he should light a cigarette, stick some jazz on, and stand in just the right spot so the blinds could cast slatted shadows across his face as he regarded it.

Even so, he needed it. The board provided a tactile, physical representation of his thoughts, each part of the investigation anchored to something real. It was a process that helped him think more clearly, to force him to slow down and examine what he had.

He turned his attention to the meagre notes he had scrawled.

The last person believed to have seen Finbar alive was Deirdre's brother, Adrian Dunphy. He had been travelling in a car along the Falls Road when he had spotted his nephew walking in the opposite direction. Adrian hadn't stopped, and the only thing he had been able to tell his sister was that Finbar was alone.

Unfortunately, any hope Jacob had of gleaning further information from Adrian was a dead end.

"He passed," Deirdre had answered quietly, her slight shoulders sinking as she spoke. "During the troubles."

She offered nothing further and Jacob didn't pry. Prior to Adrian, the last confirmed sighting of Finbar was at the borstal in Millisle the evening before, December 23rd, 1981.

"The staff saw him at lights-out," Deirdre explained. "They had to do a headcount every night. They told me he rigged a couple of pillows and stuffed them under his blanket." She was able to give a proud smile at her son's deception. "They didn't discover the trick until the next morning."

That brought Jacob to his second thread. Entering Hartley House into Google, the top result returned was for an urban exploration website, theirishrover.com. He clicked on the link and saw the rover had visited the location within the last year and had not only posted pictures, but had also provided a detailed history of the place.

The first paragraph confirmed for Jacob that Deirdre had been half-right about the borstal serving as a training facility for the Northern Ireland Prison Service. It had indeed been a training college, but the prison service had transferred their facility to the young offender centre at Hydebank Wood in Belfast a number of years back. Hartley House now sat empty, an apparently enticing attraction to people who liked to hang out in abandoned buildings.

Hartley House, according to the Irish Rover, was an Italianate mansion built in the 1800's and had passed through several generations of the same family before falling into disrepair. The mansion, and the forty-acre site it sat on, had been taken over by the state in the fifties, and converted into a borstal.

Clicking through the pictures snapped by the intrepid explorer, Jacob could see that even derelict, Hartley House was an imposing structure. The front entrance had a curved bow at one end, a projecting wing at the other, and a central, three-storey tower incorporating a porte-cochére for vehicles to pass under. Aerial drone shots showed that the mansion branched off into two wings that appeared to be add-ons to the original construction. Jacob could only imagine how the sprawling, ancient building would have looked to a busload of young inmates being ferried towards it.

Although the bright white paint had faded over the years, battered by the winds coming off the Irish Sea which looked like it was only separated from the house by a public road and narrow strip of beach, the grand facade and large bay windows had stood the loss of its occupants well. Judging solely from its outward appearance, Hartley House had not yet fallen victim to vandals or time.

Jacob scrolled on. In the mid-seventies, as a response to the spiralling violence, the prison service constructed a new building to the rear of the property; Lisvardin Training School.

The urban explorer had captured some suitably depressing pictures of Lisvardin. It was circled by high metal fences topped with barbed wire. Inside, grilles controlled movement on the landings. Rows of cells lined both sides of the corridor, while cameras watched every movement within. The barred windows, flimsy wooden chairs and concrete bed frames in each cell would have done little for whatever morale remained in the populace. It was obvious to Jacob that the training school was a prison in all but name.

Lisvardin wasn't meant to be welcoming. It was a closed borstal, and according to the Irish Rover, it was the goal for inmates to be promoted to the more liberal regime within the old mansion, where the boys slept in dormitories and enjoyed a degree more freedom.

In the early eighties, the prison service converted the dormitories into classrooms and the open borstal in the mansion closed. Lisvardin remained in use until the late nineties when the inmates were transferred to a more modern facility in Bangor.

Jacob scribbled down 'Simon' in his notebook. Whilst his father and uncle had walked the thin green line with the RUC, and later the PSNI, some of Jacob's family on his mother's side had made a career in the prison service. His cousin, Simon, was a senior officer at HMP Maghaberry, once dubbed the most dangerous prison in Western Europe, something Simon invariably managed to drop into conversation every time he told a new acquaintance what he did for a living.

His cousin could be an arse, Jacob knew, but he could be helpful in trying to track down where the records for the borstal were now held, or if they even still existed. Simon's name in his notebook was his reminder to reach out and ask.

By now he was at the bottom of the web page and belatedly realised there were no pictures of inside the mansion itself. The Irish Rover noted that although there was no on-site security, someone had shown up before he could get into Hartley House. He made a vague mention of an entrance to the mansion but wouldn't reveal where it was, in the hope it would prevent would-be vandals from accessing the site.

Jacob scrolled back to the top of the page and began once more from the start. According to Deirdre, Finbar was a frequent absconder. It stood to sense he would have spent the majority of his time in the closed unit. But if that was the case, how had he been afforded so many chances to escape?

Clicking through the website, Jacob saw the urban explorer

had a short 'About Me' section. The page revealed a name, Terry Lunn, and an address for Lunn's gallery on Bedford Street in the city centre. Jacob took note of both.

A further scan of Google didn't turn up much more info about Hartley House or the site it sat on. There was a page from a paranormal research group, but aside from the ghostbusters and Lunn's website, most of the returned results were years-old articles regarding a rumoured redevelopment of the site.

With nothing else about Hartley House to be found online, he turned his attention back to Finbar Skelly. A scan of the major social media sites didn't come back with any hits, and there were no unidentified bodies listed on the NCA's missing persons database for Northern Ireland. Helen would do a wider search to cover the whole of the UK.

The PSNI had a list of around thirty missing people on their website, but the oldest of those cases.was from 1987. For whatever reason the list didn't go any further back. After forty odd years the police probably guessed the missing person was not for turning up. Jacob ignored what this meant for the prospects of his case.

He brought up an online map of the Falls and Whiterock Road. Jacob was well acquainted with the area from his policing days and knew it would take, at most, fifteen minutes to make it from where Finbar was last seen to his home address.

This brought up something that had been gnawing at him from the moment Deirdre had mentioned it. Belfast in the early eighties. The violence of the Troubles was at its zenith. People were suspicious. Housing estates and streets were divided among religious lines. A stranger in the community stood out, yet someone had seemingly snatched a child off the street without anyone noticing.

Certainly, no member of the prison service was going to be taking a trip up to West Belfast to enquire after a juvenile absconder. The task would be given to the police, but as Deirdre had said, anytime they had caught Finbar previously, it was with an army escort. If a police patrol had intercepted Finbar between the Whiterock and home, it would have drawn attention, not to mention a few bricks and bottles coming their way.

Jacob glanced back at his notepad and the name he had scrawled.

Ned By Night.

Deirdre gave a wan smile when he had asked who he was. "From before your time. It was a story our parents told us when we were wee. Make sure you're home by dark or else Ned by Night would snatch you up."

"Why would Finbar be shouting that?"

"I wish I knew."

"Was it a story you told him?"

"Aye, not that it did much good. The kids then were too clever to be scared by some made-up monster and sure, there were worse things on our streets by then."

"Did Finbar ever mention him before?"

"No. Never." She paused for a beat and then said softly; "When stars are cloaked, and the moon slight, a figure wanders, cloaked in white. Through misty alleys and streets so bare, the wraith roams, a spirit of despair."

Jacob had leaned closer but had said nothing.

"His coat is tattered, his hat askew, a phantom of night, in foggy dew. Silent he moves, with gaze so hollow. A bandaged ghost in twilight's dark follow. A whispering breeze, the floor's soft creak, a hall's faint echo, the door's gentle shriek. Guard those you cherish, hold them near, for when the night deepens, Ned is here. Craving revenge by moon's ghostly light, stalks the tormented soul of Ned, by Night."

Jacob read the name again, felt a cold shiver creep across his chest and then felt utterly ridiculous for it. He opened his emails and quickly composed a freedom of information request addressed to the PSNI, regarding any investigation into the disappearance of Finbar Skelly and whether the case was still considered open. He was about to send it when he stopped, and saved the message to his drafts instead.

He brought up an online newspaper archive. Narrowing the search to just local papers and typing Finbar Skelly into the search bar produced only two results, both from the Belfast Sentinel. The first was from a week after Finbar went missing, a brief article on the fourth page. The same picture Deirdre had provided Jacob with now sat in black and white next to an appeal for anyone with any information to contact Andersonstown RUC Station. Jacob noted that the piece incorrectly stated Finbar was last seen at Hartley House Borstal, not the Falls Road.

The second article was from 1985, four years after Finbar's disappearance. This time Finbar's picture was accompanied by three others, all teenage boys, all roughly the same age as Finbar, and all missing.

Jacob sat forward. The article was written on the back of a fresh appeal by the RUC, trying to obtain any information about their whereabouts. Finbar had been the first of the quartet to go missing. The last, Richard McBride, had disappeared in 1983.

Aside from the appeal, there was little information other than the names, ages, and where the boys were last seen. The article ended with the police appealing for them to return home and for anyone with any information about their whereabouts to come forward.

No suggestion of foul play was mentioned, nor was there any hint the boys knew each other. The article stressed that it was not believed the disappearances were linked. Of the three from Belfast, one, Desmond McClure lived over in the East of the city. Another, Craig Fullerton was from the Village, not far from the Skelly home on the Whiterock. The Village however, was staunchly loyalist and Jacob doubted too many kids from there and the Whiterock palled about with each other back in those days.

Jacob scanned back up to the pictures sat by the byline. All were faded, low quality black and white copies. He wondered where the originals were sitting now. Over a mantelpiece in a battered frame, the picture held within fading along with the memories of those who knew them? Or were they forgotten already, gathering dust in an attic, or thrown away by a relative who never knew the person in the frame and didn't want the memento after clearing out the house of the deceased relative who did?

How many still remembered? How many still talked in hushed tones about Finbar or Desmond or Craig?

He took each name in turn and entered it into the archive. The other boys had rated at least five articles related to their individual disappearance. An anniversary would occasionally bring up a slightly updated piece but by the mid-nineties, none of the boys were ever mentioned again.

Jacob entered a few different combinations of the names into Google but nothing of relevance came back. The boys were forgotten to history.

He sat back in his chair. Four disappearances in two years. All unexplained, all seemingly unsolved. Belfast was blood-soaked in the eighties, but this seemed like an oddity.

Back in his emails, he pulled up the draft of the message he had composed to the PSNI. He edited it to include the details of the three other missing boys and hit send. The standard response time was twenty working days. Such was the nature of the job. Paper trails and waiting.

Darkness had fallen outside by the time Jacob pulled himself away from his screen. He leaned back into his chair as he rubbed his eyes and considered what he had. An idea was forming.

He picked up his phone, found the number in his contacts and dialled before hanging up after the first ring. He debated the reason why he was really making the call, ignored his rational side telling him exactly what he was doing, and phoned again.

By the time it hit the fifth ring, Jacob decided he would give it seven.

She picked up on the sixth.

"Well, hello stranger."

3

Jacob thanked the young waitress as she set his coffee down and left him alone to people-watch those shuffling past the window, hunched against the cold.

He stifled a yawn. It was a little before nine but he had been on a job and hadn't got home until almost three that morning. After making his call, he had driven over to a little side street off the Stormont Road. From there, he had tailed a Mrs. Louise Grady from her swish apartment complex to the car park of a local gym.

Ninety minutes passed before she exited the gym accompanied by a man at least fifteen years her junior. Jacob had snapped some pictures. Tanned, toned, and much too good looking in Jacob's grudging assessment, the man shared a few words with Mrs. Grady before getting into his own car.

It had seemed that on this occasion, the suspecting spouse was wrong, and fidelity was about to enjoy a rare win. Jacob was halfway through reprimanding himself about the job turning him cynical as he watched Mrs. Grady follow the man's car out onto the road and in the opposite direction of her marital home.

Jacob followed her to a modest semi-detached in Dundonald. Toyboy's car was already in the driveway. Jacob snapped a few more pics of Mrs. Grady entering the property and waited. She emerged a few hours later, looking a good deal more flushed than she had been after her gym session.

The client, the woman's rightfully suspicious spouse, was on business in England, but had insisted on an update as soon as Jacob had anything. He had transferred the pictures from his camera onto his laptop and emailed them to the husband, along with a text message to check his inbox, as soon as he got back to his apartment. The payment for killing another marriage was in his account before he had sat down in the café.

A dull melancholy took a sudden hold. He had been riding high in the summer. In a business that dealt with deceivers, swindlers, and cheats, he had brought home a case that had mattered. And yet, here he was, less than six months later, pursuing the same investigations once more.

The door opened and a chill swept through the coffee shop as Natalie Amato stepped in. Her smile was enough to lift Jacob, at least temporarily, from the sullen reverie. As she approached his table he was transported to their first meeting in his office and how suddenly he had fallen for her.

He had never acted on those feelings and Natalie had never given any indication she considered him anything other than a friend. So they had continued as such, even after the podcast had wrapped. They met for coffee, swapped stupid Instagram videos, and she even threw a bit of research work his way. On one occasion Natalie had invited him to climb Slieve Donard, Northern Ireland's highest mountain, with her and her son, Dillon, a fourteen-year-old whose moroseness was matched only by his ungainliness.

As was standard with Jacob, he was not upholding his end of the friendship. It wasn't that he pushed people away, it was that he let them slide by. It had happened with school friends, uni friends and his police friends, save for one. If he didn't buck up his ideas he knew it would happen with Natalie too, and the prospect hurt him more than he cared to consider.

"You don't write," she said, with mock hurt in her voice. "You don't text, and when you call, it's only with vague allusions to a tantalising mystery."

"Turnabout is fair play, Miss Locked Room Murder."

"Fair," Natalie acknowledged with a wink as she shrugged

off her coat. The overhead light reflected off the stainless steel of her Breitling chronograph watch, half-covered by the sleeve of her sweater. Natalie Amato was a successful woman but modest about it. The expensive watch was one of the few outwards signs she allowed herself to indulge in. "You look good," she said, appraising him as she sat.

Jacob, never comfortable with receiving praise, mumbled a thanks. He waited as she gave the waitress her order before her attention turned back to him. Her warm hazel eyes danced with barely contained excitement. She had found her lot in life with her podcast and Jacob had to admit that he had read her wrong when they initially met. He had thought her a journalist with a killer idea. In truth, she was a bona-fide investigator, who lived for a good case, for the thrill of a mystery needing to be unravelled.

There had been numerous times last summer where Jacob had expected her to throw her hands up, or at least take a step back. Yet every step further into danger only seemed to increase her resolve. Considering the case had ended up with her drugged and kidnapped from her own home and tied to a chair in a derelict factory while her would-be killer described how he was going to get away with her and Jacob's murder, then one might have expected her to have run a mile the instant Jacob called. Instead, he had barely made it past hello before she told him she was in. This coffee shop rendezvous first thing the next morning was her idea.

"So," Natalie said, spreading her hands. "Let's hear it."

Jacob had covered it briefly on their call the night before but now gave her a more comprehensive rundown while she listened without interruption.

Four boys. Four disappearances. No resolution. There was no link, at least in the sparse information available, between the quartet. Even so, the less than three years spanning their disappearances was odd, even for Northern Ireland in the early eighties.

"Finbar Skelly," Jacob said, holding out a finger as he consulted the notebook he'd brought. "Last seen on the Falls Road. Disappeared without trace, Christmas 1981, after escaping from the Hartley House borstal in Millisle. Desmond

McClure, last seen Lower Newtownards Road, 1982." He tallied the name of each boy on a new finger. "Craig Fullerton, left his grandmother's house on the Castlereagh Road in November 1982 and Richard McBride from Carrickfergus, January 1983."

"Carrickfergus?" Natalie said, noting the same discrepancy that Jacob had.

"Richard McBride was from Carrick but, and I'm quoting the Belfast Sentinel here, so don't shoot me, was 'feeble-minded.' He went to a special school in North Belfast, Saint Joseph's. Took a bus from outside his house, up to the Antrim Road and then walked the short distance to the school."

Natalie nodded as she considered the information. "Let's assume for now, the disappearances could be linked. Is there any sort of connection?"

"I'd been thinking the borstal initially. Finbar Skelly was serving time at Millisle. Desmond McClure also appears to have been a bit of a tearaway." He passed her one of the articles he had printed from the archive. "Police initially dismissed his disappearance as nothing untoward and going by the language used in that report, believed he'd turn up eventually. There's no mention of it, but I wouldn't be surprised to find he served time in a borstal too."

Natalie set the sheet down. "Alright, that seems plausible so far."

"With Craig Fullerton, the newspaper archives really don't tell us a whole lot. But by all accounts, Richard McBride was an introvert. He went to school, came home and played with his toy trains."

"So unlikely to have been in a borstal."

"Exactly."

The waitress returned with Natalie's coffee. Natalie thanked her and waited until she was out of earshot. "It's certainly an interesting premise, but we also have to be open to the possibility that there is no link."

"It's likely there isn't," Jacob acknowledged, "And I'll be honest, at the minute I don't have much to go on."

"But?"

"But, I figure if I rope you in, I get some added help for

Finbar Skelly's case, the one I've been hired for, and you might get an episode or two for your podcast. As far as I can tell, no one else has looked into these disappearances."

Natalie lifted her mug and took a drink. "Tell me more about this Ned by Night."

"An old urban legend, but I can't find anything about it online."

Natalie crossed one leg over the other as she sat back. "I like it as a hook. We could tie it into the borstal."

Jacob frowned. "How so?"

"Jacob Kincaid." Natalie took a chiding tone. "Don't tell me you haven't done your homework."

"You've lost me."

"You didn't know Hartley House is one of the most haunted buildings in Ireland?"

Jacob feigned surprise. "I did not."

"Well, don't just take my word for it, you can ask the good people at the Ulster Paranormal Research Society.

Jacob recalled a web page about the borstal being haunted during his Google search but had continued scrolling. Natalie was apparently a good deal more thorough in her background checks.

"The mansion has been the scene of two murders," Natalie continued. "A maid killed by her married lover in the 1800's, and an infant, slain by an intruder on the grounds in the 1920's. It also served as a convalescent home during the first world war."

"Oh, so it's brimming with ghosts," said Jacob

"What, you're too big to get spooked?"

"I didn't say that," said Jacob as his mind drifted to an old memory of a lonely winter night in New Burnley police station. "Do you know what a sangar is?"

"Like an armoured hut, right?"

"Yeah. Most stations over here have them at the front gate to let cars and people in and out. When I was response in Coalburn, part of our detail was manning the sangar up at New Burnley."

"I thought they'd have civilians do something like that."

"Depends on where the station is. If the threat in the area

is still high enough, like it is in West Belfast, they stick police officers in the sangars so they can shoot back should the station or their colleagues entering or leaving come under attack. Anyway, one night, probably ten years ago, I was detailed up to the sangar at New Burnley. It's a two-man post but the other guy down for it had phoned in sick, and our sergeant had no one spare to send up."

New Burnley was a sprawling site, but its use had been scaled back over the years. Sitting in the shadow of Belfast's Black Mountain, and on the edge of a Republican estate which had witnessed some of the bloodiest events of the troubles, on a winter night it was particularly desolate.

"Sangar duty is an easy gig," Jacob continued, "Especially in New Burnley. There a single TSG unit assigned there and nobody else."

"TSG?"

"Tactical Support Group," Jacob explained. "They're usually the ones you see doing public order or deploying to riots. Anyway, this night, the TSG were on a rest day, meaning the entire site was empty, save for myself. I had a horde of junk food, and whatever Netflix show I was watching at the time downloaded on my tablet.

"I don't think I saw anyone all night. Crews would sometimes call in to use the fuel pumps but I don't remember anyone stopping by. By three a.m. I was wrecked. I couldn't concentrate on my phone or tablet, so I tried to make himself comfortable and will the next four hours to pass quickly."

Natalie had leaned forward slightly and now rolled her eyes at Jacob's dramatic pause. "And?"

"And that's when I heard the footsteps. Heavy boots and a baton jiggling on the hip, walking towards the sangar from the direction of the old station building. It took me a few seconds to catch on to what I was actually hearing. The footsteps kept coming until they reached the bottom of the three steps leading up to the sangar and stopped.

"I remember turning in my chair, certain I would see someone looking back through the small porthole in the door but there was no-one. I opened the door, nothing. I swung the cameras around every inch of the site and saw no sign of anyone. How could there be? The only way in was through the twelve-foot-high gate I had been manning for the past six hours."

Finished, he spread his hands to invite comment from Natalie.

"Jacob Kincaid." Natalie's smile turned teasing. "You believe in ghosts!"

"No, no. I'm just telling a story."

"A ghost story."

Jacob tutted, annoyed at getting needled. "I didn't see anything and I don't believe it was a ghost. It's just a weird thing that happened, that's all."

"Alright," Natalie relented. She tapped her notebook. "Let's think about real life. We have our mystery. What's our first investigative step?"

"Well, I left my car back at the apartment."

"The flying deathtrap still going strong?"

Jacob ignored the unfair jibe towards his stalwart Renault Clio. "Do you mind taking a drive with me over to Ballyhackamore?"

*

Jacob had phoned ahead and his uncle greeted them both warmly, slapping Jacob on the shoulder and hugging Natalie. She and Harry had first met at a small shindig after the recording of their Followers of Eden podcast had wrapped. Harry had been charming, gracious, and had the younger crowd in stitches with his caustic wit. He had stolen the show from Jacob who hadn't minded in the slightest.

As he ushered them into the living room there was a faint scent of stale body odour, not fully hidden by air freshener. However, the telltale signs of creased blankets or stacked cushions at one end of the sofa suggesting Harry was back sleeping in the room were absent.

"Where's Noreen?" Jacob asked.

"Ah, just popped to the shop."

"Back soon then?"

"Well, it was three days ago, so who knows? But I remain ever hopeful. Anyway, long time no see, Natalie," Harry said, quickly changing topic. "Are you keeping well?"

"As well as can be expected with weather like that."

"Aye, it'd depress you quick enough. Get either of you a tea or coffee?"

Jacob and Natalie both declined and sat themselves on the sofa while Harry made himself a mug of tea in the kitchen. He came back in and sat slowly on the chair opposite.

"Like I told you on the phone, Jacob, I don't think I'll be a lot of help. The last of those boys went missing when I was still in the depot, and I only got posted up to Belfast a couple of years after that."

"I'm more looking for your take, Harry," said Jacob. "For one, how did the police treat reports of missing kids back in your day?"

Harry took a sup of tea as he considered the question. "I guess one thing to think about would be where they're from. This Finbar kid, even if his parents came to us, there wouldn't be a lot of people from the local area willing to help police."

Natalie frowned. "Not even for a missing child?"

"Different times," Harry said.

Jacob knew that wasn't entirely true. He had policed the same area as his uncle and although separated by twenty-five odd years, the ethos of not talking to the cops was still shared by many, even those too young to remember the bad old days.

"If we're being honest," Harry continued, "Back then, missing kids wouldn't be treated as seriously as now, especially boys. Lads will be lads, that sort of thing, ye know?"

"What would procedure have been?" Jacob asked.

"Christ, let's see. The station duty officer would take the initial details, complete the C6, send the missing person template to get the details circulated by radio. A local peeler would be assigned as IO and do the needful. Get details for friends and next of kin, find out if he's been reported missing before, where was he found..." he waved a hand. "You get the drift."

"So not that different from now," Jacob said.

"Technology aside, I expect not. Misper details would also be placed in the briefing book, but I'd guess briefing books went out with dinosaurs like me. If there was suspicion he was a victim of crime then the matter would probably be escalated to CID. Likewise if he didn't turn up within a day or two. You said this Skelly boy was living off the Whiterock Road. Somewhere like that, you'd always be wary of a come-on. Wouldn't be in the area in anything other than an armoured Land Rover and an army escort."

"Anything else?" asked Jacob.

Harry scrunched his nose. "Disappeared off the Falls in broad daylight?"

Jacob nodded. "Sometime around nine in the morning."

His uncle shook his head. "Sneaky beakys with their undercover surveillance, army patrols and our own, not to mention the 'Ra spotters keeping dick on every strange vehicle and person. It doesn't seem plausible to me."

"I'd been thinking the same thing," Jacob admitted. "And you never heard of the case?"

Another shake of the head. "But like I said, before my time in the West and I don't remember hearing about it when I got posted there. Sorry, Jacob, not sure what else I can tell you. Bit of a head scratcher you have."

"You don't know the half of it, Harry. Disappearances in broad daylight, haunted buildings, and a boogeyman to cap it off."

"Boogeyman, eh?"

Jacob knuckled an eye, the late night catching up to him, and murmured an affirmative. "What the kid was screaming the last time his ma saw him. Ned by Night."

Harry narrowed his eyes and set his cup down. "Ned by Night?"

"That's right. Some old urban -"

"- I know the story."

"You do?"

His uncle rubbed his jaw as if considering something before he stood suddenly and then disappeared into the kitchen without another word. Jacob heard the back door opening and Harry reappeared with a metal ladder under his arm.

"Christ," Jacob whispered to Natalie, "He's finally lost it."

She nudged Jacob in the ribs and the pair followed Harry into the hallway and up the narrow staircase. Harry had set the ladder under the attic door. Jacob stood on the bottom rung of the ladder to steady it as Harry climbed, pushing the trap door aside before he hauled himself out of sight.

Jacob listened to his uncle moving about for a full minute before he asked the question. "What are you doing, Harry?"

The answer came in the shape of a cardboard box a few seconds later. A cloud of thick dust jumped into the air as it hit the landing with a heavy thud.

Harry reappeared and quickly climbed down. "C'mon."

He lifted the box and hurried back downstairs, leaving the ladder in place. Jacob and Natalie reached the kitchen just in time to watch Harry stab a pair of scissors into the box, slicing the masking tape that had sealed it.

Jacob could see now what was inside; police notebooks. A lot of them. "Uh, should you have these?" The question earned another nudge in the ribs from Natalie, whose mind was firmly on the investigation rather than any boring data protection issues.

Harry didn't answer, fixated on the contents of the box as he began to search, picking one notebook out at a time, checking the date on the front and then setting it aside.

The notebooks had changed little between his uncle's time in the police and Jacob's own. They had the same beige cover and a space for the officer to note their name, rank, number, station and the date of issue and date of completion. The only difference was the RUC Crest in place of the PSNI one.

He picked up one of the discarded notebooks and peered inside. The writing within was in compact but tidy black ink. He was impressed. His own notebook scrawlings would have required a graphologist to decipher if they had ever fallen into the wrong hands.

"Here!" Harry thrust an open notebook towards them, his finger tapping the underlined date, Friday 22nd February 1985.

Jacob took the notebook and with Natalie leaning in, quickly read the entry.

Friday 22nd February 1985

0800. Commenced duty. Handover received from DS McCartan. Missing person, Edith Galbraith, DOB: 25/06/68, last seen Foxhill Lodge Children's Home, Stewartstown Road. Failed to return to home. Handbag found in alleyway, Lenadoon Avenue with Ms. Galbraith's ID. Suspected victim of foul play.

"Edith went missing and never turned up." Harry said. "We suspected she was abducted but never had proof. No blood, no sign of a struggle, no witnesses."

"I won't pretend that I'm some profiling expert, Harry," Natalie said carefully. "But I've picked up some casual knowledge over the years. If you're assuming a link, Edith doesn't fit. Different gender, and a gap of two years between her disappearance and the last of the boys."

Harry failed to hide a triumphant smile. "Check the entry for two days after."

Jacob turned the page.

Sunday 24th February 1985
Follow-up enquiries re: Edith Galbraith. Second round of house-to-house enquiries carried out, negative results. No update from Foxhill Lodge. No update from Edith's grandmother. Coalburn Station security cameras re-checked. Edith does not pass station in given time-frame.

The line after was a departure from Harry's neat writing. The ink was smudged on the page, the lettering jagged, written in a hurry.

Graffiti gable wall, Lenadoon Avenue:
Who took Edith Galbraith?
When stars are cloaked, and the moon slight,
Stalks the tormented soul of Ned, by Night.

"Holy shit," Natalie said, uttering a rarely heard curse.

'Holy shit indeed,' Jacob thought. "That, is a hell of a coincidence."

"There's more," said Harry. "A few months before, there

was a girl walking home on the Donegall Road."

"Another disappearance?" Jacob asked.

"Not this time. The girl, God, I can't remember her name..." Harry trailed off as if trying to recall before he gave a shake of his head. "Anyway, she remembers hearing footsteps behind her and then something being forced over her face. A rubber mask, like the kind dentists used way back when to sedate you before they yanked your teeth."

"Any link between her and Edith Galbraith?" Natalie asked.

"Not that I was aware of, but the girl," Harry snapped his finger, "Emily. Emily Goddard. She got a look at her attacker. Said his face was wrapped in bandages."

"Tutankhamun maybe." Neither Natalie nor Harry laughed. Jacob cleared his throat. "So, what's the link?"

"You didn't look into this Ned By Night?" Harry's question held a note of exaggerated shock.

"He's really half-assing this one, Harry," Natalie put in flatly.

Jacob ignored her. "Only what Finbar's mother told me. It was some sort of story kids were told to scare them into getting home before dark. Can't find anything about it online."

Harry nodded. "Aye, it's an old story. I hadn't heard of it before either. Seems like it didn't really travel much further than West Belfast. Supposedly this fella, Ned, was suspected of killing a farmer's daughter. A mob chased him back to his cottage. He barricaded the door, so they set it alight and watched it burn with him inside. When they picked through the ashes the next morning they don't find a body. A few nights later, the children of those who set the fire start to go missing, taken by a man wrapped in bandages."

A figure wanders, cloaked in white.

Jacob felt a flutter in his chest. Pieces falling together, the picture slowly forming. "Were you involved in the investigation for the failed abduction?"

Harry shook his head. "Not my patch."

"What about Edith?" Natalie asked.

Harry sighed. "Never turned up. Never got close to figuring out what happened to her."

"At least two of these missing boys seemed to be

tearaways," said Jacob. "Probably in and out of borstals."

"Edith had been in trouble with the Police a few times. Petty stuff. Her mother was a smack addict, not really in the picture, and her grandmother couldn't control her, so she ended up in Foxhill Lodge. Emily Goddard came from a well to do family though. He da was a barrister, as far as I recall."

Jacob scratched his beard. As with the missing boys, the link between Edith's disappearance and Emily's attempted abduction was tenuous but it was there all the same.

Harry opened a drawer and rummaged around until he produced an address book. "I have someone you might want to talk to. An old DI by the name of Breen. It was through him I learned about Emily Goddard's attempted abduction. He was investigating a string of missing girls and thought Edith could be connected to them.

"How?"

"Ned by Night. The graffiti found near where Edith was last seen wasn't the only time it appeared."

4

Hector Breen lived in Moira, a commuter village twenty miles outside of Belfast. A cold, driving rain had begun to fall as Jacob and Natalie took the Westlink out of the city and grew heavier as they followed the M1 countryward. The weather forecast on the radio suggested another freeze was coming, likely with heavy snow.

"How was Christmas?" Jacob asked as they exited the motorway and followed the sign towards Moira.

"Good. Me and Dillon spent the morning at the house and then we went to my parents for turkey and too much wine. How about you?"

"Same old."

When Jacob had been in the police, Christmas Day had meant bouncing from domestic to domestic as the festive cheer wore off but the drink continued to flow. His last Christmas in Coalburn had seen him tussling with a father who had originally phoned the police on his son. Junior had not found an X-Box under the tree as expected and decided to deck his father rather than the halls.

The dad had taken sudden exception to his son getting arrested for common assault and tried to lamp Jacob. He missed, Jacob tackled him, and both men went tumbling into the Christmas tree, bringing it down with them in a tangle of limbs, plastic branches and broken baubles.

The matriarch of the family decided this was the best time to grab a carving knife, to put it out of harm's way as it transpired, and not as Jacob's colleague had initially feared, to start stabbing all around her, and got a faceful of CS spray for her trouble.

Still, if Jacob had been offered the choice between the bruises, the three-hour wait in the vehicle dock at custody, and the mountain of paperwork that followed, versus the grey Christmas he had endured at the Kincaid residence, he'd have taken the holiday brawl and asked for seconds.

With no one buying the excuse that he was working, he had spent Christmas Day with his parents, stayed just long enough not to be rude, stopped in at his grandmothers to wish her a happy Christmas, and was back in his apartment by five. Alone, lonely, and ready for the day to be over.

"I thought I'd see you at the party," Natalie said.

He had forgotten about the Christmas Eve do at her place. It had promised strangers and small talk, two of Jacob's most keenly avoided matters. He had backed out by text the morning of the party with a fabricated family event.

"You get lucky under the mistletoe?" he asked, deflecting the subject from his flakiness.

"Well, it was mostly extended family, so no, thank god."

"Next year."

She scoffed. "Not if Dillon has anything to do with it. Bad times when your love life is so desolate your fourteen-year-old son is pushing you to go out and meet someone. He said it'd be good for me, if you can believe that. I..." Natalie began before stopping with an embarrassed chuckle. "I did sign up to an online dating site."

"Oh yeah?" Jacob said neutrally. "How's that working out?"

"A lot of dicks. Literally and figuratively."

Jacob made a face. "Men."

"They're the worst," Natalie agreed. "Although there was one guy who I've-oh! Is this it?" She pointed to the roundabout they were approaching, the conversation forgotten.

Jacob, who had found himself sitting suddenly straighter, glanced at the map on his phone. "That's it."

Natalie took the first exit into a large but tidy development of modern homes. They followed the road until Jacob pointed to a house with a gleaming silver Volvo in the driveway.

They huddled under the small awning above the front door as Jacob knocked. Footsteps, heavy on the floor, sounded from within. A large shadow fell over the frosted pane of glass. A lock clicked, followed by the sound of a bolt sliding across. Clearly Hector Breen took his home security seriously.

The man who answered the door would have been a bruiser back in his day. Harry had said Breen was pushing mid-seventies but he still held his large frame well. His ruddy nose and cheeks were a mess of broken capillaries, in stark contrast to his sharp blue eyes that radiated a keen cunning as he looked from Jacob to Natalie.

"Yes?"

Jacob noticed Breen kept his left arm out of view behind the half-open door and wondered if he had a weapon close at hand. Old RUC men could be a suspicious sort, often with good reason. "Hector Breen?"

"Who's asking?" The voice was gruff and age had done little to soften the strong north Antrim accent, a broad brogue with a notable Scottish influence thanks to geographical proximity separated by only a few miles of Irish Sea.

"My name is Jacob Kincaid. This is my partner, Natalie Amato. I'm a private detective and-"

"-And I'm not interested."

Before Jacob could reply the door was slammed in his face. The bolt slid back into place a second later.

Jacob looked to Natalie who offered a shrug as the heavy footsteps faded. He knelt and pulled the letter flap open. "Mr. Breen, I believe you knew my uncle, Harry Kincaid?"

He listened for any sign the name carried weight. It usually did with ex-cops of a certain vintage, but apparently not with Hector Breen.

"He told me to look you up," Jacob continued. "I'm looking into the disappearance of missing girls in Belfast in the eighties." Not quite true, but he could work around a little white lie if needed.

Natalie crouched next to him, listening. Jacob caught a

whiff of perfume as she leaned closer. "Mr. Breen. What do you know about Ned by Night?"

The name seemed to hang in the empty hallway. Jacob was about to give it up as a bad job when footsteps lumbered slowly back towards them. The door opened and Hector Breen took his time in regarding them both. Jacob got the impression he wasn't impeded by age but rather the fact he didn't rush himself on account of anyone.

"Maybe you should come in," he said finally.

He led the pair into a spotless living room and motioned for them to sit on the sofa. "I was about to open a bottle of red. Care to join me?"

"No, thank you, Mr. Breen," Natalie replied.

"I'd take a glass," Jacob said.

Breen's grunt may have passed for admiration. "Good man yourself."

Natalie checked her Breitling as Breen left the room. "A bit early, no?"

"Extremely. But I get the distinct impression Hector Breen isn't the most open person. If I need to ingratiate myself by choking back a glass of wine at eleven in the morning, I can rise to it."

"Such dedication."

"You know it." Jacob said, turning his attention to the room they were sat in.

There were no pictures of children or grand-kids, but plenty of Hector and a woman. Jacob could trace their life together through the pictures, from the black and white wedding photograph, through the changing fashion trends of the seventies and eighties, holidays, birthdays and anniversaries all the way through to grey hair and wrinkles.

"My wife, Nora." Hector said as he returned and noticed Jacob taking stock of the pictures. "She passed eight years back. Cancer."

"I'm sorry," Natalie said as Breen handed Jacob a glass.

Hector shrugged his massive shoulders and sat slowly. "So, a private detective you say?"

"That's right," Jacob replied. He reached into his wallet and handed his business card to the older man.

"You as well?" Breen asked, turning to Natalie as he set the card down on the arm of the chair.

"My lead investigator," Jacob cut in quickly before Natalie had the chance to answer. He didn't want to get tripped up by Breen taking issue with the fact he was talking to a journalist. They had an in, and Jacob didn't want to jeopardise their footing with the man at such an early stage.

Hector regarded him with those keen blue eyes once more before he shook his head. "Ned by Night. Christ, I haven't heard that name in a long time."

"But you've thought about it," said Jacob.

"You're right on that. One of few cases I could never get over. Those girls...."

"So," Jacob began. "On your doorstep, I wasn't exactly truthful."

The blue eyes fixed on him.

"What I mean," Jacob said quickly, "Is that I'm not investigating the missing girls but rather the disappearance of a teenage boy from a few years before."

"And you believe it ties in?"

"Maybe it does." He shrugged. "But maybe it doesn't."

He recapped Finbar Skelly and the other three missing boys, covering the same ground for the third time that day. No geographical link, no personal link, no anything. They had the name of a Boogeyman lost to history, which thanks to Harry, now linked Finbar, however flimsily, to at least one missing girl, and the attempted abduction of another.

"I remember your uncle," Breen said once Jacob had finished. "He was a peeler's peeler. I reviewed the Edith Galbraith file too, it was good work."

"And you thought Edith's disappearance was linked to what happened to the failed abduction on Emily Goddard?"

"Them and many others," said Breen. "Emily would have been the first, had she not been so lucky. All told, at least eight young women went missing in Belfast without explanation, the last a little bit before 1992."

Natalie leaned forward as if she hadn't heard him correctly. "Eight?"

"Linked?" Jacob asked.

Breen nodded. "No sign of struggle, nothing left behind. Emily was drugged and only escaped by the grace of God, and the good timing of two random fellas happening upon them."

"Do we know who they were?" Natalie asked.

"No, they got Emily home but cleared off before the police arrived. They'd done their good deed and didn't want to undo it by talking to the cops."

"Helpful," said Jacob.

Breen gave a *what are you gonna do* shrug. "There's more. The graffiti your uncle found after Edith Galbraith went missing wasn't the only instance. There were at least three locations that were tagged with a poem. Christ, how'd it go?"

"When stars are cloaked, and the moon slight, stalks the tormented soul of Ned, by Night," recited Jacob.

Breen clicked his fingers. "That's it."

"Hoaxsters?" Natalie offered.

The old man shook his head. "A couple of these girls were never even reported as missing. The authorities thought they'd just ran away."

"So what does that mean?" Natalie asked.

"That means no searches, no media campaign, no leaflet drop," said Breen.

"No public knowledge," added Jacob.

"So," said Natalie. "The person writing the graffiti must have known something about the disappearances?"

"Exactly," Breen replied.

Jacob scratched at his chin. "You said some of these girls were never even reported as missing. How did you find out about them?"

"Touts, intel documents, local peelers hearing a bit of gossip. Eventually word got back to me and I added them to my investigation."

"What happened?" Jacob asked.

"I kept working it. For a while the bosses were happy to let me tear away. Something to keep me busy. But when the last girl went missing, Eden Hennessey, well, let's just say I was shit upon from a great height."

Natalie frowned. "Why?"

"Started asking the wrong sort of questions. I suggested

there was a link between the disappearances and the fact almost all the girls were in care, and got hauled over the coals for it. I was given a choice, drop it and concentrate on live investigations, or spend the last years seeing out my service on some remote border station." Breen's chuckle was humourless. "I did what I could. Kept working it on the down low. Tried to give it a good go once I retired but without the resources, I didn't have much hope."

"And the girls never turned up?" Natalie asked.

Breen sighed deeply. "I keep in touch with Eden's mother, send her a card every Christmas." He got up from his seat and crossed to the mantle where a row of Christmas cards sat. He lifted one. "She still holds herself responsible. Was a junkie you see, that's why Eden was in care, but getting herself cleaned up. Just a little too late. She's managed to stay sober all these years since. Christ knows how." He cleared his throat and set the card back.

Jacob took a polite sip of the red, a drink he didn't enjoy even at a socially acceptable hour. "What about other possibilities? Maybe at least some of them did run away. Across the water or down to Australia."

"It's a nice fantasy, but I don't think so. No means to support themselves, or the finances to travel."

"Well-" Jacob began

"-And I know what you're thinking," Breen's raised voice cut him off immediately. "But turning tricks means you'll eventually flag up on police systems somewhere, be it here, or on the mainland, or over the border. Every one of these girls vanished into the ether."

"What about the paramilitaries?" Natalie asked.

"Targeting random women? Even if it was someone going off the reservation, all those groups were riddled with touts, no matter what side they were on. Some word would have got out."

"Maybe it was Poddy Sweeny," Jacob offered, more to himself than anyone else in the room.

Natalie and Breen both looked at him.

"Who the hell is Poddy Sweeny?" Breen asked.

"Poddy Sweeny?" Jacob said, affecting surprise. "The ultimate criminal mastermind? The scourge of West Belfast?"

"You've lost me," Breen replied.

"That makes two of us," Natalie said.

"It's a name I came up with back when I was stationed at Coalburn," Jacob explained. "You see, it was never that the police were too slow to respond to a call, or that the bad guy outran us, or that people didn't want to co-operate with the peelers. It was because of little Poddy Sweeny. He was a criminal savant. Anything that happened in West Belfast that we didn't have a suspect for, it had to have been Poddy Sweeny who carried it out. There wasn't any other logical explanation."

Breen's laugh was genuine, so Jacob continued.

"And there was nothing he didn't turn his hand to. Nicking cars, shoplifting, burglaries. When two big-time drug dealers got it in the head in the Shamrock social club with no CCTV and no witnesses, we figured Poddy Sweeny had turned hitman. Just for the day though. The next night, he was doing donuts in a stolie down in Albert Street."

"Sounds like another boogeyman story," Natalie said wryly. "Only this one you tell to your local policeman before he goes to bed at night."

Breen ran a hand over his face and Jacob sensed some of the man's guard towards them having slipped. "Tell me this, Kincaid. Are you going to give this investigation into your missing boys a fair shake?"

Jacob let his smile and the memory of Poddy Sweeny fade. He made sure to meet Breen's eye. "Absolutely."

"Then I want to help. I can't get past this Ned By Night connection between your Skelly kid, and my girls. Give me a day or so. I'll dig out my old notes and speak to Mrs. Hennessy, see if she'll talk to you. Maybe she'll have something to pass on."

It was more than Jacob would have hoped for before making the journey out to Moira. They shook hands and Jacob reminded Breen his number was on the card he had given him. The old man saw them to the front door and then locked it behind them.

"What do you think?" Jacob asked once they were back in Natalie's car.

"I think we have something," she said quietly. "I'm not

convinced this Ned by Night angle is anything other than fortuity, but we have something to work on."

"You alright?"

"Yeah, I'm fine. Missing children. It's just... heavy."

"I know. Sorry about cutting you off in there. I just thought-" He was interrupted as his mobile buzzed. Helen was calling. He answered with a "What's up?"

"I think you should come back to the office," Helen said. "The police are here."

5

"You want me to come up with you?" Natalie asked, her journalistic curiosity thoroughly piqued by Helen's call.

Jacob shook his head. "It'll be nothing to get excited about. I'll give you a shout when I hear back from Hector, alright?"

She reluctantly agreed and Jacob raised his hand in a quick wave as she pulled away. Keeping his head down against the rain, he hurried towards his office.

Helen hadn't been able to tell him much on the phone other than a detective was waiting and would speak only to him. Jacob assumed it was related to one of his recent cases. The police paying a visit wasn't an uncommon occurrence. Usually, it was someone on the wrong end of one of his investigations, a spurned spouse or a benefits cheat, reporting him for some sort of imagined impropriety, which was quickly filed without any further action.

Normally it wouldn't have worried Jacob, but the fact it was a detective taking an interest, rather than uniformed officers, had given him pause.

He took the stairs two at a time up to the office and found Helen sitting at her desk, face like thunder. She was alone.

"They're gone?"

Helen answered by pointing towards the closed door of his own office.

Jacob strode across the small space and yanked the door

open to find a lone woman inside. She had her back to him, studying the cork pinboard on the wall that held the scanned image of Finbar Skelly, an impressive array of takeaway flyers, and not much else.

The woman turned slowly, apparently unphased by Jacob's attempt at an angry entrance. She was young, early thirties at a guess, and although he wouldn't have described her as classically pretty, there was something about her that Jacob was immediately drawn to, even while stomping into a room.

Her fair skin contrasted against dark hair in a sharp pixie style that accentuated high cheekbones and the determined set of a strong jawline. She wore a tailor fitted double-breasted slate blazer with matching trousers and no jewellery, bar a midsize two-tone watch that gleamed on her left wrist. Rolex.

"Jacob Kincaid?" Intelligent grey eyes sized him up, as if matching him with whatever information she was already in possession of.

"That'd be me," Jacob said as he slowly took her offered hand. She had thrown her coat over the back of his chair. A beige folder sat on his desk. "I hope you're not too surprised to see me. You know, standing in my office and all."

She ignored the weak jab. "Your secretary –"

"–Business manager," Jacob said, plucking the two words out the ether and deciding they worked. Helen might not have an official title, but secretary certainly wouldn't cover it.

The woman with the fair skin held up a hand. "Apologies, business manager. She was quite protective. When I wouldn't furnish her with the details about what I wanted to discuss with you, she turned somewhat...passive aggressive."

"Helen, really? Usually she's just aggressive aggressive."

"I thought it best to wait for you somewhere I wouldn't be underfoot, so to speak."

"You couldn't have left a message?"

"I thought it better to talk in person and sooner rather than later."

The detective, who still hadn't deigned to introduce herself, stood with her back straight and shoulders squared, yet there was a relaxed fluidity in her stance that belied any stiffness. Her arms were loosely crossed in front of her, a gesture that

Jacob read as both casual and assertive.

He walked past her, lifted the coat off his chair and handed it to her, before seating himself. "The mysterious woman act is a bit old hat for me these days. I've certainly seen it done better, so can we cut to the chase?"

"We can." She produced a business card from the pocket of her trousers.

"Detective Chief Inspector Zara Steele," Jacob read the card. "Cold Case Unit." He turned the card over and then looked at Steele. "The PSNI has a cold case unit?"

"We're new. Well after your time on the job."

Jacob met the grey eyes. Intelligent and completely confident. She was letting him know she was aware of his past, establishing an early dominance as the one with the information. He pushed the card back across his desk with a finger. "A new name for the Historical Enquiry Team?"

Steele shook her head. "We deal with crimes that aren't considered legacy. There's plenty of unsolved crimes that weren't committed by terrorists. No name should be forgotten."

"Nice speech. What do you want?"

"I've been notified of your freedom of information request."

Jacob tried to keep his expression neutral. The standard response to an FOI took weeks and when the reply came, it was in writing, not a personalised visit from someone as high up the food chain as a Chief Inspector. "And?"

"And I did some digging." She slid the beige folder towards him.

Jacob lifted it and found two sheafs of paper inside, each fastened with a clip. He lifted the thinner sheaf and leafed through it quickly. "Photocopies of the original notes for the disappearance of Finbar Skelly."

Steele nodded. "And copies of the briefing book. It's a - "

"- I know what it is," Jacob interrupted sharply. Too sharply. His eyes flicked up to her. "Sorry."

Steele waved the apology away as Jacob turned his attention back to Finbar's notes. They were brief. No statement from Deirdre Skelly, no witness details, no record of contact with Deirdre beyond the initial receipt of the missing person report.

"The original IO?"

"DC Craddock. Deceased."

Jacob grunted. So much for that line of enquiry. He put the thin sheaf of papers down and lifted the other.

"Richard McBride," Steele explained. "The last of these missing boys."

There was a good deal more information in McBride's file, including statements from friends, family, teachers at St Joseph's, even the bus driver for his last journey from Carrickfergus to the Antrim Road.

"How about the IO for this?"

"DI Philpott." Steele shook her head before Jacob could even ask the question if the man was still alive.

Even a brief glance at the two sets of notes told a story. Richard McBride had warranted a thorough investigation headed by a Detective Inspector. Finbar had rated a DC and little else.

Jacob set the notes down. "The two other names, McClure and Fullerton?"

"Working on it." Steele said and then made a face. "Truthfully, I'm having trouble tracking down where their files might be stored."

Jacob put the paperwork back in the folder and then slid it back across to Steele. "What do you want?" He repeated the question Steele had deftly avoided just a minute before.

"I want to find out what happened to these boys."

"And?"

"And for the Police to get a share of the credit."

Jacob steepled his fingers and allowed himself a humourless smile. "Just the Police?"

Steele returned his smile. There was no point denying her angle, and to her credit, she made no effort to.

"Why me?"

"I know you," Steele replied. "Or of you, rather. You were highly thought of during your time on the job."

"Not highly enough for them to keep me around."

She ignored that. "And my team was briefly involved in the

aftermath of your investigation into the Followers of Eden."

Jacob rubbed at his chin but stayed silent.

"Look," Steele said, her voice softening as she leaned on Jacob's desk. "My unit is small and presently swamped, but I believe we want the same thing here."

"What about your superiors? Aren't they worried working with a private detective, one who was kicked off the force, would sully the good name of the PSNI?"

"Let me worry about my superiors," Steele replied. "I think a partnership could be mutually beneficial. Unless your investigation has already turned up so much information that you're able to turn away help?"

"I've only been on it a day," Jacob said sullenly and felt his cheeks redden at his defensiveness. Steele was right though. Aside from the boogeyman angle, he had nothing to go on. He thought for a second. "There's a name that's come up in my initial research. I'd like his address."

"I can't do that," Steele said.

"Partnership already paying dividends," Jacob replied, sinking back into his chair with feigned resignation.

Steele laughed. "That is a trap." She pointed an accusatory finger towards him. "You know I can't give out that info, but if I tell you I will, then you can assume that I'm not on the level."

Jacob smirked. She was canny enough. Giving him the address would have breached any number of data protection laws and a police officer didn't have the same flexibility in bending the law that Jacob enjoyed. A police officer who wanted to stay gainfully employed, at any rate. The fact she was laying out her boundaries from the outset, lent her proposal a degree of legitimacy.

"What I'm suggesting," Steele said, "is that you work the case and I'll try to see how I can assist, within the law, and the code of ethics." She held her hands up. "That's my pitch."

"I have a partner on this investigation. Natalie Amato. You already know about our investigation into the Followers, so I assume you know the name. Just so you're aware that if anything comes of this, it might get a lot of exposure."

Steele's expression didn't shift.

Jacob grunted. "You were counting on the fact I'd brought

Natalie on board."

"I had been planning to suggest it," Steele admitted if you didn't bring it up beforehand. Look, I won't bullshit you, Jacob, I want to help you find what happened to those boys, and I'm looking to get a share of the credit if we do."

"Well, I respect your honesty."

"Good," Steele replied. "You have my number. Call me when you make your decision. For now, I won't take up any more of your time."

Helen stood as they exited Jacob's office. Steele to her credit, steadfastly ignored the daggers following her across the room, and turned to Jacob as she reached the door and held out her hand.

"I look forward to hearing from you." Her grip was practised and strong.

Helen waited until the younger woman had shut the door behind her. "Well?"

"Wants to help with the Skelly case." Jacob replied. It was a stretch of the truth he knew, and although he felt guilty about the deceit, he didn't want the lecture from Helen reminding him they had been hired by Deirdre Skelly to look into the disappearance of her son, and only her son. He hadn't mentioned about bringing Natalie on board yet, or the angle with the other missing boys.

"Why?" Helen asked. "What's her angle?"

"Ambitious ladder climber."

"In it for herself."

"Oh, very much so. Sees her name in the papers that one."

Helen folded her arms and leaned against her desk. "She's using you." The thought of Zara Steele using him wasn't particularly unappealing to Jacob. Helen sensed his mind had shifted to the gutter and rolled her eyes. "Grow up."

Jacob smirked as his phone buzzed. It was a message from Simon, telling him he was in town. Jacob fired off a quick reply, asking to meet in The *Spaniard* in twenty minutes.

"Before you rush off," said Helen. "The priest you were looking for?"

"Pettigrew?"

"Might have located him." She beckoned Jacob around to

her side of the desk. On her screen, an old article from the BBC news website was open.

BBC News Northern Ireland
Monday, 24 January, 2005, 09:19 GMT

Jeremiah Pettigrew, a former priest accused of abusing young boys at a school in West Belfast, has been located at an address in Whitehead, following an extensive investigation by victim advocacy groups.

Pettigrew, 59, who worked at St. Martin's School in the 1980s and 1990's, was named by several former students who have come forward with allegations of sustained physical abuse.

Allegations against Pettigrew first surfaced in the early 1990s but were quietly handled by church officials. Pettigrew was reportedly removed from St. Martin's and reassigned to another diocese before leaving the priesthood entirely.

"Deirdre said he left the parish," said Jacob, as he read. "Interesting that he left the priesthood altogether." He scanned the rest of the article but nothing further caught his attention. "Nice work, Helen."

"There's more. The 2013 phonebook shows a Jeremiah Pettigrew, still with an address in Whitehead. I'll ping it through in an email."

Jacob nodded and reached for her mouse, quickly scrolling back down the article. Going by what the BBC reported, the priest would be pushing eighty now and very possibly no longer among the living. Still, it was a trail worth following and Jacob decided to hit Whitehead in the morning.

He asked Helen to lock-up, said goodbye and walked to The Spaniard. The bar was quiet. Simon had got there before Jacob and secured one of the tables in the little snug at the back.

His cousin was touching forty with a generous gut and a hairline retreating even faster than Jacob's. "Well, what about you?" he said as Jacob reached the table.

"All good. Thanks for meeting me."

"Not a problem." He moved a pint of beer towards Jacob.

"We missed you over Christmas."

That was a lie. Jacob and Simon's wife, Clara, had never got on. Clara was of the opinion Jacob was a sarcastic ass who clouded any social engagement she hosted, and Jacob was of the opinion Clara was Clara, and Clara was someone who he took measures to avoid.

"Our busiest period," Jacob said, lying right back. "Never stopped." He flipped open his notebook before he could spew more fibs. "I've been hired to look into the disappearance of a teenager. Went missing back in the eighties."

Simon let out a low whistle. "Good luck. How do you think I can help?"

"He was an inmate at the Millisle Borstal."

"Alright, fire away but fair warning, I'm not sure how much help I'll be."

"You worked at Hartley House when it was the prison service training college, right?"

"Aye, just before the college moved to Belfast. 2014 or thereabouts. Thought it'd look good for the promotion board."

"What was it like?"

"How do you mean?"

Jacob shrugged. "It as haunted as they say?"

"Oh absolutely."

"Come on," Jacob scoffed.

"Hey, no lies here. It was a weird place, Jacob. Spooky as fuck. There were store rooms on the second floor and a file room on the third, none of the staff would go up to them alone. And I mean not a one. I'm talking about hairy-arsed prison warders here. These boys had been through some shit in the old days at the Maze and the Crum, but at quitting time, most wouldn't stay in the building by themselves."

"And you believed it?"

Simon held up his right hand as if taking an oath. "I stayed behind my first day. I'd already heard the stories back when I was going through training and laughed them off. I lasted ten minutes."

"Why?"

"The vibe. I can't explain it, but the place isn't right."

"You ever hear anyone talking about Ned by Night?"

"Who?"

"Never mind." Jacob took a long drink of beer, a buffer between topics. "What about the Lisvardin? When did that get closed down?"

"Before I joined the job, and that's going back fifteen years. I was up in it a few times, they used it for training scenarios. Cell takeouts, hostage negotiation, stuff like that."

"Anyone around the college ever work in the place when it was still a borstal?"

"A couple, yeah."

"They ever talk...I dunno...about anything untoward?"

"Untoward?"

"You know what I mean."

Simon took a drink of his beer and then snapped his fingers. "As a matter of fact, they did. From what I remember, it was in between the lessons on prisoner escort and landing routine. Oh by the way, a few lads got diddled here back in the day."

"Funny."

"Oh come on, what's got your balls in a twist?"

Jacob shrugged, not quite sure himself. A heaviness had attached itself over the case from the moment he had laid eyes on Deirdre Skelly. He let his attention drift over the random tat that adorned the walls of the pub. Photos of sunnier climes competed with band posters, crosses, and religious memorabilia fought for limited space. "The kid escaped by stuffing a couple of pillows under a blanket."

It took Simon a second to realise Jacob had jumped back to the missing boy. He harrumped. "Keys and numbers."

"Come again?"

"The most important thing for any warder. All keys present, all numbers correct."

"So what are you saying?"

"Well, different times and all that. But some routines don't change, for good reason. At night, we do hourly checks of every prisoner. At night we do body checks, specifically checking for a sign of life from every prisoner, even if it's just a chest rising and falling. Pillows under the blanket are good for movies, but it doesn't pass mustard in real life."

"Maybe the borstal staff weren't as rigorous."

"Maybe." Simon didn't sound convinced.

"I know it's probably a long shot, but who could I speak to about accessing the records from Hartley House?"

"For the trainee officers?"

"The inmates, Simon. Why would I need the records of trainee prison officers?"

His cousin frowned at the snapped reply.

"Sorry," Jacob said, rubbing a hand over his face. "Were they kept on site?"

"This job of yours is getting on top of you, mate," Simon said quietly.

Jacob didn't disagree.

"The records *were* kept on site actually," Simon continued. "Very top floor of the tower. One of those rooms no one went near. Don't know why they were never moved." He smiled. "Maybe they didn't want to bother the ghosts."

"Well, where would they be now?"

"Still there."

"C'mon, Simon, don't take the piss."

"I'm not."

"They just left the files sitting in an empty building?"

"Why not? The borstal in Hartley House was shut down in the eighties, and Lisvardin was closed in the nineties. What good are old juvenile records going to be?"

"This isn't America. Juvenile records don't get sealed. They stay with you."

"They do," Simon agreed. "They're probably on any number of digital databases, but I'm telling you, the original paper records will still be in Hartley House."

Jacob shook his head. "I don't buy the prison service would just leave cabinets full of documents at their arse."

Simon smirked into his beer. "Then I think you severely underestimate the ineptitude of our esteemed management in the Northern Ireland Prison service."

6

Jacob took a ragged breath, knowing he was losing a battle against sheer exhaustion. He tried to push away, to create separation but he had nothing left.

The thumb pushed into his throat as his attacker tried to sneak an arm around to choke him. Grunting with desperation, Jacob blocked it, his own arm weaker than a wet noodle as he grabbed at the other man's wrist.

Suddenly, the weight on his back lifted. Too late, Jacob realised what was happening. He tried to spin with the movement but was too slow. He gurgled as the fabric of his clothing was pulled across his throat tighter than a vice.

Spots began to dance in front of his eyes and Jacob knew he was going out. With the last ounce of strength he possessed, he did the only thing he could think of, and reached out to tap his hand on the ground.

The release in pressure was instant and Jacob sank down to the floor, sucking in lungfuls of air.

"Good roll, mate."

Jacob felt the friendly tap on his shoulder as last night's dinner threatened to make an appearance. He managed to raise his head an inch off the mat. "Thanks."

"Hey, you almost made it the full three minutes," the man said.

Man. Jacob doubted his sparring partner was old enough to buy a beer. His smile was infectiously happy. The rest of the morning's class had headed for the showers, and the youngster had asked if anyone fancied a quick roll. Only Jacob had offered. He now realised why.

"Next time," Jacob said.

The kid's smile grew wider and he patted Jacob on the shoulder one more time before heading for the changing room.

"Well, he made you look like a dickhead."

Jacob turned his head to find Michael Healy standing at the edge of the mats. He had just finished the last shift on a set of four nights and looked every inch of it, his poster boy handsomeness somewhat diminished by the pale skin and heavy eyes that only night shift exhaustion could bring.

Thirteen years before, Jacob had found himself sitting next to Michael on their induction day at the police depot. They had been friends ever since. Lucking out, they had been posted to the same section at Coalburn station and had learned the ropes together. Jacob, once he felt he had a sufficient grasp of on-the-ground policing, had made the jump to detective and the Major Crimes Team. Michael, on the other hand, had never harboured any ambition to go beyond response, and was still in the same section he and Jacob had originally been posted to.

"He's been doing this since he was in nappies," Jacob replied, breathing still laboured.

"I thought this was your sport."

Jacob flopped onto his back. "That was Judo, and that was fifteen years, and several bad lifestyle choices ago."

He had been a reasonably fit man when he was younger. Thanks to the tutelage of his uncle Harry, Jacob could boast he was a judo black belt and mediocre boxer. Sports had taken a back seat after he joined the police but he had kept himself fit through gym work. Apathy, and if he looked back honestly, a touch of depression after the loss of his policing career, had killed any athletic endeavours in the almost five years since. The gym was a rarely visited location, and his diet quickly fell away to takeaways and junk food.

The turning point had been his hike on Slieve Donard with Natalie and Dillon where he had seriously considered asking her to carry him up the last half of the mountain. After allowing himself the appropriate time to recover and deciding something needed to change, Jacob had gone back to his old Judo club, thinking the time was right to pick the sport up again. He was promptly chucked on his head seven times in the first half hour, puked in a bin outside, and came to the conclusion the sport had perhaps passed him by in the intervening years.

Not wanting to give up completely, he had signed himself up for Brazilian Jiu Jitsu, a grappling sport with more emphasis of ground submissions and less on him getting launched through the air against all reasonable understandings of physics. To his own surprise, he had stayed reasonably committed to his new hobby and usually managed to drag himself onto the mats a few times a month to get stretched and roughed-up.

A fleeting thought of taking up pickleball went through his mind as he slowly stood up on jelly legs. He fetched his bottle of water and took several long gulps. "How long were you standing there?"

"Long enough to see a child take you down and watch you flop around the mat like...." Michael paused to search for the appropriate description.

"...a beached whale?"

"God, no. Nowhere near that graceful."

"Thanks, chum."

Jacob took a quick cold shower and stuffed his sweaty gi into a sports bag. Once changed into a hoody and tracksuit bottoms, he led Michael to a nearby cafe where they claimed a free table.

"Zara Steele," Michael said as they sat. "You never heard of her?"

"Should I have?"

"Probably came on the job a couple of years after us."

"She doesn't look much over thirty," said Jacob. "I take it she's on the fast track?"

Michael nodded and Jacob grunted. By its nature, fast tracking meant candidates were raised above their level into roles they did not have experience in, to act with an knowledge they did not have. Some rose to the occasion, others floundered.

His friend seemed to sense what Jacob was thinking. "From what I've heard, she was actually a pretty decent peeler when she was on the ground. Ambitious as fuck, but decent."

"Where did she go out of the depot?"

"Bangor."

Jacob gave a sarcastic whistle. "The wilds of North Down."

Michael smiled. "You remember Jonny Martin?"

"The ball bag from E Section?"

"The very same. He was in Steele's depot squad. I remember him telling me they all had awful luck with where they got assigned to. Everyone got the rough spots. North or West Belfast, Derry, Lurgan."

"But not her."

"Nope. Only one of the twenty to get sent to the mean streets of Bangor. Caused a bit of a stink."

"How so?"

"She comes from some sort of money."

"Money? Like rich parents?"

Michael shook his head. "Oh no. There's rich, and then there's the level above that. When she got her posting there was talk of backs being scratched, stuff like that."

"Oh yeah?"

"Probably bullshit, about the back scratching, I mean. But the money part is true. She turned up for her first day at Garnerville driving a vintage *Porsche*. A 911 at that."

Jacob had little interest in cars but a Porsche 911 registered, even for him. The fact it was being discussed twelve years after the fact, spoke to how it was received at the time. Steele would have been noticed from the very beginning of her career. Not ideal in the training depot where the safe advice was to play the grey man.

He rubbed at his chin. "How did she fuck up and get pushed into running a cold case unit?"

"No fuck up. The unit's her baby. I mean, think about it, people love mysteries. How many listeners tune in to Natalie's podcast every week? When one gets solved, it makes the news, generates interest. She wants her name out there."

Which married up with what she had said in his office, Jacob thought. Fast tracker, from money, and with enough clout to create her own unit. She was either a potentially useful ally, or a positively deadly enemy.

"She's already been on TV you know."

"Sorry?"

"Local tv," added Michael.

"Doing what?"

"Presenting."

"Fuck off."

"I'm serious," said Michael. "It was on *UTV* a few years back, one of those shows where they appeal for information on different crimes. She was meant to be the police consultant but ended up being a co-presenter. She's either for the very top, or sidestepping onto the speech circuit, or consultancy, or something."

"Has she had much success with the cold case team so far?"

"Some," said Michael. "The unit's probably only a couple of years old and very small."

"So she's looking for a big win."

"Four missing teenagers? She cracks this and her name will be in lights."

The waiter arrived with their breakfast and they both tucked in.

"You hear from Natalie lately?" Michael asked, as he went to work on his smashed avocado.

"I'm actually working with her on this." Jacob noticed the immediate curl of Michael's lip. "What?"

"Nothing."

"Come on, out with it."

"No, nevermind." Micheal grinned before finding his game face. "And how did she get involved?"

"I asked her."

Michael sighed and lowered his fork. "You've got it bad, boy."

"Fuck off."

"Look, as a committed and reasonably content homosexual, I'll admit I'm not too familiar with the way of women folk, but why not just ask her out?"

"That moment has passed." Jacob watched Michael shoot him a despairing look before returning to his breakfast. "I thought that maybe there was something there," he continued, "when we were working together last summer, but I talked myself out of acting on it."

"How come?"

Jacob shrugged. "I dunno. She's gorgeous, smart, funny, successful..."

"You're funny."

"Cheers for that."

"Oh, come on, don't get in a twist." Michael stabbed a loose piece of toast with his fork and then pointed it at Jacob. "You know what your problem is?"

"Where to start?"

"You've built her up in your mind into some sort of ideal woman with no faults."

Jacob knew there was some truth to that but wasn't going to admit it. "You think I put her on a pedestal?"

"Do I think you put her on a pedestal? I think if she farted in the car you'd wind the window up and ask for seconds."

They finished their breakfast. Jacob picked up the bill as a thank you for picking his brain, and let Michael get home to his bed. He walked back to his apartment and changed into a pair of jeans, a sweater, and a heavy coat. Collecting his Clio from the multi-storey, he made it out of the city without much difficulty, the majority of the morning traffic coming in the opposite direction.

Whitehead was a small coastal village, sat on the northern end of where Belfast Lough opened into the North Channel. Jeremiah Pettigrew's last known address was on a promenade that stretched from the edge of the village, along the shoreline, and ending at the foot of the Blackhead Lighthouse, one hundred and fifty feet above. Jacob left the Clio at a car park and made for the promenade on foot.

It was a beautiful walk, aside from the temperature. Jacob pulled his coat tighter and shoved his hands deep into his pockets, cursing himself for forgetting to bring gloves. The wind coming off the sea was sharp, and Jacob could almost taste the salt on his lips.

He was glad when he came to a stop ten minutes later. The cottage was a dump. If he hadn't checked the number on the gate against the address Helen had given him, he would have believed it to be derelict. Paint peeled from the exterior like aged skin and the single pane windows would have done little to stave off the cold. The garden was overgrown and the stone path leading up to the cottage was treacherously slippery from lingering overnight frost.

The wooden door felt soft to the touch when he knocked. It was answered by a peculiar looking man. Burly and wide in the chest, his physique contrasted sharply with a pair of delicate, almost infantile eyes, unnaturally small in his wide, ruddy face.

"What?" The word came out like a bark.

"I'm looking for Father Pettigrew," Jacob said.

A door slammed in his face for the second time in as many days. From within he heard voices before the door re-opened. Baby Eyes remained but he was now stood behind a much older man who Jacob could only assume to be Jeremiah Pettigrew.

The priest had smooth skin that belied his advanced years, and a full head of hair with a poor dye job. Grey eyes, intelligent and piercing looked out from behind a pair of well-worn glasses. Jacob caught a whiff of Old Spice.

"How can I help you?" the old man asked.

"My name is Jacob Kincaid. I'm a private investigator."

Pettigrew didn't reply.

"I'm looking into a disappearance," Jacob continued. "A teenage boy from -"

"- Finbar Skelly."

"That's right." He frowned. "Were you expecting me?"

"No, but a thing like that you tend to remember. Come inside."

The cottage interior was damp and musty, and the chill in the air was somehow more pronounced than when Jacob had been standing on the promenade with the wind whipping off the sea. Pettigrew led him to a living room. The carpet underfoot had faded into grey and had worn so thin in places that the threads had given way, creating patchy bald spots.

"No one has called me Father in many a year." Pettigrew

motioned for Jacob to sit on a threadbare sofa.

Jacob decided to play dumb. "You're retired?"

"Laicized. That is, removed from the clerical state."

"Why?"

Pettigrew groaned as he seated himself in the chair across from Jacob, ignoring his question. From the door, Baby Eyes watched for a moment before turning away slowly and disappearing. Footsteps climbed on creaking floorboards.

Jacob turned back towards the former priest and tried to disguise an unease that had gently gnawed at him since stepping over the threshold of the dilapidated cottage. There was an atmosphere in the air, a disquiet that he couldn't quite put a finger on.

"It was Deirdre Skelly who told you to look me up, I assume."

"Why would you say that?"

"Who else would care? She felt I wasn't as helpful as I could have been in finding Finbar. That I was holding back information."

"Deirdre told you this?"

"Her brother."

"Adrian."

"That's right. Not sure why she didn't give him a hard time, given his connection to the movement, tenuous as it were."

"The movement?"

"You're young, Mr. Kincaid, but don't have me spell it out for you."

"Finbar's uncle was in the IRA?"

"More of a hanger-on."

Jacob considered this new information. Deirdre had told him that the police weren't involved, but meagre as the paperwork was, Finbar's disappearance had been reported. She had not followed up, either by her own decision, or due to pressure from another party not to cooperate with crown forces. Now knowing she had a brother linked to the IRA, he had a feeling he knew which.

"Don't get me wrong," Pettigrew continued, "I lived in the area and I was sympathetic to their goals."

Jacob grunted. "What about their actions?"

Pettigrew's shrug was easy. "No war is bloodless."

"What can you tell me about Finbar?" Jacob asked, moving the conversation on.

"Probably nothing more than what his mother already has."

"Deirdre didn't work in the borstal."

"No," Pettigrew conceded. "I suppose that's a fair point. Is this where I tell you about the abuse? The beatings?"

"If you like." Jacob had taken a dislike to the priest, the haughtiness, the sense of superiority he carried himself with. The attitude against the squalid surroundings he lived in, only enhanced Jacob's aversion.

"Well there's nothing to tell. Millisle was a hard environment but so were the boys who were incarcerated. They weren't there for good behaviour. They needed discipline, regime, structure, and when required, a firm hand. I was certainly no friend of the justice system but the boys at Millisle were treated fairly. Were there bullies on the staff? Maybe, but a bad apple shouldn't spoil the bushel."

"What did you think of Finbar?" Jacob asked, keen to get an opinion he assumed would be a tad more unbiased than Deirdre's.

"He was a hood, Mr. Kincaid. God forgive me for talking ill of the dead, but that's what he was."

"So you believe he's dead?"

"Going on forty years I'd say it's a safe assumption, wouldn't you?"

"Deirdre said you and Finbar were close while he was in the Borstal."

A fleeting grimace passed over Pettigrew's features. "Finbar knew me from back home. I suppose he gravitated towards a friendly face."

"The hood and the priest?"

"A different world, Mr. Kincaid. He might have been the big man at home, but in Millisle he had no friends and no protection from his family." Pettigrew leaned forwards "Did you know Millisle was the only institution in Northern Ireland where the youths weren't separated because of their religion? A fine idea, but Finbar didn't get on with one of the lead

Catholic boys, and most from the other side weren't going to pal about with a Fenian, so Finbar was isolated. Not big enough to defend himself, and not crazy enough so that the other lads were afraid to pick on him."

"I understand he was a frequent absconder."

"He was."

"How? I've seen pictures. The closed unit seemed pretty secure, and I imagine after his first bout of Steve McQueen-ing, he would have spent most of his time there."

"I spoke for him. Every time they dragged him back, I encouraged the governor to get him back into the open borstal."

"Why the interest in Finbar?"

"I already told you. I knew the family. I worked in his community. Perhaps I felt a kinship of sorts."

Jacob nodded, scribbled some notes. "How long did you work at Millisle?"

"Until the early nineties."

"Around the same time you moved out of the West Belfast parish?" Jacob kept his eye on his notebook.

"Thereabouts."

"How did the borstal respond to his escape?"

"The governor asked me to reach out to the family, try to appeal to them to turn him in. Obviously he never turned up, so he was UAL as far as they were concerned."

"UAL?"

"Unlawfully at large. As far as I know, he stayed that way, right up until the borstal closed."

"Do the names Desmond McClure, Craig Fullerton or Richard McBride mean anything to you?"

"Should they?"

Jacob clenched his teeth at the non-answer. "They were boys who went missing around the same time as Finbar. They've never been found."

"They were in the borstal?"

Jacob didn't want to admit that he didn't know and quickly pushed on. "What about Matthew Connelly?"

"That name I do know. Finbar's friend."

"You know what happened to him?"

"I'd wager nothing good. He was already a lost soul by the time he was fifteen. If he didn't drink himself to an early grave I'd be shocked."

"Did the Police ever speak to you about Finbar's disappearance?"

"No. Why would they?"

Pettigrew's annoyance at the question was genuine and Jacob felt his time was suddenly limited. "Maybe for an insight into Finbar's mindset before he disappeared?"

"The RUC didn't care about a missing boy from West Belfast, Mr. Kincaid."

Jacob felt Pettigrew was holding back. He looked up. "I hope you're not withholding anything."

"That almost sounded like a threat, Mr. Kincaid."

"No threat, but for the sake of openness, I'm working with a lady called Natalie Amato for this investigation. I don't know if you ever heard of the Miss Gumshoe podcast but it has a healthy listening audience. Maybe you'd like to avoid your name featuring."

The hardball didn't play. Pettigrew stood. A signal that their meeting, and his patience, were at an end.

Jacob followed the former priest to the front door and turned as he stepped onto the cracked front step. "One last question, as someone from Finbar's community."

The sigh was weary. "What is it, Mr. Kincaid?"

"What can you tell me about Ned by Night?"

It was fleeting, just a flicker, barely there. Pettigrew's lips pressed into a thin line, his gaze darting away, before he caught himself. "I pray to our Lord above that you bring more than ghost stories to Deirdre Skelly."

The door closed without another word and Jacob ambled up the slippery garden path. He glanced back to the cottage as he reached the gate and caught the twitch of a curtain from an upstairs window.

7

Helen called as Jacob approached the tail-end of a traffic jam on the outskirts of Carrickfergus.

"Might have a name for you, courtesy of the 2012 phonebook this time. Eileen McClure, same street Desmond McClure was listed at in one of those old newspaper articles. Maybe a mother or sister?"

Jacob reached for his notebook and set it on his lap, scribbling the address down. "This the only one you could find?"

"So far, but there's not a lot to go on."

"I know. I'll stop in with Ms. McClure when I get back into the city and then work from home the rest of the day."

"You mean you're going to sit in your underwear and play video games?"

"Enjoy your weekend, Helen." Jacob ended the call, a tad too abruptly. He wasn't in the right mood for Helen's banter, his disposition soured by the cold cottage, the old priest and the man with the strange baby eyes.

A gathering storm hammered his car with cold rain and the late morning sky was growing darker by the minute. His phone vibrated again, this time it was a text from Natalie enquiring how he was getting on. He pulled in at a petrol station, phoned her, and quickly filled her in about his meeting with Pettigrew.

"What's your thoughts?" Natalie asked once he had

finished.

"About the priest? He's hiding something, I just have no idea what. It was a bit odd."

"With him?"

"With him, his house, his living arrangement, his history. Everything." There was a pause on the other end of the line as Natalie considered this. "Helen just called," Jacob said, filling the silence. "She has an address for a relative of Desmond McClure. I'm going that way now."

"Let's go together. We're a team after all, and I can't have you doing all the running."

"Alright. Want me to pick you up?"

"Well, I can't make it today," she said, her tone apologetic. "But I'm free tomorrow morning if you don't mind putting it off?"

"Not even remotely." The case was in no way time sensitive and with a mood dropping faster than the temperature outside, Jacob was happy to put off visiting the family of a long-missing child.

Natalie told him that she would collect him the next morning. They said goodbye and Jacob was home within half an hour to an apartment that had chilled during the day, its familiar stillness greeting him like a waiting companion.

He flicked the thermostat to full blast and the heating system responded with a soft, reassuring hum that slowly spread warmth into the room, chasing away the cold.

It was the start of the weekend, a time that should promise respite. Instead, an uneasy weight settled in Jacob's chest. He tried to relax, attempting to push the heavy thoughts of missing children out of his mind. He knew well that some cases had a habit of hanging on. The postponement, if only for the evening, was a much needed separation, a moment to breathe, even at this early stage.

He ordered in from the local Chinese takeaway. The portion was big enough for two, but he still tucked most of it away, and indulged in the last of a packet of caramel squares for dessert, despite feeling full.

It was a crutch he frequently fell back on, using food to fill up some lacking happiness he could never quite pinpoint. He knew it and in response, would drag himself to the gym, and now the BJJ mats, to fight a rearguard action against the excess.

Unable to eat another bite, he ran a scalding bath and jumped in with an old Elmore Leonard novel. He lay there, submerged in the warmth, letting the water soothe his tired muscles as he listened to the wind hammering through the streets below.

Once out of the bath he sank a large mug of tea. He was scunnered but his lonely bed held no allure. Instead he fired up the PlayStation and played until the small hours.

His mistake, he realised the next morning as Natalie hammered on his door, had been in not agreeing on a set time. He stumbled out of bed, glanced at his phone to find it was a wholly unreasonable hour, and quickly pulled on a hoody and a pair of tracksuit bottoms.

"You're keen," Jacob said, rubbing sleep from his eye as he opened the door.

"Time is the most valuable thing a man can spend." She tapped the face of her watch for emphasis.

"Oh yeah?" Jacob stifled a yawn. "Who said that?"

"Theophratus."

Jacob nodded. "Think I lifted him for possession of class B one time."

Natalie smiled. "Had to leave Dillon off to a basketball game over at Queens PEC. Didn't think there was much point heading back to the house, and I thought you'd be ready for the road."

"You thought wrong." Aside from the plastic containers of the leftover Chinese on the coffee table, the place was thankfully halfway presentable. "Why don't you get the coffee on the go." He nodded over to the machine in the kitchen. "I have a couple of travel mugs in the cupboard."

He returned to his room, brushed his teeth and showered quickly. When he returned to the kitchen, a coffee sat waiting on the counter. Natalie was standing at the open door of the balconette, peering down into the piazza below, deserted at such an early hour.

"This is where he fell then?" she asked as Jacob joined her.

Her coffee was cupped tightly between her hands.

"This is it."

The summer before, a man, assisted by a member of Natalie's podcast team, had entered Jacob's apartment with the intention of murder. He and Jacob had fought, and the man had plunged over the balconette and onto the piazza four storeys below.

"You ever think about it?"

"Wouldn't do much good." Jacob replied, dodging the question. They hadn't talked about the fight in his apartment, or her abduction, since the recording of the podcast.

"You ever get any update on how he was?"

"Brain dead. Not sure how they can tell. I didn't get the impression he had much brain before he fell."

Natalie didn't laugh.

Jacob moved a step closer. He moved a hand towards her shoulder but stopped short and then dropped it to his side. "You alright?"

"Fine." She shivered slightly. "With everything that happened when..." she waved, "You know..."

"Sure."

"It all went down so quickly that I didn't have time to process it properly, not really. Between the police interviews, throwing myself into the story, hiring Mairead's replacement, getting the podcast ready for YouTube, I didn't stop. *Haven't* stopped."

"Is that why you were so keen to jump in with this investigation?"

She turned to look at him with a wry smile, the rare moment of vulnerability already forgotten. "Maybe." She playfully pushed against him with her shoulder and stepped away. "Nice place you have here, Jacob."

It was a clumsy change of subject. She had been to his apartment before. Jacob closed the balconette door. "So everyone keeps saying. I'm not sure at what point I should start to feel insulted."

Natalie moved across to the bookcases that took up most of the space on the far wall and took stock. Aside from a few fantasy and space opera novels, the majority of Jacob's reading collection was made up of crime and mystery fiction, or true crime novels.

She stopped and with a genuine chuckle, pulled a book from the shelf, holding it up to Jacob. "I've heard great things about this one."

It was Natalie's own novel, *Caught Red Handed*, a thriller about a Belfast-born solicitor solving two seemingly unconnected crimes in London. It had made a number of UK best-seller lists.

"Just a shame the author won't give us a sequel."

"The author has enough on her plate, or so I hear."

Jacob scratched at his eye. She seemed to sense he had something to say and turned to face him. "So, the police officer who called at my office?"

"Yeah?" Natalie slid her book back into its place on the shelf.

"She wants in."

"In?" Natalie frowned. "On what, this case? How would she even know about it?"

"I stuck in a freedom of information request for anything the police had about the missing boys. She got wind of it and now wants to work together."

"Ok. Does she realise we come as an investigative package?"

"Oh, she's banking on it."

"Ah." Natalie's tone suggested she understood immediately. "And who is this clout chaser?"

"Detective Chief Inspector Zara Steele. Head of the PSNI's cold case team."

"And what is your read on Detective Chief Inspector Zara Steele, head of the PSNI's cold case team?"

"Well, she didn't deny what she's after by wanting to work with us. That gives her some credibility in my eyes, and having a Chief Inspector at our disposal could be a huge benefit."

"But?"

"But any involvement she has will be constrained by the fact she has to uphold the law."

"Uphold the law? Jesus, it's not like we're criminals, Jacob."

"No, but there's a certain flexibility in my line of work that she doesn't have."

"And when those times come, we just won't tell her."

"Now, that's the type of law-bending sentiment I can get behind."

Natalie smiled. "Let's play it by ear. See how much she can be relied on not to get in the way. For now, time's a-wasting. Let's go."

Eileen McClure lived on a narrow street on the lower end of the Newtownards Road, in one of an identical row of small red-brick terraced houses pressed tightly together. The red, white and blue painted on the kerbs for the summer marching season had faded, and the asphalt on the narrow street was cracked in places, patched together over the years with uneven repairs.

"What?" The question was a barely audible croak as Eileen regarded the two strangers at her front doorstep. Her face was etched with wrinkles, her grey hair dishevelled and unkempt. Gnarled hands were stained with tobacco, but the stench of smoke on her clothing did not cover the stale smell of vodka on her breath as she spoke.

"Mrs. McClure? My name is Jacob Kincaid. This is Natalie Amato. We're private investigators looking into the disappearance of a teenage boy."

Eileen stood a little straighter and folded her arms around her skinny body. "Does this have to do with my Desmond?"

"Maybe," Jacob replied. "Can we talk?"

Mrs. McClure motioned for them to come inside. The curtains in the living room were drawn and the flickering television cast the room in a dingy light. Newspapers and magazines littered the floor, as did empty bottles of vodka and food containers. An ashtray on the arm of an ancient chair overflowed with cigarette butts.

She didn't invite them to sit. A small mercy, Jacob thought, as any free space on the cluttered sofa looked to be covered in a thin layer of grime.

The old woman lit a cigarette with a shaking hand. "No one's mentioned Desmond in forty years."

"What can you tell us about him?" Natalie asked.

"He was a bad rip. His da wasn't around and I couldn't control him. Got mixed up with a wrong crowd who got him doing all sorts."

"Like what?" Jacob asked.

"Thieving, mostly."

"The boy whose disappearance I'm investigating, his name was Finbar Skelly. Does that mean anything to you?"

McClure shook her head. "Desmond wouldn't have been running around with Fenians."

"Lovely," Jacob said to Natalie under his breath.

The old woman heard him and shrugged. "It's true."

"Is that where you drew the line?" Jacob made a show of looking around the room.

"Fuck is that supposed to mean?" Eileen looked up sharply, her voice straining. "You think you know me, do ye?"

"Mrs. McClure," Natalie cut in, her tone placating. "When was Desmond last seen?" She gave Jacob a quick look as she spoke, a signal to back off and let her take the lead.

"On his way to school."

"Where was that?"

"The school was in Dundonald but it closed years ago. Last anyone saw him was on the Newtownards Road."

"Waiting for a bus?" Natalie asked.

"Who the fuck knows? He bunked off more often than not."

"When did you report him missing?"

Mrs. McClure took a deep drag of her cigarette and watched the blue smoke dissipate into the murkiness of the room.

"When Mrs. McClure?" Jacob prompted.

She stubbed out the cigarette angrily. "He'd not come home for days at a time. How was I to know he was missing?"

Jacob moved to speak but Natalie put a hand on his arm. Eileen McClure watched him warily from the side of her eye. Natalie took a deliberate step forward, putting herself between the old woman and Jacob, acting as a buffer and focusing McClure's attention on her alone. "I take it the police were contacted?"

"Aye, they came out. Took a description. I've no idea why. The peeler they sent had been here plenty of times before. Said they'd keep an eye out for him. Seemed to think he would turn up. He never did, and the police stopped calling."

"Was Desmond ever at Millisle?" Natalie asked.

"What, the borstal?"

"That's right."

"Aye, a couple of times. For all the use it did him."

Jacob and Natalie shared a look "How long was it between Desmond getting released from Millisle until he went missing?" Jacob asked.

Eileen looked up at him and for a second Jacob thought she wasn't going to answer. "Six months," she croaked. "Thereabouts."

Natalie turned to Jacob who shrugged in return. He had nothing further to ask.

She didn't see them out. They left Eileen McClure sitting in her grotty chair. Stepping out into the brisk morning air was a welcome relief.

"What do you think?" Natalie asked as they walked towards her car.

"I think we have a connection," Jacob replied. "Finbar and Desmond were both at Millisle, maybe not at the same time, but in the same date range." He stopped as they reached Natalie's car. "Question is, what's the link to their disappearance?"

"Pettigrew?"

"If Desmond was anything like his charmer of a mother, I'm not sure he'd be hanging around a priest."

"She got to you in there."

"She did," Jacob admitted. "Look at her, nothing in her life but can still muster some hatred for them 'uns." He looked back towards the house, almost feeling a twinge of embarrassment for the bitter old woman. "Sad auld bitch," he muttered quietly before getting into Natalie's car. "It didn't bother you?"

"Why, because I'm the Catholic on this team?"

"Basically."

"I feel bad for her actually. Dealing with that loss for all those years. You can see the effect it's had."

Jacob grunted. "I don't buy it. She said herself it was days before she reported Desmond missing. She didn't give a shit then, and I don't think she really gives one now."

"Harsh."

"But true."

His phone began to vibrate in his pocket. He pulled it from the pocket of his jeans. The screen told him it was an unknown number. "Jacob Kincaid."

"Kincaid, it's Hector Breen."

Jacob knuckled an eye. "Hector, hi. What can I do for you?"

"It's what I can do for you, actually. I have an address."

"For Eden Hennessy's mother?"

"Better. For Emily Goddard."

Jacob glanced at Natalie. "The failed abduction victim?"

"One and the same. I've already spoken to her."

"You've already -"

"- She has an office in the city centre. I'll text you the address and I'll see you down there in an hour."

"See me?"

"I'm on for this, Kincaid. I need it. Don't even think about telling me no."

Before Jacob could even think about telling Hector anything, the line went dead.

"I believe," Jacob said slowly, as he put his phone back in his pocket. "We have a new partner."

Natalie started the engine. "Another one?"

8

"What is that?" Natalie asked, nodding to the cardboard tub in Jacob's hand as he got back into her car.

He set the can of Pepsi held in his other hand on the dash. "Chicken."

"Chicken?"

"Chicken in a box." Jacob lifted the lid to reveal the assortment of battered and breaded chicken he had managed to squeeze into the tub.

They had stopped at a petrol station to pick up something to eat. Natalie had elected for a protein bar, whereas Jacob had bee-lined for the hot food counter.

"I'm not sure I trust chicken from a petrol station."

Jacob lifted the top goujon from the tub and pointed it towards her. "Snob."

"Battered chicken and a Pepsi." Natalie watched as he took a bite. "The breakfast of champions."

"It's really more of an early lunch."

Natalie shook her head and quickly finished the remainder of her protein bar. Jacob worked his way through his tub of chicken as she drove to the address Hector had texted to Jacob.

Emily Goddard's office was located in the Ormeau Business Park on what had once been the Belfast gasworks. On a Saturday afternoon the site was almost deserted. Breen was awaiting their arrival in his Volvo and Natalie parked next to him.

"She's in her office," Breen said as he slowly pulled himself out of the car. "Was a bit taken aback by my call, but wanted to help as soon as she heard what it was about."

"Must be a dedicated lady," Jacob said, wiping his hands on his jeans before shoving them deep into the pockets as the cold bit at them. "Working on a Saturday." He glanced at a nearby sign. Judging by the names listed, most businesses based in the park appeared to be in the IT or tech sector.

"You see Emerald Futures on there?" Breen asked.

Jacob scanned the sign and found the name. An arrow pointed towards the modern red-bricked building closest to them.

Hector led the way in long, purposeful strides that had Jacob and Natalie hurrying to catch up. "How goes the investigation?"

"About as slowly as expected," Jacob answered. "We just spoke to the mother of one of the other missing boys just before you called, but she was as much use as a chocolate kettle. I also talked to the priest who used to work at the borstal. Pettigrew."

The name stopped Breen in his tracks.

"Not Jeremiah Pettigrew?"

"Yeah," Jacob said. "You know him?"

"I remember the name," Breen said, stepping into the awning over the door of the building. "Provo sympathiser and suspected of getting his hands dirty when they required."

"How do you mean?" Jacob asked.

"Stashing weapons, delivering equipment, shit like that. Never caught him at it of course. What did he tell you?"

"Not a lot, although he was kicked out of the clergy in the early nineties."

"Fiddling?"

Natalie's nose scrunched. "Fiddling?"

Breen brought up his hands but Jacob cut off the incoming apology. "Some type of abuse. I get the impression the news articles either aren't telling, or don't know the full story."

"You know what those..." Breen trailed off as his rosy cheeks turned scarlet. "Uh, nothing against any Catholics here," he added quickly. "Never had time for any religious nonsense. Back when I was still on the job I lifted a lay preacher for murdering his wife and her lover and rigging it as a suicide pact. Pinched the local Methodist minister for buggery too. Just so you don't think I'm biased or, you know-"

"- Pettigrew also mentioned Finbar's uncle was associated with the IRA," Jacob jumped in before Hector could stick his foot fully down his throat.

"Oh yeah?" Breen quickly seized on the reprieve. "You have a name?"

"Adrian Dunphy."

This got a hearty chuckle from Breen. "Oh yes, I remember Adrian alright."

"He's the last person to see Finbar, that we know about," said Jacob. "But he died years back."

"He did. You weren't told how?"

Jacob shook his head. Deirdre hadn't gone into detail.

"Adrian was on the fringes of the provos," said Hector. "Think he did a bit of time up at the Maze for weapon possession. Not the brightest penny in the jar but useful for grunt work. One day, the higher-ups handed him a grenade, and told him to lob it over the wall at Andytown RUC Station. Adrian obliged, snuck up to station and..." Hector made a throwing motion. "Unfortunately for him, he undersold it. The grenade hit the lip of the security fence and came straight back down. Took his head off at the shoulders."

"Jesus," said Natalie.

"Aye," said Breen. "They didn't send their best when they sent him. Local commander at that time was a fella called Dolan. Seamus Dolan. One evil bastard. Last I heard, he was still kicking, but barely. Hit the bottle hard. I guess all those ghosts that were chasing him finally caught up. If you want to knock Dolan's door, you might get something."

"Former IRA commanders being the notoriously sharing sort," said Jacob flatly.

"You got much else?" Breen didn't bother to wait for Jacob's reply as he pushed the intercom next to the sign for Emerald Futures.

"Mr. Breen?" The question was static tinged.

"That's right, Ms. Goddard. I'm here with my two partners."

Partners, Natalie mouthed silently to Jacob.

The door buzzed as the lock released. "Anything else I need to be brought up to speed on?" Breen asked, holding the door to allow Jacob and Natalie to step past him into the lobby.

"Actually, yeah," Jacob said. "A detective came to my office yesterday, Zara Steele. She's a DCI with the cold case team."

The elevator dinged before any further questions could be asked and Emily Goddard stepped out. Her hair was a natural silver, styled in a chic cut that flattered her angular features, while her suit accentuated a tall, lithe frame. The smile was warm and welcoming as she extended a hand to Hector and then Natalie and Jacob. She waited as Hector made the introductions.

"A pleasure to meet you both." Her voice was deep and melodious, with a touch of gravel that suggested a life well-lived. "Shall we?"

The quartet shuffled into the tight confines of the elevator and Emily hit the button for the third floor. The doors opened to an empty office and Emily led the way to a conference room at the far end of the floor.

"How long has your company been in business?" Natalie asked.

"Ten years or so," Emily answered. "I followed my father into the family practise out of university but I never had a passion for the law. I kept at it long enough to ensure I had a safety net when I made the jump into something I did care about."

"And what's that?" Jacob asked.

"Environmental advocacy." Emily waited until her guests had seated themselves before doing the same. She straightened out her top and sighed. "Your call this morning took me rather by surprise, Mr. Breen."

"Hector, please."

"Were you aware of a link between the attack on you and other women?" Jacob asked.

"Not initially." Emily clasped her hands together and now looked at them, rather than anyone around the table. "As far as

I understand it, I was the first. I only became aware of any sort of connection when Hector reached out to me a few months later."

"Had you heard the urban legend?" asked Jacob.

"Only after the fact. My mother knew the story though."

"Where was she from?"

"The Clonards," said Emily.

"West Belfast," said Jacob.

"That's right."

Natalie leaned forward. "Is there anything you can remember from that night? Anything you might have missed telling the police at the time?"

"It's been so long since I thought about it. Tried not to dwell, as far as that were possible. I saw the shadow move from behind a tree and dismissed it as, I don't know, just me spooking myself. It was only when he was..." She paused and took a steadying breath. "I didn't see him move towards me. It was as if he hung in the air, floating."

"Floating?" Jacob asked.

"It was the bandages you see. In my memory they're flowing, almost as it they were...ethereal. Truth be told, I wasn't sure I would be believed. Even forty years later I feel like I'm describing a ghost rather than a man."

Jacob rubbed at his beard. "When I first heard about this, I had an impression of a man hiding injuries. But what you're describing seems like more of a costume."

"Someone playing up on the legend," Natalie said. "It's not unheard of," she continued as the group turned towards her. "I mean there was a brief craze a few years back with idiots dressing up as scary clowns and chasing people."

"But why so obscure?" Jacob asked. "It seems like the story is only known by people of a certain age from a certain part of the city."

"It may sound silly but it's the mask I remember more than anything," Emily said. "The one used to knock me out, I mean. The smell of rubber, even now." She shook her head at the memory. "So sickly sweet. I remember my vision swimming, the sensation of floating away and then nothing but blackness."

"What about the two men who found you?" Jacob asked.

"I never learned their names. They told me they never got a look. Just a shadow crouched over me when I was on the ground. He took off running and lost himself in the back gardens of the houses."

They asked more questions but Emily couldn't provide them with much else other than a drug-fogged, four-decade old memory of a bandaged phantom. They thanked her and left her to her work. The rain had picked up and the trio paused in the lobby before braving it.

"Emily was knocked out and at the mercy of whoever jumped her," Jacob said. "Blind luck or sloppiness on the part of her attacker that she got away?"

"Luck," Hector replied.

"Agreed," Natalie said, although her tone was guarded as if knowing Jacob had more to say.

"Or we're dealing with an unrelated case," said Jacob.

Natalie quirked her mouth. "Dressed like an obscure urban legend from decades before?"

"If Emily remembers it correctly," said Jacob.

Breen stiffened. "She's a smart lady. If she says she saw it, I believe her."

"I'm not saying I don't believe her," Jacob replied. "Just that maybe the memory has been affected by the drugs and all the talk about Ned by Night. Reality, memory, and imagination has all mashed together over the years.

"Let's say Emily's memory is accurate," he continued. "And let's say the missing boys, the missing girls, and Emily's attack are all linked. We have what, a dozen instances of abductions without a trace, without evidence, without witnesses. The failed attempt on Emily was committed by someone whose costume would in no way blend in. He sounds like someone who wanted to be noticed. To have the story told." He paused and looked at Hector. "How much did you release to the press?"

"Not a lot. Just a couple of paragraphs about an attack on a woman and an appeal for the two fellas who helped her to come forward. The bandages, the rubber mask, all that was left out."

Jacob nodded and then considered what they had, which

was very little. He felt he was picking at strands, tangentially connected without anything concrete. "What about this Dolan?"

Breen's posture took a sudden rigid edge. "I think it's a door worth knocking. Maybe not for the missing girls, but at least as far as this missing Skelly kid goes."

"Think you can get us an address?"

"Don't need to. He's lived his whole life in the same house up in the Ballylo'".

Jacob grimaced. The Ballylogue estate. Insular, staunch, and not welcoming to outsiders asking questions.

"Let's hit it now," Natalie suggested, keen to keep their momentum going.

"It's a rough spot," Jacob replied.

She spread her hands. "Okay."

"Really rough."

Natalie frowned. "What are you saying? You think I'm too delicate to go into a housing estate?"

"It's not that," he began and then stopped, realising he didn't have a solid reason, other than the guilt he still harboured about what had happened to her last summer.

"There's a leisure centre on the Whiterock Road," Hector said, understanding the decision had been made and wanting to head off the potential for a brewing argument. "Let's meet there and head into the Ballylo' together."

Jacob agreed and the trio hurried to their respective cars. Natalie waited until they were inside before she spoke.

"You know, it can be a fine line between chivalry and chauvinism."

"That is not what I was getting at," Jacob said, his hackles rising at the accusation. "I thought you'd know me better than that."

She studied him for a moment before her features relaxed. "You're right, I'm sorry."

They lapsed into an awkward silence. Back in the earliest days of their investigation into the Followers, Jacob had asked Natalie if she was willing to accept the consequences of what they might uncover. She had said she was, and together the pair had ploughed ahead, the ever-increasing danger of their investigation seemingly spurring them on.

They had been reckless, Jacob had realised once he had time to take stock. Reckless. And lucky. And stupid. They had let themselves enjoy a victory without being attuned to the danger still lurking. It had almost cost them their lives.

They had talked about it in the days after, and covered it during the podcast. Natalie had made it clear the only person she held accountable was the man who had kidnapped her. Six months later Jacob's guilt had still not assuaged.

"You know the leisure centre Hector mentioned?" he asked, keen to break the silence and move on.

"I do." Natalie moved the stick into drive and was about to move off before she stopped and put it back in park. She turned slightly in her seat to face him. "This police detective."

Jacob felt his guard rise. "Steele."

"Right. You didn't think to mention that at any point before this morning?"

"Thought it could wait until we spoke in person. Give me a chance to consider if there's any benefit to her working with me."

"Us," Natalie corrected. "This isn't like last time, Jacob. I haven't engaged your services. You came to me and when you did, I joined up on the understanding this investigation is a partnership. We work together and we don't keep things from each other."

"You're right. I'm sorry," he said echoing Natalie's words from a couple of moments before.

She nodded, satisfied with the apology and followed Breen's Volvo towards the exit. "Seems like Hector is part of this too now. Do you think the disappearances to those girls are linked to these missing boys?"

Jacob thought on that for a while. "I don't think so," he answered slowly. "At this point, we're not even sure of any connection between the boys. I suppose Finbar has a connection to Hector's missing girls, through Ned by Night but that seems shaky until we get something more concrete."

"Well," said Natalie. "Maybe this Seamus Dolan can connect some dots."

9

Traffic was light as they travelled across town. Belatedly, Jacob realised the route they were taking, along the Falls Road and towards the Whiterock, followed Finbar Skelly's last journey.

He peered out the rain-streaked window and tried to picture it. A winter morning, just like this one. A child huddled against the rain. Cold, wet, hungry. Unseen as he vanished into memory.

Hector was waiting for them at the leisure centre car park. The choice of which car to take was made unilaterally. The former detective was already out of his Volvo before Natalie had even came to a stop. He gave brief directions to Dolan's house as he climbed into the back seat.

"So, do private eyes usually work in pairs?" he asked as they moved off.

Jacob glanced at Natalie. She quirked her mouth and Jacob decided to drop the pretence. "Hector, you should probably know-"

"-That Natalie isn't actually your partner. That she's the host of a rather well-known podcast show?"

Jacob frowned. "You can just say podcast."

"How'd you figure it out?" Natalie glanced up at the rearview.

"Give me a bit of credit, you pair. I'm old, not daft. I knew something was off the moment Jacob introduced you, and I knew who you were about five minutes after you left my house."

"Why didn't you say anything earlier?" Natalie asked.

"Biding my time. From the moment Jacob started talking in my living room I knew I didn't want to be on the outside looking in on this. I figure after bringing you to see Emily Goddard, and now to Dolan, I'm a part of this. Although I'd prefer to be kept out of any podcast."

"Don't want your fifteen minutes, Hector?" Jacob asked.

"Made a lot of enemies through the years. Seamus Dolan included. More than a few people would relish the chance to bump me off, even after all this time."

"What can you tell us about him?" Jacob asked.

"Dolan? Big man in the movement in the seventies and eighties. When peace came, he was one of the hardliners opposed to it, but by then he was on the outs."

"How come?"

Breen grunted. "Who knows with these groups? Republican or Loyalist, they could be singing your name one week, toasting the fact you took a bullet in the brain the next. He was probably happy enough to stay alive and on the fringes."

"And you two have history?" Natalie asked.

"I lifted him, more times than I could count. Never got a thing from him. He was a bastard. God knows how many souls he put in the ground." Breen smiled grimly. "It caught up to him though."

They pulled off the Whiterock and followed a road narrowed by cars parked on either side. Two minutes later, a bilingual sign welcomed them to the Ballylogue estate. The place had changed little in the years since Jacob had last been in it. The same murals were still on the gable walls, a little more weather-worn, the same terraced houses still packed tightly together.

A familiar feeling fluttered in his stomach. They were being watched, he knew. Strangers in a strange car. Natalie drove slowly. Her posture had stiffened. She sensed it too.

"How long were you on the job for?" Breen asked.

Jacob turned in his seat. "Who said I was?"

Breen smiled. "I notice you didn't ask what job."

Jacob turned back to face the road. "Eight years."

"Miss it?"

He let out a slow exhale. "Yeah. How about you?"

"Didn't know anything else. That was the problem. When it's gone and all you have left are memories and some shiny bits of tin. Suppose I'm dragging around a few ghosts myself."

Jacob didn't know what to say to that, so kept quiet.

"Take it from an old man, Jacob. Don't let this consume you."

"The case?"

"The work. Make your bread but make sure you get to living too."

Jacob felt Breen watching him, as if waiting for a response. "Back in the day, we'd only have been in the Ballylogue with two armoured Land Rovers," he said, trying to change the subject.

Breen slumped back into his seat as if unsatisfied with the response, but after a few seconds said, "Back in my day we'd have only been in here with a full army patrol."

A group of teenagers, all with their hoods up, leaned against a graffiti-covered gable wall, sizing up the Audi and its passengers. Further down the street, two men stopped mid-conversation to take stock of the unfamiliar vehicle. One leaned casually against the concrete wall of his front yard, elbows resting on the rough surface. His gaze was steady and unblinking. The other man stood on the pavement, his stance less relaxed, feet planted firmly as if guarding an invisible line.

"They used to bang the old bin lids whenever we came in here," Breen said, breaking the silence. "Signal for the kids to come out and start throwing rocks. Guess it's all changed now."

"Must have been quite the racket," said Natalie.

"You didn't mind," said Hector. "It was when the kids didn't appear that you began to worry."

The long street culminated at a dead-end, stopping at a high wall that separated the estate from the Springfield Road. A number of small cul-de-sacs branched. Hector directed

Natalie to the furthest of the branches. She turned in and brought the SUV onto a free space on the kerb.

Jacob touched her arm lightly. "Park it facing out."

She sighed but complied, turning in the confined space until the vehicle was facing back out towards the main drag.

"Old habits die hard," said Breen, an amused tinge in his voice as Natalie finished the manoeuvre.

A woman, hard-faced with a bad dye job, stood on the front steps of the house opposite where they had parked. She watched silently as the trio approached Seamus Dolan's house and disappeared inside as Breen knocked the door.

"We won't have long," Hector said, inclining his head toward where the woman had been standing.

There was no answer to the door and Breen knocked again. As each second passed, a stab of anxiety burrowed itself deeper into Jacob's gut. They weren't welcome here. He was just about to suggest they give it up when the door finally creaked open.

The man who looked out from behind it was a wreck. An old shirt hung loosely around an emaciated frame. A cigarette burned in his hand, its smoke curling upwards in a lazy dance. Tobacco had stained his fingers a deep, mottled yellow. Jacob could make out the faded tattoo of an Irish tricolour on the man's wrist. The rest of the tats on his skinny forearms had blurred into indistinct smudges on wrinkled skin.

But it was his eyes that caught Jacob's attention. They held a vacancy, a detachment from the present and the three people standing on his front step. Breen took a step forward and the man shuffled aside, letting him pass without objection. Jacob held a hand out and the man wordlessly followed Hector into the house.

Inside, the stench of tobacco mixed with the acrid, bitter, and unmistakable aroma of piss. The scent seeped from the corners of the worn armchair where Dolan now ponderously seated himself.

Jacob wondered what it was about this case that had brought him to so many utterly depressing homes in the last couple of days.

On the far wall in a battered wooden frame sat a copy of the Proclamation of the Republic. A wooden harp with the words

20-Maghaberry-05 etched into its base sat above the fireplace. Presumably a memento carved in the prison workshop when Dolan, or a relative, was incarcerated there.

Do you remember me?" Breen asked.

"Peeler." Dolan's answer was flat, lifeless.

Breen nodded. "Aye, a long time ago." He allowed himself a few seconds to take in the room. "So, this is how you ended up? Glad I got to see it for myself."

Dolan looked up at them. He frowned but the eyes remained vacant.

"Least you had your chance to live," Hector continued. "How many others did you rob of that?"

"Hector," Jacob said with a hint of reproach.

Breen got the warning. He straightened up and took a step back, allowing Jacob to take over.

"I'm looking for information about a missing boy," Jacob said. "Finbar Skelly."

Nothing changed in Dolan's features.

"I believe you knew his uncle," Jacob continued. "Adrian Dunphy."

At this something did register in the old man's fuddled mind. Some fleeting flicker of recognition, some snatch of memory.

Jacob leaned in closer. "Adrian was the last person we know of to see Finbar before he disappeared."

"Nothing happened around here back in the day without it getting back to you, Dolan." Breen snapped.

Outside, a car door slammed shut.

"He doesn't know anything," Breen said.

Jacob bent down and locked eyes with the old man. There was nothing there. "No," he agreed. "He doesn't. Not anymore."

They left Dolan in his chair. By the time they stepped back outside a small crowd of five men and as many teenage boys had gathered around Natalie's car. One of the men who had been watching their arrival, nudged another who had his back to them.

The man turned. He was unremarkable in almost every way. Short and skinny, his greying hair had been sheared to the scalp. A gold chain glinted around his neck. Yet as their eyes met, Jacob felt his stomach tighten as some ancient, primeval animal instinct told him to run. The eyes that met his were of a killer. A man who knew the weight of a life, and how easily it could be snuffed out.

Behind the killer, the other men began to spread out, boxing them in, preventing them from reaching the car. The boys hung back, a couple sharing excited glances at the trouble brewing.

"What's your business here?" The man with the dead eyes asked. His Belfast accent was hard and clipped.

"Talking to your uncle," Breen answered. His voice held no hint of fear.

The man's expression went slack for a moment, as if only just noticing the older man. "Jesus Christ, Hector Breen. Fuck me, you can't imagine the number of times I've dreamt of having you standing in front of me, you sleekit fuck."

"Nice to see you remember me, Martin."

"Oh aye, I remember you well, Breen. Don't you have no worry about that." The man called Martin turned back to Jacob. "You a Peeler too?"

"Not anymore." Jacob answered, his throat dry and tight.

"So what the fuck are ye doing here?" One of the men in the rabble demanded.

"Talking to your uncle about a former comrade," Breen replied. He said comrade with an impressive amount of derision. "Adrian Dunphy."

"A brave man," said Martin. "Long dead."

"We're investigating the disappearance of his nephew." Natalie's voice was calm, unflustered. It drew the attention of everyone. "Finbar Skelly."

Unlike Dolan, Finbar's name registered with Martin, if only for a second, before he caught himself.

"Adrian's gone, like you said," Natalie continued, "but we were hoping he might have said something to your uncle."

"And what would Seamus know about that?"

"Because nothing happened around here back in the day without him knowing about it." Hector was completely unphased by their situation, much to Jacob's disbelief. They were in imminent danger of violence, which meant Breen was working on pure bravado and attitude.

"We've got a problem here." Martin's voice dropped but the threat in it had only increased. "Two old peelers sneaking around, asking questions, sticking snouts where they don't belong. I thought you'd be long dead, Breen. Ate your gun years back. I'm going to enjoy putting you down."

Breen laughed. "Out here in the street?"

"What? You think the people here will be talking to the peelers? You think people here will be toutin' on me?"

"We're looking for a missing boy," Natalie said, trying to bring some sense into the conversation.

"I don't give a fuck what you're looking for." Martin shot back.

The crowd began to close in around them. One of the men made a sudden grab for Natalie, as if trying to pull her out of the way. She wriggled free and stumbled back into Jacob.

The sound stopped them, the trapped and the advancing, as one. Jacob recognised it instantly and wasn't sure he'd heard anything so sweet in his life.

It grew louder, and a second later, a PSNI Land Rover rumbled by the cul-de-sac entrance. The driver glanced in the direction of the crowd and Jacob waved his arms frantically as the vehicle disappeared from view.

Jacob held his breath as time seemed to stand still. Brakes squealed followed by the shifting of gears. The Land Rover reappeared, stopping at the edge of the cul-de-sac. He could see the driver and front seat passenger taking in the scene before them.

The passenger, a woman, reached for the radio attached to her flak jacket and spoke into it briefly before opening the door. She climbed down and paused to put on her forage cap. She waited until she was joined by a second officer from the rear of the vehicle before approaching the crowd warily.

"What's going on here?" The question was asked with a confidence Jacob admired.

Most of the rabble had taken the chance to remove themselves to the other side of the street. They watched the police officers with mute but unmasked hostility.

"Private investigators," Jacob said. "We're being prevented from leaving. I'd appreciate it if you stuck around to make sure we do."

The officer looked from Jacob to the gathered crowd. Jacob knew what she was thinking. Strange circumstances and a potentially hostile crowd who outnumbered them significantly. He had no doubt the message she had sent on the radio had been asking for another crew to join them, but who knew how far away they were? She nodded slowly.

Jacob, with a hand around Natalie's arm, guided them towards her car. The crowd slowly parted. A few watching from across the street began to jeer as the trio made it to the relative safety of the Audi.

"Get us out of here," Breen said, closing his door.

Natalie didn't need to be told twice.

10

It wasn't until they passed the sign welcoming them to Ballylogue that Jacob allowed himself to relax.

"You two okay?" Breen asked from the back seat.

Jacob rubbed a hand over his face. "When my ass stops twitching like a rabbit's nose, I'll let you know."

"Lovely," said Natalie, her own voice tight.

Blue lights flashed behind them. The Land Rover that provided their timely rescue had followed them out of the estate and was now signalling for them to pull over.

Jacob wasn't surprised. The officers had stumbled upon a strange scene and the police would want to know who they were, especially when seen in the company of a few of the local players.

Natalie stopped on the side of the road and the trio in the Audi waited as the female officer and her colleague approached the driver window.

The officer ducked her head down to look into the car. "Alright folks, you've been stopped under Article Twenty-One of the Justice and Security Act..."

Jacob zoned out as the officer launched into a spiel he was more than familiar with from his time on the job. In a flat tone that suggested she had done this countless times before, she explained why they had been stopped, the power that allowed the police to do so, and a few other necessities. In essence, Article Twenty-One gave the officer the power to stop and question a person for as long as it was necessary to ascertain that person's identity and movements.

Names and addresses noted from each of them in turn, the officer asked the trio to remain in the car while she checked the provided details on her police-issue Samsung phone. Jacob knew she would be able to access a record of all their previous interactions with police, previous arrests, outstanding warrants, and warning flags.

"So," Jacob said, turning in his seat to look at Breen. "What's the story with your man back there?"

"Martin Closkey," Breen replied. "You might have heard him say Dolan is his uncle. Well, Dolan might have been a hard bastard, but I'll give this to him, he believed in his cause. Closkey might say he did, but he got his kicks from killing."

"And you two have history?" Jacob asked. It wasn't much of a leap judging by what he had just seen.

"Suppose you could say that. Back when I was a wet-behind-the-ears Detective Sergeant over in Coalburn, a mate from the depot got posted over to my team. We got a call about a burglary one morning. I gave Nige the job. It was a come-on. They had a gunman lying in wait." Breen stopped, as if taking a sudden interest in the waste-ground they had stopped beside. "They told me he was dead before he hit the ground. Didn't suffer. I suppose that's something."

"Fuck," said Jacob.

"Closkey got picked up for it. We knew he was the gunman but the case never made court." He shook his head, the hurt still evident. "I sort of made it my mission to get after him any way I could. The year after Nigel was murdered, I nailed Closkey's brother on an armed robbery charge. Got sent down for ten years. A few months in, he realised he couldn't do his whack and ended up topping himself."

"He held you responsible," Natalie said quietly.

Hector kept his gaze on the window. "Not long after, Special Branch got word of an imminent attack planned against me. Woke us up in the dead of night, told us to pack up what we could." He let out a slow exhale. "Nora loved that house. Told me when we bought it that it was our forever home. We never went back."

Jacob glanced in the mirror. The officer was still absorbed in her phone. Closkey was the type of man you didn't forget in a hurry, yet Jacob couldn't place him. "I did the guts of five years over here and I've never heard of him before."

"Left years ago," Breen replied. "Some sort of internal feud. Heard he was back in town about four years back. Gave some of the Belfast dissident groups a shot in the arm."

Natalie turned to look at Hector. "You've very clued in."

"I like to keep abreast. Old habits." He sighed. "Old habits."

In the mirror, Jacob watched the officer tuck her phone away into a pocket on her flak jacket and approach. He was expecting her to tell them that they, and the car, would now be subject to a search, but apparently any suspicions had been allayed, and she wished them a good day.

The Land Rover waited for them to pull away. A minute later, they were driving into the car park of the leisure centre to retrieve Hector's car when Jacob's mobile buzzed. It was an unrecognised number.

"Hello?"

"Jacob, it's Zara Steele."

"DCI Steele," Jacob said, loud enough for the benefit of the others in the car. "What can I do for you?" He didn't recall providing his phone number and figured she must have grabbed a card while she waited in his office.

"We need to talk."

"Alright. I'll be back in the office first thing Monday -"

"-Now."

"Now?"

"I'm working from home today, catching up on some admin. I have the call screen open and see something come in up at the Ballylogue estate. Imagine my surprise when curiosity gets the better of me, and I click in and see your name is now attached as one of the people saved by police from a mob of some well-known paramilitaries."

"Well-"

"-I'll be at your office in thirty minutes."

The call ended and Jacob pocketed his phone. "Take it you both heard that?"

"Looking forward to meeting her," said Natalie.

Jacob nodded and glanced at the time on the dash. "Alright. Hector, I'll give you a call in the next -"

"-Not on your life, Kincaid. Give me the address of your office and I'll meet you there."

Jacob didn't argue. Furnished with the location for Kincaid Investigations, Hector exited the Audi and got back into his own car. He signalled to let Natalie pull away first.

They drove in silence for a few minutes before Jacob spoke. "That was a bit hairy."

Natalie huffed out a laugh. "You have a talent for the understated."

Jacob sank back into his seat, trying to shake the lingering tension from the confrontation with Closkey and his goons. He was relieved they were safe but angry at himself. Less than an hour ago he was lamenting how reckless and lucky that he and Natalie had been on their last investigation together, and now here he was, once again thankful for a timely intervention that had saved them from their own recklessness.

The trip to the Ballylogue had gotten them nowhere. Martin Closkey's reaction to Finbar's name could have had any number of reasonable explanations, and Seamus Dolan was a little more than a shell, who, even if he could remember something useful, would never have divulged it to strangers.

By now, they were back in the city centre and within a couple of minutes Natalie found a parking space close to Kincaid Investigations. Somehow, Hector had managed to beat them there and was waiting by the locked ground floor door.

"What's the java like?" he asked, nodding to the coffee shop the office shared an entrance with.

"Awful," Jacob lied. Hector stared him down expectantly. He sighed and handed Natalie the office key. "Three cappuccinos?"

Custom was mercifully light for a Saturday morning and Jacob got his order quickly. He took the three coffees up the narrow staircase to his office. Hector had seated himself on the sofa while Natalie remained standing. He had just handed out the coffees when the door opened and Steele entered.

The suit was gone, replaced by a casual coat with a subtle sheen that suggested a high-quality label, along with a pair of smart jeans and leather boots.

"Afternoon, everyone." She spoke as if she had entered the room to address a briefing of her subordinates. Jacob almost felt himself reaching for a notebook.

Natalie stepped forward first and took Steele's offered hand. "Natalie Amato."

Steele's smile was polite. "Zara Steele, it's a real pleasure to meet you, Natalie."

"A fan of my podcast?"

"I've listened to a few episodes. I was also in the audience for your talk at the Women in Leadership conference last year. I was very impressed."

Hector stood up slowly and held out a meaty hand. "Hector Breen."

"Now you, I don't know."

"Used to be on the job," Hector said.

"Mr. Breen is assisting me with my case," said Jacob.

"This case." Steele said the words wearily. "Not sure I expected it to lead to you being rescued from a baying mob in the Ballylogue. How did that even come about?"

"Following a lead," Jacob replied.

"What lead?" Steele asked.

"Just hold on a second," Natalie cut in before Jacob could answer. "What are we doing here? This is our investigation." Natalie motioned to the two men. Jacob noticed how Natalie had deftly included Breen as part of their group. She was letting Steele know she was well out-numbered.

"And I never suggested anything different," said Steele.

"Good. So let's not start trying to run the show," replied Natalie.

Steele held up two hands. "I'm thinking maybe we got off on the wrong foot."

Natalie crossed her arms. "And maybe that's not entirely your fault," she said, her posture relaxing a fraction. "For what it's worth, we haven't decided if we even want the aid of the PSNI. How constrained are we going to be by having direct police involvement?"

"I've already covered this with Jacob."

"And Jacob isn't the sole authority on this investigation."

Steele's smile was one of patience. "Assuming you're not going to rob a bank or have any shootouts in the middle of Victoria Square, I don't think you need to worry. I want to help, not direct."

Natalie leaned on the edge of Helen's desk and gave Jacob a slight nod. She could live with it.

"Looking like a damn fine quartet of investigators, if you ask me," said Breen.

"I suppose we should get you up to speed, Detective Chief Inspector," said Jacob.

"No need for the formalities. Just call me Chief."

Jacob smirked. She had jokes. "I located someone who might be of interest."

Steele raised her brows. "That was quick work. Who?"

"Jeremiah Pettigrew. The former borstal chaplain and from Finbar Skelly's neighbourhood. He left the priesthood in the mid-nineties, with all sorts of allegations seemingly hanging over him."

"Not to mention in thick with the provos back in the day," said Hector.

"Wow, alright" said Steele. "Where does this Pettigrew live now?"

"Whitehead. Some ramshackle cottage on the promenade. Managed to track him down through the old phone books. He's living with a younger man. Seems like a strange set-up."

"How much younger?" Steele asked.

"Maybe around fifty or so," Jacob guessed.

Steele nodded, digesting the info and then glanced at Hector. "If you don't mind me asking, Mr. Breen, how do you connect to this investigation?"

"I was the investigating officer into the disappearance of a number of girls and young women not long after these lads went missing."

Doubt creased Steele's features and she looked back at Jacob. "So you're trying to tie them altogether?"

"Well, they have a potentially common thread," said

Natalie. There was a testiness in her tone, no doubt due to Steele directing her question to Jacob. "Ned by Night."

"What Finbar Skelly was talking about the last time his mother saw him," Jacob put in for Steele's benefit. "Graffiti with that name also went up in a few areas close to where these girls disappeared."

"So the connection is some old urban legend?" Steele asked.

"That's right." Jacob was surprised. "You know it?"

"Yeah... A bandaged man who stole children, something like that?"

"Close enough," Breen replied. "Just prior to our little jolly into the Ballylogue, we stopped in with a lady called Emily Goddard. She was the victim of an attempted abduction by a man clad in bandages and who I believe, was the first of this string of female victims.

"I see," Steele replied, doubt obvious. She seemed to realise this and quickly said, "Well, this is your investigation, and I suppose every lead needs bottomed out. Although with all the names already being bandied about, I'm worried we're spiralling beyond the scope of the four of us."

"So, let's split it," said Hector. "I have an attic full of notebooks and old case notes about the missing girls. I'll see if I can find anything that was missed in the original investigations. Maybe I'll touch base with your uncle too, Jacob."

"I'm sure Harry would be delighted," said Jacob. "If you do that, me and Natalie can focus on Finbar, and Zara, you can maybe concentrate on what can be found about the other three boys."

Zara acquiesced to the suggestion with a nod. "Speaking of which, I have something. The last of the missing boys, Richard McBride? I tracked down his mother and made her aware that a police investigation might be reopening. She's agreed to meet. Now, I can't let two private citizens have her address. I am however willing to bring one of you along."

"That's hardly standard procedure," Jacob said.

Steele laughed. "That's an extremely diplomatic way of putting it. But I want to show you that I'm on board with this investigation, that I want the same answers, and that I want to work with you, however..." She paused and turned to Natalie. "Mrs. McBride is a rather private woman. At this stage, I think it best not to bring around a podcaster with a six-figure listening audience."

Natalie folded her arms slowly and turned to Jacob. "I guess that means you."

"I guess it does," he replied.

"How does tomorrow afternoon suit?" Steele asked.

"I can move some things around in my diary."

With a plan in place, Breen and Steele said their goodbyes and took their leave. Natalie waited until their footsteps had faded on the narrow staircase.

"Quite the eclectic team you've managed to assemble," she said.

He grunted. "Easy to do when people invite themselves onto your investigation."

She gave a half-smile and turned to look at the pinboard. Jacob had cleared the takeaway flyers, leaving only the copy of the under-saturated picture of Finbar Skelly on the cork.

"You have anywhere to be?" Jacob asked.

"Not urgently, why?"

"Was thinking the pinboard needed an update."

"Oh my, and I'm allowed to witness?"

"Consider yourself blessed."

Natalie waited as Jacob booted up his computer, located the saved article from the Belfast Sentinel and printed out the pictures of the three other missing boys. He then went back to the Irish Rover website and snipped a picture of the outside of Hartley House.

He grabbed a stack of post-its and began to write down names. DESMOND McCLURE. RICHARD McBRIDE. CRAIG FULLERTON. JEREMIAH PETTIGREW. EDITH GALBRAITH. EDEN HENNESSEY. EMILY GODDARD.

On the next post-it he had written OTHER MISSING GIRLS. He unpeeled it from the stack and then stopped. He realised he not asked Hector their names and it suddenly felt wrong to refer to them so abstractly. He should know their names. He scrunched up the post-it, dropped it into the waste bin by his desk, and mentally reminded himself to ask Hector who the other girls were.

On the final post-it he wrote, NED BY NIGHT.

Collecting the pictures from the printer, he attached the individual images of the other missing boys next to Finbar Skelly's. He then took the three post-its with their names, and pinned them under the corresponding picture.

He placed the Post-its that held Edith, Eden and Emily's names on the opposite side of the board. The NED BY NIGHT post-it went to the centre.

Retrieving a roll of red twine from a drawer in his desk, he cut off two strips and pinned one next to the boys, and the other next to the girls, leading them both to point to Ned by Night.

The image of Hartley House went below the picture of Finbar and Jacob cut another piece of string to connect the borstal and the escapee. Finally, he placed Pettigrew's post-it between Finbar's picture and Hartley House.

Finished, he waited for Natalie who studied the completed board for a few more seconds before turning to him. "You know, there are apps that would do that for you."

Jacob smirked. "I did it for our first investigation."

"No, I remember. At the time I just thought you were trying to impress me with your private eye vibes."

"I like laying it out like this. Let's me see where we're at."

"Yeah, a computer screen definitely couldn't do that."

He gave her a playful shove on the shoulder. "What are you thinking?"

Natalie considered the pinboard once more and scrunched her nose. "A whole lot of names."

"And not much else."

They both stared at the board. Perhaps waiting to be struck by a divine clue that would break the whole thing open. Nothing came.

"Well, it looks nice at least," said Jacob.

Natalie laughed. "Before I forget. The Miss Gumshoe crew are coming to mine tonight. A little get together to welcome Giselle onto the team officially."

"Sounds nice."

"Come over. Say hi to the guys."

Jacob, caught out by the invite, scrambled for an excuse as to why a mostly normal guy in his thirties didn't want to socialise on a Saturday night and came up blank. "What time?"

"Eight or so."

"I suppose I can move some things around."

11

Jacob locked the office and walked back to his apartment. The air was bitingly cold, carrying a sharp tang of salt from the sea and the promise of impending snow. The streets were subdued, as if Belfast itself was bracing against the chill.

He threw his coat over the sofa and blasted the remnants of the previous night's takeaway in the microwave. He shovelled it down and watched the sun dip out of view. Streetlights cast a golden glow, fighting back against the encroaching darkness. He briefly thought about crying off from Natalie's little shindig. But he knew there was only so much tolerance she would have for his flakiness.

Letting go of a sigh heavy with resignation, he selected a bottle of wine from the rack, some Peroni from the fridge, and jumped on a bus over to the Belmont Road. It was a five-minute walk from the bus stop to Natalie's house; a large, detached Edwardian style construction, sitting well back from the quiet upmarket street.

Natalie met him at the door. She had changed into a button-down shirt and a pair of chinos. Jacob offered the bottle of pinot and followed her inside.

The rest of the party had beaten him there. Ciaran and Arjun seemed happy to see him, with the latter going so far as to climb down from his seat to pull Jacob into a friendly hug. Giselle, who Jacob had only met on a couple of brief occasions previously, was more reserved in her greeting. So long as she didn't attempt to seduce him in order for him to be murdered, Jacob considered her a marked improvement on the person she had replaced.

The talk, once Jacob had said his hello's, seated himself, and opened a beer, was inevitably of work. It soon turned to their current case and the plan for it to be the next project of Miss Gumshoe.

Jacob, who had recounted versions of the story multiple times over the past couple of days, let Natalie do the heavy lifting in bringing her team up to speed. From the way they listened, it was obvious they were all immediately on-board. As had been the case with Natalie, the combination of true crime and urban legend, was a tantalising prospect.

"How did you start looking into this?" Giselle asked Jacob once Natalie had finished.

"A mother of one of the missing boys approached me. She didn't know, or at least didn't mention the other boys, but the short timeframe between the four disappearances caught my attention.

Giselle nodded. "You know, I'm not sure I've met a real-life private detective before."

Jacob leaned forward. "Well..."

"-We are private!" Natalie and Ciaran shouted in unison before descending into cackling hysterics. Arjun booed and threw a Dorito chip at Jacob.

Jacob blushed and took a swig of beer. "That felt like a set-up."

"Oh, it absolutely was," Natalie said, her smile wide as Giselle offered an apologetic shrug. "Take it as friendly advice, you need new material."

Dillon entered the kitchen as the laughs slowly subsided. He kept his head down, found a can of coke in the fridge, and caught Jacob's eye on his way back out the door.

"What's happening?" Jacob asked.

Dillon turned, already smiling. He motioned to the party. "Busy?"

"Never too busy to take you to school, kid."

He excused himself and followed Dillon into the front room to find he had the game already set-up.

Back in October, a week or so after Natalie had first floated the idea of a series about their investigation into the Followers of Eden, she and Jacob had been at her place, trying to come up with an accurate chronology of events to work into an episodic podcast structure. As the evening wore on, she had suggested they order some food. They had been joined by Dillon who appeared from upstairs a second after the delivery guy rang the doorbell. Just as they were finishing up, Natalie got a call, leaving Jacob and Dillon alone at the kitchen table.

The awkwardness had stretched until Jacob made a final, Hail Mary attempt at conversation and asked the kid if he liked video games.

Dillon admitted that he did, and explained to Jacob that his game of choice was a long-standing football franchise. Dillon, most likely assuming Jacob, as a man in his thirties, with relevant interests, was being polite when asking the question. He even went as far to offer Jacob a friendly match.

Unfortunately for Dillon, Jacob, without burdens like a social life or girlfriend, was more than familiar with the game, having purchased almost every annual iteration since the days of the first PlayStation.

Jacob had eased up after the fifth goal without reply and even allowed Dillon a consolation. Their rivalry had continued online over the next couple of months with Dillon improving his virtual footie skills to the point where Jacob's perfect record was in peril.

He picked up the controller that Dillon had left on the sofa. United for Jacob, Spurs for himself. Dillon had inherited his loyalty from his dad. Rough deal.

"Could make it easier on yourself," Jacob said, flicking through his lineup. "Pick someone other than Spurs, and you might have at least some chance of winning."

Dillon smirked, unbothered. "You sound like mum."

"Your mum's a smart woman. Wants to save you a lifetime of disappointment. She never try to talk you out of it?"

"Nah. It was Dad's team, so it's my team." He kept his voice casual. Jacob knew that Dillon's father had died when Dillon was just a baby. Support for Spurs tied him to the man he never had the chance to know.

Jacob understood that loyalty, the kind that didn't always make sense. "I'll take you to a Northern Ireland game sometime," he said. "Show you some real hardship."

The virtual players kicked off. Within seconds, Dillon scored with a scrappy shot. Slow, awkward, completely saveable. Jacob scowled at the screen and tightened his grip on the controller.

He worked the ball around, playing patient football, waiting for his opening. He got it just before halftime. A well-timed interception in midfield sent the ball out wide to his right winger, who danced past one defender, cut inside, sent Dillon's last man the wrong way with a deft feint, and then lobbed the goalie. It was a sublime goal, and he told Dillon so.

The game continued but Jacob found his mind drifting. Back to the missing boys. They had been Dillon's age. Too young to fight back, too vulnerable against the kind of men who preyed on them. Boys who had been victimised, stripped of their futures, buried under years of silence.

You know how to fight?" he asked suddenly.

Dillon, sitting cross-legged on the floor, flicked a glance over his shoulder before turning back to the game. "What?"

"Fight. I mean, if you had to. Could you?"

Dillon shrugged, adjusting his grip on the controller. "I dunno. It's not something I've ever thought about."

Jacob figured as much. Dillon was sharp, quick-witted, analytical. He was fit, Jacob knew he ran cross-country and played basketball but physically, he was willowy, slight.

"I could show you a few things. If you're interested."

"Yeah?"

"Yeah."

Dillon's eyes remained on the game. "Mum said you got beat up a whole bunch last summer."

"Well, I wouldn't say a whole bunch..."

"Alarmingly frequent; was how she described it." He was enjoying himself.

"I feel your mum might have left some context out."

"Sure," said Dillon. He waited a beat and then said. "I'll think about it. The fighting lessons, I mean. Thanks, Jacob."

"No worries."

The sound of controller buttons being tapped filled the silence for a few seconds before Dillon spoke again. "It's been a while since you've been around."

"Yeah," said Jacob.

"How come?"

"Me and your mum finished the podcast, and then work got busy."

Dillon's attention stayed on the TV but he nodded. "I think mum missed having you about."

"She said that?"

"No."

"Oh."

"But she did talk about you a few times. Just an impression I got. You and her doing a new show together?"

"Maybe. We'll have to see how it pans out."

Dillon kept tapping on his controller. "Cool."

By now there were only seconds on the clock. Dillon picked the ball up on the halfway line but another sloppy pass by his midfielder was cut out by Jacob, just as his phone vibrated in his pocket. With one hand he answered the call, using the other to try and pass the ball back to his keeper

"I found quite a few Matthew Connelly's," Helen said by way of greeting, oblivious to the struggle on the other end of the line. "I think I have a likely candidate though."

"Shite!" Jacob hissed as his goalie shanked the clearance.

"Excuse me?"

"Sorry," Jacob said as Dillon played his centre forward through on goal. He turned away from the screen and the inevitability of what was to follow. "What makes this guy stand out?"

"Supported living scheme," Helen answered. "For ex-offenders. I don't want to assume but..."

"But he was already in the system as a child. He probably never made it out on the straight and narrow."

"Exactly," Helen said.

Jacob made a mental note of the address Helen gave him,

thanked her, and bid her a good night before ending the call. He turned back to the tv. Dillon's striker was pumping his hips back and forward in a vigorous goal celebration.

"Games forfeit," he said as he stood, ignoring Dillon's crowing that followed him out of the room. He met Natalie just as she emerged from the kitchen.

"Just seeing if you needed rescuing," she said.

"As a matter of fact, yeah, from a gloating fourteen-year-old. Helen just called."

"On a Saturday night? She's a dedicated lady."

"She is, and she's come through with a potential address for Matthew Connelly."

"Awesome. Tomorrow?"

"Tomorrow." Jacob echoed.

Natalie smiled. "Thanks for coming tonight. It's good to have you-"

A piercing scream from the kitchen cut through the air. Natalie took a startled step towards Jacob, her hand going to his chest for a fleeting second before she caught herself.

Jacob burst into the kitchen with Natalie only half a step behind. Giselle looked around, utterly perplexed but reasonably calm. Belatedly Jacob realised it was Ciaran who had screamed.

"Ciaran says there was someone at the window," Arjun said. "Looking in at us."

Jacob headed for the front door. He sensed someone following and glancing behind, saw it was Arjun. He told him to check the back garden as he went to the front of the house. There was no one in the front garden, nor in the street.

Natalie's street was a cul-de-sac that ended at a low fence corralling a small copse of trees. Jacob used his phone's torch to make sure no one was lurking there before jogging to the far end of the street. The junction led onto another equally quiet road. Jacob counted five other streets within twenty metres of where he was standing, each offering a quick escape into the suburban maze.

Arjun was waiting for Jacob by the front gate. "Anything?"

Jacob shook his head. "Long gone."

"If there even was anyone there," Arjun said quietly. "I

mean, Ciaran's a few drinks deep."

"Deep enough to think he saw someone staring at him through the window?" Jacob didn't believe it, and he doubted Arjun did either, even if he wanted to tell himself otherwise. He walked up the side of Natalie's house and took in the expansive back garden.

"You checked out the whole yard?"

"Of course," Arjun replied, a little too quickly.

The rear patio was bathed in a warm glow from outdoor lighting, but beyond was a deep blackness, made altogether more ominous by the supposed spectre Ciaran had glimpsed.

Shadows merged and shifted as the tall hedges that bordered the garden swayed with the night breeze. Jacob was almost prepared to accept Arjun's assertion, but a niggling worry forced him forward.

He searched the garden until he was satisfied they were alone. There was no evidence of freshly trodden grass, disturbed soil, or trampled plants. Letting out a breath he hadn't realised he'd been holding, Jacob returned to Arjun, glancing at the camera above the patio. He had already noted another over the side entrance and a third above the front door.

"You'd think one of them would pick up whoever it was," Arjun said, following the same train of thought as Jacob.

"You'd think," Jacob agreed.

"A burglar maybe?" Arjun continued. "You know, casing the joint?"

Jacob gave an amused grunt. "Casing the joint?"

"Well, that's what they say, isn't it?"

"I'm sure they do, somewhere. But," Jacob gestured towards the house where a light was burning in almost every room, "place like this, they'd wait until the house is dead to the world."

"So then, who?"

Jacob didn't know, and didn't like it. "C'mon, let's get back inside."

Natalie was waiting for them by the front door, her arms folded across her chest. "Well?"

"Nothing," answered Arjun.

"Okay," she said, some tension lifting from her shoulders.

"Good."

"Your cameras," said Jacob. "Think we could get a look?"

"We could, but are we sure Ciaran just didn't see his own reflection?"

"It'd make me scream," Arjun said.

Natalie waited until Arjun went into the kitchen. She gently closed the door behind him and then turned back to Jacob. "You seem concerned."

"Someone snooping around your house? Of course I'm concerned."

"Oh, c'mon. What are the odds that I get kidnapped from my home twice in the space of six months?"

"That's not funny."

Natalie's wry smile curled. "No, I suppose not, but let's not jump to conclusions either." She led him towards the living room. "Could have been some drunk idiot who wandered up the wrong driveway."

They entered the living room. It had been vacated by Dillon whilst Jacob was outside.

"Dillon alright?"

"Not even slightly fazed," Natalie replied, shaking her head. "Asked what was happening, took advantage of me being distracted to grab another can of coke, and disappeared up to his room."

"Ice in the veins," Jacob said.

Natalie smirked and nodded in the direction of the kitchen. "More than we can say for some."

"Did our scream queen tell you what he actually saw?"

"Just someone pressed against the glass. Said he had a white face, but then said that it was probably the light reflecting onto the window."

She picked up the remote Dillon had left on the floor and pointed it at the TV. The blank standby screen changed to a crisp, high-definition, black and white video of the front of her house. The camera angle took in the front steps and most of the front yard, but not the far side of the driveway. There was a twenty-four-hour timer on the bottom right of the screen.

"Is the time accurate?" Jacob asked.

Natalie glanced at her Breitling, then the TV and then back

at her watch. "Maybe five seconds slow."

"Can we take it back half an hour?"

"Sure."

With a few taps of the remote, the footage jumped back in five-minute spurts. Natalie let the footage play at double speed, periodically changing the view to the side of her house and then to the patio; well-lit and empty. She flicked back to the front of the house and after a minute began to cycle through the cameras again.

Jacob wished she would let the footage play on just one camera but kept quiet. Natalie brought the footage back to the front of the house once again and had raised the remote to start a third cycle when Jacob saw it.

"There!" He jabbed a finger towards the TV. It was brief, but he was certain he had seen a shadow flicker at the edge of the camera's field of vision.

Natalie rewound the footage a few seconds and let the video play back at normal speed.

It was brief but it was there, a whisp of movement, gliding along the edge of the screen. Natalie changed the view to the side door in time to catch the shadow again, this time lingering a fraction longer before vanishing. The edges of the shadow blurred into the darkness, skewing its proportions.

Without prompting, Natalie switched the feed to the third camera. "He'll have crossed the patio to get to the kitchen window," she said quietly. "We'll see him then."

They watched in silence as an inky smudge, almost indiscernible against the night, flitted around the patio, and the border of the third camera, before fading away once more.

To Jacob, the calculated movement of the shadow was evident, appearing at the edges of the camera's range, never venturing into the full view, smart enough to avoid revealing any identifiable features.

Natalie let the footage play out, well past the time Ciaran would have seen the figure at the window. Slowly, she set the remote down and turned to Jacob. "What are you thinking?" She began to fiddle with the bezel of her watch, her one tell when she was nervous.

"That this person is savvy enough to notice the layout of

your cameras," Jacob said. "And that they're careful enough not to get seen clearly." He clicked his tongue. "Anyone you've pissed off lately?"

"No. The last few Miss Gumshoe shows have been international stories, and older ones at that."

"What about the Followers? The trial is going to see a lot of people fall. Money lost, reputations ruined. Have you been getting any attention from them?"

Prior to Natalie engaging Jacob's services for their first investigation together, she and a colleague, Roisin Dunwoody, had released a three-part expose on the Followers of Eden, with an intention to release a separate podcast, hosted by Roisin, going deeper into their misdeeds.

As a result, both women had experienced a course of intimidation and harassment from the cult. Roisin had borne the brunt of the conduct, which had eventually culminated in her murder, but Natalie had also told Jacob about threatening letters and believing she saw someone hanging around her house.

She considered his question and then shook her head. "Ever since Huber got arrested, they've hunkered down and have been steadily screaming persecution. I don't see them changing tactics now."

Jacob shrugged his agreement.

"Which means," Natalie said, "That it's maybe to do with this case."

It took Jacob a second to realise what she was referring to. "What, Finbar Skelly?"

"Well, it's not just the Finbar Skelly case anymore, is it? Between us and Hector, we're dealing with up to ten known disappearances. Who have we spoken to so far? Seamus Dolan, Emily Goddard, Jeremiah Pettigrew, and Eileen McClure." Natalie counted the names off on her fingers.

"I think we can rule out Emily and the lovely Mrs McClure, and Seamus Dolan's mind is mush."

"What about the nephew?"

An uncomfortable shiver crept over Jacob at the thought of Martin Closkey and his dead eyes skulking outside Natalie's house. "But why?"

"Scope out who we are, why we're asking questions. His uncle's an ex-IRA commander who has strangers coming to his door asking questions about some missing kid from forty years ago. For all we know, he could be involved. It's not like they don't have form for making people disappear."

It was a possibility, Jacob supposed, but it was remote. They had got nothing from Dolan and Closkey and his goons had put enough of a scare up them that they wouldn't be returning any time soon. Which sat fine with him. Getting tangled up with paramilitaries was not something he wanted to consider.

Jacob gestured towards the TV, "Whoever this was, seemed to know where your cameras were. Closkey or one of his minions would have a seriously tight timeframe from meeting us today to using that knowledge tonight."

"Which leaves the priest."

Pettigrew. The old man's presence had put Jacob on edge in a way he couldn't quite explain. There was something unsettling about the way he carried himself, the way his gaze lingered just a fraction too long, assessing, weighing. His demeanour had been calm, almost passive, but Jacob hadn't bought it for a second.

But then there was the obvious problem. Jeremiah Pettigrew was old, at least eighty and in no way spry. Would he still have the physical capability to avoid the cameras and then escape before Jacob and Arjun ran out of the house?

He shook his head. "Pettigrew unsettled me. But he's old. And frail. I just can't picture him doing this."

Natalie didn't look convinced. "You don't have to be strong to make a phone call," she pointed out. "To tip someone off."

Jacob's jaw tightened. She was right. He thought about the baby-eyed man who lived with Pettigrew. Could it have been him?

"And aren't we forgetting someone else? This police detective of yours."

"Of mine?" Jacob suddenly realised he was on shaky ground and not exactly sure why. "Natalie, are you suggesting Zara Steele, a chief inspector, is snooping outside your house?"

"No, not really. I'm just looking to point score."

"About what?"

"About you not telling me about her, Jacob. You sat on it for two days."

"I thought we'd moved past this."

"So did I, then she swans into your office this afternoon like she's running the show."

"I think it'll be good to have a police source on our side." His reply sounded more defensive than he had intended.

"I'm feeling like a broken record. When I agreed to join this investigation, I agreed it on the condition that I-"

"-That you were an equal partner," Jacob interrupted. "I know."

Her look hardened and Jacob held up a hand. "Sorry. What do you want me to do? Tell her we're not interested?"

Natalie sighed. "No. I think you're right, having a police source could be a major help. Besides, I'd bet even if we tell her we didn't want her assistance, she'd dig her heels in and either get in the way, or make life difficult."

Jacob said nothing. He'd had the same thought when Steele had made her pitch back in his office. He followed Natalie back into the hallway. She reached for the handle on the kitchen door and stopped, turning back to him.

"Do you trust her, Jacob?"

The question caught him by surprise. "Why? Don't you?"

"I'm not sure." Natalie pressed the handle down and they stepped back into the kitchen.

"Well?" Arjun asked. "Anything?"

Natalie lifted her wine glass. "No. Not a thing."

12

Jacob woke from a fitful sleep early the next morning. As everyone else said their farewells at Natalie's, he had taken the opportunity to make a round of the ground floor, checking every door and window, confirming all were locked tight.

Although the theory of the drunk wanderer seemed the most likely, it wasn't a particular comfort. Neither he, nor Natalie, could offer any other potential candidates. By her own admission the last few episodes of Miss Gumshoe hadn't ruffled any feathers. Jacob followed the podcast enough to know that himself and he had discretely asked Ciaran, once he had climbed down from high doe, about future plans. There was nothing scandalous in the works.

He had offered to sleep on the sofa but Natalie, although appreciative, wouldn't hear of it. She could be rigidly independent. Jacob supposed being widowed at twenty-three, with a newborn and a burgeoning journalistic career in London would do that to you, but at times he wished she would lean on others, just a little.

She thanked him for the offer and then pulled him into a hug. He had paused on her front step until he heard the double lock on the door clicking into place.

Jacob showered and made breakfast. Natalie phoned a little after nine to say she was waiting downstairs. It was a dry morning, but it came with a bite that suggested the anticipated snow storm might not be too far away.

She nodded to a cup in the holder as Jacob climbed into the Audi. "Petrol station special, I'm afraid."

"You know me, I'm not picky." Jacob took a swig and grimaced. "Jesus."

"You're welcome. So, where are we heading?"

"Malone Road."

Natalie made an impressed sound. In Belfast, Malone Road was shorthand for affluence and influence.

"The other end of the Malone Road," Jacob said, meaning the end closer to Queens University and the tightly packed terraced houses of students and migrants.

The building where Matthew Connelly lived was a three-story Victorian style construction, sitting across the road from the university's computer science lab. Connelly's flat, and the others that made up the supported living facility, were a modern add-on to the original house, stretching far down a side-street.

Natalie found a parking spot beside the building. It was a Sunday morning and the streets were quiet. Many local students tended to travel home for the weekend, usually with an armful of dirty laundry and ready for mummy's cooking. Those who remained were likely still tucked up in bed, nursing cocktail jug hangovers.

Jacob had lived not too far away in student digs in his first and only year at Queens, before he ditched his studies for a career with the police. He remembered the night shifts of his early twenties, casting envious looks at others of the same age out on the lash. The laughter spilling from pub doors, the flirtatious glances exchanged under the dim streetlights. They were carefree. He was in an armoured car wearing a flak jacket with a Glock at his hip, bouncing from domestics, to road traffic accidents, to overdoses, to suicides, and whatever human misery Belfast could dredge up.

He often wondered if it would have been a different life, had he stuck to his law degree. A respectable job. Married to Catherine. Lazy Sunday mornings at home before taking the kids to the park, and then around to the in-laws for a roast beef dinner. Instead, many of his Sundays were an echo of his weekdays, laden with the weight of other people's crises and problems.

"You alright?" Natalie was halfway out of the car but had stopped when she noticed Jacob wasn't following.

"Yeah, fine." He released his seat belt and followed her.

The front door to the building was unlocked. It led to a reception area with an empty office behind a plexiglass partition. To the right of the office was an open door into the bottom corridor of the flats, and to the left, a row of metal letterboxes, each with a name scribbled beside them. Jacob found Connelly's name next to the box for flat twelve.

They took the stairs to the first floor. Flat twelve was the second one along the corridor. Jacob rapped the wood and the door opened slowly a few seconds later, as though the person behind it wasn't used to finding someone on the other side.

The man who peered out had blotchy skin and a whiskey nose. His balding head was shaved close to the scalp. Watery blue eyes regarded them with suspicion.

"Matthew Connelly?" asked Jacob.

"Who's asking?"

Jacob held out a business card in reply. There was nothing on the card other than his name, occupation and office phone number, but Connelly took his time reading it.

"You're not the police?"

"Private investigators, just like the card says. We're looking into the disappearance of a boy."

"We believe you knew him," said Natalie. "Finbar Skelly?"

Jacob, who had enough doors shut in his face to recognize the signs, stuck his foot against the frame, pre-empting Connelly slamming it closed by a second.

"Matthew," Natalie said gently. "We just want to talk."

"No, no, I can't."

"We know you and Finbar were close," Natalie continued. "We think you can help us in finding out what happened to him."

"You don't know what you're dealing with."

Natalie put her hand on the door and leaned in close. "So tell us."

Jacob watched the fight suddenly die inside the man. It was

a look that somehow seemed to suit him, like he was used to the world throwing him obstacles he couldn't overcome. Connelly's shoulders slumped and reluctantly, he beckoned them inside.

The small flat wasn't what Jacob had been expecting. The furniture was worn, the appliances old, but it was well-kept and neat. It was a home.

"Finbar," Connelly said as he motioned for them to sit. That's a name I spent about four decades trying to drink away." He noticed Jacob taking stock of his apartment and the lack of any bottles. "Ten months sober. Part of the conditions of them allowing me back here after I got out of Maghaberry. My driest spell since I was eleven years old."

"So, you and Finbar were friends," Natalie prompted.

Connelly lifted a pack of cigarettes from the coffee table. He pulled one out and then held it up. "You mind?"

"It's your pad," Jacob replied.

"Aye, we were mates," Connelly said once he had the cigarette lit. He stopped to take a drag. "Place like that, you tend to gravitate towards anyone who'd tolerate you near them."

"What can you tell us about him?" Natalie asked.

For the first time Connelly smiled. "Like a coked-up Duracell bunny. Never sat still. Got him in trouble more times than I could count. Mischievous wee fucker, had a temper too, but he was too soft for the borstal."

"How so?" Jacob asked. Pettigrew had told him something similar.

"Just a mummy's boy, I suppose. I remember the first time she came up to visit and Finbar crying himself to sleep that night." Connelly shook his head. "Jesus, what were we doing there? Just fucking kids is all."

Neither Jacob nor Natalie replied, both sensing he had something further to say.

"My first day, one of the screws told me that I was now only a number. Six Seven Two, that was me. He told me I was a number, and that I was theirs for ten months, and then he punched me in the belly. I was fourteen." He took another puff of the cigarette, lost at some moment in his past. "I'd always hoped he'd got away, you know? When he didn't turn up again...But I knew, even if I didn't want to admit it."

"What was Finbar in Millisle for?" Jacob asked.

It was a question he had decided not to pose to Deirdre, afraid she would think he was judging her boy. He knew it didn't really matter. The crime Finbar had committed to get him sent to Millisle had no bearing on his case but he was curious to know a little more about the boy. Pettigrew had referred to him as a hood so Jacob had assumed it was either car theft or burglary.

"Assault."

"Assault?" said Natalie. "Must have been serious enough to get a custodial sentence."

"Aye. Don't know the details but it was on a girl. Maybe it got treated more seriously, I don't know."

Jacob said, "When you say assault...."

"Physical," said Connelly quickly. "Only physical. Finbar wasn't a root, I would have stayed clear if he was. He told me it was some wee girl he knew from back home. She was giving him grief, so he slapped her."

"They don't send you to borstal for a slap," said Jacob.

Connelly shrugged. Defensive. "That's what he told me. I didn't ask any more about it. Wasn't surprised though, he had a temper, like I said."

"Did you know a Desmond McClure?" Jacob asked.

"Aye, I knew Desmond. One of the big lads on our wing."

Jacob drummed his fingers on the arm of the sofa. "He also disappeared. Never turned up."

"Good." Connelly noticed their look and shrugged. "He was a fucker."

"What about Craig Fullerton?" Natalie asked.

Connelly frowned. "Maybe. McClure was the main boy on the wing, and he had his own wee gang. I think there was a Fullerton he palled about with."

Another possible link to Millisle, Jacob thought. "How about a Richard McBride?"

This time Connelly shook his head.

"So Finbar had a hard time at the borstal?" Jacob asked.

"We all had a hard time." The tone in Connelly's reply was

testy. "But aye, I suppose Finbar had it worse than most. There was this one screw, Higgins. Big fella and a nasty fucker to boot. Always took every chance he could to bully the lads. Finbar got the worst of it."

Jacob nodded along. Pettigrew had given him the impression that he had looked out for Finbar. "So he had no one to look after him?" he asked, wondering Connelly would volunteer the name of the priest.

"The matron did. Patricia Winslow. Lovely woman. She was about the only person in that place that didn't treat us like shite on the bottom of their shoe. Finbar loved her. She didn't take any guff. Even Higgins left Finbar alone when Ms. Winslow was about."

"Don't suppose you know what happened to Ms. Winslow?" asked Jacob

"She left, not long after Finbar..." Connelly trailed away and then pretended to clear his throat. "Suddenly too, we were never told why."

"Did you know Father Pettigrew?" Jacob asked, believing Connelly wasn't going to bring the priest up unprompted.

"To see, aye."

"Were him and Finbar close?"

"Not particularly. They were from the same part of Belfast though, I remember that. Pettigrew tried to use it as an in with Finbar, but Finbar gave him a wide berth."

Jacob sat forward slightly, a familiar sensation fluttering in his belly. The crack in an account, the faint discord in a story that didn't quite line up with what someone else was saying. "Why?"

"Well, why the fuck do ye think? That priest was a wrong 'un."

"Finbar told you this?"

"No, it was just known. He never seemed to be out of the borstal and he had a few favourites. Boys he'd keep close to. There was one boy in particular, Chambers. Eddie Chambers. Followed Pettigrew around like a puppy. About twenty years ago, I'm down in the city centre and who do I see but Pettigrew. And who's carrying his shopping? Eddie fuckin' Chambers."

Jacob thought back to the strange man who answered the

door in Pettigrew's cottage. "What'd he look like?"

"Who? Eddie?"

"Yeah."

"Jesus, I dunno. He was a bit of a weird looking fella. Big, but not solid if you know what I mean. His face was...big...ah fuck, I'm no good at this."

"You're doing fine, Matthew," Jacob reassured him. He pointed two fingers towards his own face. "Small eyes?"

"Aye!" Connelly brightened. "That's right, eyes too small for his face, like they hadn't grown with the rest of him. How'd you know that?"

Jacob didn't see any benefit to be gained by lying to the man. "Him and Pettigrew are living together. I was at their house two days ago looking for info about Finbar."

Connelly shifted. "And what did Pettigrew tell you?"

"Very little, and what he did, I'm beginning to question."

"Matthew," said Natalie. "Did you personally see any impropriety from Father Pettigrew towards any of the boys?"

"No," Connelly replied. "But it'd hardly be surprising in that place."

"How do you mean?" asked Natalie.

Connelly went to speak and then stopped. He angrily stubbed out the butt of his cigarette before lighting another as tears suddenly pricked the corners of both eyes. "You don't know, do youse? About..."

Jacob and Natalie shared a look, both lost. "About?" Jacob prompted.

Connelly rubbed at his eyes with his free hand and then buried his face there, before lifting it slowly. "Fuck it. They used to have these parties, towards the end of every month. Men from the outside, trustees, they called them, part of some charity group." Connelly swallowed hard, his eyes narrowing as if visualising the scene anew. "They'd pick a few of us, the younger ones usually, to serve drinks. Put us in these ridiculous little uniforms and have us wait on the guests. It was demeaning, but you didn't dream of saying no. It was either do that or face the consequences."

Jacob's gut twisted.

"Some of the boys, we'd get taken aside, led off to a private room."

"And the staff knew?" Natalie asked quietly.

"It was the same two. Higgins and another screw, Hussey. You see, Finbar and me, we were in the open borstal, in the mansion. Up there, after lights out, it was nightwatchmen on patrol, not the prison officers. My guess is they paid a couple of them off to look the other way."

"And no one did anything?" Natalie asked.

Connelly ran a hand over his face. "There was one officer, McCarthy. It was maybe a week after the first time it happened. I told him what happened, what I'd seen, and he believed me, God bless him for that. He didn't even question it. He told me he'd get it sorted. A week later McCarthy was shot dead by the IRA, driving into work. They pulled up alongside him when he was stopped at some traffic lights and raked the car. Higgins caught me up by the laundry, give me a proper kicking and says to me, 'see what happens when you talk.' After that I kept my fuckin' mouth shut."

Jacob frowned. "Higgins suggested he was involved in this other prison officer getting killed?"

"He never came out and said it but what he was saying was clear enough."

Jacob nodded and decided not to press. He had no doubt the IRA had murdered McCarthy but Connelly's belief that Higgins had something to do with it, seemed like a long shot. The IRA saw prison officers as legitimate targets for murder. That, and the notion that Higgins would set one of his own colleagues up, was hard to stomach. More likely in Jacob's opinion, Higgins had used the killing, fortuitous timing and all, to frighten the kid.

"Was Finbar at these parties?" Natalie asked.

"Finbar was a favourite." Connelly looked as if he was about to say something else but paused.

"What is it, Matthew?" Natalie asked gently.

"It wasn't just the parties. There were times, someone would come to the borstal to see him. Higgins would come up to the dorm and take Finbar away. He always knew it was coming. You'd hear the car pulling up. It was always late, after midnight, so there would be no one coming into the borstal at that time."

"One of these trustees?" asked Jacob.

Connelly shook his head.

"Did Finbar ever talk about-"

"-Never."

There was something in Connelly's reply. Something not said.

Jacob asked, "Did Finbar say who he was? Did he give a name?"

Connelly's lip trembled. "Oh, Jesus."

"Who was he, Matthew?" Natalie asked softly.

"I don't know. I only saw him once, the night he took Finbar."

A chill crept up Jacob's spine.

"I don't understand," said Natalie, looking from Jacob and then back to Connelly. "You were on the Falls Road?"

"The Falls? No, no. Finbar disappeared from Millisle."

"Finbar's mother said he was last seen on the Falls Road-"

Natalie was cut off by a vehement shake of the head from Connelly. "They brought him back."

"Maybe you've got mixed up-" Natalie began

Connelly slapped the table hard. An ashtray bounced, spilling butts. "I haven't got anything fucking mixed up. Christmas Eve. How the fuck do you think I'm ever going to forget a thing like that?"

"Okay," Jacob said quietly. "Who brought him back? The police?"

"These were no coppers. They were rough looking fuckers. From our dorm room you could see the front gate, and we were right above the reception. I saw them drive up and drag Finbar out of the car and into the building."

"And that's the last you saw of him?"

Connelly couldn't meet his eye.

Natalie reached across and touched him gently on the arm. "Matthew."

"That night." Connelly's lip trembled and he took a steadying breath as his eyes lost focus at some point on the wall behind him. "Christmas lights in the window, carols on the radio down the corridor. Little Drummer Boy. I still can't listen to that song. The car on the gravel. I got up, crept to the window. They dragged Finbar out, shouting and screaming. I know the rest of the lads in the dorm were pretending they couldn't hear. He stepped out of the car...."

"Who?" Jacob asked.

Connelly didn't seem to hear him. He was lost in the past. "Covered in bandages. Pits for eyes. The head snapped up to right where I was standing. No way he could have seen me, but he knew I was there and that look pierced my soul. By the time I got enough guts to look again, the car was gone. And so was Finbar."

13

Jacob wasn't sure how long they sat in Natalie's car without a word from either of them. They had left Connelly in his flat, alone with the memories they had dredged up,

Natalie broke the silence. "Just what have we stumbled into?"

Jacob had no idea how to answer. A paedophile ring at the borstal. A witness who had seen Finbar get taken. The abductor dressed like this urban legend that hovered over the case since the beginning.

"Where do we go from here?"

Jacob rubbed a hand over his face as he considered her question. "See if we can't look up this matron," he said slowly, trying to plan their path ahead. "If she's still alive, see what she knows."

"What about Higgins?"

"Hold off, I'd say. He's a suspect in Finbar's disappearance. He might not have taken Finbar, but it sounds like he set it up." They lapsed into silence again. "There is one thing bothering me," Jacob said. "And it's been bothering me since Deirdre Skelly walked into my office. We know Finbar was picked up somewhere in the vicinity of the Falls Road."

"Right."

"Who could have done that? Falls Road in daylight in the eighties? Connelly said it wasn't police who brought him back?"

"Undercover army unit?"

Jacob shook his head. It seemed unlikely that an undercover unit would have been used to apprehend a fourteen-year-old delinquent. Even if they had, surely someone would have seen it, and some sort of word would have gotten back to Finbar's family.

Which led him to his next thought. Maybe people had seen who took him, and were too scared to say. He voiced this to Natalie. "From what Hector tells us, Seamus Dolan was a man to be feared back in the day."

"But why would an IRA commander return a kid back to the prison service?" Natalie asked. "They would have hated them as much as they hated the police and army. Not to mention Finbar's uncle was involved in the movement."

Jacob leaned back into his seat. "Another thing to consider. Deirdre Skelly believes her son was last seen on the Falls Road."

"She didn't know he was brought back to the borstal."

"Exactly."

"So, what are we thinking, cover-up by the borstal staff?"

"Maybe," Jacob said. "But I'm thinking, something like that, they'd try to involve as few people as possible. Connelly said Higgins and another officer were involved in arranging these parties which took place after the other officers would have gone off duty. I'm guessing they either bribed or intimidated the nightwatchmen into silence."

"So, a small contingent of rogue staff? Makes sense, I suppose."

Jacob shifted in the seat. He was leaving the hardest to believe point to last. "Connelly saw this man in bandages then taking Finbar."

"Apparently," Natalie said it with a shake of her head. She wasn't doubting what Connelly had told them, Jacob knew, but was struggling with the reality of what they were hearing. Along with Emily Goddard's account, they now had two confirmed sightings of this supposed urban legend.

They were now facing the reality that there may be a kernel

of truth to the idea that some sort of masked man in the eighties had abducted a slew of young men and women, and had apparently gone undiscovered.

"Hartley House," said Jacob. "The records are still there. Maybe they can tell us something."

Natalie scrunched her nose. "You think they just left records sitting in a derelict building?"

"That's what my cousin told me. Even if he's wrong, I feel like I need to go, get a feel for the place or something."

"Alright. When?"

Jacob puffed his cheeks. "Tomorrow night?"

"Ok."

"Any pressing plans right now?" Jacob asked, reaching for his phone.

Natalie tilted her wrist to check her watch. "I have to be at the studio for noon. There was an audio issue on a recent advertisement recording. We need to fix it before the episode release on Tuesday. Why?"

"I need to make a stop."

The Focal Point Gallery was on the ground floor of an ancient brownstone building just off Bedford Street in the city centre. The owner had replaced the original architecture with a sleek minimalist design, with long windows displaying an array of environmental and urban photography prints.

The gallery itself was deserted, save for a man sitting behind the counter. He offered a nod as Jacob entered, and then perked up considerably when Natalie came in half a second behind him.

Rising with an easy confidence, his shoes echoed on the polished wood as he approached. He was handsome and knew it, with deep-set eyes and dark hair peppered with silver. A crisp, dark blue shirt fitted over an athletic frame, and was tucked into a pair of smart looking trousers.

"Hi there, can I help you?"

"Hi there, and hopefully," Jacob replied. "Would you happen to be Terry Lunn. The guy that runs the Irish Rover urbex website?"

"That's right," Lunn replied. "You saw something online that you'd like to purchase?"

The man kept his attention on Natalie as he answered. She in turn, took a sudden interest in the prints furthest away from where they were standing.

"Not quite," Jacob said once the man's attention focused on him. "I saw your post about the old Millisle Borstal and found it rather interesting."

"Thank you." Lunn's tone suggested a forced politeness now that he sensed a sale wasn't forthcoming.

"I'm wanting to check it out myself, but I saw on your post that it's well secured and there was only one way in."

"And you want me to tell you where that one way is?"

"Basically."

"I'm afraid I can't do that. Urban explorers have a code of sorts. We want to preserve the buildings, their history, their soul even. Part of ensuring that is preserved, is by limiting who goes in."

"That's actually sort of noble."

"Thank you."

"I'll bung you fifty quid if you tell me."

Lunn frowned. "I have to say, I'm rather peeved that you think my principles could be bent for fifty pounds."

"Then I'll offer a hundred."

The Rover clucked his tongue, thought on it, and fetched the card machine from behind the till. Evidently his principles didn't extend to three figures. He input the fee and held the machine out to Jacob who inserted his card and input his pin.

"Would you like a receipt?"

Jacob ignored him. He should charge the fee to Deirdre as an investigative expense, but knew that he wouldn't. "So, how do I get in?"

"The old canteen. Go up to the face of the mansion that's facing the sea. Follow the building all the way around to the right side and you'll spot the canteen by the old delivery doors. There's an unlocked window directly under a heating unit."

"Is there anything I should know?"

"Such as?"

"Oh, I dunno, any old files lying about?"

The Irish Rover grimaced and leaned forward slightly. "To tell you the truth, I didn't see much of the inside."

"Right," Jacob said, recalling the post on his website. "The security guard."

"Yeah...no. There was no security guard. I made it as far as the first corridor and then left."

"Why?"

"Vibes. The whole place felt heavy. You know it's supposed to be haunted?"

Jacob thought back to what his cousin said, about the old, hard-nut warders who wouldn't stay in the place by themselves after nightfall. About his own experience with the phantom footsteps of New Burnley police station. He could sympathise with the Rover, but on the other, he also thought the man was a bit of an arsehole.

He leaned forward to mimic the other man's pose. "Aren't you a little old to believe in ghosts?"

Lunn's look hardened and Jacob thanked him for the information. He motioned for Natalie that he had got what he needed, and held the door open for her as they stepped back out onto the street.

"Seemed simple enough," she said. "What'd it cost?"

"Your phone number."

"Funny, Jacob." Deadpan but a small smile cracked the facade as she checked her watch. "Right, I need to get over to the Wheelman. Want a lift back to your place?"

Jacob shook his head. "I'm going to see if our friend Cora Adebayo will give me a few minutes of her time."

She nodded slowly and Jacob thought she was working towards questioning this step. Instead, she said, "Alright. You've got the thing with Steele and Richard McBride's mother tonight, and then we'll hit Hartley House tomorrow evening. What time should I pick you up?"

"I'll drive tomorrow night. You've been ferrying me all over Belfast the past few days. About time I did my bit."

Natalie pursed her lips. "The flying deathtrap has heat, right?"

"Heat, four tyres, several gears, and it can go both forwards and backwards. What more do you need?"

"Comforting. See you around eight or so?"

"See you then."

Jacob waited until her car had pulled away before walking in the direction of Cora's office. He had her number and texted ahead. It may have been a Sunday, but he'd have bet the house that even if Cora was not in work, she'd have her phone close to hand. The reply came less than a minute later, telling him she'd meet him there.

It took ten minutes to make the short walk to Great Victoria Street. The building Cora worked out of was an utterly nondescript seven storey, sandwiched between two other equally sized, and equally boring buildings.

Inside, the small lobby was welcomingly warm. The sole occupant, a white-shirted security guard seated at a desk, didn't look up as Jacob entered, but did reach for his phone, speaking briefly into the receiver.

Twenty seconds later, the elevator door at the far end of the lobby opened and Cora Adebayo stepped out.

"Jacob Kincaid." Her English accent was refined, educated. "To what do I owe the pleasure?"

"Hoping to run something by you."

He held out a hand towards the elevator. Cora offered a wane smile and held out her own hand, indicating the door back out to Great Victoria Street. She guided him towards a small coffee shop and within ten minutes, Jacob had recounted what he had so far.

"It's an intriguing story," Cora said, her tone practised neutral once he had finished. "I can see why Natalie is interested."

Jacob clicked his tongue at what was being left unsaid. "But not you."

Cora held up her hands.

"Four missing boys, two with a connection to the same borstal? Allegations of a paedophile ring in that borstal? Not to mention a number of missing girls, possibly connected to all this."

"Connected? Take a step back and see how thin that particular thread is."

"We have a woman who was a victim of an attempted abduction and a man who saw his friend being taken. Both of them describe a man wearing white facial bandages as the culprit. That's a connection." Jacob jabbed a finger against the table to emphasise his point. Cora said nothing, so Jacob continued, "Are you telling me that, whoever it is you work for, isn't interested in finding what happened to these children?"

"We're talking about four decades ago, Jacob."

"So they don't matter?"

Cora sat up straighter. "I didn't say that."

Jacob knew he had blundered with the accusation and slouched back into his seat, feeling the battle was already lost.

"We have an interest in things that threaten the security of this country," Cora said. "This is a sad story, and I hope the families get their answers, I really do, but-"

"-But it's not for you."

Her sigh carried what might have been a twinge of regret. "I'm sorry, Jacob."

He reached for his coffee and shook his head. "The borstal. I just can't believe nothing ever came out about these allegations. About the parties."

"Jacob, you heard this from one person."

"So?"

"So, from what you told me, the man is a recovering alcoholic and a habitual criminal. Have you or Natalie considered that he could be lying?"

"He's not lying."

"How can-"

"-He's not," Jacob said firmly. "I believe him."

An uncomfortable silence descended over their table. Jacob felt he had stretched the limits of their relationship by coming to Cora. The fact that she had now refused, made it all the more awkward. His phone vibrated in his pocket with a timely incoming call. It was Natalie.

"Jacob." Her voice was tight. He heard her take a breath. "Can you get over to the studio?"

"What's wrong?"

"You can see when you get here." She disconnected before Jacob could press further.

"Problems?" Cora asked as Jacob rose to his feet.

"Always." He thought for a moment and then bent down towards Cora. "This borstal. We have a catholic chaplain sympathetic to the IRA, not to mention more than a few of the detained boys were likely rising stars in the paramilitary group of their choice."

"Ok?"

"There must have been some intelligence gathered on the place as a matter of routine."

"Jacob, I told you-"

"-Just for your own curiosity," Jacob interrupted. "If nothing else. Thanks for the coffee."

It was a five-minute walk from the cafe to the Wheelman Studio. The pedestrian gate to the business park where the studio was located was open, but there was no one in the guard hut. Jacob spotted Natalie outside the studio building. She had her arms wrapped tightly around herself as she paced. Worry wormed its way through Jacob's stomach.

"You here alone?" Jacob asked.

"I texted Giselle and told her not to come in." She waved for him to follow in the direction of the studio.

The Wheelman was eerie in its silence. Natalie still hadn't told him what had happened and Jacob didn't press her, guessing she wanted to show rather than tell.

Jacob's first hint something was amiss came not from sight, but from smell as they approached the door of Studio A. It was a sharp, chemical odour that he recognised immediately.

The graffiti stretched across the entire length of the wall, executed with a precision that suggested whoever wielded the spray can was more artist than vandal.

The phantom loomed over them, with bandages that appeared windblown and frayed, giving the apparition a motion-like effect, as if caught in a gust of wind. His mouth was a jagged line, and his eyes were empty sockets that still seemed to follow Jacob as he moved.

Below the phantom, the artist had added an urban streetscape. Foggy, twisted versions of familiar buildings were depicted, with shadowy alleys slithering over them.

Three words had been sprayed below the graffiti.

NED IS NEAR.

14

Jacob paced, trying to temper the unease coiling through him. This wasn't just vandalism. Someone had gone out of their way to send a message, and had chosen Natalie's place of work to do it. It was targeted at her and it had him rattled.

The front door of the studio opened. A chilly wind followed Zara Steele as she stepped into the lobby.

"Are you okay?" Her question was directed to Natalie.

"Fine." Natalie managed a smile. "Mostly."

A bored looking police officer poked his head out from a door further down the corridor, scene log in hand. He looked their way long enough to satisfy himself the newcomer wasn't the crime scene investigator he was waiting on, and ducked back into his hiding spot.

"What do we know?" Steele asked.

Jacob brought her up to speed. Natalie had entered via the front door, went straight to Studio A, found the graffiti, and called Jacob. She had been certain the main entrance had been locked when she had arrived at the building. The fire exit door however, was only on the latch, and this is where Jacob assumed the intruder had gained entry.

The initial attending officers had agreed with Jacob's assessment about the point of entry. The graffiti vandalism, combined with the trespassing, upgraded the crime to a burglary, so they had cordoned off the Studio A, and requested

CSI. Calling Steele had been Jacob's idea.

"Was there anyone else here?" Steele asked Natalie.

She shook her head. "Not on a Sunday. The studio's manager gave me a key last year so we can work on the show late night, or over the weekend."

"Want a look?" Jacob inclined his head down the corridor to where the painted phantom lurked.

"Not sure I should announce my presence."

Jacob understood. To see the graffiti, she would have to enter the boundary of the scene. That meant signing the log. Steele didn't want the headache of trying to explain what a DCI from the cold case unit was doing here.

"We spoke to Finbar's friend," Natalie said to Steele, steering the conversation away from the vandalism, some of her previous guardedness to the other woman apparently fading.

"Anything interesting?"

"Oh, you could say that," said Jacob. He filled her in on what Connelly had told them about the parties and watched the creeping disgust spread across her features.

"So," said Steele once he had finished, "We must consider it a strong possibility that there's a connection between Finbar's disappearance and these parties."

"Not just Finbar," said Natalie. "Connelly also told us at least one of the other missing boys, Desmond McClure, was also an inmate at the borstal."

"Jesus," said Steele.

"It gets better," said Jacob. "We'd been working with the belief that Finbar was snatched on the Falls Road. Matthew Connelly says Finbar was actually brought back to the borstal, and then taken out on the same night."

"By a man with facial bandages," Natalie finished.

This time Steele gasped. "Ok," she said slowly. "This is getting weird fast, right?"

"Weirder by the second," said Jacob.

Steele crossed her arms and lost herself in her own thoughts. "But I don't get it," she said eventually. "Have either of you mentioned the supposed connection about this Ned By Night to anyone outside our investigation?"

"Just the priest I think," said Jacob.

"I think we can safely rule him out," said Steele dryly.

"Why?"

"Well, he's ancient, isn't he?"

"I never said that," said Jacob.

Steele rolled her eyes. "No, you didn't, but call it a confident guess."

"Fair enough," conceded Jacob, "And for what it's worth, you're right. I think we can safely rule Pettigrew out as the culprit for this. To get access to the studio, the vandal would have needed to scale the fence bordering the business park.

"What about his companion?" asked Natalie. "What did Matthew say his name was?"

"Eddie Chambers," replied Jacob. His mind had gone the same way. It was a simple process of elimination between who they had asked about Ned by Night, and who may actually be capable. Chambers hadn't been there when Jacob brought up Ned by Night to Pettigrew, but he had no doubt the former priest would have mentioned it. There was nothing else to do in that cottage but converse. At least, nothing Jacob wanted to think about.

"What do you know about him?" Zara asked.

"Nothing," Jacob said, "Just that he was at the borstal at the same time as Matthew Connelly, and maybe Finbar." He chewed on his lip. "I only mentioned you in passing to Pettigrew," he said to Natalie. "This and then the thing at your house -"

"-Sorry," Steele cut in, "What thing at your house?"

"Someone skulking about," Natalie said. "Last night."

"Wow, hold on a second here," said Steele. "Someone at your house and now someone breaking in to where you work?"

"The two might not be related." Natalie caught Jacob's eye and gave a resigned sigh.

"Have you told the police about the person at your house?" Steele asked.

Natalie folded her arms. "No."

Steele looked back toward Studio A. "Give me a moment."

Jacob and Natalie watched as she walked up to the door where the police officer was waiting and went inside. She returned half a minute later.

"One of the officers is going to get some statement pages from their car. I asked him to get a serial started for the intruder, and suggested that he requests your house gets some passing attention from local patrols, at least for the next few days."

Natalie nodded, clearly miffed at Steele making the decision for her.

"It's for the best, Natalie," Steele said gently.

"Agreed," Jacob put in. She had refused to call the police last night, and he had reluctantly gone along with it, but the passing attention from local officers would put his mind at ease, if not Natalie's.

Steele glanced at her Rolex and made a face. "I hate to rush off, but we're late to meet Mrs. McBride, Jacob."

"I'll be alright," Natalie said, noticing Jacob's immediate hesitation. "Just keep me updated, ok?"

Jacob said he would and Natalie in turn promised to let him know when she got home safely. He and Steele left her in the care of the police officers and walked to Zara's car, a sleek BMW M2.

"How straight did yer man stand when you flashed your warrant card and he saw the words 'Chief Inspector' in big bold letters?" Jacob asked.

Steele laughed as she unlocked the car with the push of a fob. "Like his chair had an ejector function."

Jacob smiled as he got into the passenger seat. "Have to admit, I'm still a bit surprised you're letting me come along on this. I take it you told Mrs. McBride that I'm not police?"

"I did. Like you said back in your office, it's hardly standard procedure, but I made her aware that I have an external partner acting as a consultant on the case. I gave her the option of speaking to both of us or me alone. She chose us both, I suppose thinking the more people on it, the better."

"Consultant? That's got a nice ring to it. Makes me sound like I charge three times as much and wear jeans without a coffee stain."

Steele followed to where he pointed towards the dark splotch at the crotch and snorted her amusement.

He smiled at the reaction, seeing some of Steele's front break down, if only for a moment. "What was your initial read on Mrs. McBride?"

"Nothing out of the ordinary. She was surprised, more than anything. I got the impression she'd managed to move on."

"Move on?" Jacob said doubtfully.

"It was a brief phone call, Jacob and I could be wrong, but it has been forty years. Maybe time healed some wounds."

Jacob eased back into the seat. His mind immediately and invariably went to Natalie, and the knot of worry that had been alleviated by Steele's arrival at the studio, now began to gnaw in his stomach once again. The prowler at Natalie's house, and now the break-in where she worked. They had only begun to prod at this case but someone had been unsettled and was now trying to put the frighteners up them.

"So, what's the deal with you and Natalie?" Steele asked, as if sensing his thoughts.

"The deal?" They had travelled in silence for a couple of minutes and the unexpected question caught him by surprise.

"Don't be coy."

"I'm not," Jacob said. "There is no deal."

"I see."

"You see?"

She pursed her lips momentarily. "The pair of you are hard to get a read on. Just got a sense there was something there."

"Are you sure you're a detective?"

"My mistake. Must have picked it up wrong."

"How come you're so curious?"

"Just getting a feel for who I'm working with, that's all."

"Uh huh."

He noticed a sudden colour on her cheeks. "So, you're committed to the single man lifestyle?"

"Me? I'm the bachelist bachelor whoever bachelored, which might be the most tragic thing I've ever uttered." Steele laughed all the same and Jacob tried to decide if he should pursue the direction their conversation seemed to be going. "How about you?" he attempted to affect an air of casualness.

She shook her head. "Just me and my lonesome."

"I'm surprised."

"Because I'm such a catch?"

"Basically, yeah."

Steele kept her eyes on the road but Jacob saw the faint curl of a smile.

By now they had crossed the River Lagan at the Queen Elizabeth Bridge. Jacob expected Steele to take the sliproad onto the M3, which would lead onto the M2, and towards Carrickfergus. Instead, she continued on Middlepath Street, and took the next sliproad, also leading onto the M3, but in the opposite direction, towards the City Airport.

"Mrs. McBride and her husband divorced a year or so after Richard went missing," Steele said, reading his mind once again. "She left Carrickfergus and settled out in Helen's Bay," she continued, naming the upmarket village, perched on the edge of Belfast Lough. In the summer it was overrun, mostly by drunken teenagers hopping on the train from Belfast, flocking to its two golden beaches. In January, the village was dead, its narrow streets empty.

They made it to the village in a little over ten minutes. Following the map on her phone, Steele soon came to a stop outside a house hidden from the road by a concrete wall flanking an automatic gate. The gate had a natural wood finish that had weathered over time to give it a rustic look.

Steele was halfway out of her car when the gate slowly began to open. Mrs. McBride had apparently been anticipating their arrival. The driveway beyond the gate was cobblestoned and led towards a modern two-storey home of clean lines and broad surfaces overlooking the lough.

Mrs. McBride was waiting for them by the front door. She was nervous, that was clear as Jacob and Zara stepped out of the car, hugging her arms tightly to her chest. She was dressed in dark denim jeans paired with a grey cashmere sweater.

"Detective Steele?"

"Zara, please." She motioned to Jacob. "This is the person I was telling you about. Jacob Kincaid."

"Hello, Mrs. McBride." Jacob said as extended his hand.

"Eleanor." Her handshake was fleeting and she quickly returned her arm to the same posture as before. "Come in, please."

She led them through the house into a living area with large bay windows overlooking the water. In the darkness, Jacob could only make out the white swell of the waves lapping below. He and Zara were guided to a long sofa where they both politely declined Eleanor's offer of tea or coffee.

"I'm not sure there's anything much I can help with." Eleanor had remained standing and was wringing her hands together slowly. "I told the police everything I could forty years ago."

"We understand that, Eleanor," Steele said gently. "But I'm new to this investigation and still putting some of the pieces together in my mind." She motioned for the older woman to sit.

Eleanor took a chair on the other side of the room. "Ask away, I suppose."

"We understand Richard went missing on his way to school," Steele said. "From statements obtained at the time, it was confirmed he got off his bus on the Antrim Road, but never made it to the school."

"That's right."

Jacob kept his attention on Eleanor. Steele was the police officer and was the only one with any sort of legal authority in regard to the case. He was content to let her lead.

"We know the RUC canvassed the local area between the school and the bus stop, but was there anyone Richard knew who lived in that area?"

"No, no-one. My ex-husband and I are from down the country and we lived in Carrickfergus. We tended to stay clear of Belfast for the most part."

"Any enemies?"

"Richard? No, he never bothered anyone."

"What about you or your husband?"

Eleanor shook her head.

"Where is your husband now?" Jacob asked.

"Dead." The word was said bluntly. The message was clear; she did not want a follow-up on the topic.

"I understand Richard was a quiet boy," Steele said. "Could be he kept any issues at school to himself?"

"No, St. John's was a school for children with certain needs. They were closely monitored and would have been alert to any bullying behaviour."

"St. Joseph's," Jacob said.

"Pardon?" Eleanor shifted her attention to him.

"The name of the school," Jacob replied, sensing Steele tensing next to him.

"Forgive me," Eleanor said icily. "St John's was my brother's school. I got the name confused. It's been forty years."

"Sorry," Jacob mumbled, unable to meet the woman's eye and equally unable to come up with a reason why he thought it would be a good idea to correct the mother of a missing child over such a minor slip.

He turned his attention to the coffee table next to him. The surface of the table had a thin layer of dust, save for two perfect rectangles. Picture frames, Jacob guessed, recently moved.

"Eleanor." Steele said the name softly, deftly drawing the focus back to her, and not the bumbling buffoon to her right. "Did the school have anyone reach out to you following Richard's disappearance? A head of year? A teacher?"

She shook her head. "No, no one from the teaching staff. The chaplain did make contact. I don't know if he was acting in any official capacity, but he was very kind."

"The chaplain," Steele said as she scribbled in her notepad. "Do you remember the name?"

"Oh god, no, I don't think so. It began with a *J*, um, Jeremey or something like that."

Jacob immediately forgot about dust marks on coffee tables. "Jeremiah? Jeremiah Pettigrew?"

Eleanor took a moment to think and then nodded. "Yes. I think so."

Steele continued scribbling, as if she'd never heard the name before. Jacob made a note to not play her at poker.

"When was the last time you spoke to Father Pettigrew?" Steele asked.

"Just that one time."

"And you never saw him again?"

"No." Eleanor shifted in her seat. "Why are you so interested in the priest? Did he, did he have something to do with..."

"We're not saying that," Steele cut in quickly. "But we're aware of him. At this stage, I can't tell you much more than that presently. I'm sorry."

Eleanor settled back into her seat, clearly not happy with the non-answer.

"Do you remember what Father Pettigrew said when he spoke to you?" Zara asked

"Nothing really. Just said that Richard never turned up to school."

"Did it strike you as strange that the chaplain called you and not the principal or head of year?" asked Jacob.

"I suppose I didn't think about it." Eleanor's jaw tightened.

"Did Richard ever mention Father Pettigrew?" asked Zara.

"Often enough. He used to take some of the boys on camping trips."

"Did Richard ever go on any of these trips?

"A couple. He was starting to come out of his shell a bit. Before..."

Before. Jacob thought. Before Richard and these other boys disappeared into the ether.

"What about ghost stories?" Jacob asked, jumping in as Steele continued to jot her notes. "Did Richard ever have an interest in them?"

"Ghost stories?" Eleanor frowned. "What's that got to do with what happened?"

"We're not sure yet," Steele replied. "Just another avenue we're exploring."

She moved on quickly and asked a few more questions, but Eleanor McBride could not provide them with anything else of note. As she led them towards the front door, Jacob stopped.

"Mrs. McBride, do you have any photos of your son we could use?"

"Photos? How do you mean?"

"Well, the only one we have to work with is the picture in the newspaper archive and as you can imagine, the image quality isn't great."

She glanced at Steele. "What would you need a photo for? How would that help find Richard?"

"Well, for one, a good quality picture could be of great help in age progression software," said Jacob.

Eleanor already had one hand on the door. "No, I don't have anything. I shut that part of my life away. Pictures, they'd be too painful."

"That's fine, Mrs. McBride," said Steele. "We won't ask you to bring up bad memories when they can be left alone. We can work with what we have."

Eleanor bid them a curt good night and then shut the door behind her. The automatic gate began to open before they reached Steele's car.

She waited until she had pulled out onto the road, as if worried Eleanor McBride would somehow overhear her. "Holy shit! Pettigrew was involved at Richard McBride's school."

Jacob shook his head, not quite believing the large piece of the puzzle that had just fallen into their lap. And yet, it all seemed a little too easy.

"What's bugging you?"

He rolled his mouth. "What did you make of her in there?"

"Eleanor?"

"Did she seem a little off?"

"She had two people landing at her door asking about the disappearance of her son from forty years ago."

"She'd hidden pictures."

"What?

"On the coffee table. There were marks in the dust where frames had been lifted."

"So?"

"So, I don't know. Just struck me as odd."

"Jesus, you're a suspicious sort."

"Based on past experiences, yeah."

His phone vibrated in his pocket before he could ruminate further. "Hector." Jacob said, answering the call.

"Jacob," Breen replied "How's it going?"

"Fine, Hector. What's up?"

He heard Breen tut on the other end of the line. "Someone's been sniffing around my place."

Steele turned, the volume on Jacob's phone loud enough for her to overhear.

"Sniffing around?"

"Aye. Gate in the back garden was left unlocked. Noticed it this afternoon."

"You see anyone hanging about?"

"No, and I like to think I'm still alert enough these days to notice something like that."

"What about your friends from the Ballylo'?"

"To be honest, that's what I was thinking. Martin Closkey and about twenty others of his ilk would love to put me in the ground. Thing is though, I was careful about heading home after coming to your office, and I was watching out for tails. Even checked for any tracking devices on my car."

"It's good to keep up to date with the techniques of the modern terrorist," Jacob said.

Breen's grunt sounded almost half amused. "Maybe it was a burglar on the prowl, trying his luck, hoping to find an unlocked door. I would have put it down to that but the timing is just a little too weird for me."

"Not just you." Jacob filled Hector in on the prowler at Natalie's house, and the graffiti at her studio.

"Looks like we've ruffled somebody's feathers," Hector said.

"Yeah, just a shame we have no idea whose."

"Keep your head on a swivel," Hector said. "Both of ya's."

"This is getting worse," Steele said once the call had finished. "Maybe the three of you need to back off."

"Back off? It's my case. If you want to end our arrangement, feel free, but I've been hired by Deirdre Skelly to get answers. I won't be backing off, and although I don't speak for them, I imagine Natalie and Hector will tell you the same."

That seemed to end the discussion and the car lapsed into silence. It wasn't until they were approaching the edge of Belfast that Steele spoke again. "What's the next step?"

"Hartley House," said Jacob. "Apparently the old files are still stored there. We found a way to get in-"

She held up a hand. "If you're about to describe how you're planning to commit a burglary to a serving police officer, I'd advise you not to."

"Is it going to be a problem if I come up with something useful?"

"Well, let's cross that bridge when we come to it. For now, I won't ask too many questions."

She dropped him off a street away from his apartment. The temperature was hovering just above zero and the night was bitterly cold. Jacob turned his collar up and buried his hands as deep as his pockets would allow.

Something within his consciousness prickled. The rhythmic patter of his footsteps on the pavement were accompanied, slightly out of sync.

Jacob slowed and threw a quick glance over his shoulder. There was nothing there, just a sparse row of trees that lined the street rustling as a sharp gust of wind brushed through them.

Chiding himself for getting spooked but quickening his step all the same, he was now within sight of his apartment building. But the closer he got, the stronger the sense of another presence lurking behind him grew. He could almost feel the weight of a gaze on his back, invasive and calculating.

The piazza was empty. Lights blazed in the windows of the gym and in a number of the restaurants but the cold had seemingly kept both diners and athletes at home. There was no one sitting by the windows of any of the eateries, nor was there anyone on the row of treadmills overlooking the piazza from the gym's first floor.

Jacob didn't slow as he crossed the piazza and into the entryway leading to his apartment building. As he reached the entrance to the lobby, he risked another look behind. The piazza was still, bathed in the cold white of artificial light. With a shiver that was in no way from the cold, Jacob slipped inside the safety of the building.

He didn't slow on his ascent up the stairs and locked the apartment door behind him. Crossing over to the balconette, he pressed himself against the glass to see the piazza was utterly deserted.

He paced and then decided to distract himself. He rang Simon.

"Jesus, twice in a week. Is someone dead?"

Jacob laughed dutifully and then said, "It's a long shot, but did you know anyone in the prison service called Higgins? He would have worked in the borstal in the early eighties."

"Actually, yeah. Donald Higgins. He was the assistant governor at the college when I was there in 2014 and I remember him telling me the borstal had been his first posting. He's a Grade A arsehole."

"Oh yeah?"

"Spent most of his career in transport and visits, but to hear him talk you'd think he was super screw."

"Is he still alive?"

"I think so. Him and my da worked together for a spell in the Crum. Da couldn't stand the sight of him, but my ma became friends with his wife. Well, friends is a bit strong maybe, but they send each other Christmas cards every year."

"You think you can get me the address Aunt Marion sends her cards to?"

"Sure," said Simon. "This about that missing boy?"

"No flies on you."

Jacob ended the call and set his phone down. A restlessness pawed at him, spurred on by the fleeting suspicion he had been followed down in the street. Now, in the safety of his apartment, the unease hadn't faded. If anything, it had settled in deeper. Something was off.

He paced and flicked through YouTube videos. An hour later Simon texted with an address for Donald Higgins over in East Belfast.

It was a little before midnight when Jacob finally climbed into bed. Slowly he drifted away and woke with a start. The apartment beyond the bedroom door was bathed in blackness. A nagging feeling told him to check his front door, even though he knew he had locked it.

Jacob climbed out of bed. As he crossed the living area he heard footsteps on the tiled corridor outside. They were not the usual, lethargic drag of weary legs returning home, but a frantic pounding, growing rapidly louder, echoing off the walls with a staccato rhythm that spiked Jacob's heart.

Each footfall was a harsh slap against the cold tile. The crash against the door was so sudden and fierce that Jacob flinched. The wooden door frame creaked in a deep, groaning protest. The door shuddered a second time, a brutal, jarring thud. A force, desperate and unrestrained, began to hurl itself against the barrier, intent on breaking through.

Jacob retreated back into his bedroom. An admin error when he left the police had meant no one had thought to ask for him to return his baton. It had, save on the rare occasion where Jacob risked bringing it on particularly sketchy jobs, in particularly sketchy parts of town, stayed buried in a box at the back of the wardrobe.

Scrabbling blindly, he felt the soft touch of the rubber grip handle and pulled the baton out. The weight of it in his hand was reassuring. Flicking it down by his side, the baton racked and locked in position.

The attack on the door continued, the sound closing the walls in. Jacob moved to the living room and drew the baton back.

And just as abruptly as it had started, the pounding stopped.

The sudden calm was somehow more unsettling. Jacob strained his ears, but there were no retreating footsteps, no sound of movement at all, only a smothering silence. He exhaled slowly, forcing himself to move. Edging toward the door, he leaned in and pressed his eye to the peephole.

Nothing. The peephole had been covered.

He reached for the lock with a sweat-slicked hand. Slowly, he eased the door open. The corridor outside was pitch black. The motion-sensitive light should have come on the second he opened the door, but the hallway stayed dark.

Jacob took a single step forward and turned to his door. A thin strip of crisp white bandage had been fixed over the peephole.

His skin prickled with the unmistakable sensation of being watched. He strained his eyes down the darkened corridor, scanning for any hint of another presence. He saw nothing, but the feeling didn't leave.

He heard it then. Or thought he did. A flutter of a voice, carried on the still air. The words were too faint, barely more than a whisper.

"Ned is near."

15

Jacob didn't sleep. He didn't try, and spent the remainder of the night on his living room sofa, baton close to hand.

At first light he ventured out into the hallway, tucking the collapsed baton into the waistband of his trackie bottoms. The lights were still off. Jacob walked to the far end of the corridor where the switch to activate them was located. It had been turned off.

"Fucker," Jacob muttered.

He flicked the switch back on, returned to his apartment and phoned Helen. She was about as stubborn as he had expected and point blank refused to consider avoiding the office for the day. Jacob gave up on the notion of convincing her otherwise, and compromising, went down to meet her at the multi-storey where she parked her car, and escorted her to the office.

Kincaid Investigations was a secure spot, which eased some of Jacob's worry. As well as the metal security door on the stairs, his grandfather, back when The Troubles were in their full, violent swing, had also fitted every window with wrought iron bars. Jacob had never seen fit to remove either the grille or the bars. They were holdovers from bad old days, best forgotten, but still served a purpose, and Jacob rather enjoyed the aesthetic.

By half nine the sleepless night had fully caught up to him.

A can of *Red Bull,* followed by a double shot espresso from the coffee shop downstairs, hadn't made an impact on his malaise, but seemed to be doing a number on his guts.

He looked up as Helen knocked on his door. She was holding out a piece of paper. "The matron from the borstal."

"That was quick," Jacob said as he took the paper. He had only asked her to try to track down the matron fifteen minutes before.

"I have my ways. You should know that by now."

He took the note and read it. *Carneybaun Care Home, Antrim Road, Belfast.*

"Someday you'll have to tell me your secret."

"So you can get shot of me? Yeah, nice try."

Jacob's smile turned into a gaping yawn which he hid behind the crook of his arm.

"Attractive. Go home, Jacob. I'll be fine here." Helen grabbed his coat from its peg and held it out, having made the decision for him. "I'll lock the security grille when you leave, and won't open it again until I'm closing up."

He took the coat without protest and knuckled an eye. "No walk-ins. Anyone comes calling, you send them away."

"Got it," she said as she walked him across the office and took her seat.

Jacob made it as far as the door before stopping.

"Yes?" Helen asked without looking up.

"Bit of research, Helen. St. Joseph's school, just off the Antrim Road. Give them a call and try to find out if anyone on the staff was there in the early eighties and if so, would they be willing to speak to me. If not, ask if they'd think about diving into their old records and coming up with someone."

"Those are both long shots."

"This whole investigation has been a long shot."

He walked back towards his apartment and phoned the management company en-route, providing a vague account of what had happened during the night.

"I see," said the cheery rep on the other end of the line once Jacob had finished. "And how can we help?"

"I'd like to get a copy of the footage."

"I'm afraid we can't do that."

"What?"

"We can release the footage, but only to the police. If you'd like to contact them, they can apply to access the footage. I'm sure they will-"

Jacob cut the call and immediately felt lousy, taking his frustration out on a woman only doing her job. He could call the police, but what would he tell them? Someone banged loudly on my door and then ran away. The PSNI were undermanned, overworked, and would dismiss what had happened as a prank.

Furthermore, he was certain the person at his door was the same person who had graffitied Natalie's studio, and who had prowled around her garden. He was just as certain, as had been the case at Natalie's house, that person would be too canny to get caught on CCTV.

He decided to nix the idea of police involvement, but by the time Jacob made it back to his apartment he had ordered a doorbell camera from *Amazon*. He locked the door behind him, kicked off his shoes, threw the coat over a chair, and fell into an exhausted and fitful sleep on the sofa.

It was late afternoon when he woke, and somehow he felt more tired than when he had passed out. The light outside was already fading and the apartment had chilled without any heat since the early morning.

He had a missed call from Helen and phoned her back.

"No go on St. Joseph's," she said by way of greeting. "Closed down twenty years back and got bulldozed. I'll do some digging, see if I can turn up some alum or former teachers."

"Thanks, Helen."

"No worries. You remember you have that job on tonight?"

"Job?" Jacob asked before remembering. "Ah, shite. The fraud case."

"That's the one. The lucrative and consistent one, I should add. You have something going on for the Skelly case, I take it."

"Yeah." Jacob thought for a moment. "Give Laffs a call. Tell him it's worth two hundred."

Tommy Lafferty had been in Jacob's response section at Coalburn. Like Jacob, he was now former police, but unlike Jacob, he had pulled the pin voluntarily after five years, deciding the job wasn't for him. He'd bounced between different jobs since, security mostly, and had never really settled. Jacob had always thought Laffs a talented peeler, when the mood took him. Someone who could read a situation in seconds but rarely put in more effort than necessary.

Still, Laffs was reliable, and over the past couple of years Jacob had thrown bits of work his way whenever he was tied up with a separate case or needed a second hand.

Tonight's job was straightforward, and as Helen had rightly pointed out, a consistent earner for the business. A mid-size insurance firm had engaged Jacob to check out claimants who they suspected were double-dipping, dishonestly claiming disability while working cash-in-hand jobs on the side.

The job mostly involved staking out addresses, snapping the required incriminating photos, and making sure the company had enough evidence to justify an investigation. Nothing glamorous, but Laffs had no qualms about spending a few hours in a parked car if it meant getting paid.

Helen said she'd reach out to Laffs. Jacob thanked her, dragged himself into the shower and let it run hot and long. Once dried and changed, he fixed himself some fried eggs on toast and pottered about until it was time to go. At half seven he texted Natalie and told her he would be with her in twenty minutes.

When he pulled up at her house, he could see her silhouette watching for his arrival from the front living room. She emerged a few seconds later armed with a thermos and an eager look. There was a short list of people, one to be precise, that Jacob knew who would be so keen to go poking around an abandoned house on a cold winter night.

Natalie slid into the passenger seat, setting the thermos between them. "Coffee," she said before frowning. "And you look like you need it."

Jacob was impressed, if a little stung, by the astute observation made in the dim confines of the car. "So..."

"Ah, Jesus. Anytime you start a sentence like that I get an immediate sinking feeling."

He filled her in on the happenings of the night before; the pounding at his door, the blocked peephole, the corridor in darkness when it should've been lit. He kept the whisper he wasn't entirely sure he hadn't imagined to himself.

Natalie waited until he was finished. "Someone is really doing their level best to rattle us."

"They are."

"Well, their bad luck that it's going to take more than spray paint and knocks on the door to scare us off."

"Not much more."

Natalie laughed at that. "Please, I know what you're like when you get the bit between your teeth."

He shot her a sideways glance. "I guess I can be a little stubborn."

"You're thran to the core, Jacob Kincaid."

Traffic was light, and before long they were out of Belfast. Jacob followed the road that skirted around Bangor, through Donaghadee, and then through Millisle five minutes later. The road from Millisle curved along the coast, and Jacob was soon able to spot the white facade of Hartley House looming ahead.

Both sides of the road were bordered with narrow grass verges leaving Jacob nowhere to park. He could have ditched it at the closed gate of the old vehicle entrance, but that would likely draw the attention of the security company who managed the site, or any locals mindful of trespassers. He made a U-turn on the road and parked the Clio in a gravel lay-by about two hundred metres away from the mansion grounds.

They got out and Jacob opened the boot. Unlike the rest of the Clio, the boot was organised and clean, with two stacks of neatly ordered boxes containing all the tools he needed for his trade. He lifted the top box from the left stack and set it down, popping the plastic locks and opening the lid to reveal an assortment of torches.

"Bulk discount?" Natalie asked.

Jacob smiled and indicated for her to pick one. She opted for a slim model with a good beam strength. He was about to make a similar choice but after a moment's hesitation, instead decided on an ancient Maglite. It wasn't sleek or modern, but its heft was reassuring in his hand. Jacob knew from experience that the old torch was a useful makeshift weapon should the situation require.

Natalie didn't comment on his choice, but he could see the amused quirk of a smile. Turning the Maglite over in his hand, Jacob twisted it, checking it still worked. The beam was strong and steady.

They walked the short distance to the old borstal in silence. Hartley House was protected from the road by a wall of dark, irregularly shaped stones, each bearing the marks of weathering, with moss and lichen creeping over their surface. The white mansion stood stark against the clear night sky.

Jacob waited until there were no headlights coming up the road. He squatted against the wall and cupped his hands for Natalie to boost herself onto the top of the wall. Jacob handed her his Maglite, stepped back a few paces and took a running start, hauling himself up to the wall's lip with Natalie's assistance.

They dropped into what had once been a flowerbed, now overgrown with weeds. Jacob pointed to the central tower, a square structure with its own steeply pitched roof and ornamental railing. "That's where we're heading apparently."

"I still find it hard to believe the prison service would have just left these files sitting here," Natalie said quietly.

Jacob agreed, but didn't say so. He led the way around the back of the mansion, hoping they hadn't wasted a trip because of his cousin's exaggerations.

The kitchen was marked by a sign above what Jacob assumed had been the service entrance, and, just as the intrepid Irish Rover had said, an old heating unit was fixed to a wall, right under a set of double windows.

Jacob climbed onto the unit, which gave a low groan at the unexpected burden, and pressed lightly against the left window. It swung open silently. He shone the Maglite into the darkness beyond and waited.

And waited.

"Are you going in?" Natalie prompted.

A prickling unease gnawed at Jacob. "I guess so."

He dropped down to the floor below. What had once been the canteen was now a barren space where stale air hung heavy. Natalie landed beside him as Jacob's torch beam danced across the ceiling. The skeletal remains of light fixtures dangled precariously, their bulbs long gone. The paint in the ceiling had peeled, and thousands of green chips littered the maroon lino where they had fallen.

They moved out into the corridor. To their right was a massive oak door and a small foyer, presumably the main entrance when the building was still functional. To the left, the corridor turned a corner, leading deeper into the guts of Hartley House. The hallway was silent, broken only by the occasional drip of water from an unseen leak.

The first room they came to was cavernous. The wall furthest from the door was dominated by a monolithic fireplace with an intricate crest carved above it. Two rearing horses flanked a central shield. The shield itself was divided into three parts, each adorned with a cross. In the centre of each cross lay a tiny heart. A crown sat above the shield, and atop the crown was a motto, inscribed on a ribbon-like scroll.

FIDES ET VIRTUS

"Seems out of place," Natalie said.

"Used to be a stately home," Jacob said.

"No, I know. I'm just thinking about the contrast, the aristocrats and then the delinquents. The boys like Finbar and Matthew Connelly. I wonder if they ever saw this and wondered who these people were, so rich that they thought they were important enough to rate a crest and some stupid motto."

Jacob, keen to be on the move, less keen to ruminate on class disparity at this particular moment, stepped back into the corridor. There was an open space on the left, leading into another unmarked room. The beam of his torch swung lazily into the black and glided over the man hiding in the corner.

"Fuck!" The word came out in a strangled shout as Jacob stumbled back, his foot catching on a loose bit of plaster.

Natalie whirled around. "What?" Her voice was tight with sudden fear. "What is it?" She raised her torch towards the room. "Hello?" The call was a demand as much as a greeting. The beam of her torch swept the room before landing on something out of Jacob's line of sight.

Her bark of laughter was startlingly loud in the darkness. "Oh, Jacob. Did you get spooked by our friend here?"

Feeling the flush already spread across his cheeks, Jacob stepped forward. The male was naked and stood rigid. His head was tilted at an unnatural angle, as if caught mid-nod, the blank eyes of his featureless face staring into nothingness, devoid of expression yet somehow accusatory.

"A fucking mannequin! What's it doing here? Apart from scaring me shitless, I mean."

Natalie knelt down and picked an object off the ground. She held it out to Jacob. It was a blue plastic sign. The word MUSEUM was printed in yellow letters. "Must have been part of a display."

Jacob took the sign and lobbed it into the darkness.

Natalie patted his shoulder. "You just stay close to me."

"I think this place has me on edge."

"Because you believe in ghosts."

"I don't believe in ghosts," he shot back. "There's just something heavy here. Gives me the jeebies."

"Uh huh."

Natalie shone her torch over the rest of the room. To one side was a wooden cabinet, its glass doors reflecting the beams from their torches, its interior empty save for shadows.

With nothing else to see, they returned to the corridor and pressed on. The corridor was covered in debris. Pieces of plaster and broken glass crunched with almost every step they took.

Eventually they came to a staircase. The blue railing was coated with dust and rust. Coils of wire were sprawled untidily near its base, abandoned mid-task by someone long gone. A breeze whispered through the floor above. Jacob made sure to be first up the stairs. It was a sad attempt to save some face after being surprised by the mannequin, and Natalie probably knew it.

At the top of the stairs, a sign affixed to the wall told them that the rooms beyond had once been classrooms. They stopped at the first one. Like the rest of the rooms they had seen so far, it was large and empty. The walls, once a soft cream, were now marred by streaks of damp that spoke of the building's slowly losing battle against the elements. Hartley House was dying. Vandals and thieves had been kept at bay but time and neglect were still slowly breaking it down.

The curtains by the open window fluttered with the light gusts of air that forced their way through, carrying with them the faint scent of brine.

Jacob realised before it had been a classroom for would-be prison officers, this room, and its neighbours, would most likely have been the dorms where boys like Finbar slept, dreamt, and cried into their pillows.

Moving up the corridor, Jacob came to a stop in another room. He walked to the window and swung his torch towards the long-closed front gate, following the driveway that led from the road down to the mansion. He realised this was the room where Matthew Connelly watched his friend being taken.

He hadn't been there that night and yet, memories hung heavily in the room. Jacob felt the hairs on his neck stand suddenly on end, half-expecting to see a shadow move in the periphery of his torch's reach.

Natalie hadn't stopped and Jacob quickened his step to catch up with her further along the corridor. They continued, but soon came to a dead end. Doubling-back, they came upon a narrow hallway they had originally missed. It seemed that the original architectural intentions of Hartley House had been obscured by later additions like the corridor they were now in.

The corridor branched but they continued straight until coming to a set of five steps that brought them up and through an open doorway, which in turn led to another staircase that ascended into the darkness above.

The stairs looked as though they hadn't borne weight in decades. A creaking chorus from the aged wood followed them all the way up to a single room at the top of the staircase. It was packed with rusty metal filing cabinets.

"Not a bad view," Natalie said, as she stepped up to a small, grimy window that overlooked the road and the sea beyond. The beam of her torch shone out into the night and Jacob quickly reached out and gently pushed it to point at the floor.

He turned his attention back to the room. In one corner sat an old wooden desk, its surface layered with scattered paperwork and an ancient typewriter. A broken chair lay on its side next to the desk, one leg snapped off.

The walls were adorned with old photographs and maps of Hartley House. The photographs showed groups of boys but were so faded that individual features were almost impossible to make out.

Jacob opened the top drawer of the nearest cabinet and couldn't quite believe what he was looking at. It was as Simon had said, the cabinet was crammed with yellowing folders, their labels barely legible after years of being forgotten.

He moved along the cabinets until he came with a torn label affixed to the top drawer. **UAL**.

The door opened with a low squeal. The drawer was packed tight with paper folders, crammed together with no discernible system. Each contained a surname, prison number, and the date they had absconded.

He was three quarters of the way through the drawer when he finally found what he was looking for.

Skelly, F. H435
UAL 24/12/1986

"That's hefty," Natalie said as Jacob lifted the bulging folder from the drawer. A canvas strap and buckle had been used to keep all documents held within in place.

"Yeah," Jacob said. "Now. let's get out of here," Jacob said.

"You'd almost think you were in a rush."

The staircase groaned. They both turned towards the dark doorway, shared unease passing between them like a silent whisper.

"Old building," said Jacob.

"Right," agreed Natalie. "Still, maybe time to go, all the same."

Jacob went first and shone the torch down the staircase. There was nothing there, but that didn't offer much comfort. Some primeval urge tickled Jacob's neck. Something wasn't right.

Natalie sensed it too. Wordlessly, they picked up their pace when they reached the bottom of the stairs and hurried down the narrow corridor. Jacob took a left and quickened his step. The hallways were suddenly disorientating. Each corridor had the same sterile, peeling paint, the same heavy doors with frosted glass revealing nothing of what lay beyond.

Turning a corner, they came to a halt. The hallway split into two, and neither path looked familiar. Jacob's brow furrowed as he tried to recall their previous turns, but the sameness of the surroundings muddled his memory.

"Did we come from the left or the right?" Jacob asked.

"No, we kept straight after the classrooms," Natalie replied, her voice tight and low.

"Then why didn't you -" he stopped himself, knowing it would do no good. Cursing quietly, Jacob took the left fork, hoping to find another staircase to take them back to the ground floor. He made it only a few steps before he felt Natalie's fingers digging into his arm.

"What?"

She pointed her torch at the wall ahead.

The graffiti had faded with time. Ned looked down on them with his jagged-line mouth and empty socket eyes. Instead of an urban streetscape, the phantom hovered over a twisted version of Hartley House.

They turned without a word. Eventually, they found the narrow corridor that led back towards the old dorms and with familiar surroundings, their pace quickened once more. Taking the stairs to the ground floor two at a time, they passed the old museum and jogged across the canteen and towards the still open window. Jacob was about to squat down to give Natalie a foothold when he stopped.

It was a patter of sound, a subtle disturbance in the profound silence of the old mansion. Distant. Slow.

"You hear that?"

"Just the wind," Natalie said quickly. "C'mon."

"Right." He squatted and hoisted her up through the gap. Natalie gave a small grunt of effort as she pulled herself through the window and onto the heating unit just as the sound returned, closer. Louder.

"Footsteps," Jacob whispered.

"Don't be daft!" She held out her hand as the sound kept coming.

Jacob took Natalie's hand and felt her brace to help him up.

The slow, methodical cadence of the distant steps suddenly picked up.

He knew he had to move, but the growing proximity paralysed him. Every instinct screamed at him to flee, and yet he remained rooted to the spot.

And then the footsteps ceased abruptly. The sudden silence was more unsettling than the noise.

"Jacob!" Natalie hissed his name through her teeth, the grip on his hand tightening.

His eyes darted back towards the far end of the canteen, half-expecting to see a figure emerge from the shadows. He held his breath, listening for any sign of movement.

The footsteps resumed. Quicker. Urgent. They were coming towards him. For him.

Fear bolted him loose. Jacob leaped for the window and pulled himself onto the old heating unit.

They both started running.

16

Jacob only broke stride to lob the folder over the wall before throwing himself at it half a second later. He dropped to the wet grass on the other side, scrabbling to pick up the folder. Natalie had beaten him over. He hadn't noticed her climbing the wall, but given the speed at which she had been moving just prior, he wouldn't have been surprised if she had simply cannoned through it to save time.

The wall was a buffer between them and the old mansion, but they still took off towards Jacob's car at a dead run. Gravel mashed under the wheels as the Clio shot onto the road and Hartley House faded in the rearview. Jacob waited until they made it through to the other side of Millisle before pulling over.

"What's wrong?" Natalie asked.

"Nothing, but we should call Zara."

"Why?"

"To tell her we found Finbar's file."

"It can't wait?

Jacob glanced up at the mirror. His heart was thudding but the road behind was empty. "There's a couple of miles between us and the borstal."

"That's not what I meant."

Jacob had already pressed dial on his phone. Zara picked

up on the second ring and Jacob quickly filled her in, telling her to meet him at the office in half an hour. He noticed Natalie's look as he ended the call. "What?"

"Nothing. You're quick to keep her appraised."

"Why not? She's part of the case."

"Alright. Are you calling Hector next?"

Jacob put his mobile back in his pocket. "What's up with you?"

Natalie sighed deeply. "Nothing. Still on edge from back there."

"You think someone followed us in?" he asked.

"Maybe..."

"What?"

She turned back to him. "Footsteps?"

"Yeah?"

"Footsteps." She said the word slowly.

"Ye-es." Jacob matched her cadence.

"Are you sure you heard them?"

"Yes, I'm sure. I mean, you heard them as well. Right?"

"I heard something, I think." She scrunched her nose. "But I think maybe we spooked ourselves."

"Oh, c'mon."

"It's a real thing," she said quickly. "It's called agent detection. Humans have evolved to detect threats in ambiguous situations." She swatted at the dismissive hand Jacob waved close to her face. "Just listen. In an old mansion with creaking stairs, wind passing through cracks, echoes, curtains fluttering in the breeze, we get hyper-vigilant and maybe we hear something that we take as a threat, that really wasn't there at all."

"You ran!"

Natalie laughed and slapped his shoulder. "Because you ran!"

Jacob gave an amused grunt, the fear from only a few minutes before suddenly gone. It was easy to laugh now, locked in a car with the bright, comforting lights of Millisle village just a couple of hundred yards behind them.

Of course, it had just been the wind. Or the mansion settling. Or...agent detection. And yet, when he thought back to the person at his door the night before, and the figure in Natalie's garden, and the break-in at her studio, his smile faltered.

He pushed the thought away. "C'mon. Let's get back to the office and see what we have."

The city centre was quiet, and Jacob had no trouble finding a parking space close to Kincaid Investigations. The coffee shop was still open, although winding down for the night. The sole customer at the table closest to the door stood as Jacob glanced in. It was Zara.

"DCI Steele," Jacob said as she joined them, "at least try to play it cool."

Zara gave a wry smile. "Well, you've got me intrigued. Maybe a part of the mystery is unravelling, if only a little."

"I know the feeling," Natalie said. "Never seems to get old."

"Let's not get too excited," said Jacob, tempering his own expectations until they could actually get a look at what they had.

He unlocked the security gate and led the two women into the office. It had cooled in the hours since Helen had left, and they kept their coats on. He set the folder on his desk and unbuckled the canvas strap. The documents within were dogeared and faded.

Organised into several sections, each section was held together with paper clips and rubber bands. The first contained a condensed report of Finbar's criminal history, a long litany of thefts, joyriding and then the assault Connelly had mentioned.

A Polaroid mugshot was clipped to the cover page. The cheeky grin from the photograph Deirdre had provided was gone. Instead Finbar looked back into the camera with wide, wet eyes, and a hanging mouth.

"There's a lot, isn't there?" Zara said.

"Let's split it." Jacob lifted the first few sections and set them aside. Taking a similar sized sheaf, he handed it to Natalie and then passed the remaining paperwork to Zara.

He seated himself at his chair and began to work through what he had. The first section was basic information. ID, date of birth, any known aliases, physical characteristics, distinguishing marks or tattoos, and emergency contact details.

Finbar's fingerprints were held on a slightly yellowed card stock, which had resisted the passage of time better than the surrounding pages. It was obviously a one size fits all document, and Finbar's prints were pathetically small in the ten individual boxes where they were inked.

He thought of Deirdre Skelly, left with virtually nothing of her son, only memories fading with time. He wondered if she might find some small comfort in having the page, the black ink capturing the unique signature of her son's touch, a permanent and tangible link to him. Each line and whorl was Finbar, probably the only physical evidence of his existence that remained.

Looking up, he saw Steele was engrossed in her stack of documents. Jacob slowly slid his desk drawer open and set the card inside before closing it, and turning back to the task at hand.

The next section was Finbar's visitor log. Each page had a typed heading for visitor names, relationship to the inmate, and dates of the visits, with the required information recorded in black ink. The only name recorded was Deirdre Skelly.

Mail and phone logs followed. Jacob flicked through it quickly. It held summaries of incoming and outgoing mail, and records of phone calls made and received. Jacob knew phone calls in modern prisons could be monitored and wondered if the same technology existed back when Finbar was in the borstal. If it did, there was no mention of it in the logs.

The final section of notes Jacob held documented Finbar's escape attempts. It was a handwritten log, updated for every attempt made, and there were a lot of them. Following the log was a series of typed reports, one for every bid for freedom Finbar had made. Some ran multiple pages when the attempt had been successful and evasion sustained. A number of rough maps with highlighted areas showed locations where he had hidden but been picked up before making it home to his mother.

Once finished, Jacob rubbed at tired eyes and leaned back into his chair. "How are we getting on?"

Natalie looked up. "Medical records. Nothing significant

on the physical side of things but his psychological assessments are of note. They describe him here as intelligent but dangerous, and with a complete lack of remorse for his crimes."

She set the sheaf of papers to one side and lifted the other. "This also has something that sticks out. Finbar's conduct record. He was in trouble a lot, and I'm not just talking about escape attempts. There's vandalism, theft, general disciplinary issues. There are at least five reports where its recommended he's transferred over to the closed borstal."

"Which we know he wasn't," said Jacob.

"Right," said Natalie. "Because someone always spoke up for him."

"Pettigrew," said Jacob.

Natalie shook her head. "Not just Pettigrew. Higgins."

"Higgins?" Steele asked. "The officer who was responsible for the parties?"

"Yep. I've got three different reports from Higgins asking the governor to consider allowing Finbar to remain in Hartley House."

"He wanted to keep him there," said Jacob.

"Certainly looks that way," agreed Natalie.

Jacob filed the titbit away before turning to Zara, who had seated herself on the small sofa in the corner of his office.

She rested her hand on an untidy pile of notes. "I have legal documentation, charge sheets, copies of original arrest warrants and court proceedings. Length of the sentence and any conditions, such as probation details or fines. There's a lot here, but on first scan nothing interesting as far as I can tell.

We also have work and education programmes. This was lighter reading because there isn't much. Art was the only class he made any effort to attend, and the teacher noted he was quite talented. Work assignments all last a few days at most. No vocational training, no qualifications, no record of any learning."

"So, what does the file tell us?" asked Jacob. "For one, despite repeated discipline issues, Finbar was kept in the open borstal at the urging of officer Higgins, most likely so he could be used for the parties."

Natalie nodded her agreement slowly before yawning,

hiding it behind her hand.

"It still boggles the mind that these documents are just sitting there," said Zara.

"The whole thing is bizarre," said Jacob, who then yawned in solidarity with Natalie. The adrenaline dump after the tension at the borstal was now hitting them both.

"Look," said Zara, "it's late and there's a lot here. I don't want to miss anything because we're tired and losing concentration."

"Agreed," said Jacob. "Let's pick it up tomorrow afternoon. We can go over the file in minute detail."

"Why not in the morning?" Steele queried. "Pick it up fresh first thing."

"We've tracked down the matron from the borstal," Jacob answered, "Me and Natalie will go and talk to her first. See if she can tell us more about Finbar and Hartley House."

"So, give me the folder," said Zara. "I like burning the midnight oil and can get a head start tonight."

Jacob looked at Natalie. "Alright," she said, tidying the documents she had pored over. "What's our plan for tomorrow?"

"I'll pick you up at nine," said Jacob, as he handed Steele his stack of papers. "Zara, you can meet us here with the folder at noon. But if you could actually solve this case between now and then, it'd be appreciated."

Zara smiled as she carefully placed the complete stack of documents back into the folder. "Count on it." She secured the buckle, said her goodbyes and left.

"Get you home?" Jacob said to Natalie as Zara's footsteps faded on the stairs.

"Yeah, please. I think I'm in an adrenaline freefall."

Jacob turned out the light to his office "What do you think?" he asked as he closed the door behind him.

"About the folder? Well, it gives some credence to what Matthew Connelly said, but there's no smoking gun. Or if there is, we haven't seen it yet."

"Maybe Zara will catch something we missed."

They crossed the main office. Jacob's phone buzzed as they reached the door. It was Zara.

"Jacob." She said his name sharply. The faint echo of hurried footsteps followed in the background, sharp taps against pavement. "Are you still at your office?"

Jacob's hand tightened around the phone. "What's wrong?"

"I think I'm being followed."

"Followed?" He was already halfway down the stairs. "Where are you now?"

There was a beat of hesitation on her end, the pause stretching just long enough to set his nerves on edge. "Callender Street. I doubled back to try and get back to your office."

Only a street over, Jacob thought. "Can you see anyone now?"

Zara breathed. "No, I think I lost him. I'll come back to you."

"No, stay hidden. We'll come and find you."

"It's ok, whoever it-"

Jacob heard the sharp sound of Zara's breath catching in her throat and then a muffled scream.

"Zara?"

There was a brief struggle on the other end and then a muted gasp.

Jacob took off running. His breath came in sharp gasps, the cold air biting at his lungs as he pushed himself to go faster. Natalie kept pace beside him, her coat flapping behind her as they rounded the corner and slowed.

Callender Street was a busy spot during the day. At night any vibrancy was sucked away by shuttered shop fronts, leaving an unsettling quiet. The only illumination came from weak streetlights, casting long shadows across the pavement.

Jacob squinted into the darkness. He could just make out a figure on the ground. Zara. A silhouette crouched over her unmoving form.

"Hey!" Jacob bellowed the word.

The silhouette jumped to their feet, a flash of metal in its hand catching the weak light as they turned and took off running, immediately disappearing into the shadows and out of sight.

Jacob closed the final few metres to Zara and came to a skidding halt where she lay on the cold ground. Her complete stillness, the unnatural slack of her limbs, jolted fear through Jacob that she was badly hurt. Or worse.

He knelt beside her, touching her shoulder gently. "Zara." The word came out shaky. "Zara, can you hear me?"

She groaned softly and her eyelids fluttered. "Jacob?"

"Yeah, it's me. I'm here." His hands hovered over her, unsure what to do with them. Zara rolled to her side with a groan and tried to push herself up, wincing as she did so. Jacob guided her into a sitting position.

"What happened?" Her hand reached up to touch a spot on the back of her head.

"You were jumped," Jacob said.

Zara shook her head, clearing cobwebs, and then touched her left wrist. Confusion slowly morphed into realisation, and then a sharp anger. "My watch."

The flash of metal in the figure's hand Jacob realised. It wasn't a knife, as he had first feared. It was Zara's Rolex.

Natalie crouched next to Jacob. "That's not the only thing," she whispered into his ear. "The folder's gone too."

17

"I really think we should call the police," said Natalie. "And an ambulance. I'm not fussy in what order."

Zara shook her head. "I'm fine."

It was the same mantra she had repeated since the trio had returned to Kincaid Investigations. She had managed to walk there under her own power, which Jacob had taken as an encouraging sign. He had, however, hovered at her elbow the entire way should she have keeled over, and he firmly agreed with Natalie's assessment.

"She's right." He handed Zara a glass of water. "Even if you don't want to go to hospital, this needs to be reported to the police."

"And I will," Zara replied tersely, her patience with their needling concern at an end. "Once I process the embarrassment of the whole thing."

"You have nothing to be embarrassed over," Natalie said gently.

"I'm a police officer who just got knocked out cold, had her watch stolen, as well as the file you both entrusted me with, less than two minutes after leaving here with it." She grimaced as she touched the tender spot on the back of her head. "Let's be honest, my pride has taken a bit of a kicking."

"Don't worry about that now," Jacob said.

Natalie nodded. "The important thing is that you're safe."

Zara slouched back into her seat, equal parts angry and frustrated. "Stupid."

"Did you get a look at him?" Jacob asked.

Zara shook her head. "It was a man though. Broad, I think." She took a sip of the water and looked at Jacob. "You have thoughts, I take it."

"Well," said Jacob, "Either a mugging for your watch, and the file just happened to be taken, or -"

"-Or the file was what they were after and the mugging was just for show," Zara finished.

"Had to be the file," said Natalie. "I know we hate the word, but it's too much of a coincidence."

"I don't think I'm shocking anyone when I say it's clear we're being watched," said Jacob. "The stranger in your garden, the graffiti at the studio, the person poking around Hector's house, whoever was banging on my door."

"You think they followed us from the borstal?" asked Natalie.

Jacob rubbed his chin. "No," he said slowly. "There wasn't much traffic, I'd have noticed a tail."

"But someone knew we were here," Natalie said. She pulled up her sleeve to check the time on her Breitling. "It's going on midnight. We got here maybe around eleven, and you normally close the office by what, half four?"

"Who else knew you were going to the borstal?" Zara asked.

"Just you," replied Jacob.

"Look, let's focus on the immediate issues," Natalie said. "Like getting Zara home. She shouldn't be driving." She turned to the other woman and pointed a finger. "No arguments."

"Wouldn't dream of it," Zara replied, managing a tired smile.

"What about you?" Jacob asked.

"I just ordered an Uber," Natalie replied. "It's a minute out."

"Not sure I like the idea of you heading home alone after what just happened," said Jacob.

"Dillon's there and the house is locked. I'll get him to meet me at the front door and I've got passing attention from my local police station thanks to Zara. I'll be fine, but I appreciate the concern."

Jacob walked her down the stairs. Arthur Street was meant to be a pedestrian precinct. The Uber driver, not seeing any pedestrians to worry about, had just turned off the main road and pulled in beside them.

"I'll pick you up at ten," said Jacob. "And text me when you get home safe."

"Sure. See you tomorrow."

"Yeah, see you tomorrow."

He waited until the Uber was back on the main road before reaching for his phone and calling Hector.

"The problem with having three different partners," Jacob said, once the older man answered, "Is that it's an absolute pain in the hole trying to keep track of who knows what."

"Well, don't keep me in suspense, Kincaid. What's happened?"

"Where to start?" He brought Hector up to speed about the meeting with Matthew Connelly, and the second confirmed sighting of this bandaged man. He allowed Hector the time to find the appropriate swear word and pressed on, telling him about the graffiti at the Wheelman, the intruder at his door, Finbar's folder located at the borstal, and the attack on Zara.

Hector waited a beat once Jacob had finished. "What, that it?"

Jacob huffed a laugh. "I probably didn't even cover all of it. Anything more on your end?"

"Nothing. I've been going through my old case notes but…" He made a noise which conveyed how that was going.

"Alright, just keep an eye out."

"You too, Kincaid. Keep me in the loop."

"Of course."

"Alright. Good night."

"Hector," Jacob said, suddenly remembering. "I meant to ask you something."

"Yes?"

"The names of the other girls. I appreciate you might not recall them off-hand, but I was -"

"-Edith Galbraith, Fiona Maguire, Teresa Harte, Siobhan Hanlon, Ciara Watson, Joanne King, Eden Hennesey, Lauren

Cooke."

No hesitation, no pause for recollection. Hector didn't need time to remember, he had never forgotten. They weren't just names to him. They were ghosts, they were a weight carried, silent echoes of lives that had been lost.

Jacob thanked the old man and wished him a good night. When he returned to his office he found Zara in the kitchen, rinsing her cup. "Give me a minute?"

"Of course," she said.

Jacob crossed to his office and found the post-its. He quickly scribbled the names of the six girls he had not known while there were still fresh in his head, and pinned them with Edith and Eden. Zara had joined him, watching from the threshold of the door but saying nothing.

"Alright," Jacob said, once finished. "Let's get you home."

She brought her arms up, folding them across her chest. "I'm not really sure I want to go home alone. Not just yet, at any rate." She pinched the bridge of her nose. "Jesus, sorry, that's asking for quite a big favour. Forget I asked and -"

"-It's fine," Jacob cut in. "I live close by. Come back to mine and I can get some food ordered in, or something."

"Only if you're sure?"

"I'm sure."

Jacob locked the office and they walked together to the Clio for the short drive back to his apartment.

"Nice place, Jacob," Zara said as he turned on the light switch by the front door.

"So I've been told." He walked over to the kitchen and opened the fridge. "Beer?"

"Is that a good idea?" Zara pointed to her head.

"I don't know, and I suppose we shouldn't find out." He shut the fridge door. "Tea?"

"That's a plan."

Zara removed her coat, placed it carefully over a chair, and then sat on the sofa, watching as he brewed two mugs of dark tea.

"I've always liked that painting," she said.

Jacob followed her nod to the wall where a print of Edward Hopper's *Nighthawks* hung. A late-night diner bathed in artificial glow, three customers at the counter opposite a lone server. A man and a woman sat next to each other, together but not. Their hands rest inches apart, and yet their postures suggested the gap is impassable. The third customer sat alone, ignoring the couple, lost in his own world.

He had bought the print not long after he had left the force and made the decision to take over Kincaid Investigations from Harry. Business had been slow in those first months, and Jacob had spent most of his days sitting in the office, passing time re-reading some of his old crime fiction collection.

It had been a passage in Michael Connelly's *The Black Echo* which had caught Jacob's attention. The book's protagonist, Bosch, was also fascinated by Hopper's painting. Bosch considered himself as the man sitting alone, but wanted to be the other man, the one across the counter and alongside the woman.

Even if he was a fictional character, Bosch's simple yearning had struck a chord with Jacob. He had been alone, disengaged, seemingly without a purpose. He knew the painting, but had immediately looked it up online and felt an immediate kinship to the lonely man at the counter. A sad, solitary nighthawk, just like him.

He crossed over to the sofa and handed Zara one of the steaming mugs before sitting next to her.

"Cheers," she said.

"Cheers." He remained standing but gently clinked the mug against hers. "So...You alright?"

Her smile seemed to acknowledge the insipidness of his question. "Fine. Like I said, my pride is hurt worse than anything else. I'm sorry about the folder."

"It happens. I did something similar on the Followers of Eden investigation."

"You lost evidence?"

"Well, technically speaking, I broke it. It was on a tablet, and I bounced it off some guy's skull during a scrap. Same result."

"It's not. You fought back. But, I appreciate the effort in trying to make me feel better." Her right hand went to her opposite wrist. The tan line left by her Rolex was faintly visible.

"Did it have any sentimental value?" Jacob asked. "Like a gift or something?"

"No, I bought it for myself after I made Chief. Something I could look at to remind myself how far I'd come." She cupped two hands around her mug. "You do your research. Did you hear the tale about turning up at my first day at Garnerville in the Porsche?"

Jacob shrugged.

"It was my father's and he wasn't using it. I suppose you heard the rest too? Easy post out of the depot, didn't need to do the required two years in response, fast track, all that."

"Some."

"Yeah, most have. Like it's some sort of stick to beat me with. I was asked to leave response early for a training opportunity, and I was eligible for the fast track, and you know what, I aced the board. Same with the detective exam. What was the pass mark when you did it?"

"Fifty-five percent, I think."

"They say it's the hardest exam you can sit in the PSNI. I scored ninety. I'm not boasting, it's just a fact. I was a good detective, and when I got promoted, I was an even better supervisor. I got to where I was on my own merit. No one is taking that from me."

Jacob took an interest in his tea.

Zara sighed. "Sorry. It just wears a bit thin after a while. You think there would be the same kind of talk if I was a man?"

"Probably not."

"Probably not," she echoed.

"Still, could be worse. Better to be known for that, rather than the guy who got kicked out for..." Jacob trailed off. Nigh on five years and the pill of his dismissal wasn't any easier to swallow.

Zara motioned around the apartment. "Seems to have worked out alright, this private investigator business."

Jacob sat next to her. "Well, the money's decent but the real reward is how much it galls my father."

"Ah, unable to live up to fatherly expectations? We might be kindred spirits."

"You don't live up to expectations? You already made DCI

and you're what, thirty?

"Thirty-two."

"What was he expecting?"

"That I take a job where I could be of assistance to the family. When he found out that I'd applied for the police, he asked me how putting strangers first, helped us."

"What does your father do?"

Zara hesitated for a second. "He's a constant irritation. That's what he does."

She had avoided the question, but Jacob decided not to press. "DCI and not even halfway into your career. Seems like it was the right career choice."

"I suppose. But the fast track isn't all it's cracked up to be. You're jumping ship to a new department what feels like every few months. I'm never in one post for long, so I never made any friends in the police, and never had any time for my friends outside it. Never made any time for a real relationship. It gets lonely." Her hand reached out and gently, almost absentmindedly, she began to brush his arm. "You ever get lonely, Jacob?"

"Probably more than I'd like to admit," Jacob said, scrambling to process the sudden and unexpected turn his evening had taken.

"I can tell." Zara's smile held a tinge of sadness. She glanced back to Nighthawks and then at him. "Well, you certainly know how to make a girl feel safe. I'm sure you've got better things to do than watching over a damsel in distress."

"I'm struggling to come up with anything to be honest."

"Maybe, it takes something like tonight to realise what I've been missing out on." Her finger began to trace an idle pattern on his arm. It was a gesture both absent and filled with intent.

Slowly, as if pulled by the same string, they drew nearer. Jacob reached up to brush a loose strand of hair behind her ear, fingers lingering at her jawline. Her breath hitched at his touch, her eyes closing in anticipation.

Jacob tilted his head, closing the final gap between them, his lips meeting hers in a kiss that was gentle at first, exploratory, as if both were savouring the sensation, memorising the feel.

He pulled back and rested his forehead against hers.

"What's wrong?" Zara's hand reached up to touch his cheek.

"I'm worried that I'm taking advantage."

She let out a breathy chuckle. "What?"

"You've been through a traumatic experience, you're vulnerable, you might even be concussed. Put that all together and I start to feel a bit grubby."

"Don't."

She moved in to kiss him again and Jacob put a gentle hand on her shoulder. "Easier said than done. I can't. Not like this."

Zara closed her eyes and eased herself back. Her hand went to his chin and stayed there. "You're a good man, Jacob."

"Yeah, well, don't let it get out. It'll ruin me."

18

Jacob stifled a yawn as Natalie climbed into the passenger seat of his car. He pointed to one of the two travel mugs in the cup holder, freshly brewed just before he had left the apartment.

"Rough night?" she asked, lifting the mug and saluting him with it.

He considered saying nothing. "Stayed up too late," he replied after a moments deliberation.

Natalie raised a knowing brow as she took a sip of her coffee. "And did Zara get home ok?"

"She stayed at mine in the end."

"Did she now?"

"Nothing happened."

It was the truth, although Jacob wasn't sure why he was in such a rush to say so. He and Zara had talked. Talked about work, cases, hobbies. A lot of the time they talked about nothing at all, simply enjoying the presence of another person as their chat meandered. The lulls in conversation when they came, were easy and unhurried, before the conversation would start again, flowing without effort or urgency into the wee small hours.

Eventually, the day had caught up to Jacob and he let his heavy eyes close for a fraction too long. He woke up to find night had given way to a grey morning. Zara had slipped a blanket over him and was busying herself in the kitchen, having liberated one of his old hoodies from the wardrobe. They had shared a coffee and then he had seen her to the door.

"Thanks again," she said. "For looking after me."

She leaned forward and kissed him. This time he didn't object. It was tender and he wanted more but she was gone, her confident stride taking her down the corridor without another word. He watched her go, the lingering warmth of the kiss mixing with a pang of longing as she disappeared from view, leaving him alone with the quiet hum of the wakening city and thoughts of what might be.

"Nothing happened?" The disbelieving tone pulled him back from the reverie.

"Nothing happened," he repeated. "It was just comfortable, you know?"

"Sounds nice."

Jacob glanced across but Natalie's attention was on the road. "She's ok, I take it?"

"Yeah, she's fine. Barely fazed her."

"Probably hasn't sunk in yet," Natalie said.

"No," Jacob agreed. "Probably not."

Carneybaun Care Home sat on the Antrim Road, a long arterial route that stretched from inner city north Belfast, out to the small country hamlet of Dunadry, fourteen miles away. The home, shielded from the road by a tall concrete wall, was accessed by a short, steeply-sloped driveway.

As they got out of the car, Jacob could see the exterior of Carneybaun bore obvious marks of neglect. Once-white paint was now peeling and cracked, exposing patches of grey, and several of the window frames were visibly rotted, with panes that looked like they hadn't been cleaned in years.

The lobby wasn't in a much better state. A stale, musty odour mingled with the scent of disinfectant. The walls, painted a dull, institutional beige, were marred with scuffs and stains, and the few pieces of décor, a couple of faded paintings of pastoral scenes, seemed as forgotten as one of the residents who shuffled passed.

There was no one at reception, and nothing to signal that they were standing there. They spent a couple of minutes waiting to be noticed before an Asian woman appeared from a backroom and saw them hovering. It was obvious she was busy but she was able to force a smile as she approached. A name badge identified her as Reyna.

"Good morning," she said through a thick accent. "Visiting?"

"That's right," Natalie replied. "Here to see Patricia Winslow."

Reyna's expression shifted to one of surprise. "Oh wonderful, Patricia doesn't get many visitors." Her brow creased. "Are you family?"

Jacob pulled out a card from his wallet and waited a beat for Reyna to read it. "We're looking into an inheritance case," he said. "We believe Patrica knew the beneficiary."

"Is some money coming her way?"

"That's confidential," Jacob replied. He used a curt tone, keen to cut-off any scrutiny on their flimsy cover story.

Obviously disappointed in the answer, Reyna handed Jacob his card back. "She on the first floor, left at the top of the stairs, and then the first door you come to. Just knock and then go in." She looked as if she was going to say more but stopped.

They thanked her and took the stairs up to the next floor. Stopping at the first door on the left, Natalie rapped it twice, waited a second, and then opened it.

Patrica Winslow was seated in a high-backed chair, facing the window. She didn't turn as they entered, or seem to register their presence at all. She was a skinny figure, draped in a thin shawl that fell loosely around slight shoulders. Her posture was rigid, almost statuesque.

Jacob could see the dusty pane offered a view of the care home's garden, overgrown with wild shrubs, untended trees, and not much else.

The room, like the rest of the home, smelled stale. It was a sparsely furnished space, with a faded rug, a couple of threadbare armchairs, and a small wooden bookshelf laden with a few tattered books. The bed, positioned against one wall, had been neatly made with a floral-patterned quilt, a rare splash of colour against the drab surroundings.

There were only a couple of personal touches on display; a

framed water colour painting of a country cottage on the middle shelf of the bookcase, and a vase of fresh flowers sitting on the sill of the window the woman continued to stare out of.

"Patricia?" Natalie asked softly.

At the mention of her name, the woman's shoulders tensed. She ducked her head for a moment, before turning to face them.

Natalie gasped.

Patrica Winslow's face was almost devoid of skin. The few remnants that remained were a tapestry of scars and discoloration, uneven in texture and mottled with shades of grey and pale blue. The disfigurement extended down her throat and beneath the collar of her shirt. Her lips were gone, causing her teeth to be forever bared in a ghastly, ghostly, grin.

Natalie caught herself and offered a gentle smile. "Hello, Patrica. My name is Natalie, and this is Jacob."

Patrica said nothing as she regarded them with eyes that were a mix of expressiveness and eerie intensity.

"We were hoping to ask you about your past employment," Natalie continued. "At the Hartley House borstal."

The woman's unnerving gaze stayed on them and Jacob had to look away.

"Can, can you talk?" Natalie asked.

Slowly, Patrica opened her mouth and Jacob felt his stomach roll. Her tongue was missing, leaving a smooth, scarred hollow. As if performing a rehearsed bit, Patricia lifted both her hands, silently letting her visitors take the sight in. Every finger was missing above the knuckle. She nodded towards the bed.

By the pillow Jacob found a small pile of laminated sheets, connected by a treasury tag looped through a hole in their top left corners. Each sheet was divided into a grid layout and each square of the grid displayed a clear, easily readable word and accompanying symbol.

The top row of the board was dedicated to basic needs. Jacob saw symbols for water, food, bathroom, and bed. Each icon was accompanied by large, bold text to ensure there was no ambiguity. Below this row, there were phrases for emotional expressions like happy, sad, and worried.

One hundred and twenty or so phrases across four sheets. Jacob didn't want to even consider how isolating it had to be, to be restricted to pre-printed words, unable to articulate thoughts. He removed the treasury tag and sat the four sheets out on the table in front of Patricia.

"We're looking to track down a missing boy," Natalie said. "Finbar Skelly. Did you know him?""

Slowly, laboriously, Patricia lifted her arm and pointed to the word **YES**.

Encouraged by her affirmation, Natalie followed up. "Can you tell us about the borstal?"

Patricia paused, her gaze falling on the words. With a deep breath that seemed to muster some sort of resolve, she again pointed to **YES** and then to **BAD** and **SCARED**.

"You were scared of the borstal?" Natalie asked.

Patricia didn't move.

"You were scared of someone there," prompted Jacob.

YES.

"Higgins?" Jacob asked.

Patricia's hand moved swiftly to **NO** but then to **BAD** and **DANGER**.

"What about Father Pettigrew?"

BAD

Natalie bit at her lip. "But it was someone else who scared you?"

YES

Jacob knelt down. "Finbar?"

Patricia's hand brushed the **NO** icon before she took it away immediately. Her face creased with a sudden anguish as a low, guttural moan sounded from deep within. It was raw, distressing. She pushed the sheets away and then waved her arm in the direction of the bookcase.

Jacob walked over, unsure what she was indicating. Hesitantly, he reached for the water colour painting of the old cottage. "This?"

Patricia nodded, the movements frantic.

"Did Finbar paint this?"

Patricia hit at the table, nodding wildly.

Jacob turned the picture around to get a proper look at it.

He remembered the mention in Finbar's file about him being a decent artist. The painting was proof.

The cottage had whitewashed walls, tinged with the subtle hues of age and weathering. Dark, ominous clouds dominated the sky, swirling in shades of deep blue and grey set a foreboding mood. Heavy brushstrokes conveyed the fury of the storm, with rain slashing diagonally across the canvas in streaks of transparent blues and silvers.

"You recognise it?" Natalie asked.

In the background of the painting, a gently sloping hill with yellow gorse rose in the distance. Atop the hill stood a monument, tall and slender, reaching into the tumultuous sky.

"I think I recognise that," Jacob said. "That's the Knockagh memorial, out near Carrickfergus."

Patrica waved an arm. Jacob tapped the painting. "We go here?"

She nodded again, somehow more desperate than before.

Natalie moved beside him. "Think you can find it?"

"I think I can try."

He looked up as Patricia Winslow tapped an urgent beat with a truncated knuckle on the communication board.

DANGER
DANGER
DANGER

19

Patrica wailed. Guttural moans. Jacob picked the cardboard grids off the floor and stood by lamely as Natalie comforted the woman, holding her close and whispering soothing words until the anguished sounds slowly reduced to shaky, uneven breaths.

Natalie broke the embrace and gently touched Patrica's cheek, her thumb wiping a tear from the mottled skin. It was almost intimate and Jacob, feeling like an intruder, edged closer to the door and waited until Natalie had calmed Patricia down enough so they could leave.

"Fuck me," said Jacob once they were on the stairs.

Natalie shook her head sadly and cleared her throat. "What are you thinking?"

"Well, like I said, the painting seems to show the Knockagh monument. Assuming the painting is in any way accurate..." He stopped to get his phone out of his pocket and brought up the map app. "We should have a relatively small area to search. It should be somewhere in the countryside between Greenisland and Carrickfergus, and Knockagh Hill and Belfast Lough." He traced a rough rectangle of the search area with the tip of a finger.

"Sounds simple."

"Well, get back to me with that thought if we're still trawling the back roads in six hours' time."

Reyna walked past the bottom of the stairs and stopped

when she noticed them. "You saw Patricia?"

"We did," answered Natalie. "We had no idea about..."

Reyna only nodded.

"What happened?" Jacob asked.

"She was attacked," replied Reyna. "Long time ago."

"By who?"

"No one knows. Random."

"My god," said Natalie. "How long has she been here at Carneybaun?"

"As far as I know, since then." Reyna said.

"No family?" asked Jacob.

"A nephew, comes in a few times a year. Brings flowers. No one else." Reya's tone was resigned, as if Patricia's story was a familiar one within the walls of the care home.

Jacob felt a profound sadness settle over him. He imagined Patricia, sitting by her window, the routine likely unchanged for years, marked only by the rare visits from a nephew, her only link to a world beyond Carneybaun. He wondered about the nephew, and the flowers he brought. Did he feel affection, obligation, or a sense of familial duty? Were the flowers a token of love, or a symbol of guilt for not doing more?

"Are those cards her only means of communication?" Natalie asked. "Surely a computer with a programme would be much more efficient, not to mention enabling."

"Money," Reyna said with an apologetic shrug. "Always money."

They thanked Reyna and trudged to Jacob's Clio. Natalie stopped as she opened the door and looked at Jacob across the car roof.

"Am I alone in thinking what happened to Patricia is much too coincidental?" She smiled thinly. "There's that damn word again."

"I dunno," said Jacob. He had the same thought about the horror inflicted on Patrica being connected to Finbar's disappearance and what had happened at Hartley House. "If they, whoever they are, wanted to keep her quiet, why not kill her?"

"Jesus, Jacob. Did you see the poor woman? It looks like someone gave it a good go."

"I'm not so sure. The injuries suggest someone with a grudge."

"Who?"

He shrugged. He didn't have an answer and didn't want to dwell on the mutilated woman with the sad eyes and felt like shit for realising it.

Neither said much as they drove towards Carrickfergus. On a clear day you would have been able to see the Knockagh Monument from several miles away. Today, the hill it sat on was socked in with low clouds.

The temperature on the dash told Jacob it was only a couple of degrees above freezing. A lonely ferry navigated its way through the choppy grey water of Belfast Lough towards Scotland, as they passed Whiteabbey, and followed the road as it skirted Jordanstown and Greenisland.

He stuck to the main carriageway until they reached the edge of Carrickfergus. Natalie, with the aid of Google Maps, guided him back out to the countryside to begin their search for the cottage in earnest.

As Natalie had said, the plan to find the cottage in the painting was simple enough. The digital map displayed a relatively sparse network of roads but it soon became clear the area itself was a spiderweb of lanes and paths that twisted away into fields and woodlands without any indication where they ended.

They stopped at every unmarked laneway, reversing back onto the road when it became clear they were on someone's private farmland, or a dead-end leading to overgrown fields. The sun, a rare companion throughout the day, retreated further behind the thick blanket of clouds, leaving the world beneath it in a dim, diffuse light.

"Stop!"

Jacob, who had been miles away, slammed the brakes on instinct. Natalie was already halfway out of the car and he scrambled to follow.

The laneway, flanked by two ancient stone pillars, was almost entirely concealed by overgrowth. Beyond the thicket, stood the cottage from the painting, still and desolate. Its walls were covered in patches of moss and ivy, and the wooden door, swollen with moisture, hung on its hinges.

A narrow path snaked through the weeds to the front door. They shrugged their way through the thicket, and Jacob nudged the door to the cottage aside with his shoulder and held it in place for Natalie to step past.

She stopped at the threshold. "Footprints."

Stark against decades of grime, the muddy footprints were clearly defined, their edges still sharp. They led from the front door, across the living room and through a doorway on the far side.

Someone had been here recently, certainly within the past few days.

They moved into the living room. Faded paper peeled from the walls in large, curling strips, revealing patches of damp plaster beneath. An old stone fireplace stood cold and empty. The door on the far side of the room led to a kitchen with a rusting stove and a sagging, wooden cabinet.

Every cupboard in the kitchen hung open on rusted hinges, revealing empty shelves and a few scattered utensils. Jacob moved across to an old porcelain sink, caked in mildew. The window above the sink offered a view of the overgrown backyard.

"Jacob." Natalie had lifted a framed picture sitting on the cabinet and passed it to him. "That's Finbar Skelly."

She was right. Finbar stood on the far left of a row of six boys. They were all skinny, wearing shorts and t-shirts. Finbar was smiling but it didn't reach his eyes. An adult man stood behind Finbar, one hand resting on his shoulder.

Jacob studied the faces of the other boys, hoping to pick out Desmond McClure or Craig Fullerton, but coming up empty. He was about to put the photo back when he stopped, a flicker of recognition kindling in his consciousness.

Jeremiah Pettigrew.

The former priest was four decades years younger, his hair still its natural colour. His smile, unlike the boys he was with, was broad and genuine.

Natalie moved beside him. "Why is -"

"-I have no idea." Jacob set the picture down. An unshakeable sense of foreboding crept over him. There was a wrongness here.

A creaking staircase led to the first floor. The room immediately to the left on the landing was empty, as was the bathroom next to it. Mildew painted the walls in splotches of black and green. A mirror above the sink was so speckled with age it barely reflected their images as they passed the doorway.

The final room held only a sagging, moulding mattress and another grimy mirror affixed to the wall closest to it. The fabric of the mattress was heavily stained, and it gave off an odour so pungent, Natalie pinched her nose and remained in the hallway.

Jacob moved around the room, unsure what he was looking for. His gaze drifted and then stopped on the floorboard closest to the wall. It was slightly raised, out of alignment with the rest.

Kneeling down, he noticed faint scratches around its edges, as if it had either been frequently moved, or had things moved over it. Gripping the edge of the board, it lifted with a soft creak, revealing a small, dark cavity beneath.

There was nothing in the space. Jacob sat back on his haunches and looked at the wall. From behind, he heard Natalie crossing the room, her boots loud on the creaking boards. She reached over his shoulder, her hand feeling along the wall. She paused and then struck it twice with the palm of her hand.

A hollow sound echoed back.

Jacob put his hand back into the hidden crevice, feeling for the bottom of the wall, running two fingers along the surface. They brushed against a small, metal fixture, raised and smooth. He pressed it, and with a *click*, part of the wall swung open.

The space beyond was tiny, barely big enough for a fully grown man to crouch inside. An old camera tripod was the only thing in the compartment. A hole had been cut in the wall to fit the mirror over on the room-facing side. The backside of the mirror had a dark, reflective surface.

"Two way," Jacob said, tapping the glass.

Natalie shook her head sadly and then took her phone from her pocket. She snapped pictures of the hidey-hole, the old tripod and the filthy mattress.

Jacob rubbed a hand over his face as she finished. "Let's get out of here."

Back downstairs, Jacob stopped in the kitchen, his gaze following the footprints Natalie had noticed. They led through the kitchen to the backdoor and the overgrown yard beyond. Stepping into the yard, he looked for any outbuildings, sheds, or any other structure, but saw nothing.

Something must have drawn the owner of the footprints out here, he thought. He turned back towards the cottage and found his answer. A narrow staircase clung to the exterior wall, partially hidden by an overhanging bush. The stairs were concrete, smoother and less weathered than the rest of the building, leading down to directly beneath the cottage.

"Looks like it goes to a basement," Jacob said, as Natalie joined him.

"Should we check it out?"

Her tone conveyed the reluctance Jacob felt. The cottage had a bad mojo that plucked at his nerves. There was a residue here, just like he had felt at Hartley House. There were secrets in the walls and the ghosts of past misdeeds walked the floors.

The wooden door at the bottom of the stairs was old but sturdy. The bar slid across to lock it was just as old, but the silver padlock looped through the bar still maintained some shine.

"Why would this be the only door with a lock?" Natalie asked, as she gave it an experimental tug.

"Hang fire here." Jacob took the steps back up into the garden. A narrow path ran between the side of the building and the tangled, overgrown hedge bordering the property. He opted for that route rather than going back into the cottage. He went to his car, retrieved the old Maglite from the boot, his set of lock-picks from the glovebox, and returned to Natalie.

He was about to hand the Maglite to her so she could give him a bit of light while he attempted to finesse the lock, but stopped, and instead switched his grip on the torch. With a firm swing, Jacob brought the Maglite down on the padlock. The sound of metal striking metal rang sharply through the desolation. The lock held. With a grunt, Jacob raised the Maglite back again.

The impact sent a jarring vibration up his arms, but he barely noticed. Missing boys. Missing girls. Grieving mothers. A stained mattress in a dingy old cottage. The sudden surge of righteous rage lent strength to his arm as he struck again and again.

The padlock gave way under the strain of the assault, its body distorting enough to release the hasp. Jacob pried the broken lock off and tossed it aside. Natalie stepped forward, put a hand on his shoulder.

He took a breath and handed her the Maglite. Pushing the bolt across, he opened the door. The space beyond was dark. The thin windows had been painted over in thick, careless strokes. Natalie turned the torch on and the beam cut through the gloom, dancing over a concrete floor of uneven, discoloured patches.

Jacob knelt to inspect the floor. At first glance, the dark marks seemed like water damage. Natalie crouched beside him, her nose wrinkling at the musty, iron smell. "This looks like... is it blood?"

Jacob didn't respond. The light from the torch trembled slightly as Natalie moved it across the room, uncovering more stains. She paused at a corner and bent down at a particularly large patch of discolouration. Jacob watched as she scraped at the bottom of the wall lightly with her fingernail. The plaster flaked away, revealing deeper, darker stains underneath.

"What happened down here?" she asked quietly as she stood.

Before Jacob could answer, Natalie's gasp of fear cut sharply through the room. He whirled around to find a man standing by the door, watching them silently.

He was short and stocky with dyed blonde hair cropped short. "Ah, look at that," he said with a heavy Belfast accent. "Heard there were a couple of snoops, poking their noses around here."

"The fuck are you?" Jacob asked, his voice tremoring as he felt the previous surge of adrenaline spike, knowing something ugly was coming. He moved in front of Natalie.

The man glanced up the staircase as if looking for someone, before he turned his attention back on them, stepping forward slowly as he spoke.

"This place, it's got history, or so I've been told. And I suppose not everyone's keen on that history being dug up." Dye-job balled his fists and Jacob took a step back. The action earned a cruel smile from the man. Jacob knew the type, a bully who got off on the fear of others. "Nothing personal, you get me?"

The thug wasn't expecting resistance. He moved in, ready to mete out violence. Jacob lashed out with his right foot and caught him square in the balls

With a choked, wordless noise, Dye-job doubled over. A flailing arm reached out for Jacob, who shoved it away. He couldn't hesitate or let him recover. This man, who was going to hurt him without a second thought, would hurt him worse now that Jacob had the temerity to fight back.

He yanked Dye-job's coat over his head, trapping his arms, and hit him with a couple of clumsy uppercuts, that felt as though they hit more forehead than anything else. Dye-job swiped at air as he stumbled back.

Jacob grabbed him around the head and shoved him backwards until he collided with the doorframe. Fighting to keep a grip, Jacob rammed Dye-job's head back into the frame. The man grunted, and then went silent as Jacob crashed his head against the wood a second time, and slid limply to the ground after the third.

He grabbed Natalie by the wrist and pulled her toward stairs. There was no one waiting in the garden, but he could hear low voices coming from the kitchen.

They kept low, taking the path up the side of the cottage and made it to the stone pillars marking the entrance when they heard a shout, a harsh, startling sound that spurred them into a frantic run for Jacob's car.

He yanked the door open and fumbled with shaking hands as he tried to slide the key into the ignition. In the periphery of his vision, he could see two men emerging from the side of the cottage.

His fingers finally found their mark and the old engine sputtered to life. Jacob slammed the accelerator and the tyres spat gravel as the car jolted forward with a suddenness that pressed them back into their seats.

The road ahead twisted through dense countryside. The Clio's engine whined in protest as Jacob pushed it as hard as it would go. Behind them, headlights cut through the late afternoon murk, the beams bouncing with the uneven terrain as they sought their quarry.

The Clio's tyres screeched as Jacob took a sharp corner, the vehicle barely managing to cling to the asphalt. The road was all curves and bends, not designed for the speed he was pushing. Jacob's eyes darted to the rearview, to the relentless headlights that grew steadily closer.

The pursuing car was larger, more powerful. Jacob was certain he could hear its engine, a deep, menacing growl that seemed to mock the Clio as the distance between the two cars steadily shrank.

He pressed the accelerator to the floor when the road allowed it, but it wasn't enough. The other car was behind them now, the silhouette of its driver looming over the wheel.

As they approached a particularly tight bend, the pursuing vehicle made its move, nudging the rear of the Clio. Jacob fought the steering wheel, trying to regain control, but it was no good. The car veered off the asphalt and onto the verge, tyres losing grip on the slick grass.

Metal crunched as the car ploughed through a cluster of bushes and into a field. The Clio lurched into the air before slamming back down with an impact that jolted Jacob's vision. He could do nothing more than grip the steering wheel and hope it would stop.

It did. A jarring, abrupt halt. The engine sputtered and then died, and for a moment, everything was still.

Jacob turned to Natalie. Her head was slumped was against the window, "Natalie," Jacob shook her by the arm. "Natalie!"

Her eyelids fluttered, her brow furrowing slightly as if she were struggling to make sense of her surroundings. So focused on Natalie, Jacob only just registered the two figures closing in.

He fumbled for his seat belt and managed to unbuckle it at the same moment the leading figure reached his door and yanked at the handle. As the door was pulled open, Jacob kicked it.

The man on the other side was unfortunately a sight more competent than his companion from the basement. He dodged the swinging door with a swift sidestep that belied his size, took another step forward, and hit Jacob with a punch that connected squarely on the bridge of his nose.

Pain seared across Jacob's face as his vision blurred. He could taste the metallic tang of blood trickle down over his lips.

Before he could recover, strong hands gripped his arm, dragging him out of the car. He landed on the grass, moisture quickly seeping through his clothes. His head spun. As he tried to scramble to his feet, the man started kicking him, targeting his sides and stomach. Each blow forced the air from his lungs, pain flaring hot and bright with every strike. Jacob curled instinctively, gasping for breath, the wet grass clinging to his face and hands.

A scream pierced the night, high-pitched with terror. Jacob forced his head up. Natalie was struggling against the second man, who had one arm gripped around her waist, holding her back from reaching him.

Despite the pain racking his body, Jacob tried to climb to his feet but was stopped with a boot to the chest, pushing him back into the grass.

"Relax, hero," said the man who had just been using him as a football. He was solidly built with a shaved head and broad shoulders. "You think we'd hurt a woman?"

Jacob thought their type had hurt plenty of women, and had their names sung for it, but decided against voicing it.

"Think he's had enough?" It was the man holding Natalie who asked the question.

"He has," Jacob groaned.

"Oh, he's a funny fucker," said the man with his boot on Jacob's chest. He lifted it off and then delivered one last kick, softer than the others.

Natalie was shoved forward. She stumbled and then ran to Jacob, hugging him closely as he sat up.

"Consider this a message sent," said the man who had held Natalie. "Back off." Like his companions, he was an older man. Steely grey eyes held a calculating coldness that suggested he was the leader of the trio. There was no sign of Dye-job, which was a mercy, Jacob knew. He'd be no doubt eager to even the score.

The man who had delivered the kicking opened the fuel cap on Jacob's Clio with a swift twist. His other hand pulled a rag from the back pocket of his jeans. He stuffed half of the rag into the tank and left the rest hanging out. With a flick, the lighter sparked to life. He lit the rag which began burning with a steady, hungry flame.

Fire began to lick up the side of the car. Within moments, it had taken hold. Orange hues threw long, distorted shadows across the field. Smoke billowed up into the late afternoon sky, thick and acrid, filling the air with the smell of burning plastic and gasoline.

20

What remained of the Clio was hidden by the hedge they had crashed through. The warm embrace of the fire was tempered by the scent of petrol and scorched metal. The silence was occasionally punctuated by the windows and tyres of Jacob's car popping under the heat.

"I hope the insurance company appreciates the dramatic flair of my claim as much as I do."

Natalie's grunted reply could almost have passed as amusement. She had her arms folded together tightly against her body. Her mouth was set in a grim line and her eyes betrayed the fear of what they had just endured.

Jacob's nose, which he was reasonably confident was broken, throbbed with a sharp, pulsating pain that radiated across his face. His midsection wasn't faring much better. Even the slightest movement sent waves of sharp pain across his ribs and into his stomach.

The sound of the fire slowly faded as the minutes ticked by. It was bitterly cold and it was perhaps an hour after they had climbed back onto the road that Jacob could hear a car in the distance. A minute later it rounded the corner and slowed, coming to a stop where they stood.

Michael Healy lowered the window and looked at them. "What the fuck have you two been at?"

Jacob and Natalie climbed into the back seat of his car without a word. Michael had the heat on full blast and the hot, dry air was a welcome relief as the car pulled away.

"So, is anyone going to tell me -" Michael started until his gaze fell on the hole in the hedge made by Jacob's Clio. "-Is that your car?"

Jacob looked out the window. The flames had died, leaving behind a blackened husk of twisted and warped metal. Shattered glass lay around the car, their fragments catching the fading light.

"I'll tell you when we're back in the office," Jacob said. He turned his attention to Natalie. "You ok?" It felt like he could only ask the question now they were in the comparative safety of Michael's car.

She somehow managed a smile. "I don't really consider it a proper investigation with you until I get knocked out for the first time."

Jacob felt guilt stab through his gut.

Natalie reached across and squeezed his hand. "Bad joke. I'm fine. How are you?"

"I think I'm more hurt about what they did with my car. Lot of memories in that old thing."

Michael snorted. "Oh yeah, like what?"

"Sitting, mostly." Jacob smiled and immediately regretted it, the muscles around his nose protesting vehemently. He sank back into his seat.

The car was quiet for the remainder of their journey back into Belfast.

*

Helen looked up from her computer as Jacob stepped into the office. "Didn't expect you in today, where have-oh shit!"

"Thanks for that, Helen," said Jacob flatly.

"What happened?"

"Later," Jacob said, waving away both her concern and question as Michael and Natalie shuffled in after him. "I'll tell you later."

"Alright." Helen had shot out of her seat and now remained

standing, tapping her fingers together in a nervous manner, entirely unlike her. "Can I get you anything?"

"Coffee. Strong."

"Anyone else?" Helen asked.

Natalie and Michael both shook their head. Jacob waved them towards his own office while Helen went and busied herself in the kitchen.

Michael hesitated at the door. "Look, whatever you're about to say, as a police officer, I can't hear about a crime and not report it."

Jacob knew that wasn't strictly true. The previous summer Michael had watched the video of Natalie's kidnapping, which her abductor had sent to Jacob to lure him into a trap. He had held off on reporting that, knowing that raising the alarm would have likely meant Natalie's life.

"What crime?" Jacob asked as he sat down, wincing with the effort.

Michael scoffed. "What crime? It looks like someone used your face for a drum solo, not to mention your car is smouldering in some farmer's field."

"Would it reassure you if I told you my car gained sentience, drove itself through a hedge, and self-immolated?"

"I'll stay out here."

Jacob waited until his friend closed the door and swung his chair to face Natalie. "So."

"So."

"What do we have?"

Natalie paused, her attention fully on Jacob's busted face.

"I need to focus on this," Jacob said, pre-empting her train of thought. "Let's worry about my face later."

She bit her lip but didn't argue. "The matron from the borstal, who we know Finbar Skelly was close to, with her face sliced up by an unknown assailant."

"Unknown, and as far as we know at this stage, potentially unconnected to this case," said Jacob.

"Potentially," Natalie conceded to his point with a slight nod. "And we have a picture of Pettigrew and Finbar Skelly at the cottage."

"With their connection already known through West

Belfast and the borstal."

"But not as close of a connection as Pettigrew led you to believe. Then, in the same cottage we have hidden recording equipment pointed at a bed, and a locked basement with what looked like blood on the floor."

Jacob rubbed at his chin. "Patrica wanted us to go to the cottage. She knew we'd find something."

"Maybe it's where she was attacked?" offered Natalie.

"Maybe that's where Finbar was killed?" said Jacob.

The words seemed strange in his mouth. He had assumed from the outset Finbar was dead, had never considered otherwise. For him, the question had always been who had done it. Still, to hear the words aloud, was rather jolting.

"We need to talk to Patricia again."

"Yeah," Jacob agreed. There was more to the story there but extracting it from Patrica would be a difficult and time-consuming endeavour, if she was even mentally up for it.

Helen entered with a steaming mug of coffee. Jacob thanked her as he took it.

"Have you had a look at yourself?" Helen asked.

"I generally try to avoid it," said Jacob. "Not good for the self-esteem."

Helen fixed him with her best disapproving mother look.

He turned to Natalie. "You think you can find the cottage on the map app on your phone?"

"Yeah, I think so."

"Have a look and see if there's an exact address. I guess I'll go and get a proper gander at the damage."

He crossed the main office to the tiny bathroom, and locked the door behind him. Turning to the small mirror above the ancient sink he couldn't help but offer a wry smile at the reflection looking back at him. As it had been in Michael's car, the smile was a mistake and he was rewarded with a stinging reminder that brought water to his eyes.

Gently, he prodded at the tender skin. His nose felt hot to the touch, but he could still breathe through it, albeit painfully. He unzipped his coat and gingerly lifted the sweater and t-shirt underneath to reveal a tapestry of blue, purple and yellow bruises, blossoming across his abdomen and ribs. Each hue meant a different depth of bruising, all of which would be painful in the days to come.

He splashed water on his face and carefully dried it with a paper towel. Michael was sitting on one of the chairs in the main office, shaking his head in a familiar what-am-I-going-to-do-with-you-Kincaid fashion, as Jacob exited the bathroom. On reaching his office he could hear the low murmur of conversation from behind the half-closed door.

"-Won't let things drop," Helen was saying. "He's had a stubborn streak as long as I've known him but-."

Both women turned as he entered, the conversation apparently not for his ears.

"Got the address," Natalie said, holding up her phone.

"Good," said Jacob. "Helen, can you get down to Land and Property services? Find out who the cottage was last owned by."

She glanced at her watch. "I won't have much time before they close for the day."

"I know, but see if there's anything that stands out. While you're there, see what you can find out about Hartley House."

"The old borstal?"

Jacob nodded. "Something doesn't sit right about that place. I'm just not sure what."

Helen found a scrap piece of paper on his desk and a pen, and quickly scribbled down the instructions.

"One last thing," said Jacob. "There was a crest on one of the walls in the borstal."

"I'll probably need a little more than that."

He tried to cast his mind back. It didn't seem possible that the visit to the mansion had only been the night before. "Two horses standing on their hind legs. There was a shield between them, and I think hearts and crosses in the centre of the shield."

"And a crown above the shield," Natalie added. "There was a motto as well."

"Right," said Jacob. "Fades et virtas. Something like that."

"Fides et virtus," said Helen. "Faith and strength."

"You speak Latin?" Jacob wasn't sure why he was surprised.

"Picked it up during my brief stint as a gladiator."

"Well get on it, Helenus Maximus."

She winked and hurried out the door.

"What's our next step, Jacob?" Natalie asked.

He turned to the pinboard and considered it for a few seconds. "Him." Jacob tapped the post-it with Jermiah Pettigrew scrawled on it. "He's been too close to all of this since we started, and now he's got some of his former comrades running interference."

"You think those guys that ran us off the road were ex-IRA?" Natalie asked.

"Or current IRA, or whatever they're calling themselves these days, but yes. Hector said Pettigrew was linked to the movement and Pettigrew told me himself that he was sympathetic to their goals."

Natalie chewed on her lip. "But what would they gain from covering it up now?"

"To protect Pettigrew?"

"But why? They're not a sentimental bunch. If we're close to revealing something about him, why wouldn't they let him swing?

"I don't know, that's why we're going to go and ask him."

"Now?"

"No time like the present."

21

Michael agreed to drive them over to Natalie's house to collect her car. He parked in the street and Jacob was halfway out the door when Natalie asked him to stay where he was.

"I just need to check on Dillon first," she said. "Give me two minutes."

Frowning, Jacob sat back in his seat and watched as she hurried up the driveway. "She mustn't want him seeing me like this." He motioned a circle around his face.

Michael snorted. "Can you blame her? You look like you fell out of the just-got-my-shit-kicked-in tree and hit every branch on the way down."

Jacob didn't respond and they lapsed into silence. It was heavy, as if a conversation that should be happening, wasn't. He reached for the heating knob and turned it up to full, more to keep himself occupied than anything.

"Do you know what you're getting into, Jacob?" Michael asked finally.

"No," Jacob said quietly, still fiddling with the knob. "I don't think we do."

"Would it do any good if I told the pair of you that I think you should back off?"

As if in answer, Natalie emerged from her house and waved her car keys in their direction. Jacob offered his friend a sympathetic smile.

Michael heaved a weary sigh. "Just stay safe, alright?"

The roads were quiet as they passed through Whiteabbey, Jordanstown, and Greenisland for the second time that day. It was early evening, the rush hour was over and the majority of people who had made it to the warmth and comfort of their homes had no intention of leaving.

Ten minutes after leaving Carrickfergus behind, they reached Whitehead. They left Natalie's SUV in the car park, devoid of any other vehicle, and walked the short distance down the promenade to Pettigrew's house.

The cottage somehow looked worse in the sparse light offered by a nearby streetlight than it had on Jacob's first visit. Cautioning Natalie about the slippery path, he knocked on the door, and waited.

"No one's home," Natalie said, after half a minute. Her attention was on the window on the first floor, looking for any sign of movement.

They shared a look that confirmed neither had considered the possibility on the drive from Belfast. Natalie puffed her cheeks in frustration and turned on her heel.

"Wait," Jacob said.

"What?"

He lowered his head against the door. "I think I hear someone inside."

"You sure?"

"It sounds like they're calling for help."

"I didn't hear -" She stopped, realising what he was getting at. "An abandoned mansion is one thing. People live here." She glanced at the dilapidated building. "Allegedly."

"Someone could be in trouble."

Natalie shifted uneasily but stayed silent as Jacob tried the handle. As expected, the door was locked. Taking a firm grip of the handle, he leaned his full weight against the door. For a moment, it resisted, its hinges groaning against the unexpected force. Then, with a loud creak and the splintering of wood, the lock's old, rusted latch broke free from the frame. The door swung open, revealing the cold, musty interior of the house beyond.

"Hello?" Jacob called out. "Anyone there?" He turned to

Natalie with a theatrical shrug. "Must have been the wind."

With a last, reluctant look at the promenade, Natalie followed him inside. "What are we looking for?" she asked in a whisper.

"I'm not really sure."

Both hands shot skyward in exasperation. "Wonderful. And what's your excuse going to be if this priest comes back and finds his front door broken and us poking around his house?"

"I'm not so sure he's coming back."

"What do you mean?"

"Someone comes around asking questions about a missing boy from forty years ago. All signs point to him being involved in some way with the disappearance. I wouldn't be surprised if he's gone to ground, at least long enough for his old mates to scare us off."

Jacob reached for his phone and turned on its torch, sweeping the small light around the living room. The smell of soot and burnt paper lingered in the air. The fire had been lit recently and Jacob could see grey, flaky ash had piled up within the hearth.

The kitchen, its sink piled high with dirty dishes, lay beyond the living room. The fridge was bare, save for a bottle of curdled milk and an empty butter dish.

"Looks like you were right about them clearing out," Natalie said from over his shoulder.

The vibration of his phone was loud enough in the stillness of the house to make Jacob jump. It was Helen.

"Just got kicked out of the LPS office. Because it was closing time, not because of any impropriety," she added, the joke clear in her tone.

"What did you find?"

"Well, nothing. Not yet, at least. I can't pinpoint a clear owner for the cottage. It seems to have passed through different companies, and I didn't have enough time to dig in."

"Alright. Can you pick it up again first thing tomorrow?"

"Of course."

Jacob noticed the slight hesitation in her reply. Something was being left unsaid. "Helen, what is it?"

"It's odd. Ownership of the place got passed around a lot. Enough that I'd suggest someone is trying to obfuscate ownership."

"Obfuscate?"

"Hide."

"I know what it-" he stopped himself from taking the bait. "Obfuscate, how?"

"Like I said, it's changed hands a lot through the years. Usually to different companies, rather than private persons."

"Why?" Jacob asked himself as much as Helen.

"Not a clue. I'm going to check local planning applications when I get home. You can search them online. See if they might be able to shed some light."

"Ok, sounds good. What about the borstal, did you find anything there?"

"Didn't get a chance to look. Too busy chasing the trail for the cottage. I'll get on it tomorrow."

"Right, thank you, Helen."

Jacob pocketed the phone and asked Natalie if she got all that. She confirmed she did and with no questions forthcoming, Jacob gave the kitchen one last cursory look. Seeing nothing of interest, he led the way back toward the front of the cottage. Climbing the narrow staircase they stopped at the first door on the landing above.

Mostly certain that no one was coming home anytime soon, he flicked on the light. The small bedroom was chaotic and cramped, with every surface cluttered by magazines, forgotten dishes, and stacks of DVD and video game cases. Eddie Chambers's room, Jacob guessed.

The air was heavy with old sweat and unwashed clothes. The bed, unmade and sagging under a lumpy mattress, was pushed against the room's only window. It was the same window Jacob had felt himself being watched from when he had been leaving the cottage after his first visit.

Natalie remained at the threshold of the door, clearly not at all keen to get closer to the squalor that Chambers inhabited as Jacob began to search around the room, starting from the doorway and working clockwise.

A battered wooden dresser was his first stop. Each drawer

was slightly ajar, with clothing spilling out haphazardly. In the top drawer, amidst a tangle of mismatched socks, lay a collection of old watches, none of them working. A small desk was crammed into the corner of the room, piled high with old magazines, and a lamp without a bulb. The chair pushed under the desk was stained and torn, its cotton stuffing peeking out of tears in the leather.

He moved on to the closet, and found a mishmash of coats and shoes, some mouldy from damp, and a couple of boxes filled with assorted electronic gadgets, their cords tangled hopelessly together.

Dirty laundry had been piled at the bottom of the closet. Jacob pushed the pile aside to find three old photographs underneath, as if stashed away. He picked them up. The pictures were curled and yellowed at the edges and appeared to have been professionally taken. The first picture was of a woman, the second a baby, and the final was of the two together. The woman holding the child beamed at the camera with unabashed joy.

Jacob checked the rearside of each. On the photo of the woman by herself someone had written *Mummy, 1962* in a childlike scrawl. He carefully put the pictures back where he had found them.

"Find anything?" Natalie asked. "Other than new and exciting types of bacteria?"

Jacob sighed and glanced at the lumpy mattress. With his thumb and forefinger touching as little of the duvet as possible, he peeled it back.

"I hope you realise I expect you to jump in the sea before you step foot back in my car."

"Usually, I have a couple of boxes of latex gloves in the boot," Jacob said as he reached under the limp, dirty pillow that was nearly indistinguishable from the rest of the bedding. "I guess that's another thing I need to add to -"

He stopped as his fingers brushed against something unexpectedly hard. He took a hold and pulled it out. It was a watch.

A Rolex.

Incongruous in the grotty bedroom, Jacob could see that

although the gold and silver of the watch band were smeared with a thin layer of grime, the band and the face were unscathed.

He turned and held it up to Natalie. Her mouth fell open and she stepped forward, any aversion to the room forgotten. "So, it was Chambers who attacked Zara."

"Looks like it," replied Jacob.

Zara's mugging had been swift and calculated. He didn't normally judge a book by the cover, but he had a hard time matching his one meeting with Chambers against any action that could be deemed swift or calculating. And yet, the evidence was held in Jacob's hand that he had.

He turned the watch over and noticed the engraving on the case.

Earned Not Given
- Z

"It's definitely Zara's," he said.

"Good to get confirmation. You don't want to be finding the wrong Rolex under that pillow."

"Such snark, Ms. Amato. You've been hanging around me for too long." He smiled and then felt a kick in the guts as sudden realisation hit him. "Fuck."

"What?"

He held up the Rolex. "If they had this..."

Natalie's shoulders sagged as she followed his train of thought. "Then they had the file."

"The fireplace."

They rushed downstairs but Jacob wasn't sure why. Natalie took a poker from beside the fireplace and used it to sift through the ash. Carefully, she reached into the gritty remains, her fingers delicately teasing out several fragments of paper, their edges brittle and curled from the heat.

She handed him the largest surviving piece. Jacob recognised it immediately as part of the log used by the Borstal to chronicle Finbar Skelly's escape attempts.

"Shit!" He tossed the fragment back into the fireplace.

"There was something in that file we weren't meant to see."

"But what?" Jacob leaned an elbow against the dust-caked mantle. His nose throbbed and his head seared with a dull, pulsating pain. "The three of us went through it and nothing jumped out."

"Not deep enough apparently. We should have spent more time going over it."

Jacob kicked the hearth. "Yeah, we should have."

He glanced back up towards the stairs. He wanted to get out of there. To leave the old, crumbling house behind. He wanted to go home and shower, to wash away the stench of this case. To purge himself of missing children and grieving mothers, of old buildings and their ghosts, of blood stains on the floor and of predators who called in the night.

And yet, he knew he wouldn't. Not yet. Not when there were still answers to be found. He couldn't let things go. That was his problem.

One of many, he supposed.

So he took the stairs once more. He could hear Natalie following. He knew she would.

Pettigrew's bedroom was cold and sparse. Jacob began to search it in the same fashion as he had the other, beginning at the door and working back to his starting point.

A bedside table and wardrobe yielded nothing. As Jacob had a hoak through a creaky wooden dresser he noticed an envelope wedged at the back of the top drawer. It was yellowed with age, and bulged with whatever was held inside. He opened the loose flap and tipped the contents into his hand.

It was a stack of black and white photographs. The pictures were faded, the lighting poor. Some were grainy, others slightly blurred, but as Jacob began to flick through them, what they depicted was all too clear.

Young boys, expressions detached, eyes void. One boy in each photo. One man in each photo. The men in various states of undress.

Jacob stopped at one picture. A naked man so fat that his skin seemed to spill over the confines of the chair he was seated in, dominated most of the image. Even through the grainy, faded quality of the photo, Jacob could make out the sheen of sweat that seemed to coat the man's skin.

He smiled towards a boy who had his back to the camera. His head was bowed as if avoiding eye contact with the creature in front of him, his shoulders hunched, to shrink away from the presence that regarded without remorse or shame.

Jacob felt bile tickle the back of his throat. He couldn't face looking through the rest. He passed the photographs to Natalie.

She quickly flicked through the collection, her jaw tightening with each one. She made it to four before handing them back to Jacob. "Jesus Christ."

Jacob stood up. He felt sick, tired, and so very sad. "Pettigrew had a reason to keep these." He turned the photos over. Each had a surname and date scribbled on the back in neat penmanship. Names of the boys?

He forced himself to look at the pictures again. The boys usually had their backs to the camera, their faces often blurred by motion, or obscured by the position they stood in. They weren't the focus, who they were with was.

"Blackmail," said Jacob, with a sudden certainty.

Natalie twisted her mouth. "They're old photos. I'd guess at least thirty years or so. Why would Pettigrew keep them?"

"Aside from being a twisted old pervert?" Jacob shrugged. "Insurance maybe?"

"Against who?"

Jacob didn't have an answer for that. He couldn't focus. His mind felt fuzzy. He needed to get out of the house, to get a clean break where he could take a step back and think.

He put the photographs back in the yellowed envelope. "Let's get everyone together."

22

Jacob phoned Zara and gave her Breen's address, telling her to meet them there in an hour. She said that she'd see them there without questioning what was going on.

"Why Hector's house?" Natalie asked as Jacob ended the call. "Your office is central, rather than have three of us traipse out to Moira."

"I'm worried the office is being watched. The four of us meeting there might set off alarm bells."

"Hector thought someone was snooping around his place a couple of nights back."

"But hasn't seen anyone since, and I'm certain Hector would pick up anyone running surveillance on his house."

They made it to Moira in a shade under an hour. Snow began to fall as they passed the sign welcoming them to the village. Flakes landed silently on the windshield, their intricate patterns visible for only a moment before melting away.

Turning in to Hector's street, Jacob could see Zara had beaten them there, her silhouette just about visible behind the wheel of her car. She got out as they did.

"Oh my God -"

Jacob caught the reaching hand and held it for a second. "Let's talk about it inside," he said as Natalie stepped past and rapped Hector's front door.

It was opened immediately and Hector motioned them

inside, pointing towards the kitchen. "Bloody rotten night, the cold would skin you, so it would." He took one look at Jacob's face. "Looks like you've had a day of it."

"I'll say," Zara answered. "Last I heard, you were going to track down the borstal's old matron."

"And we did," said Jacob. "Poor woman can't talk. Had her tongue sliced out, her face cut up, her fingers amputated by persons unknown."

"Fuck me," said Hector.

"Connected to the case?" asked Zara.

"We don't know," replied Jacob. "She was however, able to point us in the direction of an old cottage out in the countryside near Carrickfergus."

"And?" Zara pressed.

"And we found a picture of Jeremiah Pettigrew, Finbar Skelly, and a few other boys," said Jacob. "Oh, we also found a secret room, set up to record whatever was happening on the other side."

Zara frowned. "What do you mean, record?"

"Well," said Jacob, "We'll come to that."

"We also found a basement," Natalie said, taking over the telling. "With what looked like old bloodstains on the floor."

"And then we were rudely interrupted by a few toughs. They burned out my car and did this." Jacob indicated his busted face.

"Wow, wait," said Zara, "They did what to your car?

"We then went to Pettigrew's house," said Natalie.

"And what did that bastard say?" asked Hector.

"Nothing. He'd already cleared out. But..." Jacob reached into the pocket of his jacket and brought out Zara's watch. "We did find this."

Zara's hand went to her mouth. The action caused the sleeve of her coat to slide down enough to reveal she had already replaced the missing watch with what looked like an equally expensive piece.

"Hold on a minute," said Hector as Zara took her Rolex from Jacob. "You found Zara's watch in Pettigrew's house?"

"In the room of his...companion," said Jacob. "Hidden under a pillow."

"So he attacked Zara?"

"Looks that way," said Natalie. "We also found the remnants of Finbar Skelly's borstal file. They burned it."

Zara's shoulders dipped. "Shit."

"That's not all," Jacob said. "We also found, well..."

He pulled the yellowed envelope from the pocket of his coat and then spread the old, faded photographs across the kitchen table.

The quartet regarded them in silence.

"Blackmail." It was Hector who finally spoke, echoing Jacob's theory. He removed his glasses and rubbed a hand over his face.

Jacob nodded. "My working hypothesis is that Pettigrew, along with a couple of warders at the borstal, were pimping boys, including Finbar Skelly. They hosted parties at the borstal and then used the cottage for more...."

"...More private meetings," said Natalie quietly. "Recorded or photographed without the knowledge of the men involved. Blackmail, like you said."

Hector folded his arms. "And you think Pettigrew was working on behalf of the IRA." He had started to go through the photos, picking each one up, studying the name on the back, and then setting it back down.

"It makes the most sense," said Jacob. "I'm guessing once we start digging into those names, some influential people are going to crop up."

Hector nodded once. "What about the missing girls? Do you think they tie in at all?"

Jacob closed his eyes. He wanted to be back in his office, looking at the pinboard so he could visualise the moving parts. How did the missing girls fit in? He hadn't studied the photos in great detail, he couldn't face it, but he was confident that all the victims were male.

"Jesus Christ." Hector stared at one of the photographs, his jaw slack.

"What?" Zara asked.

"I know this man."

They crowded around Hector. The man he was referring to was handsome, with swept back hair, a sharp jawline and a high forehead. The lines around his eyes were tight and drawn, and his posture, though seated, was rigidly upright.

His hand rested on the slender shoulder of a shirtless boy who appeared unable to meet his gaze.

"Phillip Sansom," Hector said.

"Should we know who that is?" asked Jacob.

"He was a senior civil servant in the Northern Ireland Office during The Troubles." Hector looked at Jacob. "His department worked with RUC senior management."

Jacob felt the flutter in his chest and made a leap. "The type of person, who, say for arguments sake, might be able to put the kibbosh on an investigation into missing girls."

Hector didn't reply.

"Wonder if he's still alive," Natalie said quietly.

"Oh, he's still alive," Hector spat. "Bastard sits in the House of bloody Lords." He smacked the table with a meaty fist and stood so suddenly his chair toppled over. "Kincaid, come with me."

It was said with such authority that Jacob didn't think twice, rising to his feet.

"Wait," Zara said. "Where are you going?"

"To speak to my old boss," Hector answered.

"Stop." The single word from Zara came out as a command. She stepped in front of Hector, blocking his path.

"Stop?" Hector asked incredulously.

"Emotions are running high here." Next to Hector's meaty frame, Zara was diminutive, but her eyes met his without flinching. "We need to stop and think about what we're doing next."

"I know what I'm doing next."

"No," said Zara. "Look at what we have here. Evidence of who knows how many horrible crimes. It's time to follow procedure."

"Here we go," Natalie whispered, quiet enough that Jacob was sure he was the only one who heard her.

"Firstly," said Zara, indicating the photos sitting on the kitchen table. "This is evidence. It needs to be seized and logged."

"Seized?" Jacob almost laughed. "Zara, you know how we got these, there's no way that'll stand up in court."

Zara turned to him. "I can't just let you hold onto them. It's bordering on an offence just having them in your possession."

"Oh come on," he replied, not quite believing she was serious. Zara glared hard to assure him that she was.

Hector took it as his moment to act, brushing past her and into the hallway. He lifted a heavy coat from a peg beside the front door. "Enough talking." He yanked open his front door and motioned for everyone to get out. "Former Superintendent Haywood is seeing out his days in a grand house near Lisburn. You're all free to come along, although I don't plan on talking nice."

"I'm not sure I care for that implication, Mr. Breen," said Zara.

"I couldn't give two fucks." Hector strode across to his car with Natalie and Jacob following close behind.

The snow was falling freely now as the trio got into the Volvo. Hector didn't wait to see what Zara was doing. He gunned the engine and the car shot forwards. If he had any concern about the downturn in weather effecting the road conditions, the old man didn't show it.

In less than ten minutes, he pulled the car off the road and onto a winding drive that led to a large, two-storey house with a single light burning in an upstairs room. A vintage green Aston Martin was the only vehicle in the driveway.

Breen bounced out of his car, up the steps, and began to pound on the heavy door. He continued the racket unabated for close to half a minute before a light on the other side was switched on.

The man who opened the door cautiously peeked around from the other side. He was of an age with Hector, but while Breen still carried a solid frame, the man who Jacob assumed was Haywood, was short, and slight in stature.

"Hector Breen?" God, I...it's been -"

"-A long time." Hector shouldered the door open and stepped inside. Jacob and Natalie followed. From behind, Jacob could hear a car door slamming and the sound of hurried feet on gravel. Zara had caught up with them outside Moira and had just about managed to keep pace with Hector's rallying through the back roads.

It was only when Zara entered the house that Haywood asked, "Who are these people?"

"Friends," Breen replied. "Friends who want answers."

Haywood wore an expression of absolute perplexity. "About what?"

"Edith Galbraith," said Hector. "Ciara Watson, Lauren-"

"Jesus, those missing girls? It's been forty years, Hector. You have to -"

"-Don't." Hector leaned in close to the other man. "Don't think about telling me to let it go or some other shite. I still remember that day, you know? When you called me into the office. Poured me a brandy, told me I'd done some fine work but it was time to drop it."

"You had, and it was."

"And when I resisted? When I said I wanted to keep working it? Do you remember what you told me then? Looked me in the eye and said you'd give me a choice of whatever border station I wanted."

Haywood's look hardened. "You know what your problem was, Breen?"

"Oh, where would I start?"

"You were always so far up your own arse. You were good, I'll give you that, but that's all you were. Maybe if you'd spent less time at the bottom of a bottle, you could have found what happened to those girls. But instead you want to blame everyone else for your failure. That's what it was. I didn't say it then, but I should have. It was a failure. You failed."

Breen loomed over Haywood forcing the smaller man to take a step back. "I saw the light on upstairs. Bedroom?"

"Study," Haywood replied, uneasy with the sudden change in topic.

Hector took Haywood by the arm and led him towards the stairs. "Let's talk in private. Jacob, join us."

Jacob didn't argue. This was Hector's show. As he went to follow, so did Zara. She was stopped by Natalie, who pulled her back gently.

"Just wait and see," Jacob heard Natalie whisper. Zara responded by throwing her hands in the air. She wasn't in control and hated it.

Jacob trailed the pair of older men up the stairs, along the landing, and into a plush study.

"Jesus," Hector said, only releasing his grip on Haywood's

arm once there were in the room. "This must be some view during the day." He nodded toward a large window overlooking what Jacob assumed to be rolling countryside. It was hard to tell in the dark. He walked to the window and then opened it. It swung inwards bringing a draught of sharp, cold air. "I never thought about it. Why I was pulled off the investigation, I mean. Whims of the bosses, who can tell?"

"You had nothing to show -"

"-Then I send one report mentioning the link between the care homes," Breen continued, talking over Haywood. "And suddenly the case is dead. Explain that."

"Explain what? You had nothing to show and maybe it escaped your attention, but there were other things happening in Belfast at the time. More important than some missing runaways and ghost stories."

"Ghost stories," said Jacob. "You mean Ned by Night."

Haywood looked at Jacob and then rolled his eyes. "Don't tell me you've got someone to believe your shite, Breen."

Hector reached into his coat and produced the photograph. Jacob hadn't realised Hector had taken it, and now watched the colour drain from Haywood's face.

"About the reaction I was expecting. You recognise Lord Sansom, I take it?" Hector flipped the picture over and read the date. "June 1982. Well, I suppose he wouldn't have been Lord Sansom then, just a minister with the Northern Ireland Office. You and he worked pretty closely together though, right?"

Haywood forced a laugh and looked between Jacob and Hector. "What is this?"

"This is the sound of the truth being laid bare, you bastard," Hector suddenly shouted, jabbing a finger at Haywood.

"Wh-what truth?"

"Missing children. Boys and girls, maybe a dozen or so. Bastards like your pal, Sansom, taking advantage and then getting blackmailed. Blackmailed to put the squeeze on a toad like you, to put the squeeze on me, to drop the investigation."

Haywood licked his lips. "You have proof?"

"We're getting there."

"Getting there," Haywood scoffed.

"I always thought you were a scummy fucker," said Hector.

"Did you now?" Haywood's air of boredom rang hollow.

"Scummy but not stupid. You had something."

Jacob watched the slightest shift in Haywood's posture.

Hector saw it too. He stepped up to the smaller man. "What was it?" Another almost imperceptible shift from Haywood. Hector narrowed his eyes, pushed his face into Haywood's space. "What *is* it?"

"I have no idea what you're talking about."

Hector took a breath, looked up at the ceiling as if searching for inspiration, or a divine interruption. He seemed to have found it as he suddenly grabbed Haywood by the scruff of the sweater and began to drag him across the room.

Haywood's feet scrambled for purchase, his legs kicking at air as he clawed at Hector's grip.

It took Jacob a second to realise what Hector was doing and felt his stomach drop as it clicked.

Haywood, getting ever closer to the open window, came to the same conclusion. He tried to twist his body, to wriggle out of Breen's hold, but it only seemed to tighten the larger man's grip. As they reached the window, Breen stopped and hauled Haywood back to his feet and shoved him against the sill.

"Hector, please!"

What?" Breen's look softened and the grip on Haywood's sweater loosened. "Jesus, Cecil, did you think I was going to throw you out the window?"

Haywood nodded, his cheeks reddening. "Yes, I-uh, I suppose I did."

"See! I told you that you weren't stupid."

Haywood screamed as Hector lifted him clean off his feet. Arms flailed, seeking something, anything, to grasp onto, but there was nothing but the smooth, cold rim of the window. And then he was through it, falling into the night air, only stopped from plunging to the ground by Hector's grip on his ankles.

"Hector!" Haywood wailed. "Hector please!"

Jacob stepped up to Hector's shoulder. He could see the stark terror in Haywood's eyes. Breen's face, by contrast, was a mask of absolute indifference, his jaw set, his eyes hard.

Jacob wasn't so sure he was only trying to scare the man.

"What the fuck!" Zara, apparently drawn out of the house by the commotion above, looked up at them before dashing back inside.

"You going to give me what I want?"

"Yes, yes! Please Hector!"

"Sorry, getting on a bit these days, hearing isn't what it once was. What did you say?"

"I said I'll give it to you! Just, please, pull me up!"

The study door crashed open, "Enough!" Zara strode across the room, her tone brokering no argument. "Hector! Pull him up, now!"

Hector smirked. "Give us a hand, Jacob."

Jacob complied, reaching over the window to grasp Haywood's wrist. Pushing a foot against the sill to brace himself, he and Hector lifted him back into the room. Haywood's breath came in ragged gasps as he collapsed into a trembling ball. He had pissed himself.

"What were you thinking?" Zara demanded, squaring up to Hector.

"We need answers."

"Not like this!"

"Zara." Jacob tried to take her by the elbow but she shook him off. This time there was no holding her back. She rounded on him and he held up his hands in apology. "Let Hector talk to him -"

"-Talk to him! This is how he talks?"

"The man fell through the window," said Breen. "Thank god I managed to catch him."

"Oh, fuck off, Hector!" Zara snapped.

"I'll talk to you, Hector." Haywood's voice was raspy with fresh fear. "Just you."

"Give me two minutes, Zara," Hector said. His face and his tone softened. "Two minutes."

"Not happening."

Hector clenched his teeth and took a long breath. "Talk to you?" he said quietly, inclining his head towards the door.

Zara hesitated, her eyes narrowing slightly, but after a moment she gave a curt nod of agreement. Jacob led the way out of the room. Natalie was waiting in the corridor. Jacob was only over the threshold when Zara gave a shout of surprise as she barged into him.

"No fucking -" She was cut off by the slamming of the study door and the *click* of a lock on the other side. "Hector!" Zara threw herself at the door, pounding with a closed fist. "Hector, open this door, now!"

She took a step back and Jacob saw she intended to try and kick the door in. He stepped in front of her.

"Move!"

Jacob held his ground. "Zara. Work with him. Give him the two minutes."

For a moment, it seemed like Zara might ignore him and kick him in along with the door. Instead, she shook her head and crossed her arms, glaring at Jacob.

"What happened?" Natalie asked.

"Don't ask," Zara snapped and turned back to Jacob. "You were okay to go along with that?"

"Did you see the same pictures I did?"

"Don't give me that shit, Jacob. At the end of the day, I'm looking to build a case here. How can I do that with a witness or a defendant claiming they were beat up and hung out a window. Fifteen minutes ago you were being precious about those pictures being seized, but now you think what Hector did is alright?"

Jacob didn't have an answer for that.

Zara took a breath. "I said it before and I'll say it again. We need to slow this down. We're all amped up and going at a hundred miles an hour. We need to take a step back and think about what comes next. If we rush too far ahead we could damage the investigation."

"We have momentum," said Jacob. "We need to keep it."

"That's not your decision to make -"

She was interrupted by the study door opening. Hector stepped into the corridor.

"Well?" Zara demanded.

"It's a file."

"On what?" asked Natalie.

"A paedophile ring." He paused. "At Hartley House."

The name hung in the air. No one spoke, until Jacob eventually said, "The RUC already investigated Hartley

House?"

"Apparently," answered Hector. "Haywood says the file has witness statements, surveillance reports, documentation of who came and went."

"The police knew about a paedophile ring and did nothing?" Zara's tone conveyed obvious doubt.

Jacob felt the same doubt, not to mention a rapidly rising number of questions.

"Haywood kept the file for insurance," Hector said, "Should they ever try to burn him."

"We need to see it," said Zara.

"And we will. Superintendent Haywood has seen the light. He's going to give it to me."

"No," said Zara. "He's going to give it to me."

"That's not going to work," replied Hector. He held up a hand to cut off any protestations from Zara. "He's a smart man and he's clocked you for a peeler."

"So?"

"So, he's not going to incriminate himself. He says he wants to make it right. I say he wants to stall so he can think of the best way to protect himself from the shitstorm coming his way. Me and him are going to have a long talk. There are things that need to be said. Let's meet in the morning and we can see what he has."

"That's not going to work," said Zara.

"It's the only way it's going to work," replied Breen. "Besides, we don't want to make a habit of losing important files, do we?"

Zara's expression turned stone. "Fuck you, Hector." She stormed off down the corridor.

"That was wrong," said Natalie. She fixed the old man with a measured stare and then turned to go after Zara.

Hector heaved a regretful sigh and looked at Jacob. "What a horrible thing to say. What's wrong with me?"

"Heat of the moment," Jacob said.

Hector shook his head and then smirked. "Thank God she burst in when she did. I don't think I could have held onto him for much longer."

Jacob inclined his head toward the study where Haywood had yet to reemerge from. "Do you believe him?"

"I do. Doesn't mean I trust him."

"I'd say that's smart." Jacob rubbed at his chin, bamboozled by the revelation of the file. "Hector, did Hartley House ever come up in your original investigations into the missing girls?"

"No, never. Why would it have? It was a boys only institution."

"So why would Haywood have a file on it? You worked in Belfast. Millisle would have been in a completely different district, under a different area commander."

"I know," said Hector. "Was pondering it myself, and it's a question I'll be asking." He leaned against the wall, suddenly looking every bit his age. "When you and Natalie came to my house. What was the name of that phantom criminal of yours?"

It took Jacob a second to realise what Breen was talking about. The meeting in his living room seemed a long time ago. "Poddy Sweeny."

The old man grunted. "Poddy Sweeny. I can see why you came up with a ghost story, Kincaid. Easier to get your head around that than what we deal with in the real world."

23

Jacob found Natalie and Zara waiting downstairs by the front door. "You alright?" His question was directed at Zara.

She took a slow breath. "I don't love my failures getting rubbed in my face."

"Hector didn't mean -"

"It's fine," Zara cut him off sharply and then seemed to realise she was taking it out on the wrong person. "Sorry. I have a habit of taking things personally."

"Not a bad trait to have," said Jacob.

"I'm not so sure," said Zara. She clucked her tongue. "So, what's our plan here? Just wait for Hector to come through?"

"I'm not sure what else we can do," said Jacob. "Haywood isn't going to deal with you, or anyone other than Hector."
"What's your read?" Natalie asked.

"I don't think he's going to give Hector any trouble," said Jacob. "And I don't think he's bluffing. Hector's too wily to fall for it."

Natalie shifted as she considered this. "You think he's on the level?"

"I think so," Jacob said carefully. "My issue is, why would Haywood have ordered an investigation into Hartley House?"

"Because it wouldn't have been his district," said Zara, catching on to the same issue Jacob had. "I don't like it. We're missing something."

"Maybe," said Jacob. "But I trust Hector to get to the bottom of it. For now, I say we let him and Haywood hash it out and we all get together in the morning, review this file, and decide where this investigation goes."

Natalie and Zara both murmured agreement. Seemingly surplus to requirements, the trio got into Zara's BMW and drove back to Hector's house to pick up Natalie's car.

Stopping alongside it, Natalie thanked Zara for the lift and got out. Jacob hesitated. The connection from the night before and their kiss that morning had been on his mind. He had hoped they could get a moment, but Zara was clearly elsewhere, almost certainly still stinging from Hector's unfair rebuke.

"So, talk tomorrow?" he ventured.

The words seemed to shake her from wherever her mind was. "Yeah," she said, clearing her throat. "Tomorrow." She waited until he had got out of the car before saying, "Jacob."

He poked his head back in. "Yeah?"

Zara took a breath and then waved a hand. "Don't worry, it's not important."

Jacob closed the door reluctantly and waved as Zara turned in the street and drove off. She didn't wave back.

The snow was falling harder now, and Natalie slowed to match the worsening conditions. Hot air blasted from the heater, cocooning the SUV in a comforting embrace. Jacob was done-in, the long day, the adrenaline dump of the car chase, and the beating that followed teamed-up against him now, dimming his senses as he sank down into the leather seat.

And then he was back in Hartley House. His breath came in ragged gasps as he ran through dark corridors that warped around him, sturdy lines of construction now bending at unnatural angles.

He was being chased. Could feel it behind him. A suffocating presence. A dark weight pressing on his back, urging him forwards. The figure was wrapped in crisp white bandages, pristine yet wrong, too bright against the decaying backdrop of the mansion. It hovered, moving with an eerie, deliberate pace that steadily closed the gap in its pursuit through the guts of the old mansion.

Doors loomed out of the darkness on either side, but when he grabbed for a handle, they wouldn't budge. The house groaned and whispered. Faint cries echoed somewhere deep within, fragmented voices of forgotten boys.

The corridors seemed never-ending, until at last he came to a room. A solitary person sat on the lone seat. Patricia Ambrose, her face cut to pieces, regarded him with those cold eyes.

She opened her mouth and screamed.

Jacob jolted awake.

"Perfect timing," said Natalie.

She had come to a stop on the street closest to Jacob's apartment complex. Jacob patted his cheek, willing himself to shake off the dregs of the nightmare and numbly reached for the door.

"Good night," Natalie called after him. "Give me a call in the morning."

Nerves still on edge, he hurried up to his apartment. He had just begun a search for something to eat when the door knocked and Jacob just about jumped out of his skin.

It knocked again. Jacob hurried across to his bedroom and lifted the old baton which he had left sitting on the nightstand.

"Jacob?" The voice, female, was muffled from the other side of the door.

"Zara?" He lobbed the baton onto the bed and hurried over to let her in. She was framed by the dim light of the corridor, her eyes dancing with a playfulness that immediately set his pulse jittering. "What's wrong?"

She tilted her head slightly, a faint smirk tugging at the corner of her lips. "Does something have to be wrong?"

"No, but at times it feels like the question I should lead with."

"Sorry about earlier. Lots of things on my mind."

"I get it," Jacob said, dismissing the apology.

"All the talk last night about what I was missing out on, and there I go, doing it again."

"But you're here now."

"Yes. I am."

With a deliberate slowness, Zara stepped closer, closing the gap between them. She reached up, her thumb brushing lightly along the line of his jaw. Anticipation, thick and undeniable and then, as if the tension had finally snapped, Zara tipped her chin up, and her lips met his.

Jacob wrapped his arms around her, pulling her close, feeling the warmth of her body against his. The kiss grew urgent, more insistent. Zara's fingers dug through the fabric of his sweater into sore, bruised muscles. He barely noticed. The world narrowed down to the sensation of her lips on his, the taste of her breath, the soft moan that escaped as she pressed herself against him.

A sharp, unexpected jolt of pain snapped him back to reality. Zara's kiss shifted, just slightly, pressing near the bridge of his nose. He winced as pain, sharp and hot, radiated across his face. He quickly smothered the reaction, burying the discomfort, refusing to let it break the moment.

Zara didn't seem to notice. Her body leaned into his as Jacob's hand tightened at her waist, pushing the pain in his nose to the back of his mind. As they pulled closer, her fingers brushed his jaw again, and he flinched internally, but didn't pull away. Instead, he adjusted, tilting his head slightly to avoid the most tender spot, his movements smooth enough to seem deliberate.

Zara broke the kiss and gently pushed him away. Her eyes locked on his and with deliberate, unhurried movements, she shrugged off her coat and then her sweater. She began to unbutton her blouse. Each button slipped free, revealing more of her fair, smooth skin, glowing softly in the dim light of the apartment.

She let the loose blouse falls off her shoulders, and then unhooked the bra and let it drop. She stood in front of him with an unshakable confidence that left Jacob breathless.

Backing away slowly, her eyes remained locked, inviting him to follow. He caught up to her at the threshold of the bedroom door and she let him pull her close once more, her arms wrapping around his neck as they kissed.

The sex that followed was clumsy and frenetic. The lovemaking of two lonely souls craving something they had both missed and were now trying too hard to make up for.

Once finished, they lay panting and spent, entwined in a tangle of bed sheets. The urgency that had driven them quickly faded into a peaceful lull. Zara shifted against him, her head resting on his chest, an arm draped comfortably over his waist. Her fingers traced lazy, aimless patterns on his skin.

Jacob's fingers were tangled in her short, dark hair. She drifted off to sleep. Every now and then, a soft sigh or a gentle shift in position punctuated the silence, a quiet reaffirmation of her presence in his arms. He let himself enjoy the feeling of contentment as he breathed in the scent of her hair, a mix of her floral shampoo and the faint, lingering trace of the just spent past passion.

The cold world beyond the bedroom window seemed suddenly distant and inconsequential. For now, he could forget about missing boys and shadowy men and their grubby deals. He could lie here.

24

Jacob stirred, caught in that hazy place between sleep and waking, as the mattress dipped and then rose. A chill crept over his skin as the duvet lifted, exposing his bare shoulders to cool air.

He opened his eyes to see Zara's naked figure, silhouetted against the window by the dawn light of a Belfast winter morning, padding softly across his bedroom and into the en suite. The shower started and he drifted off.

When he woke again, the shower had fallen silent, but he could hear Zara in the kitchen. He got up, brushed his teeth, regarded his battered reflection in the mirror, and took a quick shower.

Back in his bedroom, he checked his phone, hoping to see a call or text from Hector. The only message was from Natalie, telling him she had gotten home safely. Trying to ignore the flash of guilt that he hadn't noticed the message until just then, he threw on some fresh clothes and went into the kitchen.

Zara was seated at the counter, holding the Rolex Jacob had returned the night before, seemingly lost in her own thoughts.

"Earned, not given, huh?"

She looked up as he spoke, seemingly in a world of her own. "That's right," she replied, managing half a smile. "Nothing given."

He started to brew some coffee and thought about breakfast, but aside from Coco Pops, what he had to offer was embarrassingly limited. Zara had gone back to looking at her watch. "Something on your mind?"

"Just thinking," she said.

"Always dangerous. About?"

"How big this could be."

"Yeah?" Jacob glanced over his shoulder. "Getting cold feet?"

"Yes."

He turned fully at the answer, not expecting Zara's ambition to have a limiter. "What, you serious?"

"Yeah, I'm serious. We went from four missing boys, and in less than five days have somehow involved a number of missing women, the IRA, senior RUC management, and a peer in the House of Lords." Jacob moved to speak but she swiped her hand cutting him off. "Natalie's studio gets vandalised, you get beat up, your car is burned out, I get knocked unconscious, and to top it all off, Hector Breen hangs a retired Chief Superintendent out a damn window."

"Everything you mentioned is a piece of the puzzle. Everything that's happened means we're on the right track"

"Or it means everything is falling apart and we're in too deep to notice."

"This is what detective work is. You chase the leads."

Zara closed her eyes and took a breath. Jacob realised he had misspoken, lecturing her on what detective work was. "All I'm saying is, we're moving way too fast."

"Alright," Jacob said, relieved that she didn't make issue of it and not wanting to antagonise further. "Let's wait to hear from Hector. See what Haywood came up with. Then we can talk about what's best moving forward."

Zara rubbed a hand over her face and leaned back in the chair without further argument. She was tense. Jacob watched as she fixed the Rolex back on her wrist. His phone vibrated in his pocket as the watch clasped shut. He expected to see Hector's name, but instead saw it was Helen calling.

"Morning," he answered.

"Morning," she said. "I'm down at the LPS office."

Jacob lifted his phone away from his ear to check the time on the display. "Early on the go."

"It's what you pay me the big bucks for."

Jacob snorted. "I assume you have something?"

"Maybe. I stared with Hartley House and found out a bit of interesting info."

"Go on."

"The prison service never owned the house."

"That can't be right, Helen. Sure they sold it off a few years ago."

"No," Helen replied. "They may have sold off part of the estate, but from what I can see here, the mansion itself was never sold. To anyone."

Jacob felt himself squinting. "So..."

"So, bearing in mind I've only started my research and may not be in possession of all the facts, it looks like the government, and later the prison service, owned much of the grounds but presumably only rented the mansion."

"Why?"

"Who knows? Maybe the upkeep was too much for the original owners, but they didn't want to part with it, and decided they could make a profit in the meantime."

"Ok," Jacob said slowly. "So, who owns it now?"

"That's a little harder to figure out. Portions of the records are missing."

"Balls."

"Such eloquence," Helen said. "But you mentioned the crest you saw when you and Natalie were there?"

"Yeah?"

"Did a little digging on that last night when I got home. It's the heraldry of the Duke of Whitburn."

"Who?"

"The Alcorn family. The current Duke of Whitburn is James Alcorn. He's also an officer in the Order of the Garter."

"So many words, Helen, most of them not making sense on my end of the conversation."

"The crest you and Natalie saw belongs to an extremely influential family. Actual British nobility. If their crest is in Hartley House..."

"Then it's probably safe to assume they owned it, and if the house was never sold, likely still do."

"Such a clever young man."

"Does land and property have any records before the prison service took over?"

"No. At least, not that I've found yet."

Jacob thanked Helen and asked her to keep digging. Ending the call, he turned to Zara. "You get all that?"

"I did, but what does it mean?"

"That is an excellent question" Jacob replied. The aristocracy connection was an interesting aside but he wasn't really sure it was anything more.

He checked his phone again to see if Hector had called during his brief conversation with Helen. When he saw he hadn't, he phoned Natalie.

"Hi, has Hector called you?"

"And good morning to you," Natalie replied. "No, Hector hasn't called, and I wasn't expecting him to. You seem to be his point of contact." She waited a beat. "Something wrong?"

"No, just keen. I'm going to head over."

"What, to his house?"

"Yeah."

"In your car?"

"Shit." Jacob said, suddenly remembering the smouldering remains of his poor Clio and thinking he should probably call someone about it.

Natalie laughed. "Give me half an hour, I'll come get you."

"It's alright. Zara can take me."

"I can be there before Zara gets over...ah," she intoned knowingly. "She's already there."

Jacob glanced up at Zara who was listening in on the conversation. She raised her eyebrows conspiratorially.

"You crazy kids," Natalie said lightly. "Want me to meet you both at Hector's?"

"Yeah. We can sit down as a group and discuss what we have."

"Alright. See you in an hour or so."

The snowfall had stopped at some point before first light, but the temperature had continued to drop until sunrise, turning soft, powdery snow into hard, slick sheets of ice that clung stubbornly to the roads and pavements.

They moved in inches through Belfast's morning congestion. It wasn't until they got through the Westlink and past the Sprucefield exit that the traffic thinned, giving them a clear, albeit cautious, run to Moira.

Jacob had tried to phone Hector as he and Zara had left his apartment, and again while sitting on the Westlink. Neither call was answered, and a small knot of worry settled in his gut. If Zara shared his concern, she didn't voice it, keeping her attention on the road.

When they pulled up to Hector's house Jacob was relieved to see his Volvo was outside. The curtains were pulled in the downstairs living room and in the windows upstairs. It had been late when they left Hector with Haywood, and no doubt it had been the small hours of the morning before he made it home. The excitement, not to mention the physical exertion of hanging a fully grown man out of a window, had almost certainly caught up with him.

Jacob knocked on the front door and waited. The air was sharp, and the chill quickly seeped through his clothing. His busted nose throbbed dully at first, and the longer they waited in the cold, the sharper the pain became, radiating across his face with each shallow breath of icy air.

There was no answer and Jacob knocked again, louder. He took a step back, watching for any twitch at the curtains on the first floor. He glanced at Zara, who was also watching the upper floor, and then took his phone from his pocket and hit Hector's number. He pressed his ear to the door, listening for a ring tone but heard nothing.

He crouched and peered through the letterbox, but the hallway was clear.

"Walked to the shop?" Zara offered as Jacob stood back up.

"He hasn't answered his phone all morning," Jacob said. He tried the door handle and felt a sick feeling wash over him as it depressed fully. He stepped into the hallway and called out, "Hector?"

His footsteps were loud on the wooden floor. The kitchen was straight ahead and Jacob could now see a number of cabinets were lying open. On his right, the door to the living room was partially shut. Jacob stopped, and then nudged the door slowly.

The room was a wreck. Cushions were strewn across the floor, the coffee table was overturned, and a lamp lay shattered near the fireplace. Hector lay among the debris, utterly still.

Jacob heard Zara step up behind him, her breath catching as she took in the sight. Jacob's shoes crunched on broken glass as he moved to the old man and knelt beside him.

Hector's eyes were open, glazed and unseeing. His face was almost unrecognisable, swollen and mottled with bruises, his nose smashed to one side, blood crusting around the nostrils and down into his mouth, which was slightly ajar, revealing broken teeth. One eye socket appeared to be shattered, the bone beneath caved in. A halo of blood had pooled beneath his head, stark against the pale wood of the floor.

There was no pulse, Jacob knew that without needing to check and yet, he reached out a hand, touching Hector's shoulder gently, almost as if to offer some final comfort.

"Jacob," Zara said quietly. It was a gentle reproach. This was a crime scene.

He stood slowly but forced himself to keep looking, to take in the details. Hector's shirt was torn open. Unnatural angles beneath the skin told Jacob several of the old man's ribs had been broken. His knuckles were bloodied and raw, the skin split open. He had fought for his life.

Backing away slowly, careful to avoid disturbing the scene more than he already had, Jacob stopped at the doorway and tried to assess the room.

It was a story of a ransacking, although whether it had preceded or followed the murder was unclear. Drawers had been pulled out and their contents dumped, cabinets emptied haphazardly. Hector's killer had been looking for something specific.

"We need to call this in," Zara said. She touched Jacob's shoulder and guided him to the front door. Jacob stepped outside and sucked lungfuls of cold air. Tears pricked his eyes. He chewed on his lip and tried to steady his breathing.

"Hello, my name is Zara Steele." She spoke quietly into her

phone. Her eyes were wet and the hand she held her phone in was trembling. "I'm a detective chief inspector, currently off-duty. I'd like to report a suspicious sudden death."

Jacob looked back towards the house, trying to remember every detail. The beating had been savage. Violent. Personal? Or could it have been borne out of frustration that the old man wouldn't talk? Wouldn't give them what they wanted?

The search of the house appeared as frenzied as the beating. He looked at Zara again. Her focus was firmly on the phone call. Jacob ducked back inside and moved past the living room, his gaze steadfastly ahead so as not to see the dead man again.

In the kitchen, drawers had been yanked from their moorings. Utensils, documents, and glass jars were scattered across the tiled floor.

Upstairs, in the master bedroom, the mattress was off the bed frame, propped against the wall. The carpet was upturned at the edges, suggesting whoever had done the ransacking had looked for a floor safe. The wardrobe doors were wide open, clothes roughly pulled from hangers and tossed aside in heaps.

The bathroom echoed the same story. The medicine cabinet had been emptied, contents spilled into the sink and onto the floor. Dirty clothing had been dumped out of the laundry basket and sifted through.

"Jacob!" He was halfway back down the stairs when Zara hissed his name. She was standing at the threshold of the front door "What the hell are you doing? This is a crime scene. Get out, now!"

She waited until he joined her outside before throwing her hands up.

"The whole house is trashed," Jacob began. "They were looking -"

"- I know what they were looking for, Jacob. That's obvious, but it doesn't give you cause to disturb a scene. You know better."

She was angry and he knew it wasn't really directed at him. Tears welled in her eyes now and she wiped them with the back of her hand.

He pulled her close as sirens sounded in the distance.

25

The police arrived at Hector's less than ten minutes after Zara called it in. They were followed in short order by two further cars, the latter of which carried the local response duty sergeant.

The officers knew their job. The first pair on scene quickly cordoned off the house, and then placed a second outer cordon on the street to keep the inevitable crowd of gawkers at a distance.

Jacob knew the quiet street would soon be hiving with CSI examiners, police photographers, and detectives. He let Zara take the lead and hung back as she reported what they had found to the sergeant.

One of the officers took Jacob aside and led him into the back of her car. Her name-tag identified her as Constable Murphy. She unclipped the body-worn video camera from her flak jacket and pointed it toward Jacob, asking him to provide an initial account of what he had seen inside the house.

Once finished, she asked him for his name, date of birth, contact number and home address. He gave them and watched as she noted them on her phone rather than on paper.

She noticed him watching. "Digital notebook." She turned the screen towards him briefly.

Jacob nodded and wondered how the data was stored. It hadn't quite been five years, but the job was already changing in the time since he had left. It was the way the world worked, he supposed. Times changed, even in policing. The uniform he had worn, a white shirt and a navy tie, had been replaced by a rifle green top with a fabric more akin to sports-wear. At Garnerville, they had gotten rid of show parades for the recruits whose presentation was deemed to be below standard, and had even binned the passing out parade, marking the end of the initial training phase and a recruit's attestation as a police constable.

He pushed those ruminations away. "I didn't give the officer holding the scene my details."

Unlike the loss of the paper notebook and other trappings, the yellow hardback scene log hadn't changed since he had last wielded one. It contained a specific section to record the details of anyone who had been in the scene prior to it being officially set up.

Murphy looked up from her phone. "You on the job?"

"No, not anymore."

She tapped her phone screen. "I'll pass them to him."

He thanked her, and with Murphy not requiring anything else, he got out of the car. Zara was still in conversation with the sergeant and they had been joined a newly arrived Inspector. Jacob decided to stay out of the way.

"Jacob!"

He turned. Natalie was stood on the other side of the police tape, her expression confusion bordering on alarm. Jacob ducked under the tape and directed her away from the growing throng of onlookers.

"Got caught behind an accident on the Westlink. What's going on?"

"Hector's dead."

She stopped, wide eyes turning to him. "What? How?"

"Beaten to death." Jacob felt a lump in his throat, coughed it away. "His whole house has been ransacked."

"The pictures?"

"Gone. Along with whatever Haywood gave him too, I assume."

"How did they know -"

"- Haywood must have told them."

"But who? Told who?"

"I don't know."

It felt like he'd been repeating those three words a lot during this investigation. There was someone in the background, moving the pieces with an unseen hand.

He leaned against a wall. "Pettigrew has these blackmail pictures. Forty years pass and suddenly we come around asking about some missing boys. Boys who were used in his honeytrap. Boys like Finbar Skelly."

Natalie pressed her tongue against her cheek. "And we find Finbar's file in the borstal. Find the pictures in Pettigrew's house. Find the cottage where the pictures were taken."

"We know pressure was put on Hector to drop his investigation into the missing girls. We learn that Hector's superior has a file about Hartley House."

Natalie looked towards the police cordon. "A file that someone killed to get back."

Jacob rubbed a hand over his face. "We're still not seeing the full picture."

"How do you mean?"

"The graffiti in your studio. The person banging on my door."

"Trying to warn us off."

Jacob shook his head slowly. "It's too strange, like they were taunting us. The boys that did this," he pointed to his busted nose, "That's a message sent. That other stuff, I'm not so sure."

"What are you saying? You think they aren't

related?"

"I don't know." Jacob sighed. The combination of those words was becoming extremely tiresome. His phone vibrated in his pocket. "Helen."

"Jacob, I think you need to get back to the office."

Tension prickled his neck. "What's wrong?"

"Nothing," Helen said quickly. "I'm still down at the Land and Property building, but I forwarded the office phone to my mobile. A woman just called, saying she's there to see you."

Jacob glanced back at the police clustered around Hector's house. "It's not the best time."

"She's rather insistent. She said Hector Breen sent her."

Jacob and Natalie both began to walk hurriedly towards her car. "How far away from the office are you?"

"Fifteen minutes."

"Get over there and don't let her leave. Lock the door if you have to."

"Got it."

They reached Natalie's car before Jacob suddenly remembered something. "Shit, give me a minute."

He ran back to the cordon's edge and managed to catch Zara's attention. "I have to get back to the office."

"Ok," she said. She looked past his shoulder and spotted Natalie. "I can't leave yet. There's going to be a few questions about what I was doing here. Just formality," she added quickly. "But it'll take some time. Keep me in the loop?"

"Sure. You do the same?"

"Of course." She reached out and touched his arm. "Stay safe, alright?"

Natalie kept the pedal to the floor on the way back to Belfast. The Gods of parking were on their side and they found a space mercifully close to the office. Hurrying up the stairs, he found Helen had taken his instructions literally and locked the security gate.

The woman on the sofa rose as Jacob stepped

through the door. She was a slim with a sharp, angular face. Her hair was neatly pinned back, with streaks of silver running through chestnut. She clutched a bulging folder tightly to her chest.

"Mr. Kincaid?

"That's right."

"I'm Rosemary Hennessy."

"Eden's mother?" Although Hector had never mentioned her by name, Jacob assumed it was a safe guess.

She confirmed it with a nod. Jacob remembered Hector had said she was a heroin addict who had somehow stayed clean in the years since her daughter's disappearance. The hands around the folder were steady, the fingers long and delicate, but the veins were pronounced, her knuckles a little too prominent, as though her body still remembered the lean years it had endured.

He led Rosemary into his office and watched as her eyes flicked to Natalie who followed, gently closing the door behind her. "This is my partner, Natalie Amato."

Natalie offered the woman a simple nod.

"Hector asked me to come here first thing and hand deliver both of these to you personally. I was waiting for you to open, but no-one appeared."

"I'm sorry, Helen, the lady out the front, was on another-"

"-It's fine." Rosemary said, waving the apology away. "I'm just glad I could get it to you. It sounded urgent." She stopped and handed the folder over.

Jacob took it. "You said both of these. Is there another folder?"

Rosemary shook her head. "No, just this." She reached into her coat and produced a small white envelope. KINCAID was written on the front. "I didn't look inside."

Jacob carefully opened the flap of the envelope and felt his heart rate climb. It was the photos from

Pettigrew's house. Careful not to let Rosemary see the contents, he tilted it so Natalie could get a look, and then eased them back into the envelope.

"Hector said he was working with you into Eden's disappearance," said Rosemary.

"That's right," said Jacob, setting the envelope on top of the folder

"Is that..." She cleared her throat with a sharp cough. "Will that be something useful?"

"I hope so," said Jacob.

Rosemary sniffed. "Good."

"When did you last speak to him?" Jacob asked.

"Last night. He phoned and told me to meet him at Shaw's Bridge. There's a small car park down there."

"Did he say why?"

"Just that it was important. He called me two or three days back, to tell me about you looking at Eden's disappearance and that he was helping."

Jacob rubbed at his chin. "How did he seem?"

"Last night? Nervous. I've known Hector a long time, since...since Eden went missing. He was always so confident. This was the first time I had ever seen him like that. It scared me. He pushed that folder and envelope straight into my hands, along with a note with the address for your office. He told me to go home, that he was going to follow-me to make sure I got back ok." She licked at her lips, sensing something was off. "Is Hector ok?"

"No," said Jacob. "I'm sorry to be the one to have to tell you this, but Hector died last night."

It was blunt but that was the point. He had learned early in his policing career that you didn't want any ambiguity in delivering news about a death. Sombre expression, solemn tone. Remove the hat slowly, look them in the eye. Speak plainly. It's my sad duty to inform you...

"He's dead?" Rosemary asked the question with a shuddering breath. Her eyes turned to the folder on

Jacob's desk. "Because of that?"

"We don't know yet," Natalie answered gently, although they really did.

"Am I -"

"-You're safe," Jacob answered immediately. "I didn't know Hector long, but I'm certain he wouldn't have given this to you if he didn't think it was safe to do so."

That seemed to mollify her somewhat. She stood up, wringing her hands. "I hope you get the answers you are looking for."

"I hope so too," said Jacob.

Rosemary paused at the door. "Hector was a good man."

"Yes," said Jacob. "He was."

They waited until the door was closed.

"Hector knew Haywood would blab immediately," said Natalie. "He knew someone would come for this. That's why he insisted that only he could deal with Haywood."

Jacob rested a hand on the folder and nodded slowly. "Get it offside and let the consequences fall squarely on him."

"Jesus," said Natalie.

"Jesus," agreed Jacob. He glanced down at the folder. "Let's see what someone would kill for, shall we?"

He opened the flat of the folder and removed the large sheaf of paper held within. The front page was a cover sheet with the RUC crest in the centre.

CONFIDENTIAL
Case Number:
N/A
Date Opened:
12th March 1983
Senior Investigating Officer:
Detective Chief Inspector Paul Morgan

Confidentiality Notice:
This file contains sensitive information pertaining to an ongoing investigation. Unauthorised access or dissemination of this information is strictly prohibited under the Official Secrets Act 1911. Any personnel found in violation will be subject to disciplinary action and potential prosecution.
Status: *Filed - NFPA*

Natalie pointed to the acronym. "What's that?"
"No further police action," said Jacob.
He turned the page. The next sheet was a memo. It had been filled out with a typewriter that had seen better days, the letters uneven and slightly smudged.

Dear Sir,
On your direction I have concluded my investigation in regard to the Hartley House Borstal. Initial witness statements and medical reports indicate potential criminal misconduct and abuse of authority by certain members of staff. I reiterate my earlier argument that I feel this investigation has been brought to a close prematurely, and that there is conduct beyond what is covered in my report. I would be remiss in my duty if I did not present all findings uncovered by this investigation to you, and I hope you will be convinced that there is enough substance to warrant the continued investigation into Hartley House.

Jacob read on in silence. The first few pages of the file contained preliminary information about Hartley House and the closed borstal at Lisvardin, mostly relating to staff deployment, roles, and regimes.

The following two sections were interview statements led by DCI Morgan. The sections had been split between boys who had been former detainees at the borstal, and those still incarcerated. The detail and length between the statements contained in the two sections was stark. For the boys no longer held within the borstal, almost all the statements ran multiple pages in Morgan's compact and neat penmanship. In contrast, the statements from boys still detained were brief and light on anything that would resemble criminal acts. It wasn't much of a leap to assume the boys had been warned to keep their mouths shut.

Accounts obtained from those who would, or rather could, talk, recounted bullying behaviour, corporal punishment that went far beyond the scope of reasonable discipline and unchecked authority of some of the members of the staff. Two of the statements outlined experiences of being taken from their beds at night, blindfolded, and brought to a quiet room where beatings would occur for infringements made.

The file continued onto a collection of medical reports, requested by Morgan, detailing the physical condition of several boys upon their admission to local hospitals after being released from Hartley House. Doctors noted bruises, cuts, and in a particularly severe case, an indication of broken ribs.

As Morgan's investigation progressed, so too did his growing frustration with the lack of cooperation from the Hartley House administration. Requests for official records and staff rosters were met with delays and excuses that bordered on obstruction. Memos suggested the same thing Jacob was seeing; that Morgan suspected a cover-up.

Slowly, the nature of the investigation began to shift. Not satisfied with what he was getting, he began to watch Hartley House, building up a profile of people coming and going, and soon realising there was a stream of visitors who had no legitimate business being there. Among those Morgan positively identified were several prominent local businessmen, a justice of the peace, two senior police officers; two Englishmen who were officials from the Northern Ireland Office, and an unknown man who seemingly took great lengths to disguise his identity.

Jacob felt his heart stutter step. Quickly he flicked through the next set of pages of known information on each of these interlopers until he found what he was looking for.

Unidentified Individual

The individual in question is notable for their appearance, specifically the presence of extensive facial bandages which disguise identifying features. These bandages cover the lower half of the face, wrapping across the nose and jawline, with additional layers extending around the forehead and over the sides of the head. The bandages appear clean but hastily applied, inconsistent with the professional dressing of legitimate medical professionals.

Physical Description:
The figure is of medium build, approximately 5'10" to 6'0", and male based on their stature and gait. The bandages, as described, are prominent and appear deliberate, leading me to suspect they serve as a disguise rather than medical necessity. At no point did the individual appear hindered by injuries—movements were purposeful and brisk, lacking any of the hesitancy or physical discomfort one might expect from someone recovering from facial trauma.

Behavioural Notes:
The individual has been observed entering Hartley House on two occasions, both after midnight. He is accompanied by one other male, who remains with the car throughout.
The car is not stopped and checked at the gate, as is dictated by security protocol at every Northern Ireland Prison Service site, suggesting his visits are expected. Furthermore, checks of the vehicles number plate do not correspond to any registered vehicle, suggesting the plates are bogus.

Conclusion:
While the purpose of the individual's visits remains unconfirmed, the facial bandages are troubling. Such a disguise would prevent witnesses from accurately describing or identifying the wearer, which could indicate an intent to conceal identity while engaging in questionable activities. Given the context of this investigation and the allegations against Hartley House, I believe the presence of this individual, so far the only interloper yet to be identified, warrants further scrutiny.

It was the last page. There was no mention of the masked man or any hint of who he really was. Jacob checked the date of the memo and saw it had been written three days before the cover memo at the front of the file, where Morgan urged his superiors to re-consider closing the investigation.

"This is huge, Jacob," Natalie said. "Some of those names were influential people. If this had got out, if this gets out now...."

Jacob nodded. She was right, this was huge. Establishment shaking. And yet, not why he had begun this investigation. He had been hired by Deirdre Skelly to find her missing son. The best lead he had found was in this file, and the rug had been pulled forty years ago. The identity of the masked man who took Finbar, was still a mystery.

He picked up his phone and called Cora. When she answered, he told her he needed a favour. When he had finished, he went out into the main office.

"Helen." He held out the folder and the envelope with the sordid pictures. "I need you to wait here with this. Cora Adebayo is on her way. I want you to hand these to her and nobody else. Keep the door locked until she gets here. While she's here, I want you to lock up and go straight home. She's going to see you safely to your car. I don't want you back in the office until you hear

from me, got it?"
　　Helen's jaw tightened. "Got it."
　　"Where are we going?" Natalie asked.
　　"House calls."

26

"You sure this is the right move?"

It was a fair question. Two days ago, Jacob had been cautious about approaching Higgins, worried about overplaying their hand. Now he was sitting outside the man's house, intent on bracing him for information. He answered Natalie by getting out of the car and walking up the driveway towards the tidy bungalow.

The door was answered by a woman in her fifties. Her fair hair was tied in a ponytail, and she regarded them with tired eyes.

"Afternoon," said Jacob. "I'm looking for Donald Higgins?"

The woman looked warily between him and Natalie. "That's my father."

"Is he in?"

"What's this about?"

"We're private detectives. We're looking to speak to him about his old job with the prison service, specifically his time at the Millisle borstal."

"My father isn't a particularly well man. I don't think he'd want to speak to you."

She had already begun to close the door but Jacob pushed his hand against it. A look of alarm passed over her face and he shoved down the shiver of guilt it made him feel. "Tell your father we're here to speak to him about Finbar Skelly. Tell him if he doesn't see us now, our next stop is a police station."

A bluff, but it seemed to hit the mark. "Wait here," the woman said quietly.

Jacob moved his hand off the door to allow her to close it and figured if she wasn't back inside a minute, they should probably skedaddle, as the police were most likely getting called by Higgins's daughter, complaining of two suspicious types at her front door.

It was maybe thirty seconds later when she reappeared, with a face like a wet weekend. "Come in."

She led them through the house to a back living room where Donald Higgins sat on an old chair that had seen better days. Tubing from an oxygen machine trailed across the carpet, snaking its way up towards his face, hooking under his nose.

Despite the breathing apparatus, Higgins retained the broad-shouldered frame of a man who had once been physically formidable. There was no welcome in his expression, no softness in the deep lines of his face. Indeed, Jacob read a quiet, simmering disdain that lingered in the way his gaze raked over them, sizing them up as if they were intruding on something they had no right to see.

It may have worked on scared young boys forty years ago, but Higgins was an old man and held no fear. Jacob matched the stare and returned the disdain in spades.

Higgins broke first, turning to his daughter. "Maggie." The word came out in a slight wheeze. "Close the door on your way out."

Maggie wrung her hands, but did as she was told. The trio waited until the door shut.

"You have her worried," said Higgins. "Turning up at an old man's door."

"Be thankful I only named Finbar Skelly," said Jacob. "Talk of a paedophile ring would probably send her over the edge."

Higgins wheezed. "What do you want?"

"The truth. About Finbar Skelly. About what happened at Hartley House."

"Nothing happened at Hartley House. I remember the

Skelly kid, but it had nothing to do with me."

"What didn't?"

Higgins raised a dismissive hand.

"Who was he?" Jacob asked. "The man who took Finbar?"

Higgins actually managed to laugh at him. "Listen, I don't know what you're talking about or what you think you know. That Skelly kid escaped out of the open borstal one night, just before Christmas. Probably thumbed a ride with the wrong person. Got picked up by a pervert, buggered to death and chopped up into pieces."

"Bullshit," said Jacob. "I know you were involved Higgins."

"You know fuck all, both of ya's."

"Here's what I know," Natalie said as she stepped in front of Jacob and gripped the arms of Higgins's chair, the wood creaking slightly with the pressure. She leaned in close, forcing the old man back into the faded fabric. "I know I have a podcast with a hundred thousand weekly listeners. I know I have a story about the worst kind of crime. I know the name of the main man involved."

"I'm not -" Higgins began.

Natalie talked right on over him. "-I'll be shouting your name from the rooftop by the end of this week." Her grip on the chair eased as she straightened slowly.

Jacob decided to keep the pressure up. "We have statements from a number of men who were abused at Hartley House, at parties they swear blind you organised. I have a recorded interview with a man who saw Finbar Skelly the night he was taken. I have a police file detailing an investigation into the paedophile ring you organised."

He was playing hard and fast with the truth in almost everything he had just said, but Higgins had turned a shade paler and Jacob knew they had him.

"What do you want?"

"The truth," Jacob said. "We ask the questions, you tell us the truth. If we think you're lying or holding back, we're out the door and you can listen out for the story on all good podcasting sites, and wait for a knock on the door from the peelers."

"You want me to incriminate myself?"

"We're not the police," answered Natalie. "We can make a

dirty story smell so much sweeter. If you work with us."

Higgins licked at his lips. He was on the hook. "I'll tell you and you keep my name out of it."

"I guarantee it," Jacob said. It was a lie and he had no bother telling it. "Finbar's mother thought he was last seen on the Falls Road on Christmas Eve. Everyone thought that for the last forty years. Except we know he was brought back to the borstal that night, and a couple of hours later was taken away by a man wrapped in facial bandages."

"So you say."

Jacob's hand moved before his mind could catch up, whipping across Higgins's face. It was a pure, raw reaction, an explosion of frustration and anger that had been slowly building, beginning with a grieving mother and culminating with the sight of Hector's broken body.

The sound lingered in the stillness of the room. Jacob ignored the sting in his hand as Higgins mutely touched a bloody lip.

"Don't fuck me around," said Jacob lowly. "A man has been murdered, and my patience is long over."

"Just..." Higgins's wheeze seemed more emotional than physical. He took a second to catch himself. "Just ask your questions and get out."

"Finbar was brought back to the borstal on Christmas Eve."

"Yes."

"By who?"

"I don't know."

"You don't know," Jacob echoed. "Someone must have sent people looking for him. It wasn't prison officers who brought him back."

"Pettigrew," said Higgins. "He was -"

"-We know who he was," Jacob said. "So Pettigrew enlisted someone to drag Finbar back. IRA men?"

"They were hardly fucking priests." Higgins sensed Jacob tense and flinched. "I don't know, but I'm guessing so. Pettigrew was in thick with them."

"And you were in thick with Pettigrew." Jacob made no effort to hide the contempt in his voice. "A prison officer working for the IRA?"

Behind him, Natalie cleared her throat. A wordless reproach to keep on track before Higgins decided to clam up.

"The bandaged man," Jacob's pulse quickened at the mere mention of the phantom. "Who was he?"

"Fuck me," Higgins murmured. He put his head in a hand and kept it there.

"Who?"

Higgins slowly looked up. "His name was Jonathan Alcorn."

Jacob felt his skin tingle. It was the best kind of sensation, that kind could only come with the sharp clarity of a puzzle piece snapping into place. He finally had it. The man who had taken Finbar Skelly, the phantom who had haunted the edges of his investigation, was no longer just a shadow. He had a name.

He took a breath to calm himself, wary of losing Higgins before he could ask what he needed to. "As in the Alcorn's who owned Hartley House?"

Higgins looked up sharply, surprised at the depth of Jacob's knowledge. "That's right."

"What was with the bandages?"

"He was military. Got caught up in an IRA bomb over on the mainland. Tore his face to pieces."

Jacob looked to Natalie, eager for her to jump in, to let him process what he was hearing. An IRA honeytrap. A family member of British nobility. A family member of British nobility who had kidnapped a boy forty years ago.

Natalie had taken the invitation. "How did it come about, these parties?"

"Well, as you said, the Alcorns owned the mansion. The government had bought most of the land and rented the mansion back to them. The Alcorns set up a charity group, the Whitburn Society to support the new borstal. They had a motto..." Higgins trailed off as he tried to recall it. "Ah, yeah. To support the reformation and rehabilitation of troubled youth. They held fundraisers, arranged apprenticeships, sponsored camping trips."

Jacob leaned forward. "And what did they actually do?"

"You know what they did. And nobody ever questioned it

because they were the great and the good. No one questioned why certain donors kept showing up in the middle of the night when no one was supposed to be around."

"The trustees."

"Aye," said Higgins. "The trustees."

"Tell me about Officer McCarthy," said Jacob.

For the first time, something approaching shame flashed over Higgins's features. "I had nothing to do with that."

"You told Matthew Connelly different."

"I was trying to put the fear up him."

"Afraid he'd shop you," said Jacob.

"Yeah." Higgins grunted the word.

"McCarthy hears about what is happening and gets killed a few days later. You expect anyone to believe the timing was just coincidental?"

"I had nothing to do with it." Higgins reply was firmer. Too firm. He dissolved into a coughing fit that must have lasted close to a minute. "I told, I told Pettigrew we might have a problem. He told me it'd get sorted. McCarthy was dead within the week."

"Just like that?"

"Pettigrew knew some heavy hitters."

"How did you get involved?" Natalie asked.

"Pettigrew approached me. The Whitburn Society had been holding these *soirees* in the mansion since before I was in the job. Pettigrew thought I would be a good supervisor. A firm hand to keep the lads in line."

"No, we wouldn't want them to take exception to getting molested," said Jacob.

"Did you know what they were doing at these parties?" asked Natalie.

Higgins shifted in his seat. "Not at first, but it was obvious after the first night."

Jacob turned away from the man. He was sure Higgins was lying, that he knew damn well what he had signed on for. But he couldn't muster the energy to question why he didn't do anything to stop it. Why he didn't raise the alarm. "What'd they get you with?" he asked instead.

"Get me with?"

"Get you with," Jacob shot back. "How'd they convince you to supervise teenage boys getting abused while you stood and did nothing?"

"Money." Higgins scoffed like it was the most obvious answer in the world. "Got a mate to help out. The auld fella who did the gate was paid off and we told the nightwatchmen to mind their own fucking business."

"The mate," said Jacob. "Hussey?"

"Aye, that's right. Gavin Hussey. Don't bother looking for him, he ate a gun back in the nineties."

"Good," said Jacob. Higgins bristled. Jacob ignored him. "We found a cottage, out near Carrickfergus. We believe it's linked to what went on in Hartley House."

"I don't know anything about a cottage, in Carrickfergus or anywhere for that matter."

Jacob stood over him and stared the man down.

Higgins looked away, towards the window. "Pettigrew used to be a scout master. He'd take day excursions or weekend camping. Gav used to chaperone. That was the cover story anyway."

"For more discrete get-togethers."

Higgins continued looking out the window. "Apparently."

"Did you know those meetings were being photographed?"

"No."

"Did you know Pettigrew was using them to blackmail people?"

Higgins shook his head. Jacob didn't believe him, but without proof, decided not to press. "Did you know Patricia Winslow?"

"Aye, I knew her."

"You know what happened?"

"Just the basics."

"Well, that's probably more than us," said Jacob.

"She got attacked one night. Story is, she stepped out of her car and got jumped by someone. Cut her to pieces." He shrugged. "That's all I know."

"Was there a police investigation?" Jacob asked.

"Aye. Most of the staff at the borstal got interviewed, maybe they were thinking it was a jilted lover or something like that, I dunno."

"They never fingered anyone for it?"

"From what we heard, she didn't give them a chance. Never cooperated with an investigation. We did a whip-round, sent a card. Never heard what happened to her."

"Did she have any enemies?" Jacob asked.

"She was a pain in the hole," said Higgins, "But no, no-one hated her enough to do what happened to her."

"How did it end?" asked Natalie. "The soirees."

"Pettigrew shut it down. Not sure why, but I didn't argue. He left the borstal not long after. I never saw him again."

"And you just went back to work?" Jacob said coldly. "Assistant governor, was it?"

Higgins shrugged. "I did my whack and did well for myself. I put in hard time on hard landings."

"You worked soft posts, and rode the training gig for years, you spoofer. The way I hear it, you never saw the far end of a landing most of your career."

After all that had been slung at Higgins, all of it true, it was this that broke him. "Fuck you," he wheezed, nerve thoroughly touched. "Get out of my fucking house."

"Gladly. You make yourself comfortable and wait for the police to knock on the door. It'll be coming."

"You said -"

"-Yeah, I did. Shit one."

Curses and ragged coughing followed them into the hallway. Maggie stood by the kitchen, watching them leave with mute hostility.

"Sorry about that," Jacob said once he and Natalie were back in her car. He held up the hand he had struck Higgins with.

"Don't worry about it. Did it make you feel better?"

"No."

She reached up and touched his shoulder. Reassuring. "We have a name."

Jacob allowed himself a smile, but didn't feel any levity. "That we do." It wasn't a victory, not yet. But it was a thread to pull.

He got his phone out and dialled Helen's number. It rang

twice before her voice came through, clipped and slightly distant. "What's up?" The hum of the engine in the background told him she was in her car.

"I need you to dig into someone," Jacob said. "Jonathan Alcorn. Anything you can find on his background, recent activity, if he's even still alive."

There was a pause on the other end, just long enough for Jacob to picture her brow furrowing in thought. "Jonathan Alcorn? As in -"

"-As in the Alcorn family, yes," said Jacob. "He's the man who took Finbar. I don't know his relation to the grand old duke of Whitburn, but he's connected in some fashion. He's the man who took Finbar Skelly."

Another pause. Jacob could hear the faint rhythmic tick of the car indicator. "You're sure?"

"As sure as we can be," Jacob replied, glancing at Natalie, who nodded agreement. "We've got enough to connect the dots. Another thing, Helen. We think he was in the military at some point, got badly injured in a bomb attack. See if you can find anything in relation to that too."

"Alright," Helen said slowly. "I'll get back to you. Remind me what it was I said a few days ago about you making hitting the ground after tripping complicated?"

"We're still missing links here," said Natalie as Jacob ended the call. "For one, still don't know why Haywood ordered the investigation into Hartley House. He also killed Hector's investigation into the missing girls. Why?

Jacob chewed on that. "He obviously had a reason to dig up some sort of dirt on Hartley House, and had reason to keep the file."

"Leverage." Natalie said. "But against who?"

"Let's go and ask him."

27

The large house sat still. Haywood's Aston Martin didn't look as though it had moved since the previous night. Jacob ran his hand along the bonnet. It was cold.

Natalie reached for the doorbell, but Jacob caught her wrist gently. Something felt off, a familiar sense of wrongness that he couldn't place. He tried the handle. The door was unlocked. The house beyond was still.

"Haywood?" Jacob's voice was loud in the foyer.

Taking the lead, he moved to the closest door and pushed it open. It led into a living room, spacious and orderly. The air carried the faint scent of lemon polish.

At the far end, double doors stood ajar, revealing the dining room. It mirrored the living room's rigid neatness. Jacob and Natalie moved through to the kitchen. Dishes that had been left on the drying board by the sink were bone dry, the drained water staining the steel below. It wasn't much, but it was out of place against the strict order of the rest of the house.

Jacob's gut tightened, an instinctive warning hummed louder at the edge of his thoughts. Natalie sensed it too and kept close as they walked back into the foyer.

Jacob planted a foot on the bottom stair and called out again. "Haywood?" His voice echoed faintly, bouncing off the high ceilings and disappearing unanswered.

They took the stairs slowly. There was no sound, save for their footfalls on the polished wood, but the hairs on the back of Jacob's neck bristled. The sense that something was wrong was still there, but it was now matched with a primal instinct of being watched.

Once on the landing, Jacob could see the door to Haywood's study was slightly ajar and he elected to head there first.

Haywood was seated in the high-backed leather chair. His head was tilted forwards, chin nearly touching his chest, and he made no move as Jacob entered.

"Oh my god," Natalie breathed as she stepped beside Jacob. "Is he..."

"Very much so."

A trickle of dried blood had stained the collar of Haywood's shirt, stark against the pale fabric. The bullet had entered the back of his head. There was no exit wound. Jacob figured a small calibre had done the deed.

He turned his attention to the room for any signs of a struggle, but everything appeared untouched. Haywood hadn't fought. Either his killer had taken him by surprise, or he hadn't resisted, hoping for a way out that was evidently not forthcoming.

"Why?" Natalie asked.

"To shut him up," said Jacob. "I'm thinking -"

The low, soft creak in the hallway stopped. He turned to the doorway to find himself staring down the barrel of a gun. Instinctively, his hands twitched upward, an automatic gesture of surrender as his eyes rose to meet the man holding it.

"Back," Martin Closkey growled the word quietly.

Jacob was in no rush to argue. He had no illusions about how easily Closkey would pull the trigger and sleep well that night.

Closkey eased the door closed behind him, his gun trained on Jacob throughout.

Jacob inclined his head in the direction of Haywood's corpse. "Your work?"

"Shut the fuck up. What's going on here?"

Jacob looked at Haywood and then turned back to Closkey.

"Don't you think you should go first?"

Closkey took one step forward and smashed the butt of his gun into Jacob's temple. A searing white light blinded him for a second and he thought he was floating before his knees hit the floor. He felt Natalie catch him, guiding him to unsteady feet as he tried to focus his vision on the killer standing in front of him.

"Any more smart lip and I'll put one in your fuckin' mouth, and then in hers, you get me?"

Jacob gritted his teeth against the pain. Gritted his teeth about letting his mouth run away from him. "I get you."

"What are you pair doing here?"

It was Natalie who answered. "We wanted to talk to Haywood."

"You're too late."

"Apparently so," she said softly.

Jacob rubbed at his temple. "Why'd you kill him, Closkey?"

"You're not the one asking the questions here. Start talking."

Jacob bit back a bark of laughter. "About what?"

Closkey tensed, already on his last strand of patience with the meagre defiance Jacob was offering. He thought he was going to strike him again but Natalie spoke first.

"We're looking into the disappearance of a number of young people."

"So you say."

"You know we are," Natalie said. "We told you as much outside your uncle's house."

Jacob saw something flash across Closkey's features. A moment of doubt. It went quicker than it had appeared, but Closkey had let it slip all the same.

"What's your part in all this?" Jacob prompted, sensing the sliver of an opening.

Closkey set his jaw, weighing his options. Finally, he said, "I was told to meet a man called Haywood here."

"By who?"

"Never mind who. I arrived early. Heard a gunshot when I was walking up the driveway. Ducked into the bushes and waited. After no one appeared I decided whoever had pulled the trigger had got away out the back of the house and over the fields. Took a look around the house, found him here just as you two pulled up."

"Convenient. I hope you have something more believable for Hector's murder."

Closkey's cold eyes narrowed and Jacob saw the grip on the gun tighten as the study door drifted open. Jacob saw the lazy swing, assumed the door had been pushed by a draught.

And then he materialised in the threshold. More apparition than man, a face swathed in bandages that obscured all but the eyes. Metal glinted in the phantom's hand. A knife, its long blade glinting in the dim.

"Closkey!" Jacob's warning was choked, a desperate shrill.

Confusion, realisation, and something like fear all played over Closkey's features in an instant. His body tensing as instinct kicked in. He pivoted, turning his gun onto the unknown but sensed threat.

The bandaged man buried the knife in his chest. Closkey stumbled back with a choked shout. The gunshot was deafening, and the aim wild. Plaster fell as the lone bullet buried itself in the ceiling.

The phantom flinched and took off running. Closkey hit the floor. His eyes were widened with shock and pain, his mouth opening to form words that Jacob couldn't hear.

Heavy footfalls hurried down the landing towards the stairs. Jacob darted around the fallen man and give chase.

"Jacob!"

Natalie's voice. Urgent. Afraid.

By the time Jacob reached the end of the landing, the figure was rounding the corner at the bottom of the staircase. He caught a fleeting glimpse of a dark coat disappearing into the shadows below. Jacob hit maybe three stairs on his way down.

He rounded the corner, and his instincts squealed. Too late, he realised it was a trap. The bandaged man, anticipating the pursuit, was waiting.

Jacob threw himself back on reflex. Metal flashed, pain ripping up his arm in a searing line. He stumbled, his arm instinctively going up to protect his face from the follow-up.

It didn't come. Instead of pressing the attack, the phantom

retreated to the kitchen and out of sight. A second later Jacob could hear a door being pulled open and then slamming shut, the noise reverberating through the house like a taunt.

Ned by Night had escaped.

Jacob clutched his wounded arm, warm blood against his fingers and dragged himself back up the stairs.

Natalie had stayed in the study. She was crouched next to Closkey but rose to her feet as Jacob returned, swaying slightly, her arms hanging loose at her sides. Her natural honey tan, had turned ghost white. She was there and yet entirely absent, and Jacob was worried she might be about to go into shock.

"You alright?"

She nodded mutely before her eyes drifted to his hand pressed against the opposite arm.

"I'm fine," Jacob said quickly. "Just a scratch."

"That was..."

Closkey's ragged gasp cut her off. A dark stain had spread across the chest of his grey fleece, the fabric sodden with blood. Jacob thought that the wound, a brutal, jagged tear just above the heart, was mortal. Crimson blood had already pooled beneath Closkey and slowly inched its way along the wooden floor.

It was a gruesome sight but Jacob felt nothing for the man. He had killed Hector. One of many murders committed in the name of ideology to justify the unjustifiable. He knelt next to him. Closkey's eyes were glassy, and Jacob thought he was already on his way out before they suddenly snapped up to him as if sensing his thoughts.

"I'll call an ambulance," Jacob said.

"No." Closkey said the word through laboured breaths. "I'm done."

There was no point denying it. Jacob was transported back to a summer, eleven years before. A call to the Cathedral Quarter. A group of youths fighting. The combatants had fled before police had arrived, leaving behind a sixteen-year-old with a knife sticking out of his stomach. Jacob had held him, told him he wasn't going to die, and then watched as his life ebbed away before the paramedics could do anything.

He came back to the room. Shook his head clear. They

didn't have long. "Closkey, what were you doing here?"

"Family business."

Jacob frowned. Made a leap. "Your uncle?"

Closkey struggled to nod once. "If it got out...that he...that he was working for the Brits..."

"The Brits?"

Closkey's face twisted. The two words seemed to hurt him more than the wound that was killing him.

Jacob's mind raced. He needed to make the questions count. "What happened?" He immediately cursed himself. Too open-ended, too vague.

"Was told...if I did some work...they could make the proof disappear...."

"What work?" Jacob asked.

Closkey didn't answer. His eyes had unfocused, staring up at them but seeing nothing.

"The proof," Natalie said. "That's what you came here to get."

Closkey's nod was surreptitious.

"The work," Jacob said, taking another leap. "A chance to settle an old grudge with Hector?"

"Breen?" Even in his state, the confusion in Closkey's voice was unmistakable. He coughed, a horrible, gurgling sound. Blood frothed at the corner of his mouth.

Jacob chest tightened. He reached out, steadying the dying man. "Closkey, if not Hector, who?"

The light in Closkey's eyes dimmed as his head lolled to the side.

"Closkey."

His eyes were still open but no longer seeing.

He was dead.

28

Natalie had found a clean dish towel and a roll of electrical tape, the closest substitutes she could find in Haywood's kitchen in lieu of actual first aid equipment. She soaked the towel under the tap and then wrung it out. Kneeling next to where Jacob was sitting, she dabbed at the wound. The towel quickly stained pink.

Once satisfied that she'd cleaned the wound, Natalie rose and rummaged through a nearby cupboard, pulling out a second dish towel. She shook it open and knelt again. Carefully, she wrapped the towel around Jacob's arm, securing the makeshift bandage with the strips of electrical tape.

Jacob turned and flexed the bandaged arm as she stood up. "Nurse Natalie. You've got quite the touch."

She let out a small, shaky laugh, some of the tension in her shoulders easing. Most of the colour had returned to her usual tanned complexion. "Just so you know, I charge for follow-ups. So don't make a habit out of it."

The lightness from the exchange faded almost as quickly as it had come, swallowed by the oppressive weight of the house. Of what had happened upstairs.

Natalie crossed to the sink and began to wash her hands. "Do we phone the police, or is you being at two murder scenes in the space of a morning too coincidental."

Jacob had already considered leaving, but had quickly

ruled it out. If they were later traced to the scene, which they almost certainly would be, they'd have some uncomfortable questions to answer. Better to get it out of the way now, no matter how improbable his story would seem.

He knew both Hector's and Haywood's house were Lisburn PSNI's patch. It was now early afternoon. Probably around changeover time between the early and late sections. He could get lucky, and no-one would put two and two together and notice his name attached to both incidents until later.

He relayed his thoughts to Natalie.

"You think that's likely?"

"Probably not," he admitted.

"You think they'll buy your story?"

"Probably not."

"Comforting."

He grudgingly reached for his phone. "Let's make the call."

As they had at Hector's, the police arrived quickly and set up a scene. Jacob and Natalie were separated, and Jacob once again gave an account of what he seen on body-worn video.

By the time he had finished, the police presence had increased dramatically. No doubt spurred on by the fact a leading dissident Republican was found dead in the house of an executed RUC man. The place would be a circus within the hour. The scent of scandal, the whispers of intrigue, would draw journalists from London and Dublin, not just Belfast.

Any hope of slipping away unmolested were dashed by the arrival of the same uniformed sergeant who had been at Hector's house. Jacob watched the man thread his way through the growing crowd of officers, taking in the scene and no doubt wondering who he had hurt in a past life to get lumped with two murders in a single morning in a city that could go two or three years without one.

Inevitably, the sergeant's attention was drawn to Jacob, hanging around like a spare dick. There was no mistaking the recognition in the sergeant's eyes, nor the subtle narrowing of his gaze as he sized Jacob up from across the cordon. He watched the sergeant lean in towards one of his subordinates who in turn looked at Jacob, and then reached for the radio worn on his flak jacket.

Two of the burlier officers on scene suddenly materialised behind Jacob and he was escorted back into the rear of one of the waiting police cars until someone decided what to do with him.

Time ticked by. Jacob kept his attention on the driveway and waited, trying to ignore the nervous flutter in his stomach. When they arrived a few minutes later, it was not the person Jacob had been expecting, but he was relieved all the same.

He had met Colin Ambrose the previous summer. The man was squat, with broad shoulders, a barrel chest, and a broken nose that hadn't been reset. A bruiser in an ill-fitting suit, not that Jacob would ever be tempted to point that out.

Jacob waited as Ambrose's uniform escort went to find his sergeant. When the sergeant appeared, Jacob could see Ambrose speak no more than five words before the man hurried away, returning with his inspector. Apparently satisfied he was talking to who he needed to, Colin nodded towards Jacob and began talking.

Five minutes later Ambrose was walking him down the long driveway.

"What did you tell them?" Jacob asked.

"The truth, for the most part." Unlike Cora's clipped English tone, Ambrose's accent was Belfast broad.

"Where's Cora?"

"Back at the office. Perusing over that folder your friend gave to her."

"You know what's in it?"

Ambrose shook his head. "She said it'd be better if I didn't." They stopped at the entrance to the driveway and Ambrose took Jacob by the arm and guided him around so he was facing him. "You were asking a lot with this, you know?"

"Didn't have much of a choice. How does it look to be at the scene of two different murders in the space of half a day?"

"That seems like a you problem."

Jacob narrowed his eyes. "And what's your problem?"

"You." Ambrose's finger nudge was enough to push Jacob back a step. "Cora likes you. And I don't mean just for the work you did on the Followers. She respects your tenacity. Your bloody single-mindedness. And you know that, you trade on it.

She told me about you asking her to dig for info, and now this? You really think it's just a matter of one phone call and this gets forgotten about? You have no idea what goes on behind the scenes."

Jacob couldn't think of what to say to that, so said nothing.

"C'mon," Ambrose grunted. He led the way down the country road to where Natalie waited by her car. Jacob hadn't seen her since they had been seperated and hadn't seen her car being moved.

Ambrose stopped him a few feet away. "I imagine you'll be having to talk to the police again."

"Standard," Jacob replied.

The big man shook his head wearily. "Get out of here, Kincaid. Try to keep yourself out of trouble, at least for a few hours, eh?" He turned to go without another word.

"Colin. Tell Cora I said thanks."

Ambrose raised a hand without turning, offered a half-wave, and kept walking.

"All good?" Natalie asked as they climbed into her SUV.

"For now."

Natalie started the engine. "What are you thinking?" It was an invitation to work through everything since first finding Haywood.

Jacob puffed his cheeks. "I want to say that Closkey killed Hector, hoping to get the folder, and then killed Haywood, for reasons I'm not quite clear on."

"But?"

"But, Closkey seemed surprised when I suggested Hector's name. He also denied being the one to kill Haywood."

"He could have been lying."

"Could have," said Jacob. "He also said his uncle was working for the Brits."

That had confounded Jacob most of all. Seamus Dolan. Dedicated Republican. Terrorist or freedom fighter, depending on who you asked. But an informer?

"Closkey said he was there because *they* could make proof against his uncle disappear."

Natalie nodded. "But he had to do some work."

Jacob pondered if Closkey was telling the truth. "Not

Hector. Not Haywood."

"Then who?"

The question hung in the air. Jacob let it dangle as he checked his phone and saw a number of missed calls from Zara over the last hour. He phoned her back.

"Jacob." Her tone was equal parts relief and annoyance. "Are you okay?"

"Just about." He flexed his arm even though Zara couldn't see the action. "I take it you already know about what happened at Haywood's house?"

"Yes. I was still at Hector's when the call came through. Look, can we talk? I can be at your office in thirty minutes."

"Come to my apartment," said Jacob. "I need to get a new top."

"A new top?"

His phone beeped to tell him he was getting another call. "I'll explain later." Jacob ended the call and answered the incoming one. It was Helen.

"I have something."

"Go for it."

"Newspaper archive. Belfast Sentinel, tenth of March 1979." She paused to clear her throat.

"Captain Jonathan Alcorn, younger brother of David Alcorn, Duke of Whitburn, was injured in the car bomb attack at Ashford Barracks, the family have confirmed. The attack at the home of the army's intelligence corps was claimed by the Provisional IRA."

Jacob felt his pulse suddenly quicken.

Brother.

Intelligence.

Helen continued. "The attack, which claimed the lives of Nancy Vicker, 58, a member of the cleaning staff, and a second, as yet unnamed individual, has left Captain Alcorn with serious, life-altering injuries." She paused again. "A spokesperson for the Whitburn family expressed gratitude for the quick response of Jonathan's comrades and the barracks medical team, and declined further comment on Captain Alcorn's condition. The family has requested privacy during this difficult time."

"Nice work, Helen."

"Don't stop me. I'm on a roll."

"You have something else?"

"It might be of interest. From the Ulster Reporter, October 1980. David Alcorn, Duke of Whitburn, continues to uphold his family's legacy with dignity and generosity. Known for his patronage of educational reform initiatives and his steadfast commitment to upholding traditional British values, the Duke has cemented his place as one of the United Kingdom's most respected aristocrats." She stopped. "Yada, yada, yada...Younger brother, Captain Jonathan Alcorn, retired, has now followed a similar path, recently taking over the patronage of the Whitburn Society and expanding their reach to foster those same values in a number of care homes in the Greater Belfast area. Some fluff follows, but you get the picture."

"Great work, Helen." Jacob waited a beat. "You have more, don't you?"

"Of course. The Whitburn family seat is in Waterfoot. I found an online archive of old editions of the *Belfast Tatler*. It features the Duke in an issue back in the nineties. You know house tour, glossy spread, you get the drift."

"Yeah..." said Jacob, trying to prompt her on.

"There's a mention in the article of the Duke's brother living in their second property. Dunvarrick House, just outside Portballintrae."

"I know it," Jacob said. "Portballintrae, I mean. It's up on the north coast. Do we know if Jonathan Alcorn is still alive? If you searched -"

"-The newspaper archives for any obituary with his name? Already done. Jonathan Alcorn hasn't appeared in any that I can locate, so I'd say there's a good chance he's still kicking."

Jacob thanked her, ended the call and set his phone down slowly. "I'd been thinking what happened at Hartley House was an operation run by Pettigrew on behalf of his mates in the IRA. A honey-trap against prominent figures they could bribe or coerce."

"Like Jonathan Alcorn," said Natalie in agreement.

"How about a different slant on our hypothesis?"

"Go for it."

"Pettigrew was a British agent."

"An agent?"

"Either a knowing agent, or maybe an unwitting tool. Jonathan Alcorn, with past links to military intelligence. Patron of the Whitburn Society. Him and Pettigrew, two perverts in a pod. Pettigrew has ties to the IRA back home, knows the local IRA commander has a penchant for young boys. A man like Seamus Dolan would be a huge get for British intelligence."

"So Pettigrew sets up Dolan? Lures him to the cottage to be photographed in a tryst with one of the borstal boys."

"They turn Dolan into a tout. Working with the Brits, just like Closkey said."

Natalie rubbed at her jaw. "The article from the Reporter said Alcorn was retired by 1980."

"Retired from the military."

"What, you think he was working for MI5 or the like?"

"Why not? He had the connections. He had the background. He had the means. What do you bet if we sit down and trace the cottage back to the real owners, it'll be to a company the Whitburns have some sort of involvement with?"

"Where do the missing boys fit in to this?"

"I'm thinking used and then killed. Probably by someone who got too rough, or someone who thought they might talk."

"Fuck." It was rare to hear Natalie swear but when she did, it was an unvarnished and wholly accurate summation of the situation. "What about Hector's girls?"

The girls.

The one branch of this investigation Jacob had never been able to tie down. He considered it all the way back to Belfast. By the time he got back to his apartment he still didn't have an answer.

"You got a first aid kit?" Natalie asked. "That cut needs looked at."

Jacob pulled out a basic kit from the top of one of the kitchen cupboards and handed it to her. She pointed to the sofa and knelt beside him as he sat. He carefully removed his hoody as she set out antiseptic wipes, sterile gauze, and medical tape.

"Alright, let's have a look," Natalie said as she gently peeled away the electrical tape and dish towel. Jacob winced slightly as the towel came off, revealing an angry red gash on his forearm. Natalie wiped the wound carefully with a wipe. The sting of the antiseptic caused him to clench his jaw. "Sorry," she murmured. "Also, man up."

She pressed sterile gauze over the cut, and unrolling a length of medical tape, secured the gauze in place with neat strips, making sure the bandage was tight but not too restrictive.

"There," she said. "All set."

Jacob heard the small sigh that escaped her lips as she stepped back, hands resting at her sides, as if unsure of what to do next. She looked tired, Her usually bright eyes were clouded, her shoulders slumped.

"You okay?" he asked, pulling himself up from the sofa.

For a moment, Natalie didn't answer. Her eyes flicked to his arm, then without a word, she stepped forward and wrapped her arms around him in a brief, quiet hug. Her head rested against his shoulder for a second, the closeness almost surprising in its intimacy.

Jacob caught the familiar scent of her hair, something subtle, like lavender or jasmine. For a moment, everything else fell away. There was just the softness of her hair brushing against his cheek, her warmth pressed into him, and the quiet space they shared.

She pulled back after a moment, her hands lingering briefly on his shoulders before falling away, a faint, tired smile tugging at the corner of her lips. "Just needed a second."

"I get it." The three words seemed somehow familiar.

She crossed to the kitchen, dropping the old bandage in the bin before moving to the counter to wash her hands. The door rapped as she began to run the water.

"It's open," Jacob called.

Zara entered, closing the door carefully behind her. She looked as tired as Natalie, with dark shadows under her eyes and her already fair complexion a shade paler. It made Jacob wonder how closely he must have resembled a bag of shite in comparison.

"What a fucking day," she said by way of hello.

"What a day," Natalie agreed.

Zara walked to Jacob and hugged him quickly. He watched as her gaze fell to the fresh bandage on his forearm.

"Courtesy of Ned by Night. I take it you heard the major details?"

"Closkey shot Haywood, and then this masked nutter stabbed Closkey."

"Seems that way," said Jacob.

Zara's expression hardened a fraction and she slapped Jacob on his good arm. "And you chased him? What the hell were you thinking, Jacob?"

"Hopefully someone can talk some sense into him," Natalie said, drying her hands, her smile wry.

"Not sure I like this tag-team approach to scolding," Jacob said.

"I'm just glad you're ok. Both of you."

"Shall I put the kettle on?" Natalie asked. Jacob and Zara both agreed, and she went to work brewing a pot.

"Closkey and Haywood," said Zara. "Looks like someone is tying up loose ends."

"It does," agreed Jacob. "And we might know who."

Zara straightened a fraction, her fatigue immediately lifting. "Really?"

"Former military, badly injured in an explosion. Severe facial injuries, meant he took to wearing bandages."

Zara swallowed. Anticipation building. "Just..." She had to pause for a second. "Just slow down. Who are you talking about?"

"His name is Jonathan Alcorn. His family owned Hartley House. He was a patron of the Whitburn Society and had free access to the place, assisted by a couple of paid-off prison officers. Along with a conversation with one of these officers, and the evidence Hector got, we can implicate him directly."

He watched her face go slack before she caught herself. "Woah, wait. Evidence?"

Jacob looked to Natalie, keen to share the triumph. "The old RUC file," she explained. "Hector managed to get it to a safe place, along with the photos Pettigrew had."

Zara digested the new information, losing herself in

thought as Natalie set two cups on the coffee table in front of her and Jacob before returning to the kitchen and lifting her own cup. "Who else have you told about this?"

"Just you," Jacob replied.

"Ok..." Zara said, almost as if reassuring herself. "Ok. For now, this needs to have a lid kept on it. An old priest is one thing, a member of the British nobility is another."

"We're not sitting on this," Jacob said.

"We are," Zara replied firmly. "At least until we can do it properly."

"Zara's right, Jacob," said Natalie. "Pettigrew is already in the wind. If Jonathan Alcorn is a suspect, we need to play it cool, not tip our hand."

Jacob clucked his tongue. He didn't like it, but they had a point. What he had were theories. Theories backed up by credible evidence. What he needed was the full picture, or as close to it as possible.

"What about Hector?" Natalie asked.

Jacob winced as guilt stabbed at him for not even think to ask.

"MIT are keeping an open mind," said Zara. "The old man made a serious number of enemies back in the day. That's why I'm here, actually. They're drawing up a list of sorts. Looking to identify contacts, anyone who might know something. Straightforward enough, but they've had a problem with one name, probably an alias. Can't seem to find anyone who fits. I said you might know, maybe Hector mentioned him."

"What's the name?"

Zara took a swig of tea. "Poddy Sweeny."

29

"Poddy Sweeny?"

His voice sounded far away as he repeated the name, trying to treat it as though it were just another piece of information to be filed away, meaningless and benign.

Poddy Sweeny. A name he had invented in jest, a figment turned into personal folklore for crimes that lingered unanswered. A ghost he had mentioned to Hector, but not Zara.

The apartment felt smaller suddenly. He saw Natalie over Zara's shoulder, the tiniest tremor quivering through the hand that held her mug of tea.

"No," Jacob said. "No, I don't think so."

Zara turned to look at Natalie who shook her head. "Same. Doesn't ring a bell."

"Thought as much," Zara said. "Told them it was a long shot but that I'd ask."

"Sorry we couldn't be more help," Jacob said. He crossed to the kitchen on legs that didn't feel his own.

Zara waved the apology away and then set her mug down. "Natalie, the tea looks great, but I'm beat. I'm going to head home and get an early night. I'll have to attend the briefing in the morning and then have to start explaining how I'm connected." She paused to rub at her eye. "Two retired police officers and a leading dissident republican. The press are going to be all over this."

Jacob nodded and floated towards the door to open it for her. Zara paused for a moment, clearly expecting him to ask more about what tomorrow might bring in regards to their investigation.

"Give me a call in the morning, when you're done," he said instead.

Her brow creased momentarily. "Of course." She glanced at Natalie and then leaned in to kiss Jacob on the cheek before turning on her heel.

Jacob closed the door and bent down to watch Zara through the peep hole. She didn't pause or look back and in seconds she was down the corridor and out of sight. She hadn't caught on. He released a breath he hadn't realised he had been holding and rested his forehead against the door.

"Jacob...How could she know that name?"

She knew the answer as well as he did. Whoever had killed Hector had made him give up the name of the person who he had passed the folder and the photographs to. The old man had made them work for it and laid the bait.

"How?" Natalie asked when Jacob didn't reply. How is she involved in this?"

"I let her in."

"But only after you sent the freedom of information request." She shook her head. "I don't get it."

"Neither do I. But I think I know where the answers are."

"Alcorn."

Jacob nodded.

"Tonight?"

"Has to be. If we delay..." He smacked the door with a fist. "Fuck, I just told her everything. The file, Alcorn. She could kill this whole thing."

"Then we need to move."

"I can do this myself, don't feel like you have to-"

"-Don't be an idiot." She lifted her coat from the counter. "Let's go."

M2 out of Belfast. A26 at the Dunsilly roundabout, heading

north. Rhythmic thudding of wipers against windshield, fighting the worsening snowstorm and just about coming out on top. The road stretched to only a few metres ahead, obscured by fat whirling flakes of snow.

"Why do you do this?" Jacob asked. Neither had spoken for miles.

"Hmm?" Natalie asked as if not quite hearing him.

"This." Jacob motioned around him. "Everything you went through with the Followers and now this case. Someone damaging your studio, running us off the road. Hector has been murdered, and you just watched a man die a few hours ago. Why are you still here?"

"Why are you?"

"This is what I do."

"Don't give me that, Jacob. You make a comfortable living going after cheating husbands and insurance fraudsters. You could get by without being here. You ask me why I do this? Look at your face, look at your arm. Did you ever ask yourself, *why don't I stop*? I do it for the same reason you do. I want the truth, and I want the people who think they got away with it to answer. Is that good enough for you?"

Jacob eased back into his seat, stung by the rebuke and wondering what had made him ask it. "I guess I'm worried..." He began before trailing off. "I don't know..."

"What?" her voice had softened.

That I'm afraid you'll leave. That I'm afraid you'll drop out of my life like almost everyone else.

"Nothing. I'm glad I have you. To work with, I mean."

He saw the curve of a smile. "I'm glad to have you too."

They continued on, skirting the town of Ballymoney and onward through Ballybogey. A sharp junction took them along a narrow and winding coast road. By now the snow had eased, but the conditions were treacherous and with the Atlantic looming far below, separated only by ancient stone walls and a vertical drop, Natalie didn't rush.

A few minutes later they came upon Dunluce Castle, perched precariously on jagged cliffs. The castle was illuminated faintly by the moon, its pale light washing over the ancient stones.

Dunluce had its own ghost story, a banshee whose wails for a lost love could be heard from one of the old towers. It seemed fitting that they pass it, Jacob thought. Ghost stories endured, conjured up by something as simple as wind whipping through crumbling towers, or a sleep-addled brain on a night shift, or even by flesh and blood playing dress-up.

Dunluce and its banshee disappeared in the rearview, and within five minutes they arrived at Portballintrae. The little village was quiet. Many of the houses there were holiday homes, sitting cold and empty until the warmer months.

Jacob had looked up Dunvarrick House on Google Maps, trying to get a sense of its location and surroundings. The imposing mansion was perched on a headland a couple of miles outside the village, accessed by a long, winding driveway.

However, as Jacob had studied the map, his eyes had caught something else. A carpark on the tip of Portballintrae led down to a long beach which curved around the coast and eventually ended at the foot of the headland Dunvarrick House sat on.

Behind the dunes was a public path that ran alongside what looked like train tracks. An odd feature, Jacob had thought. The Northern Irish rail system was sparse, and there were no lines out this far. Eventually the path met a fork that skirted back towards the headland.

It wasn't ideal. Jacob guessed the distance from the car park to Dunvarrick House was maybe two miles over beach and uneven trail in sub-zero weather, but it was their best option. The driveway was too exposed for them not to be seen.

He relayed his thoughts to Natalie, who agreed. Following the map, Jacob directed her to the empty carpark. Natalie turned off the engine and then reached into the glovebox, coming back with two thin torches. She handed one to Jacob.

"Liberated these last night. Had a feeling we might be needing them, just not this soon."

Snow crunched underfoot as they followed an unpaved path down towards the beach. Large waves rolled in from the infinite blackness of the Atlantic, crashing with a thunderous roar that echoed across the deserted shoreline.

Crossing a narrow bridge over a shallow river, Jacob

decided to follow the wooden-slatted trail that led into the dunes, rather than the more direct, but more difficult route over soft sand.

"What are you planning to do when we get there?" Natalie asked

"It hadn't occurred for you to ask that until just now?"

"Not really."

"Lucky for me, as I'm not sure myself. I need to get a look at him. To see this ghost with my own eyes."

"Then what?"

He huffed a breath, watched it fog in the night air. "To be determined."

The path weaved through the dunes before levelling out. The train tracks appeared as they had on the satellite image and again Jacob wondered what purpose they served. The nearest station was in Portrush, a good five miles back along the coast.

It took thirty minutes before they reached the fork that led back towards the beach. The snow lay undisturbed by any footfall save for their own. Foam danced and clung to the rocks scattered along the edge of the sand, glinting briefly before being dragged back into the dark waters. A long abandoned slipway, worn smooth by time and tide jutted out towards the ocean.

Beyond the slipway, the path twisted slightly upward, and the silhouette of Dunvarrick House slowly emerged. It was imposing, befitting its position on this rugged stretch of Irish coastline. Moonlight reflected off the windows, some of which glowed faintly from within, suggesting that the house was not lifeless. The surrounding grounds, blanketed in snow, were unblemished.

Jacob couldn't help but be aware of their isolation and apprehension now prickled over him. They were alone out here, and the mansion, with its air of eerie solitude, seemed to be watching.

They veered off the main path, coming to a low stone wall that marked the boundary of the estate. He paused for a moment, suddenly seized by a worry that this was a mis-step. That he had been spurred to act without thinking. He shut it out and clambered over the wall.

Dropping into a running crouch, they approached the nearside of the mansion. There was no movement at any of the windows with light, but Jacob was sure the crunch of their feet in the fresh snow was loud enough to be heard back in Belfast.

He pressed himself against the wall next to a window of one of the lit rooms. It was large and richly furnished, with heavy curtains tied back to reveal a grand sitting area. A dwindling fire crackled weakly in the hearth, and a thick rug stretched out across the wooden floor. There was no one in sight, but a half-empty glass of milk sat on a side table next to a high-backed armchair.

Natalie touched Jacob's arm and nodded toward the next window. This one appeared to be a library or study, its walls lined with shelves packed with old, leather-bound books. A single lamp illuminated a neat desk scattered with papers, but again, no one was present.

The dull thud of a door being closed made them both freeze. Jacob ducked, pulling Natalie with him as they flattened themselves against the wall. They listened, straining to hear anything over the breaking waves. Footsteps echoed faintly from within.

Jacob attempted to the track the movement. To his ears, it sounded as though the footfalls were heading in the opposite direction. He glanced at Natalie, who apparently agreed with him, gesturing to circle around to the rear of the mansion.

They stayed crouched and close to the wall. At the corner, Jacob stopped and peered around to make sure the coast was clear before pushing on. The rear of the mansion was darker, the majority of windows unlit, save for one. Jacob moved to it and eased himself up towards the sill.

An old man stared straight at him. His face was pale and grotesquely disfigured.

Jacob recoiled instinctively, pulling Natalie down just as she was raising herself to look. His heart lurched as adrenaline surged through him, pulse hammering in his ears. They had been seen, the old man's unblinking gaze had pinned him in place.

But the seconds stretched. There was no shout of alarm. No

sound of hurried footsteps, or creak of a door. Jacob realised the old man hadn't seen him. Couldn't see him. The room's light flooded outward, and the window acted like a one-way mirror, reflecting the room back at its occupants.

Tentatively, he leaned back toward the window, his movements slow and deliberate. Natalie followed suit.

The old man was still there and Jacob now took him in properly. He was in a wheelchair and wrapped in a thick blanket. His posture was rigid, bony white fingers gripped the edge of the chair. Jagged scars crisscrossed his cheeks and brow, deep lines of raised, gnarled tissue that twisted his features into something almost monstrous. One eye was clouded and milky white. His mouth was drawn tight, the scars tugging at his skin.

He wasn't looking at Jacob. He wasn't looking at anything really. His one good eye was unfocused, as though lost in a memory.

Natalie nudged him and then inclined her head in the direction of the way they had come. Jacob nodded and they took off, pausing at a corner out of sight of any window.

"Jesus," Natalie whispered. "Is that him?"

Jacob took a moment to try to control his breathing, heavy from the spike of adrenaline when he and the old man had seemingly locked eyes. "You think that's the same man we saw in Haywood's house? The same man who killed Closkey?"

"Could he..." Natalie trailed off before she could pose the question, seemingly finding the answer herself.

"What?" Jacob asked, guessing what the question was going to be. "You want to go over and tip him out to see if he's faking or not."

Natalie managed a smile. "No, I want to get out of here before we're rumbled. Is your curiosity sated enough?"

Jacob didn't answer. He had little doubt the disfigured old man was Jonathan Alcorn. The man who had taken Finbar. Jacob was even more sure it was not the same man who had killed Closkey, or the one who had vandalised Natalie's studio, or battered on his apartment door.

They followed the wall of the mansion until they came to their tracks leading back to the boundary wall. They were halfway there when Jacob stopped, his attention drawn towards a small copse of bare trees, partially obscuring a building behind them.

Natalie, who had stopped beside him squinted before whispering, "Ice house."

Jacob moved in closer. He needed something, anything, that would justify the risk of coming here. Anything that might give shape to this ghost story Deidre Skelly had brought to his door.

He had found it in the mansion. The existence of the scarred man was something tangible. A chance to put a face to a suspect. The ice house was different. It was forgotten.

Hidden.

Natalie seemed to sense his thoughts. She looked back to the looming mansion and then nodded once. "Let's go."

As they neared the structure, Jacob could taste the musty scent of earth and a trace of something sharper, almost chemical. The stairs descending into the ice house were narrow and steep, hewn roughly from what looked like the same dark stone as the building itself.

With each step, the air grew colder and the silence deeper, broken only by the distant sound of the sea and his own steady breathing until they reached a large chamber.

Now out of sight, they both turned on their torches. A long wooden shelf ran the length of one wall. Upon it sat a row of large jars, fogged over with condensation, each sealed tight with tarnished metal lids.

Something told Jacob to turn back, to leave and not return, but the pull of his curiosity was stronger. His torchlight flickered across the jars, until he paused on one and felt his heart stop.

A woman looked back at him, her face floating in whatever fluid the container held. Her hair swirled around her like strands of seaweed. Her lips were slightly parted, frozen in a silent scream, or perhaps a final breath.

Jacob's own breath seemed to freeze in his throat, along with the rest of him as the horror took shape.

Natalie's torch beam slowly swept the row. "Oh my god."

Each face bore a different expression. Some appeared

peaceful, others twisted in a final grimace. Their features were unnervingly intact.

Jacob stepped back as his stomach rolled, trying to convince himself it wasn't what it seemed, that it had to be some twisted collection of grotesque art, but the acrid tang of formaldehyde in the air told him otherwise. Someone had taken great care in preserving them, trapping their final moments behind glass for all eternity.

He knew then what they were looking at. The mystery had tied itself together.

"Hector's missing girls," said Jacob.

30

"Let's get out of here." Natalie's voice was husky. Afraid.

"No, not yet." They couldn't leave and run the risk of their intrusion being discovered and the evidence hidden or destroyed. "Phone Cora, tell her about Zara, and tell her what we have here."

"What are you going to do?"

"Document it." He pulled his phone from his pocket and quickly brought up the camera app.

Natalie made a frustrated noise behind him. "No signal."

"Go up top."

"Right."

He grabbed her arm. "Natalie. Go back over the wall first and then make the call. Stay out of sight and wait for me. Don't come back."

"Got it."

As her footsteps retreated up the steps, Jacob brought up his phone and began to record, starting from the base of the steps and walking slowly towards the back of the chamber. Once there, he turned, now facing the row of faces and side-stepped his way back to the front of the room.

Switching to photo mode, he moved back along the row, taking a picture of each face. There had been eight girls in Hector's investigation. Jacob counted sixteen jars. Alcorn had continued his killing, no doubt emboldened by the investigation being squashed.

He was finished in less than five minutes and paused at the rear of the chamber as he scrolled though each image, making sure they were all of sufficient quality.

He was halfway through when he heard the scrape of Natalie's feet on the steps.

"I thought I told you to wait over the wall."

She didn't answer and a chill crawled down his back. He turned.

Zara Steele stood at the base of the steps. She was pointing a gun at him.

"Zara." Jacob's thumb drifted across the screen of his phone and hit record. "Thank God you're here. I was -"

"-Be quiet." She saw through the half-assed ruse before he could even start it. She removed one hand from her gun. A *Glock*, Jacob saw. Her PSNI issued personal protection weapon, almost certainly. "Phone."

Slowly, Jacob reached out.

"On the ground." She waited until he set it down, screen first. "Kick it across."

Jacob complied, sending the phone skittering across the floor. Zara bent down to pick it up, her eyes and her gun not leaving him. She tapped the screen once, ending the recording, then pocketed it.

"I remember your little investigation last summer had a bit of success with recording conversations."

Jacob shrugged. "So now we can talk freely."

"I suppose we can."

"Well, the floor is yours, Detective Chief Inspector."

"Jonathan Alcorn is my uncle."

Jacob almost choked. He hadn't been expecting that and scrambled to make this new piece of information fit. A wealthy family. A briefly mentioned father. "Meaning David Alcorn is your da?"

"That's right."

"So...you're the daughter of a duke." He blinked. "I mean, what the fuck?"

"A daughter. A bastard."

It took Jacob a moment to realise she was talking about

herself, not Alcorn. He motioned for her to continue. To his surprise, she did.

"He was pushing fifty, my mother only turned twenty. Scandalous, right? So he paid her hush money to keep it all secret and would drop by, maybe twice a year to check up on us. My mother died when I was twelve. He came to her funeral. Told me he'd support me, send me to boarding school, pay for university. He even brought me into his home eventually. All I had to do was keep my mouth shut."

"Which you did."

"Which I did. Money, jewellery, education, I never lacked for anything, other than love. Actual love. Joining the police was my attempt at rebellion, but it came across as petty and he never lets me forget it."

"Yeah, it's a real tale of woe. How does that lead to here?"

"I knew about Jonathan. Always heard the whispers about his...proclivities."

An indignant bark escaped from Jacob. "Proclivities? That's what you'd call this?" He motioned to the jars. "Where are the boys? Or does your uncle only display the women he's killed?"

"Well. I'm glad to see you're not quite as clever as you think you are."

He frowned at that. There was a piece of the puzzle still missing. "I don't get it."

"Which part?"

"Yours."

She shrugged. As she did, her open coat lifted enough to reveal a handcuff pouch clipped to her belt. "Your FOI request came to me. I knew all about you from the Followers investigation, and knew that you would be a problem."

"The cold case unit. Your way of protecting your family?"

"Don't be daft. All of this was supposed to be well buried."

For the first time Jacob saw her glancing at the jars. The front faltered. She didn't know. At least not the full truth. She seemed to shake it away, focused back on him. "The unit was a way to promote myself. I told you as much back in your office. Not with this investigation of course, but I had to do something, and the smartest play was to involve myself. Try to influence the direction it took, but events moved quicker than I would have liked. You work fast. Maybe it's Natalie's influence. I rather like her."

Jacob let out a slow breath, and began to replay the events of the last few days, from the moment he had opened the door to find her waiting in his office. "Your mugging was staged. You planted the watch in Pettigrew's house and had Finbar's file burned."

The ghost of a proud smile touched her lips. "Like I said, quicker than I would have liked."

"The borstal file, what was on it?"

Her smile widened, delighted at the subterfuge and Jacob felt his stomach lurch. "Nothing interesting, but it made for a good diversion. You like your crime novels, Jacob. What do they call it, a red herring? It put your focus firmly on Pettigrew, when you were already halfway there yourself. The watch and the burned file were supposed to give me the room to work."

Jacob thought back to his office, after the fracas up in the Ballylogue. He had mentioned Pettigrew, the former allegations, even where the old priest was living. "So, what's his role?"

"Pettigrew? Just a fall guy. You gave me the name and I saw our patsy. It was perfect really, booted out from the church, linked to the IRA, a history with Finbar."

"The pictures me and Natalie found. Were they planted too?"

Zara shook her head. "No, just rotten luck for me. Pettigrew was as guilty as anyone else as to what happened at Hartley House. That little stash of photos proves it. I couldn't believe it when Hector recognised Lord Sansom. It started to spiral then, as you may have noticed today. Lots of loose ends needed snipped."

Jacob struggled to fight through the muddle of his brain. Tried to piece together the fragments of what he knew. "Pettigrew never worked at St. Joseph's, did he?"

"No, but it was an easy lie and hard to disprove when the school's been bulldozed."

"And Richard McBride's mother? His real mother, I mean."

"No idea. I hope she's well."

He wanted to ask who the woman in Helen's Bay was. The one who had hastily removed the pictures showing her real family before Jacob and Zara arrived at her door. The one who had flubbed the name of the school her supposed lost son had gone to. He supposed it didn't matter.

"Where's Pettigrew now?"

"I don't know."

"He's not coming back."

"No."

Jacob connected dots. "Martin Closkey told me he had to put in some work. That he was blackmailed into it with the threat of his uncle being exposed as an informer. The work was Pettigrew and Eddie Chambers."

Zara worked her jaw, weighing how much to give up. "Word was passed to him that Pettigrew was going to confess about his own role with British intelligence."

"That wasn't true."

"Of course it wasn't. But as far as Closkey knew, Pettigrew was going to name a number of informers, including Seamus Dolan. He was also going to finger Closkey for his role in Finbar Skelly's disappearance."

The last part took Jacob by surprise. "His role?"

"Closkey was the one who found Finbar on the Falls Road. It was Closkey who brought him back to the borstal."

"And how do you know..." Jacob trailed off. The last piece fell into place.

"Clicked, has it?"

"Yeah," Jacob said hoarsely.

He guessed it was ten minutes since Natalie had left. By now she would have relayed to Cora what they had seen, but it would be hours before anything would be mobilized, hours Jacob didn't have. He also knew Natalie would not wait indefinitely. Eventually she would come looking for him, and Jacob didn't want her in the sights of Zara's gun. He needed to change tact.

"What's the plan here, Zara? If you were going to shoot me, you'd have done it already."

"I was hoping there was some way we could work this out."

"Work this out?"

"I don't want you...I wanted you to get out of this. Maybe if you could forget what you saw-Fuck!" She shook her head violently, already knowing whatever scheme she was concocting was doomed to fail. There was no way out, for either of them. "I was this close to tying this all off. We could have..."

The words hung in the air. "Could have what?"

"Got through it together. There's something there, Jacob."

"Jesus...There's no getting through this, Zara, but we can get a deal -"

He was cut off by a firm shake of her head. "No deal, Jacob. You expect me to throw away my life and turn on my family? No."

"Zara," Jacob said her name softly. "This place is going to be swarming with police."

Tears shone in her eyes now. "No."

"They're on their way."

"No."

Jacob read denial and regret, but not acceptance.

"Natalie already made the call."

"No, Jacob. She didn't."

Bile rose in his throat. "What do you...What did you do?"

"Not me."

"Who?"

"I'm sorry." Zara raised her gun.

Jacob looked past her and up to the steps, his expression wide with shock. "We're down here!" The call was a desperate shriek. A sudden hope of unexpected rescue.

Zara whipped towards the stairway, gun sweeping the room, ready to meet a threat that wasn't there.

Jacob lunged, caught a glimpse of fear as Zara pivoted back, realising too late she'd been fooled, and bowled into her with every bit of force he could muster, the momentum sending them both careening to the floor.

Zara hit first. Jacob landed on top of her, hard enough to force the breath from his lungs. There was a crack. The Glock skittered across the ground. Jacob raised up, grabbing her wrists to fend off an attack that didn't come.

Adrenaline roared through him, a coursing rush that pushed out everything else. For a moment, he couldn't move, his body locked in place, his mind trying to catch up with what had just happened.

Zara's head had lolled to the side, her face slack. Jacob released her wrists. Both dropped limply onto the floor. She wasn't faking this time.

He reached out, two fingers on her neck, checking for a pulse. Relieved in spite of it all to find it strong under his trembling fingers.

He reached under her coat, fumbled at her belt, and pulled off the handcuff pouch. He took the cuffs out, put one on her left wrist, letting the shackle go tight. He moved her onto her side, brought the cuffed arm behind her back, and snapped the second cuff around the right wrist.

He picked up the Glock, hit the release, and let the magazine slip out into his hand. Gleaming brass inside. He pulled back the slide just enough to see a bullet in the chamber. Zara had pointed a loaded gun at him. He let the slide fall back, slapped the magazine back into the well, checked it was secure, and took off running.

31

A lone set of footprints stretched from the ice house towards the perimeter wall. Natalie's.

Jacob followed her trail and soon spotted a second set of prints running in a wide arc, curving closer and closer to Natalie. He felt his stomach twist as the two sets converged. The pristine white of the snow was marred, kicked and scuffed in clear evidence of a struggle.

He vaulted the wall. On the other side only a single pair of footprints continued. Jacob began to run. Natalie and her abductor had a significant head start. The new prints followed the same path as they had approaching Dunvarrick, but upon reaching the railway line, crossed the tracks and pushed on towards a wooded area, rather than back towards Portballintrae.

The path dipped towards a low, frozen gully. The snow here was deeper, swallowing Jacob's shoes with each step. He slipped once, his foot catching on an icy patch hidden beneath the white blanket, and he landed hard on his hands and knees.

He pulled himself up and pushed on. Each jarring step over the uneven ground sent waves of agony shooting through his damaged nose. Every sharp inhale burned, frigid air slicing like tiny shards of glass, scraping against the inflamed membranes. His nose felt as if it were on fire, searing pain radiating to his cheeks and brow with every stride.

The path twisted around a jagged bend and Jacob caught a fleeting glimpse of movement. As the trail straightened, he saw them.

The figure was moving swiftly, despite the burden he carried. Natalie dangled over a shoulder, her arms swinging limply with the jolting movement of her captor's hurried pace.

Jacob bit down on his lip. Willed himself on.

The figure slowed, as if sensing the pursuit, and then stopped completely. With a sharp, predatory movement, he turned. Jacob skidded to a halt, still some twenty metres away.

At Haywood's, the glimpse had been fleeting, distorted by the chaos of the moment. Now, under the cold, dim light of the moon, Jacob could take him in.

Ned by Night.

Bandages wrapped tightly around Ned's head, crossing over his nose and jaw in uneven layers. They covered everything but the slits where his eyes should be. In the dark and with the distance between them, Jacob could see only black pools, and yet, could feel the gaze upon him.

Ned tilted his head. Jacob felt the unseen eyes drifting over him, coming to a rest on Zara's gun, held down by his side. Ned's posture shifted a fraction, his grip on Natalie tightening. Jacob read it a second too slow as Ned bolted towards a dense thicket of wild bushes just off the path.

"Stop!"

He raised the gun, the weapon heavy and foreign in his hand. His finger hovered near the trigger, but hesitation rooted him to the spot. Ned was already halfway into the underbrush, the thicket swallowing him and Natalie as branches snapped and rustled in their wake.

Jacob moved. Ned's shadowed form weaved through uneven terrain. Natalie slung over his shoulder, offered no resistance, no sign of life. Jacob pushed away thoughts that maybe he was already too late.

"Stop!" The shout was raw and desperate. "Drop her!" His grip on Zara's gun tightened but he knew he couldn't risk taking a shot.

The ground beneath him vanished. Jacob's foot plunged

into emptiness, the world tilting as gravity took him. The gun flew from his grasp. He crashed into a shallow sheugh, pain flaring along his side as he struck a submerged rock. The water was frigid, stealing the breath from his lungs.

He forced himself upright, gasping as icy tendrils of water seeped through his clothes. He staggered to his feet, stumbled, almost fell, before he got his footing and pulled himself back up to the path.

The gun was gone. He didn't bother looking.

The silence was suffocating, as though the woods themselves were holding their breath. He blundered on, branches clawing at his face as he pushed through the brush. He couldn't afford to stop, and could only hope that he'd picked the right direction. That Natalie and her abductor were somewhere ahead.

Then he saw her.

Natalie lay motionless on the ground, her dark hair spread across the snow-dusted earth. Ned was nowhere to be seen. Whatever his plan had been, he had abandoned it, leaving Natalie as bait to make good his escape.

Jacob ran to her, shaking fingers feeling for a pulse. His fingers brushed against her cold skin, and he felt a flicker of life within her stillness. Relief coursed through him, if only for a moment.

It was the faintest shift of fabric. The whisper of movement through the trees. Instinct kicked in before his mind could register the danger.

He dived to the side, a glint of metal slicing through the air where his head had just been.

Ned had used Natalie as bait, as Jacob had thought, but bait to lure him in, correctly guessing Jacob's concern for Natalie would override everything else.

Jacob hit the ground hard, his elbow slamming into the dirt, sending a shock of pain up his arm. Ned was on him. The knife gleamed as he slashed. Jacob twisted, narrowly dodging the blade as it nicked his side, cutting through the fabric of his jacket.

He scrambled to his feet as Ned lunged again. Jacob caught the arm, the force of Ned's attack sending both of them staggering, feet slipping, scrambling for purchase on the icy ground. Jacob's tired muscles screamed as he fought to keep the blade at bay, desperation and fear lending him strength as he tried to wrench the arm holding the knife down.

The blade flashed between them, as Ned slashed wildly, trying to free his arm. "Come on!" Jacob's shout was guttural, as much as a challenge to himself as the bandaged man. He knew his life, and Natalie's, depended on getting the knife away.

Ned snarled and shoved forward, trying to overpower Jacob, trying to drive the blade into his side.

With a final surge of strength, Jacob shifted his weight and twisted Ned's wrist sharply. A strangled grunt of pain escaped from the bandaged man. The knife fell free.

Jacob shoved Ned, kicked the knife into the undergrowth. Pain exploded across his vision as a fist slammed into his nose. He gasped, a wave of disorienting agony washing over him as the world seemed to tilt, the stars above swimming in a nauseating blur.

He tried to clear his head when Ned hit him again, flush on the cheek. White-hot pain obliterated his focus. There was a shadow of movement, the only thing he could make out. He tried to react but was too slow.

Ned slammed his weight into him. Jacob lost his footing as Ned drove him back, his feet looking for purchase on the slick ground and finding none. He collided with the trunk of a tree, the impact knocking the last gasp of breath from his lungs. His vision blurred with tears, his nose throbbing in time with his racing heartbeat.

He felt Ned grab him by the collar. Felt himself yanked off balance. Felt himself falling. His skull bounced off something hard. The world dulled. Sound and sensation faded into a distant hum.

Cold seeped into his back, numbing the sharp ache in his ribs but doing nothing to dull the throbbing in his skull. His vision swam, the twisted silhouettes of trees above him blurring as he blinked rapidly, trying to force clarity.

Ned had found his knife. Jacob tried to push himself up. His arm gave way and he tasted dirt.

The phantom loomed large. Cold, calculating intent clear in every step. Jacob's fingers scrambled along the ground for a weapon, for anything that would save him.

He came up empty.

The crunch of snow got louder. Ned drew closer. Every step was slow, deliberate. He wanted Jacob to feel fear. His hand tightened around the hilt of the knife. The glint of steel flickered as the blade angled downward, poised for the final strike.

The scream was primal. Natalie swung the gnarled branch with what looked like every ounce of strength she had. The solid crack of wood colliding with flesh and bone rang out as it slammed into Ned's skull.

He staggered. Natalie swung again. Fierce. Unrelenting. Eyes wide with fury, fear, and revenge. The branch caught Ned across the shoulder. The knife slipped from his grip, landing in the snow beside Jacob.

Ned dropped to a knee and just about managed to regain his footing. Natalie bellowed an unintelligible challenge, and smashed the branch into the side of his face.

The wood splintered. Ned fell. He rolled, stumbled up, and broke into a clumsy run.

Jacob pushed himself to his feet, his beating forgotten in the moment, a reserve of adrenaline dulling the pain that shot through his body. He went to her.

"I'm fine." She pushed him away. "Get him."

The snap in her voice pushed through the last of the fog clouding his mind. Jacob took off after the fleeing man.

His quarry crashed through the woods and emerged at the side of the railway line. Jacob closed the gap. He could hear the faint sound of laboured breaths as he drew closer.

This was a ghost no more. Not an urban legend, nor a spectre, or phantom. This was a man. Flesh, blood, and palpable fear.

Ned glanced over his shoulder a second before his foot caught on an outstretched branch of a fallen tree. He crashed into the undergrowth, the brittle branches and frosted leaves crunching beneath his weight.

Jacob lunged as Ned climbed back to his feet. They came

together hard, both grappling fiercely for an advantage. Jacob's left hand grabbed at Ned's wrist, while his right arm hooked under his shoulder. Ned shoved forward, trying to overpower him with brute strength. With a sharp twist of his hips, Jacob used Ned's momentum to lift him off the ground and send him over his shoulder.

It was far from a perfect throw. The angle was awkward, and Jacob stumbled slightly under the weight of the other man, but the effect was as desired. Ned crashed onto the frozen earth with a heavy thud.

He didn't wait for him to recover. As Ned rolled, Jacob kicked him in the face and then to the ribs as the figure clawed at him, trying to pull himself back upright.

Jacob seized him by the collar and drove a fist into the Ned's jaw. The man moaned, tried to turn his face away. Jacob's second punch caught him high on the cheek, snapping Ned's head to the side.

As Jacob pulled back for another blow, Ned's hand shot out. A finger caught him in the eye. The pain was immediate and searing. His grip on the collar faltered, loosening just enough for Ned to try and twist free.

He made a final attempt to grab at the collar but Ned shoved him hard. The collar slipped from his grasp as Ned's foot slipped on the slick surface. His arms flailed as he tried to regain balance, his body tilting further and further until gravity claimed him entirely.

Jacob reached out on instinct, but grabbed only air.

For a moment, Ned seemed frozen in place, his arms outstretched as if trying to stop the inevitable. He gasped, his body jerking in shock as the jagged branch of the fallen tree pierced through his torso, impaling him with a sickening, wet sound.

A hand reached down, trembling, feeling the splintered wood that had punctured him, as if he couldn't quite believe what had happened. Blood was already soaking through his clothing, darkening the snow beneath him.

All traces of Ned by Night now forgotten. In his eyes Jacob could see the most human instinct of all. Fear.

He crouched next to the man.

Slowly, he reached out and began to unravel the facial bandages.

Underneath, the skin was smooth, unblemished. No scars. No burns. No signs of the injuries the bandages had suggested. Like so many other parts of this investigation, it had been a lie.

The years had softened and filled out the angles of his face, but the shape of the nose, the curve of the jawline, and the hint of that same crooked smile, had remained.

"Hello Finbar."

32

Each shallow breath Finbar Skelly took was accompanied by an audible rattle, his chest rising and falling unevenly, the effort visibly draining what little strength he had remaining. Flecks of blood stained the corners of his mouth.

The bandages, now removed, clung to his neck and shoulders in ragged scraps. His thinning hair was matted to his scalp with sweat, and a faint sheen covered his skin, the cold night air failing to cut through the feverish heat of his failing body.

His eyes darted to Jacob. Fear, resignation, and perhaps, the faintest hint of relief.

From behind Jacob could hear footsteps running towards them. Natalie. She slowed and then stopped, her eyes taking in the man who had tried to kidnap her, and then slowly drifting to the blood-soaked branch protruding out from his stomach. Jacob could see sympathy in them and knew she was a better person than he.

"I got Cora," she said. "I kept it brief, but the cavalry is on the way." She looked from Jacob and then back to Finbar. "I'll call an ambulance."

She stepped away, leaving Jacob and Finbar Skelly alone once again.

Jacob took his phone from his pocket. Somehow, it had survived his tumble in the sheugh.

"What are you doing?" the voice was weak, rasping, the breathing shaky. Each inhale sounding like it was catching in his chest

Jacob held the phone out. "Taking your confession, if you're willing."

Finbar managed a wheezing approximation of a laugh, but didn't say no.

Jacob pressed the red circle. "Why?"

"Why? Why what, the costume?"

"We can start there, sure."

"All for the thrill."

"The thrill?"

"Of being the monster. Do you know what it's like to see a look of fear on a person? Utter, unfiltered fear."

"Like those girls back there. Were they scared?"

"Every single one. They screamed, and cried, and begged, and I killed them all."

"Not all."

Finbar frowned for a moment and then smiled at Jacob through red-stained teeth. "The first girl. Emily. I remember her name in the papers after. No, that was a lesson. I learned I had to be more selective."

"The Whitburn Society?"

"Care homes, shelters. My pick of the litter."

"The girls society wouldn't miss."

"That's right."

"Well they were missed," said Jacob. "That's how we got you. I want you to know that. That's why we came here tonight. A police detective called Hector Breen and Eden Hennessey's mother. They didn't forget."

Finbar's smile curled. Jacob turned as Natalie rejoined them. She said nothing and hung back a couple of metres behind Jacob.

"Tell me about it," said Jacob.

"About what?

"Christmas 1981."

Finbar's eyes seemed to glaze at a memory. "Snuck out at night. Hitchhiked back to Belfast. Made it to the corner of the Falls and Whiterock. Not even ten minutes from home when my uncle spotted me. Thought he was going to welcome mé home. Then I noticed Martin Closkey was in the car with him. I knew something was wrong then, a man like Closkey would never be in the company of an eejit like Adrian."

"Your uncle and Closkey brought you back to Hartley House?"

"Aye. Closkey jumped out the car, slapped me in the mouth and showed me a gun. Even if anyone had been watching, they were never going to tout on a fella like Martin Closkey." His head tilted back slightly against the tree that had impaled him, the effort of holding it up now too much.

"You lured Closkey to Haywood's house. A chance for revenge?"

"That's exactly what it was."

"What about Haywood?"

"A gun? Not my style. I wanted them to feel it."

Jacob was about to ask about Hector but stopped. Finbar knew he was a dead man, and he was talking. If he had done for Hector, Jacob believed he would have mentioned it. If he had nothing to do with it, he didn't want to let Finbar know Hector was dead, not after mentioning the part he had played in his downfall. No, he wanted Finbar going to his end thinking Hector Breen had bested him and lived to see a righteous result.

He took the man in. This man who had curated an urban legend, who had so skilfully amplified the fear of those who were looking for him. He felt the chill on his spine, not because the bandaged man had been supernatural, but because he wasn't. He was human, and that made him all the more frightening.

"The graffiti at the studio, the person at my door."

"And in your garden," Finbar turned his head laboriously towards Natalie.

She matched his gaze. There was nothing to fear now. It was Finbar who looked away first.

It occurred to Jacob that Finbar had been working against Zara. While she tried to lay a story and obfuscate, he was building on a legend. It had worked, he supposed. He had never made any connection between Zara and Finbar until the ice house. She had been trying to hide his existence and by extension his crimes, as much as she was trying to protect her family.

"The cottage up near Carrickfergus," Jacob said. "We found the basement and the bloodstains."

"An old haunt. I know you found the room and the hidden compartment too." He watched Jacob for a reaction. "I suppose I find the past hard to let go off. Lot of memories in that basement."

"That night in Hartley House, you were there."

"Did I scare you? I like to walk the corridors. Some days I get lucky and get the odd curious person poking around. I get to play haunted house. Never let them see me though, that would bring trouble."

The rise and fall of Finbar's chest had grown slower. His body was giving up, piece by piece.

Jacob knew time was short and he needed answers. He leaned closer. "Finbar. Where are the other boys? Desmond McClure, Craig Fullerton, Richard McBride."

"The cottage, buried in the backyard." He shook his head as he saw the question form on Jacob's lips. "Not my work. One of Jonathan's...customers. He liked to get rough with the merchandise, so to speak."

"How were they taken?"

"Money for McClure and Fullerton. The man knew them both from Hartley House. Went looking for them when they were out. Enticed them into the car with cash."

"What about Richard?"

Finbar sucked air. "The Whitburn Society was casting a wide net. Children homes, hostels, shelters, special need schools. One of the patrons took a liking to young Richard, tried to get him into his car with one of the oldest tricks in the book, sweets from a stranger. It didn't work. He called Jonathan once he realised the boy was dead. We got rid of the body."

"Jesus," Natalie said hoarsely.

Jacob fought against a sudden urge to retch. "The girls," he said, closing his eyes, trying to ignore the feeling. "Why?"

"I was let down."

"By those girls?"

"All of them."

Something belatedly clicked for Jacob. "You attacked Patricia Winslow."

"I did."

"But you didn't try to take her. You let her live. You wanted her to feel it."

"She was meant to be watching out for me. I wanted her to know it was me and not be able to speak a word."

"And you visit her every once in a while, just to remind her?"

"Did you like my little painting? I brought her back to the cottage. Jonathan wasn't using it anymore. That little scheme had run its course. I cut her face, her tits, her tongue. It was beautiful."

"So that's what this was all about? Hating women."

"My own mother." Finbar bared bloody teeth. "She sold me. That's what Jonathan told me, at least. Told me that she didn't want me. Stupid of course and I got a little older and realised it was a lie. I also realised it didn't matter, she gave me up."

"Gave you up?"

"She didn't care. Good riddance as far as she was concerned. Jonathan...he could offer me something. A home. Safety. He didn't judge me for the hurt I wanted to cause. He encouraged it."

Jacob reached across, caught his chin roughly. Made Finbar look at him. "Why do you think I was searching for you?" He leaned closer, his voice pressing, wanting to drive the words home. "It was your mother who came to me, wanting me to find her son. Forty-four years and she never forgot about you."

Finbar's lips parted. He hadn't known. His gaze shifted, no longer defiant but suddenly lost, like a child hearing a comforting truth they so desperately wanted to believe.

"Mummy..."

It carried no bitterness, no scorn. Just a fragile, broken longing.

It was the last word Finbar Skelly spoke.

33

The cafe was quiet. It was always quiet, which was why Jacob kept coming back. He wasn't sure he knew its name, or if it even had one.

He had found it nearly five years before. Insomnia and brooding kept him up most nights as he tried to figure out where his life was going. The new apartment had become too suffocating, and he had taken himself off for a midnight stroll with no particular destination in mind.

He wasn't sure how long he had crisscrossed through the streets, alleyways and entries of Belfast until he dandered up North Street.

It was not a place he often had cause to be. North Street was a forgotten part of the city centre, with most of the buildings derelict and boarded up. The cafe had stood out, not only because it was operating, but it was open late night, a rare commodity in Belfast.

At the time, North Street had been part of a proposed regeneration scheme worth five hundred million. Five years later, work had yet to start and the area had continued on its downward trajectory.

Yet, the little cafe had remained. It was a place for people like Jacob. The lonely, solitary figures who preferred the company of their thoughts. The cafe offered anonymity without judgement. You could sit for hours at one of the stools at the triangular counter with nothing more than a lukewarm cup of coffee and not draw a second glance from the staff or the other patrons. Here solitude wasn't something to be questioned or pitied.

Tonight, there was only one other patron in the place. He had his shoulders hunched and his back to the door, and hadn't looked up from his coffee as Jacob perched himself across the counter.

The cafe was bathed in a familiar amber glow from the overhead lights, reflecting faintly off the polished counter. Two large glass windows framed the darkness of the city outside. Behind the odd-shaped counter a solitary worker moved languidly, their silhouette framed by the muted glow of the coffee machine.

It had been almost two weeks since Dunvarrick.

Police had raided the place the next morning. Jonathan Alcorn was arrested and released on bail two days later. Money and influence played their part, but Jacob took solace in knowing even a member of the aristocracy would have a hard time talking his way out of the sixteen faces in jars in his old ice house, or the twenty-one bodies recovered from grounds of the derelict cottage outside Carrickfergus. A cottage that was eventually traced back to the Alcorn family through an impressive number of dummy companies and fake names.

All but two of the bodies found at the cottage were skeletons. Three had been identified as male, their bones not fully developed. Boys. Desmond McClure, Craig Fullerton, and Richard McBride had been found and would finally be put to rest.

Who the remaining skeletons were had yet to be confirmed, but it was a safe bet that eight of them were Hector's missing girls. Who the other eight might be was still a mystery and would take considerable time to identify. Finbar had chosen girls at the edge of society for a reason.

The remaining two other bodies were newer. Jeremiah Pettigrew and Eddie Chambers, both with a bullet in the back of their head.

Zara Steele had steadfastly protested her innocence from

the moment police found her handcuffed in the ice house. The story she concocted about getting jumped by Jacob hadn't washed. From what Jacob had heard from Cora, Steele was trying to strike a deal in exchange for information. She had already given up the name of three heavies who worked for her father, and the PSNI had quickly linked them to the murders of Hector Breen and Cecil Haywood.

Cora had shown Jacob the custody pictures of the men following their arrest and asked if he recognised them. He did. Dye Job and his two mates, the pair who had broken his nose and torched his car.

Talk was, at least one was willing to roll back on their employer. Sensing what was coming, the Duke of Whitburn, had put a pistol to his head and pulled the trigger. He'd botched it and was now in a coma in the ward of a private hospital, destined to see out his days as a vegetable.

Hector Breen had been laid to rest alongside his wife in a little church graveyard just outside Moira. Attendance was limited to Jacob, Natalie, Rosemary Hennessy, Emily Goddard, and a handful of men of a similar age to Hector. Old colleagues who came out to say a final goodbye to one of their own.

Jacob looked up as the door opened. Natalie walked towards him. "Thought I'd find you here."

Jacob frowned. "I told you I was."

"I know, just felt like the thing to say."

"What can I get for you?" the man behind the counter asked.

"Coffee, please," Natalie answered. "Black"

The man shuffled away and Natalie said to Jacob, "Got something for you."

"Oh yeah?"

She reached into the pocket of her coat and produced a plastic bottle with clear liquid inside. "For the new car."

Jacob took it and read the label. "Holy water?"

"To invoke God's protection, bless your vehicle and protect all those who travel within."

"Thought you were one of those lapsed Catholics."

"I absolutely am, but considering what happened to your

last car, every little helps."

He managed a smile and then tapped his phone. She had only texted him five minutes ago, meaning she had been in the area. "You checking up on me?"

Her own smile dimmed a fraction. "Maybe a little."

Two days after Dunvarrick, Jacob had taken the photograph of Finbar that Deirdre had given him, along with the fingerprint card he had retrieved from Finbar's borstal file, and travelled up to West Belfast to tell Deirdre Skelly that her son would be coming home.

Her address was an old terraced house on a narrow street of a housing estate. Jacob got out from his hire car and saw a number of people milling in the front yard, watching him approach with clear suspicion.

"I'm looking for Deirdre Skelly's house," he said, thinking he must have taken the address down wrong.

"Jacob Kincaid?" The woman who asked the question was middle-aged and stocky, with short-cropped hair dyed a shade of blonde that didn't quite suit her weathered face.

He confirmed that he was. She introduced herself as Cathy, the niece who had first mentioned Jacob's name to Deirdre. She ushered him inside. The house smelled faintly of lavender and old fabric. She led him straight into the front living room without ceremony. Deirdre Skelly was laid out in an open casket.

"When?"

"Night before last. Passed away in her sleep. We should all be so lucky." Cathy indicated towards Deirdre. "Do you want a moment? You didn't come up here for a social call."

Jacob heard the door close and waited until he had the right words. "I found him. I guess you must have felt it. That's what I'm choosing to believe. Hung on long enough to feel it. His last thought was of you. Whatever else he became, I suppose nothing changes that. I'll see to it they bring him home, lay him next to you so you can stay together."

He supposed he could take some crumb of comfort in doing that. Deirdre would have her son back.

"What's eating you?"

Natalie's question brought him back to the present.

They had spent a good bit of time together following Dunvarrick. Hanging out, a couple of home cooked meals and bottles of wine as they discussed their next steps. A podcast would inevitably follow, they had agreed as much. She had engaged his services to do some further digging into the honeytrap operation, and into the abuse at Hartley House.

Work coming his way. A mystery solved, justice served, and people made to answer. He should have been happy.

And he had been. But as the days progressed, something hollow started to form.

It had stared with Hector's funeral and gestated as the initial flurry of activity slowed, and he was left with time for rumination.

"Where to start?"

"Wherever you feel like," said Natalie.

"How about Zara? After what happened last summer, you think I'd be wise to getting played like that. Am I so starved for...something, that I fall for that kind of deceit so willingly."

Natalie paused as her coffee was set in front of her. "For what it's worth, I think Zara's interest in you was genuine. If she had it her way, she'd have buried the truth and kept her thing going with you. She tricked you, but she tricked all of us. You're being hard on yourself, Jacob."

"You think?"

"You just closed twenty-one murders, unmasked a serial killer, and brought down a member of the British nobility."

"We. Us."

She smiled again. "That's right. Us."

"Don't forget about bringing down a cult last summer. In the spring, we should consider overthrowing a central American government." He sighed and rubbed his face. He could joke, but he also knew the victory wasn't enough. Not this time. "Do you remember what Hector said to me back in your car when we were going to see Seamus Dolan?"

He watched Natalie search for the memory before shaking her head.

"Don't let the work consume you. Make sure you get to living."

"OK?"

"At Hector's funeral, there wasn't even twelve people there. A few old colleagues and us. No wife, no family. I'm not even sure there were any close friends. Is that how it'll be for me, you think?"

She reached across the table and placed her hand into his, squeezing gently before holding it firmly. "No, I don't. You're not alone, Jacob. Not when I'm still around."

Jacob leaned back in his chair, his hand still in hers as the words settled somewhere deep, and filled the hollowness he was carrying.

Natalie didn't say anything more. She didn't need to. Her presence was enough. They sat in silence, as the faint hum of Belfast endured beyond the window.

It wasn't much, but it was enough.

Author's note:

Firstly, I want to offer my deepest thanks, dear reader, for sticking with me and finishing the story. I sincerely hope you enjoyed He Calls By Night and are enticed by the promise that Jacob and Natalie will return for another investigation.

If you'd like to keep up to date with what's in store for our intrepid investigative duo, or any of my upcoming works, please check out my website at sdwhamilton.com or follow me on Bluesky, Threads or the app formerly known as Twitter.

Location plays such an important part in what I write and I always strive to give Belfast and beyond an authentic and honest feel. With that being said, certain creative liberties were taken with this book. Hartley House is a fictional location, albeit heavily influenced by the actual prison service training college, where I attended prior to my five-year stint as a prison officer. Other places, including Dunvarrick House, New Burnley Police Station, and the Ballylogue Estate, are inspired by real locations but have been adapted to serve the story. The Knockagh Monument is real, but for the sake of storytelling, the author may have overstated the winding lanes and roads in its immediate vicinity. The PSNI's Cold Case Team is another fabrication and bears no resemblance to any real-life department.

Writing a book is a labour of love, but one that is repaid when sitting down and typing up a note such as this. I want to sign off by once again thanking those who supported this book journey, and you the reader, one final time. I sincerely hope you will join me for the next one.

- Shannon

Belfast, Northern Ireland, 12th June 2025